Homecoming

SUSAN X MEAGHER

THIS TRADE PAPERBACK ORIGINAL IS PUBLISHED BY BRISK PRESS, BRIELLE, NJ 08730.

COVER DESIGN AND LAYOUT BY: CAROLYN NORMAN
EDITED BY: LINDA LORENZO

FIRST PRINTING: MAY 2015

ISBN-13: 978-0-9899895-7-2

By Susan X Meagher

Novels

Arbor Vitae
All That Matters
Cherry Grove
Girl Meets Girl
The Lies That Bind
The Legacy
Doublecrossed
Smooth Sailing
How To Wrangle a Woman
Almost Heaven
The Crush
The Reunion
Inside Out
Out of Whack
Homecoming

Serial Novel
I Found My Heart In San Francisco

Awakenings: Book One
Beginnings: Book Two
Coalescence: Book Three
Disclosures: Book Four
Entwined: Book Five
Fidelity: Book Six
Getaway: Book Seven
Honesty: Book Eight
Intentions: Book Nine
Journeys: Book Ten
Karma: Book Eleven
Lifeline: Book Twelve
Monogamy: Book Thirteen
Nurture: Book Fourteen
Osmosis: Book Fifteen
Paradigm: Book Sixteen
Quandary: Book Seventeen
Renewal: Book Eighteen

Anthologies

Undercover Tales
Outsiders

Acknowledgements

I fell in love with the Green Mountain State upon first meeting. I hope the warmth I feel for Vermont and its people shows through in this story.

Chapter One

JILL'S GLOVED HAND SETTLED on the screen door handle, but didn't pull. Her fingers dawdled for a while, caressing the layers of paint built up over so many years.

The dim porch-light glowed a lovely golden color, freshening memories of long, summer nights, lightening bugs, games of tag, capture the flag, and too many whiffle ball matches to count. Then, years later, hours spent on the swing, trying to capture someone's attention while not appearing to. Swiped cigarettes, beer, a little grass. Anything to appear more grown up than they were.

The house throbbed with sound—laughter, music, people trying to be heard over the din, a baby's cry. Abruptly, the front door swung open and the man standing behind the screen blinked at her. "Jill Henry?"

"Adam?" Shit, this couldn't be the little boy they'd repeatedly tried to ditch on the way home from school, yet he had the same brick-red hair, owlish glasses, and freckle-filled face.

He pushed the screen wide open, letting her enter. "I was just going out for a smoke. My mom won't allow it in the house." Extending the pack, he shook it until one popped up. "Want to join me?"

She did, but not to smoke. Easing into the party by talking to Adam sure did seem like a good idea, but she'd been seen, and when Lisa Byrne locked her beady little eyes on her, Jill knew she had to gut it up and go in.

"I'll catch you when you come back." She slapped him on the back as he exited. "Good to see you, Adam."

"You too. It's been too damn long."

As Jill stepped further into the house, her suspicions were confirmed. Even through the warmth of the crowd, those icy eyes cut right through her. Lisa had *clearly* not wanted to invite her.

Shit.

Lisa moved across the room, acting like she owned the place. Strangely, she looked better than she had as a teenager. Being a cold-hearted, controlling, unsmiling jerk must have prevented crow's feet. She definitely looked older, matronly might have been the better word, but her face was surprisingly youthful.

Lisa stuck her hand out for an unenthusiastic shake. "Jill. We were *sure* you weren't going to make it."

You wish, she wanted to say, but pasted a smile onto her face and added a burst of vigor to the shake. "You look great!" she said, hoping to disarm her with a compliment. "I'd never believe it's been almost twenty years since we've seen each other."

"Oh, I've seen you," she said coolly. "Or at least your car. You always have a nice one."

"Where…?" Jill never went to any of the businesses in town. How would Lisa be able to pick her out in a moving car?

"Your parents' driveway," Lisa said. "I always take a look at the houses of people I know. Kind of a neighborhood watch thing."

There was a reason they called her the town crier. If a tree fell on Chester Road, Lisa heard it way over on Middletown. Jill didn't mention the fact that her parents' home was up a long, curving drive, with the house difficult to see from the main road. Lisa must have parked and scampered up the hill just to keep her eye on things.

"You should have stopped by. I'm always happy to see an old friend."

"Oh, you know how it is." She paused as an evil smile pulled the corners of her mouth up. "Ooo, that's right. You wouldn't know what it's like to have to juggle family obligations. You don't have kids, right?"

Being sarcastic or passive aggressive wasn't a good idea, but sometimes it was worth it. "No, I don't, and I can't figure out why. I guess I've got to double down and try harder."

"That's funny," Lisa said, her expression completely devoid of any amusement. "You've still got that sharp wit."

"I try." She looked over Lisa's shoulder, perversely happy about being a few inches taller, and peered around the room. "Where's Mark hiding?"

"He's around here somewhere. Maybe with one of the kids. You haven't met them, have you." That wasn't a question. She knew damned well Jill hadn't.

"Nope. I guess I've got my work cut out for me. Excuse me," she said as she slid past, going deeper into the room. A quick turn had her in the den, where she added her coat to the piles that filled the chairs and sofa.

When she went back into the living room, she scanned the place carefully, getting her bearings. The house had never been large enough for seven kids, two dogs and a bunch of cats whose number rose and fell with the seasons. Tonight it nearly burst at the seams.

All of the furniture had been pushed against the walls, which helped a little, but it was still tough to wade through for a drink. And Jill truly needed a drink. The bar was just ahead, the dining table having been called into service, but she had a hell of a time traversing the short path.

The evening had been warm—for February—but now that Jill was in the fray, she wondered if it hadn't been the heat billowing from the house that had warmed up the whole neighborhood.

She'd excused herself a few times, grabbed a few waists to create a little space, and guided a couple of kids in the opposite direction to make progress across the room. She was nearly at the dining room table when someone tugged on her pant leg. Looking down, she expected one of the many children scampering around to look up at her. Instead, a striking woman met her puzzled look. Jill squinted to see that she was sitting on a bean-bag chair. Then the woman held up a bottle of vodka and a glass filled with ice and something red. Maybe cranberry juice?

"Are you the bartender?" Jill asked, bending over so she could be heard.

"Yes and no," she said, her voice low and soft. "When it got crowded, I swiped some supplies and plopped myself down. I've been waiting to snag someone I want to talk to." She jiggled the bottle in her hand. "I've got an extra chair…"

After giving way to a guy carrying a crying child, Jill hoped for the best as she turned and dropped what seemed like several feet. She lucked out and hit the beanbag right in its sweet spot, then turned to take a better look.

3

The ad hoc bartender was cute. Really cute. Or maybe sexy was the better descriptor. Shiny, shoulder-length auburn hair, Cupid's bow mouth, fair skin tinted with a scant amount of blush, and lipstick that was the perfect choice for her skin-tone. As Jill leaned closer, she saw the woman had spent a lot of time making her greenish eyes look deep-set and mysterious. And those lovely eyes were twinkling—at her. The last thing Jill expected was to have a really nice looking woman hit on her at this particular party, but she was game. You had to take your swings when you were up at the plate.

"What am I drinking?" she asked.

The extra glass was placed in her hand, then a healthy measure of vodka splashed over the cubes. "Vodka and cranberry. It's not very creative, but better than light beer or cheap wine. Lisa was in charge of the bar," she added, a flicker of distaste flashing across her attractive features.

"What are you in charge of?" Jill took a drink, nearly rolling her eyes in pleasure. She didn't drink vodka often, but every once in a while you needed something strong to arm you for battle.

"Not much. I appointed myself unofficial greeter. When I see someone get waylaid by her royal pain in the ass, I try to cheer them up."

Jill looked her over once again, guessing this really attractive woman could cheer a person up quickly. "How many times have you had to do that?"

"You're the fourth."

Sticking her hand out to shake, she said, "I'm Jill."

"I know." They shook, and she added, "Lizzie."

"How do you know me?"

"Everyone knows you. You're the missing Davis. Mark's abandoned twin."

Stunned, Jill almost dropped her drink onto her lap. "I am?"

"Uh-huh," she said, a sly look settling on her face. "Until Lisa ran you off."

That made her smile. "I think that's an exaggeration. Mark chose to distance himself. He was a big boy."

"He's still not a big boy," Lizzie said. "He's got middle child syndrome in the worst way. He didn't get enough attention from his mom, so he found a wife who treats him like a child. And he laps...it...up." She stuck her puppy-pink tongue out and licked a stripe up an imaginary object.

Lizzie'd probably had a drink with each of the four people she'd rescued. That wouldn't normally slow Jill down, but here...at the Davis house? It was bad form to pick up a tipsy stranger at an old friend's birthday party, wasn't it? But it was really, really tempting...

"How do you know so much about Mark and his marriage?" Jill asked, trying to keep things neutral until she could be sure the bartender was looking to be picked up. She wouldn't have had a doubt if Lizzie didn't look so straight. It wouldn't be the first time a straight woman had flirted with Jill—either trying to prove she had the nerve or to make a boyfriend jealous. Jill had never played the game. Too complicated.

Lizzie took a long sip of her drink, then set it down on the floor, with Jill reaching out to grab it right before a large shoe stomped on it. With a smirk, she held it up triumphantly. "Saved one."

"You've got great reflexes," she said, giving Jill an adorably foxy smile. "Is that from playing whiffle ball all summer?"

"How do you know about that? I know I was good, but I didn't know the whole town knew how awesome I was."

"You're famous. Really," she insisted. "You're a professor, right?"

"I taught for a while, but I didn't make it to professor. I'm at the U now, but I don't have to tell you that, since you know everything about me."

"Not everything," Lizzie admitted, narrowing her gaze. "You came in alone, but I don't know if you're married or serious about someone."

You had to love a woman who cut right to the chase. Lizzie didn't seem like she was trying to make a guy jealous, and she clearly had the nerve to flirt with a woman. Time to get into the game. "Never married. Not currently serious about anyone." Putting on her best seductive smile, she added, "But that could change at any minute."

Lizzie's head cocked, her pretty auburn hair languidly slipping across a shoulder. "You still prefer the fairer sex, right?"

"Yeah. That's a pretty strong preference. I'd say it's a requirement." She tried to sit up straighter, but it was impossible to do in a friggin' bean bag. "How do you know that?"

"*Everyone* knows that." She waved a hand, then removed her drink from Jill's hand and tipped it towards her mouth. "Your being gay started the whole mess, you know. If Mark hadn't had such a crush on you, Lisa wouldn't have had to yank his leash so hard. It's sad," she said, looking a little melancholy. "I don't think he ever believed you wouldn't eventually fall for him. So silly."

"Who *are* you?" Jill asked again, trying to turn so she could face her.

"I already told you. I'm a very interested observer of the goings on in the Davis family." She pointed towards the opposite wall. "Speaking of which, you need to get across this room and talk to the person who made sure you were invited."

"I need to go now?"

"You do. But I'll be waiting for you when you're done." She grasped Jill's drink and held it as she tried, unsuccessfully, to stand. "Tim!" Lizzie called out. "Pick Jill up."

A tall, strawberry-blond man stuck his hand down and nearly ripped Jill's arm from the socket when he lifted her. Then his arms were around her, hugging her hard. "Jill Henry!" he said, loudly, into her ear. "I'll be damned."

When he let her go, she could focus on Mark's younger brother. "Look who's turned into a handsome man! How are you, Tim?"

"He's fine," Lizzie declared. "Get moving."

Jill looked down at her for a moment, then found herself doing as she was told, with Tim patting her on the back as she left. She passed Adam, Chris and Donna, more Davis siblings, on the way, but didn't stop to chat. Clearly, she was under some sort of time crunch. The crowd separated to deposit her right in front of one of her favorite people in the world. "Mrs. Davis," she said, beaming with delight.

The years had been kind to her. Silver hair had replaced the brown, but her pale blue eyes were as sharp and alert as ever. They still exuded a gentleness that had always made Jill feel she was very much a part of the clan.

"I've been waiting for you all night." She reached out and grasped Jill's hand, then pulled her close for a kiss on the cheek. Patting the empty space on the sofa, she demanded, "Sit right here, next to Mike."

How had she missed him? As Jill let herself take in her favorite history teacher, she realized he'd nearly faded away. No longer the hale, hearty, endlessly patient man she'd spent so many hours with, now he was thin, with a sunken chest and a sweater that hung from his bony shoulders. The poor guy couldn't have been much more than seventy, but he could have passed for eighty—easily. He'd always been a chain-smoker, and the habit had clearly caught up to him. An oxygen tank sat next to the sofa, with little tubes going into his nostrils.

"Jilly," he said, his voice thin but clear as he took her offered hand and squeezed it. "I knew you'd grow up to be a looker."

"She was completely grown up the last time you saw her," Mrs. Davis said, giving him a sidelong glance. "And she's always been a looker." She turned to Jill. "Sit right down here and talk to me."

Jill obeyed, finding herself uncharacteristically easy to boss around tonight.

"Look at this hair," Mrs. Davis said, touching the ends that had fallen across Jill's shoulder. "Not a bit of gray. Remember when Bethie used to say your hair was like chocolate pudding?" She laughed. "It still is."

Jill had no memory of that, but she smiled, then grasped Mrs. Davis' hand and squeezed it. It was thin, but not much different than it had felt twenty years ago. The woman got most of her calories from baked goods and chocolate, but had always been reed thin. "I'm *so* glad to see you again. Really. It was hard losing Mark, but..." Damn it. She was determined not to cry.

Mrs. Davis' chin trembled like she was about to cry too. "It was hard for all of us. I wanted to go behind Mark's back to keep in touch, but that didn't seem right. You were his friend...technically."

"I was. But my fondest memories are of being here with the whole family. How many hours did you and Chris and Donna and I play cards at the kitchen table? I still love bridge, thanks to you" She smiled as the memories started to fill her head. "And I still listen to the Red Sox, just like I did with Mr. Davis."

"Stop with the Mister and Missus. We're all adults. Call me Janet. Please."

"I'll give it a try, Janet," she said, the name feeling odd on her tongue.

"Good," she said, her twinkling eyes reflecting the lighthearted approach to life Jill was so fond of. It was fantastic to see that hadn't dimmed.

"Tell me about your life. I know you teach, right?"

"Not exactly," Jill said. "I did for a while, after I got my master's in public administration. But I've been on the administrative side at the U for a long time."

"I never thought about a university needing anything but teachers."

Jill knew she was teasing. Janet was as sharp as a tack, and very aware of things that were outside of her experience. "Yeah, they need a few of us around. It's a good job," Jill said. "But, like any job, it's a lot of work."

"And you don't get summers off. Your favorite time of the year."

"No, I definitely do not," she said, charmed that Mrs. Davis, *Janet*, recalled that about her. "But I'm not complaining. Summer's pretty slow. I can take enough time off to keep myself happy."

"And when you take this time off, who do you spend it with?"

Her silver hair showed off her sparkling blue eyes more than her formerly brown hair did, and the lines that had formed around her eyes and mouth somehow gave her features more definition.

"Right now? My friends. A year ago? My girlfriend."

Janet patted her leg fondly. "Who'd let a beauty like you go?"

"Actually, I let her go," Jill admitted, feeling a little embarrassed to admit that.

Without a word, Janet urged Jill to continue. Her level gaze just made you want to talk. "We got along fine a lot of the time. But when we had trouble…" She tried to think of a quick way to characterize her last relationship, but couldn't manage it. "We couldn't work our way through a single problem."

Leaning forward, Janet caught her husband's attention. "You can't live a life filled with only sunny days, right Mike?"

"Right," he agreed, nodding like he'd heard what led up to her comment, which he couldn't have.

Janet patted her leg. "I'm surprised you're still on the market, kiddo. You've got a big heart, a big brain, and a good temperament. That's a tough slate to beat."

"I'm pretty picky," she admitted. "But I'm going to buckle down and search a little harder. Most of my friends are married or serious about someone, and it'd be nice to be partnered again." She looked out at the group, seeing various members of the Davis family threading through the crowd. "Are all of your kids married?"

"Almost. Beth's the only holdout."

"She's too young to get married," Jill scoffed. "Actually, I can't imagine her dating."

"Oh, she dates, but she's single at the moment. All of the other chickadees have feathered their nests. Only Donna and Kristen left Vermont, so we've got a raft of grandchildren nearby." She leaned forward again. "How many grandkids do we have in Vermont?"

Mike furrowed his brow, thinking. "Eleven?"

"Yes," Janet agreed. "Eleven. We were out of our minds having seven kids." She threw her head back and laughed. "Can you imagine? We *caused* climate change."

"You had some help," Jill teased. "How many do Mark and Lisa have?"

"Three." She lowered her voice. "I don't know how they do it. Lisa doesn't work, and Mark's only got the shop."

"Shop?"

"Didn't you know? He took over the blacksmith shop years ago."

9

"He's Mr. Rooney?" Jill thought her eyes would bug out of her head, images of the ancient, gruff blacksmith of her youth flooding her mind. Even thirty years ago he sat around most of the day, and there were still quite a few workhorses around back then. How much business could there be now?

"Why don't you know these things? Doesn't your mother keep you up on the news?"

"No, she really doesn't," Jill admitted. She could have gone on, but there was no need. It was kind of nice that Janet thought her mom was interested in acknowledging other people in town and might care enough to recount their adventures.

"How's she getting on?"

"My mom? She's all right."

"We don't see her in church any more. It's been *years*."

"Yeah, she stopped going a while ago." She shrugged. Another fact she had a tough time explaining. "She just stopped."

"I've asked around, but no one seems to know if she's ill or what."

"No, she's not ill." Jill twitched under the questioning. "I guess she's happier at home."

Janet frowned, her probing eyes seeming like they were able to ferret out all of Jill's secrets. "She's not very old, honey. Isn't she only around sixty?"

"Sixty-two in June. My dad's turning sixty-five soon. I guess he needs to start thinking about retirement."

Trying to move the focus from her mother didn't work. Janet's pointed questioning continued. "I know your dad's gone a lot. Does your mom have anyone come by to check on her? We could arrange something at church, you know. We visit about two dozen people every day."

"No, no, she doesn't need that." She smiled and shrugged her shoulders. "My dad's around most of the time, and she's not much for visitors." Now *that* was an understatement. "But I'll tell her you mentioned it."

"All right, honey." She leaned over and kissed her on the cheek. "I sure have missed you. With so many of my own kids, it hardly makes sense that I have the time, but I always felt particularly close to you."

"Me too, Janet. I'd love to reconnect and spend some time with you."

"Then stop in when you're down here. You don't have to call first. We're always home."

"I will." She shifted nervously. "But I'm not down very often." She was tempted to say that her mother's dislike of visitors extended to her, but she hated to beg for sympathy. "I'd like to find the birthday boy at some point. And say hi to all of the other kids."

"You've got to keep moving if you want to get them all in. Beth held onto you too long."

"Beth?"

Janet laughed, then leaned forward and said, "Jill didn't recognize Beth, Mike."

"That was Beth?" Now she was certain her eyes would pop out. Beth was a snot-nosed little kid who idolized her older brother and could never understand why he—and Jill spent most of their youth evading her. When they had to keep an eye on a younger sibling, they'd always called dibs on Adam or Tim, leaving the older girls to try to keep Beth at bay.

"Yes, that's my baby. I think she's half in the bag. She's been down in the dumps, and it looks like she's taking advantage of the fact that she doesn't have to drive home." She patted Jill on the back, giving her a slight shove. "Go keep an eye on her will you, honey?"

"Sure. But if you see Mark…"

"I'll send him your way." Janet pulled her close and kissed her cheek again. "Come see me. Promise."

"I do promise," she said soberly. "And I always keep my promises."

"Go," Janet urged. "She's getting up for more ice. Take her for a walk or something."

"I'm on it." Jill got to her feet and tried to get her emotions in check. Seeing Janet again had brought up so many feelings, she didn't have anywhere to put them all. As she moved across the room she did an emotional double-take. She'd thought Beth was hitting on her! The little squirt was still fucking with her all these years later.

After forcefully pushing through the crowd, she intercepted Mark's little sister as she was filling up her glass with ice. "Hey, *Beth*," she said pointedly. "You knew I didn't recognize you!"

"Sure did," she said, smirking. "Not my fault you didn't know I'd changed my name."

"Your parents don't seem to know either," Jill pointed out.

"Eh. They forget. You know how parents are. Want a refill?"

"Not right now. Hey, will you help me find Mark? I'm driving back to Burlington tonight and I want to make sure I have a few minutes with him."

"All right. But you'd better not try to pawn me off on one of my sisters. I know your tricks." They struggled through the main floor, finding themselves in the spacious kitchen, where a cold breeze blew in around the ill-sealed door. "Let's take a breather. It's stifling in here."

"Let me get my coat."

"Take one of these," she said, going down a couple of stairs.

The entryway was, as it had been twenty years ago, covered with coats hanging from hooks. Jill didn't know if guests or family members had hung this particular bunch here, but she quickly found a parka that fit. Beth put on a big, dark wool coat that had to have been one of the boys'. *Lizzie. She wants to be called Lizzie.* "I'm right behind you."

As they went out into the moonless night, they had to pass through a clique of smokers huddled close to the house. Heading for fresh air, Jill could hear the river and knew they were just a few yards away from the fourteenth hole. Her heart rate picked up and she headed right for it, even in the dark. Her hand caught the net, hearing the reassuring clink as the metal strands collided. "God, we had fun playing Frisbee golf."

"We all still play," Lizzie said. "In the summer everyone from my mom on down is out here. If my dad didn't have to tote that damned oxygen tank, he'd still be playing."

"It's pretty unique. You've got to admit that."

"That's small-town Vermont for you. Eighteen different neighbors, all allowing a bunch of people to traipse along their property, whooping and hollering when a disk lands in the net."

"Sugar Hill is too small for me," Jill admitted, "but sometimes Burlington's too big. Know what I mean?"

"I do. I live there, you know."

"Burlington?"

"Uh-huh. I moved about a year ago. For a *guy*," she emphasized. "Never a good idea."

"What happened?"

Lizzie turned and headed back towards the house, but when they got close, she stopped. "I need a little light to be able to talk."

A vivid memory, of the older kids torturing the baby of the family, formed in Jill's head. "Still afraid of the dark?"

"Of course not. I just prefer light."

Jill could see she'd offended her. Probably because she was still afraid of the dark at…god, she had to be thirty now. "So, I had a good job at the Gardner Museum in Boston, but I met this super guy who convinced me to move to Burlington when he got a big promotion to be brewmaster at Camel's Hump Brewery."

"Oh, right in town. I know just where that is."

"Yeah. It was a good job, but it didn't work out between us."

"Was this a recent thing? Your breakup?"

"Really recent, but I haven't made a point to tell everyone. My mom knows, but she usually keeps things to herself—unless she has some other purpose in spilling your secrets."

Jill laughed. "Now *that* sounds like your mom." She looked at the way the unflattering bulb in the porch-light made Lizzie's fair skin take on a green tinge. "What happened, if you don't mind saying."

"Mmm." She seemed to think for a minute, or maybe she was deciding how much to tell. "I want to have kids, right?"

"Uhm, sure. Most people do."

"Right. So I've spent the last five years looking for a guy who'd be a good father, and damned if I didn't find him."

"The brewmaster."

"Yep. He'd be an awesome dad. Reliable, patient, gentle, fun-loving. All of the things you wish your dad had been."

"I wish mine had been home," Jill said, wincing when she caught herself. "Sorry. I shouldn't bitch about him."

Lizzie put a hand on her arm and looked up, empathy showing in her pale eyes. "It must be a bitch to have your dad be the town slut."

Jill couldn't help but laugh at her term. "Yeah, it was hard, but…" She started to laugh. "It must not be very hard now, since he's home a lot more."

"He wore it out," Lizzie agreed, laughing even harder. "Oh, that's good." She wiped at her eyes and took a breath.

"I always wondered how much people talked about my dad and his… hobbies. Apparently, it's common knowledge."

"Pretty much," Lizzie agreed, her smile having vanished. Her eyes held a certain sadness, or maybe that was sympathy Jill saw in them. "Do you remember my mom's mom? Grandma Sophia?"

"Sure. Of course," Jill said, thinking of the spritely, no-nonsense old woman.

"Have you seen her?"

"Here?" Jill's eyes bugged out. The woman would have to be well over ninety.

"Where else? She and my grandpa are still going strong. Go find them. They always liked you."

"I will. I'll get right on it."

"Oh," Lizzie said, obviously recalling she'd been telling a story. "Anyway, I was at the market with Grandma one day, and your dad came in. I remember her saying, 'That man's too good looking for a town this small.'"

Nodding, Jill said, "She might have had a point."

"I was just a kid," Lizzie added, clearly finding the incident funny. "I didn't know what the heck she was talking about. But it stuck with me." Her gaze grew more focused as she cocked her head to one side. "Probably because you looked so much like him. I didn't want you to be in trouble for being good looking."

"Not to worry," Jill said, laughing at the concept. "I might look a lot like my dad, but I didn't inherit his need to take a bite of every apple."

Lizzie let out a sigh, looking a little melancholy. "Good old reliable Jon would never have cheated on me. I'm certain of that."

"But he wasn't right for you?"

"Not sure. But I clearly wasn't right for him. It turns out that I have to find a guy who wants to put up with me for fifty years, *then* make sure he'd be a good dad. I had my priorities screwed up."

"I'm sorry it didn't work out," Jill said. "Like I said, I'm single—again. It's no fun."

"We should get together and have coffee. I work at Hollyhock Hills. Are you anywhere near there?"

"That's no art museum. What do you do there?"

"I milk cows."

Eyes wide, Jill just nodded. "I guess someone has to…"

Lizzie slapped her on the arm, a little harder than was necessary. "I work in development."

"Oh, you're the one who tries to talk little old ladies into leaving you their estate. So other people can milk the cows."

"Something like that. I've been lucky to work for organizations I love. Even though it didn't work out with Jon, I'm going to stay in Burlington. I missed the hell out of Vermont."

"That makes two of us. I feel a little sorry for people who live in the boring states."

"I haven't traveled around the US much, but I've never been anywhere I like better."

"Same goes for me. I've never gone far from home, but I'm settled now. Burlington's been a great home for me."

"Home," Lizzie said dramatically. "I wish I could afford a home. I'm competing against thousands of students for a decent rental. I was hoping Jon would let me stay and pay rent for a while, but he wanted me out by sundown."

"Ouch. I'm lucky enough to own a house close to work. I can walk when it's not below zero or a white-out."

"Didn't we have a great winter?" Lizzie asked, rolling her eyes. "I never thought I'd miss a Boston winter."

"All part of the charm of Vermont." Jill inclined her head towards the house. "You don't think your brother left, do you?"

"He might have," she admitted. "He hates crowds. I can't believe he came at all, but then I can't believe his wife threw a big party for him. I'm not sure if she thought he'd like it, or she was punishing him."

"I'll do another loop and try to track him down." She put her hand on Lizzie's shoulder and gave it a squeeze. "Give me a call one day. We'll go have coffee."

"Got a card?"

"Sure." Jill pulled her wallet from her back pocket and extracted a business card.

Lizzie took her hand from her pocket, and flicked the card between her fingers. "Comptroller, huh? No wonder you can afford a house."

"I'm also old," Jill teased. "If I remember correctly, you used to call Mark and me old, mean jerks."

Smiling brightly, Lizzie said, "You don't seem like a jerk...now. Or mean."

"I'll take that compliment, even though it was backhanded." As she walked towards the house, she said one last time. "Don't forget to call. Spring is just around the corner, and it doesn't last long."

❧

It took two hours to make the rounds, but Jill was buzzing with the high of being welcomed so warmly back into the family, from nonagenarian grandparents to a darling little girl who was the current youngest Davis.

Chris, Adam and Tim had set up a plumbing and heating shop close to Bellows Falls, and each one made it a point to demand she come visit. Donna, the eldest, and her husband lived in Portland with their five kids, and they were equally insistent on extracting a promise to visit. Now Jill stood next to Kristen, trying to get used to how a twenty-eight year old fresh-faced third grade teacher looked now that she had a smattering of gray in her dark red hair, and crow's feet etched upon the corners of her eyes. Kristen was...forty-six, Jill decided, always having to take her own age, add eight years for Donna, then work her way down the line.

"You're still teaching?" Jill asked.

16

"Oh, sure. You can't get out once you start. The retirement benefits are too good. I'll get nearly half of my salary if I stay for another six years."

"That's pretty young to retire," Jill said.

"Yeah, it is, but my oldest, Jeffrey, is getting married in April. I assume he and his wife will have a baby or two in the next six years. I could be happy babysitting for them."

Jill forced herself not to look shocked. Jeffrey had been in kindergarten the last time she'd seen him, so imagining him old enough to marry was tough. More than that, it struck her how differently you looked at the world when you had kids. She was just six years younger than Kristen, but she felt like she'd just barely gotten to where she wanted to be at work, with one more promotion a real possibility. Retirement was something far, far off in the future. You could be more selfish, and more career-defined when you were childless.

After she and Kristen parted, Jill moved around the cramped room, still searching for Mark. There were so many redheads moving around, she kept thinking she'd seen him, but it was always a twenty-something guy, probably one of Janet's grandkids. Damn, the Davises clearly didn't have a problem with fertility. Maybe Lizzie didn't need a husband. She could just click her heels together and a baby would appear.

After a few hours, Jill had to concede that Mark didn't want to be found. She'd spoken to everyone she knew, and wasn't in the mood to track down everyone's kids to spend a few awkward minutes trying to remember names. Since she hated making her way around a crowd, saying the same pat goodbyes to everyone, she had, over the years, perfected the fade out at parties. She slipped out without a word, then called the hosts the next day, apologizing for not saying a proper goodbye. Now seemed like the perfect time to execute her move.

A couple with a sleeping baby in tow were slowly heading for the front door, pausing to say multiple goodbyes. After moving as quickly as she could to retrieve her coat, she went out and held the screen door open as they wrangled a carseat out, then followed them to the street.

The neighborhood was packed with cars, bumper to bumper all the way down to the river. Her car was down close to the babbling stream, and she took advantage of the opportunity to stand on the rock-covered bank and simply listen. It was damned cold, with snow still blanketing nearly everything, but she'd gotten overheated at the party and was happy for the chill.

As she stood on the very familiar road, lifting the collar of her jacket against the wind, she opened her senses and took everything in. There might have been nicer sounds than a gently flowing river, but she hadn't heard them yet. The scraggly saplings along the banks were stripped bare, and they swayed, naked, in the breeze. A cold winter's night smelled so damned good, with wood smoke wafting along on the wind and tickling her nose.

Jill took her phone from her pocket and checked the time—11:25. She counted down the distance to her house each time she made the trip, knowing it was 138 miles from Sugar Hill to her front door. She'd only had one drink, but was worn out from socializing. With an unhappy grunt, she got into her car and drove to her parents' house. She almost referred to it as home, but that was a slip. Home was Burlington. And maybe, if things worked out, a little piece of the Davis home could be hers once again.

Chapter Two

THE LIGHTS WERE ON, which was good. Or bad, depending on the day. At least her mother wouldn't call the cops, which was always a possibility when she was startled. The police must have had the house on the top position of their GPS. The thought made her laugh to herself. If you needed GPS in Sugar Hill, you shouldn't be driving. Six hundred people, many of them Davises, maybe twelve roads, some of them unpaved.

Jill closed her car door loudly. Yep. There she was. Her mother stood in front of the picture window, peering out at the driveway. By the time Jill reached the front door, it was open.

"What are you doing here?"

She flinched a little. This was what she was used to, but after being treated so kindly, it was jarring.

"It's too late for me to drive home. You don't mind, do you?"

Her mother was still fully dressed, protected against the sixty-two degree temperature she always had the thermostat set at.

White turtleneck, dark blue cardigan, blue and black lumberjack plaid woolen over-shirt and gray corduroy slacks. Her basic uniform from September until June. Then she changed to an oxford-cloth shirt and khakis. If Jill ever woke from a long coma, she'd be able to tell if it was summer or winter by her mother's clothing. That is, if her mother took the trouble to go all the way to the hospital. That wasn't a slam-dunk.

"I guess not," Nancy Henry said, stepping back to let her only child in. "But you should have called. I wasn't expecting you."

"I know, Mom. And I'm sorry. But I know you'd rather I surprised you than fell asleep at the wheel."

"That's a stupid thing to say," she snapped. "Who'd want that?"

"Exactly." Jill scooted past her mother to head for the bath. She'd had to pee for an hour, but wasn't about to wait in a huge line for one of the two bathrooms at the Davis house.

When she emerged, her mom was sitting in her preferred chair in the living room, watching one of her favorite channels. Yet another frantic emergency room with a shooting victim being tended to. For someone who didn't care much about people, she sure did like to see doctors working furiously to save strangers' lives.

Standing there as her mom's attention was fixed on the screen, Jill spent a minute looking at her. She wasn't a bad looking woman by any means, but anyone would agree that Rich Henry could have done better.

She was just past sixty, with surprisingly dark, long hair that she'd always worn in a braid. She'd decided long ago that doctors caused most health problems, so she'd avoided them almost completely, proud of the fact that she hadn't been inside a doctor's office in twenty years. Luckily, she was seemingly healthy, and had very good habits. No smoking, no drinking, low stress, a moderate diet and plenty of sleep.

Even at that, she looked older than she was. Her pinched expression and the permanent lines etched between her brows definitely added to her years. From the few pictures Jill had seen, the sour expression had always been there. Even as a child, a camera had never caught her genuinely smiling. Maybe she had good reasons to seem so unhappy. If she did, Jill wasn't privy to them.

"I'm going to head to bed," Jill said, starting for her room.

Annoyed, her mother impatiently waved her aside. Jill hadn't realized she'd blocked her view, and she moved four feet, just to be sure she was out of the way.

"Are you leaving in the morning?"

"Yeah, I guess so."

With a scowl, her mother said, "I'd like to know your plans, Jill. I've got a life too."

"Yes," she said, decisively. "I'm leaving in the morning. Probably before you're up."

"All right. I'll see you next time."

Jill stood there for a second, not sure if she should go for a hug or not. Sometimes her mother wanted one, sometimes she acted like she was being molested if you tried to touch her. Not wanting to screw up, Jill opted out. "Okay, then. See you."

There were no complaints as she went down the hall, so she'd made the right choice. Nearly forty years of guessing had to result in some successes, and she gladly took the win.

As she closed the door to her room, she conceded that she'd fibbed a little with Lizzie. Her dad was still out trying to find female companionship most nights, but she'd told the truth about his increasing failure rate. At least, she assumed he was striking out more often. His snoring presence, before midnight on a Saturday, was a pretty recent phenomenon. Jill would never know if her mother liked his being home more or not. There was truly no way to tell.

⤙⤚

The poem said that April was the cruelest month, but Jill voted for February. It had been cold since November, and wouldn't even begin to truly warm up until May—maybe even June if they didn't get lucky.

She sat with her defroster running, trying to decide where to go for breakfast. Back to town was the smart move, but that would put her close to the blacksmith's shop, and she wasn't sure she even wanted to see Mark. Why bother to invite her, then go out of his way to hide?

Softening, she conceded that he'd always been a hider. His passiveness was one of the parts of his personality that she'd liked. Getting nothing but grief at home, it was nice to hang out with a kid who never pushed, never argued, never gave anyone a bit of trouble. Mark praised every decision she made, loved every musical group she favored, every book she read. Maybe Lizzie had been right. That might have been a crush. Poor guy! It'd be just like Mark to pick a clueless lesbian to crush out on.

Making up her mind, Jill headed for town. If Mark didn't have the guts to face her, he'd have to run from his own shop.

The town was just waking up, with a few cars on the main road and a bunch of tourists driving around, probably looking for the cross-country ski trails. People from all over came to Sugar Hill to rent equipment and trek over the bucolic landscape. Or they might have simply been driving around, sightseeing.

To her, it was just home. Home back to at least her paternal great-grandparents. Her mother's side were newcomers, down from Canada around the early 1900s. But Sugar Hill was also a town captured in amber.

In the sixties, an investment banker with local ties created a charitable entity dedicated to preserving small-town Vermont life. Over the years, the Foundation came to own most of the few businesses, along with a good portion of the land. A significant minority of the population worked for the Foundation and its businesses, the only thing keeping the town buoyant. Tourism was their lifeblood and, without complaint, they had to allow for slow-moving groups of hikers and bicyclists to stop and take pictures in front of one of the covered bridges. That was the only real downside of living in a picture-postcard, once-common way of life.

The barn door of the shop was open a crack, and Jill could see Mark building a fire in the huge hearth. He must have been making a lot of noise, for he didn't pick his head up when she closed her car door. When she crossed the threshold though, his head snapped up and she was pretty sure he was actually going to take off. Then he shuffled over to her, looking like a kid being sent to the principal's office.

The years hadn't been unkind. Mark actually looked better than he had when they'd graduated from UVM. Work had made his shoulders broader and square, and his bare forearms rippled with muscle. He'd put on a little weight, but he'd needed to, always being bean-stalk thin. And he finally had a decent haircut, with his wavy dark red hair lying down neatly. The mustache and goatee were a surprise, with the hair there brown with a little gray mixed in.

"I'm sorry I was such a wuss," he grumbled, staring at the aged stone floor.

She put a hand on his shoulder and pulled him in for a hug, with his body relaxing against hers as they held each other for a minute. "It's all right. I know you hate parties."

Jill released him and he moved back over to his big, brick forge. The same one old Mr. Rooney and his predecessors had labored at. The fire had started, but without him tending it, it wasn't up to snuff. Jill watched as Mark expertly arranged another course of kindling and paper, then added a split log as the small pieces caught. He stepped back as the flames rose, then clapped the dirt from his hands.

"Yeah, I was uncomfortable, but that's no excuse." He shrugged. "I saw you come in and was going to come over, but I thought I'd wait until you were finished talking to Lisa." Shrugging again, he said, "Then you got waylaid by Beth, and I couldn't stand to be in that big crowd any longer."

"Where'd you go?" she asked gently.

"I was out in the backyard for a while, then went down by the river." His eyes met hers.

"You saw me go to my car, didn't you."

"Yeah. But by then it was too late. That would have really looked stupid."

Jill once more gripped his shoulder. "I've seen you eat paste. You don't ever have to worry about looking stupid around me."

He started to laugh, finally loosening up a little. "Yeah, I guess that's true." He poked at the fire, acting like it needed constant attention. "Lisa told me you don't have kids, my dad told me you were gorgeous, my mom told me you were single, and Beth told me you had a big job at the U. Anything else I should know?"

"Yeah." She put her hands on his shoulders, just to hold him still. "I was hurt. Very hurt, when you ditched me after we graduated. But I'm over that. I love you and I love your family. I'd like to see all of you again. What do you think?"

"I…" He sucked his lower lip into his mouth and chewed on it for a few seconds. "I'd like that." Their eyes met. "You *know* that, right? You know I never wanted to…" His cheeks flushed, their color almost matching his hair.

"I know Lisa's not crazy about me. I can't say why, given that I barely said two words to her in high school, but…whatever."

"Maybe that's it," he said, clearly guessing. "She was a year younger. Maybe she wanted you to notice her."

"Yeah, maybe." She wasn't going to tell Mark that she'd always thought Lisa was a prissy jerk, but he couldn't have been dumb enough not to have noticed by now. Lisa was a decent looking girl, but she had an ugly mean streak that she always wrapped up in her religious convictions, which she wore on her sleeve. "Are you guys still involved at church?"

"Oh, yeah. Lisa spends most of her day over there, when she's not dragging the kids around. She's got a hand in everything."

"I bet she does." The fire had settled down, and Jill watched Mark tend it for a few seconds. "I recognize some of these machines," she said, when she had his attention again. "But some of them are new."

"Yeah, this TIG welder's pretty new. Old man Rooney did everything by hand. But I'm trying to expand the business." He went over to a side bench and picked up a graceful candelabra made from forged iron. At the end of each curved rod was a marker for a lobster trap. "I'm making these for a woman who runs a shop up in Maine on the coast. She sells all I can make."

"Nice," Jill said, admiring the piece. "This wouldn't fit in my house, but I'd love to have one of your creations."

"I'll make you whatever you want," he said, eager, as always, to please.

"How much does the lobster buoy go for?"

"Four fifty."

She almost dropped it. "Four hundred and fifty dollars?"

He winced as he took it back. "It takes me at least twenty hours labor for this. That's not including materials." He tapped the buoy. "These are antique. Not that plastic stuff they use now."

"Hey," she said, placing a hand on his back. "I didn't mean to insult you. I just can't imagine people having that kind of money to spend on a lamp." Gripping his heavy flannel shirt, she pushed him a bit. "And you're not going to give me something that costs four hundred and fifty dollars!"

She poked around the shop, finally holding up a wrought iron toilet paper holder. "What do you charge for this?"

"Fifty bucks," he said, his voice reflecting uncertainty.

"Can I buy it? It'll fit perfectly in my bathroom."

"Take it. Please," he said, almost begging.

"Deal." She slipped the piece into her coat pocket. "Next time, I'm going to take the forge if you skip out on me."

24

He looked like he thought she was serious, and it dawned on her that despite being invited back, things might not have changed a bit. "Are we going to be able to be friends again?"

He shoved his hands in his pockets, the epitome of indecision. Thank god he'd changed his mind about being an accountant. He'd still be trying to close the books from his first year in practice. "I think so. I hope so. Can we see how things go?"

"Yeah. No problem." Jill put her arms around him and gave him a brief hug. "But I'm going to reestablish a relationship with your mom. I promised I would, and I always keep my promises."

"We both promised we'd always be best friends," he said, looking at her with true pain in his eyes.

"Maybe we will be," she said, cuffing him on the chin. "I'm ready when you are."

⁂

The first of May turned out to be a perfect day for a wedding. Jill stood on a slight incline next to a gorgeous, turn-of-the-century building they called a barn. This barn, built to house coaches and wagons, was beautifully shingled and roofed with copper, now turned green with age.

Jill turned to watch her co-worker, the VP of Legal Affairs, shed her super-serious work demeanor to dance like a woman possessed. Co-workers' weddings were often revelatory, and this one was going according to form.

Cari Hunt, one of Jill's employees, sidled up next to her. "Did you have any idea Karina could dance?"

"I had no idea she could smile, much less dance."

"Too true," Cari agreed. "I think she might have had one too many glasses of champagne."

"No such thing at your wedding." Jill held her flute up. "But I'm stopping at two. I've never been an afternoon drinker."

Cari was avidly watching the dance floor, but she narrowed her eyes and said, "I can hit any afternoon pretty hard if I'm with a group. But then I go to sleep by about seven. No matter where I am," she added, laughing. "My friends almost left me on an island last summer when I was so trashed they couldn't wake me."

"You can still get away with that," Jill said. "When you do that in your forties, don't be surprised if your nearest and dearest show up for an intervention."

Cari's amused expression showed she was fairly sure she was never going to age. "I've got plenty of time left to be a screwup."

Jill noticed that her speech was less crisp than normal. And admitting to your boss that you were a screwup was never a great idea. To save the kid from further indicting herself, she said, "I need to find the bathroom. Catch you later."

"If you're not gonna finish that champagne..."

Clutching the flute to her chest, Jill waved her off and walked towards the barn, stopping abruptly when she got close. Lizzie Davis was standing by the entrance, surrounded by a small group of people, all late middle-aged, all prosperous looking. Squeezing money out of people on a Saturday afternoon? Jill hadn't given much thought to what it would be like to work for a foundation that ran and operated a farm, but it must have been worlds different from working at an art museum, Lizzie's previous job. However, no matter the organization, they all needed people donating on a consistent basis to keep the doors open.

Moving across the drive to stand under one of the tents the wedding party had rented, she watched Lizzie work. It was always interesting to see someone you knew plying her trade, even though she had to admit she barely knew Lizzie at all. When Jill and Mark had left Sugar Hill for college, Lizzie was just in second or third grade, simply a kid who got in the way when they were at the house. The main thing Jill recalled was that Lizzie was terminally afraid of the dark, threw a fit about going to bed, and was always trying to get Mark to notice her.

As Jill watched her try to charm big bucks out of some well-heeled folks, she didn't see much of Beth the Brat. Instead, a composed, mature woman cocked her head, listening patiently as one of her guests asked a question. Jill stepped back to look at her as she would a stranger—not too great a leap in this case.

Somehow Lizzie had escaped the various shades of orange or red hair that her siblings had, as well as the freckles. Those looked adorable on kids, but must have been tough for a woman trying to look mature. She wore a fashionable, not flashy, dress, and heels low enough to let her walk along the gravel paths without twisting an ankle. She could have passed for forty, in a good way, not having any of that overly-enthusiastic, self-deprecating, flustered stuff that so many young professionals struggled with. No, Lizzie had grown into an adult. A true adult—at least when she was at work. She'd definitely acted her age at Mark's party.

She finished her spiel, then urged the group to continue up the path to the main house. Striding along at the back of the group, she put her hand down by her butt and wiggled her fingers, acting like she had a tail. Jill burst out laughing, and when Scott Simmons, the University Budget Director came up beside her, he said, "Do you know that woman?"

"Yeah. Old family friend."

"Cute," he said, narrowing his eyes as he checked her out.

"Yeah, she is. She's looking for a husband. Interested?"

"Why not? How old?"

Jill turned to him, and tried to guess the point of his question. "Is there an age limit?"

"Yeah," he admitted, laughing a little. "I want to have kids, so I'm not interested in anyone who's down to their last egg."

"Really nice," she said, patting his cheek a little harder than she should have. "I'm sure Lizzie has plenty of eggs, but I don't think I want her to waste them on you."

"Come on," he insisted. "I'm a great guy, and she's got a really nice caboose. Introduce me."

She stepped back to get a good look at him. "Caboose? Seriously?"

He turned to watch Lizzie's group move up the gentle hill. "Tell me I'm wrong."

Jill refused to even look. "She's my friend's little sister. As far as I'm concerned, she's caboose free—if I were crass enough to use that term. Which I'm not."

"Uh-huh," he said, his soft laugh annoying her. "It's all right. I won't tell anyone you were looking at her ass. Your secret's safe with me."

"I was not!" she said, drawing looks from a few people. "I was not," she added, quieter this time. "How would you like your friends checking out your sister's ass?"

"Fine by me. It's her ass to do with as she sees fit." He leaned close and shook his head mournfully. "I believe in treating women like mature adults. Maybe you should talk to someone about your need to control other people."

"What?" She started to snap off a retort, then realized he was screwing with her. "Okay, okay." She took in a breath, embarrassed at her reaction. "I'll see if she's interested in a nice looking guy with a good job"—she gave him a big, fake smile—"who thinks of women as parts of a train."

❧

The party was still rocking as the sun started to set. It had been unseasonably warm, probably over seventy, but Jill knew people would begin to head for their cars as the temperature dropped. She was sitting at a big table of people from various parts of admin when someone tapped her right shoulder. When she turned her head, no one was behind her. Another tap, this time on the left, and she whipped around to see an impishly grinning Lizzie. Maybe she did still have a little of Beth the Brat hiding inside that mature facade.

Jill stood and tried to decide, in a split second, whether to offer a hug. Lizzie didn't lean in, so she let it pass. They really didn't know each other well enough to make one an automatic gesture. "What are you doing here on a Saturday?" Jill asked.

"I work weekends a lot. Especially during the spring and summer. That part kinda sucks."

Jill moved away from her table, mostly to avoid having to introduce Lizzie to a bunch of people she'd never see again. "I thought you were going to call."

"I'm going to. It's only been a couple of…months." She shrugged, not looking embarrassed in the least. "Busy season."

Jill let her gaze travel around the rolling landscape, the year's first grass crop rendering it a stunningly beautiful shade of green. "It's gorgeous around here. I've been in Burlington on and off for twenty-two years, and this is my first visit."

"You're kidding!" Lizzie looked like she'd confessed to never having tasted maple syrup. "Everyone comes to Hollyhock Hills."

"Not everyone, since I haven't. But my co-worker, the bride over there getting her groove on, decided to get married here, so I finally had a reason to come."

Scowling, Lizzie said, "She didn't just *decide* to have her wedding here. She won the lottery."

Jill laughed. "It's a nice wedding, but I don't think she had to win the lottery to pay for it. She's got a good job."

Lizzie rolled her eyes. "When I was a kid, I was sure you were really, really smart. I guess age gives you better perspective. You know, like how your grade school seems tiny when you look at it years later?"

Jill play-punched her in the arm. "So my brain seemed big then, but its shrunk?"

"It must have." She took Jill by the elbow and led her out of the tent. "Let me walk you around. You're not going to get the whole picture if you stay here."

Jill almost begged off, but the party was winding down, and she was about to do her fade out anyway. They started to walk towards a very large, beautifully constructed house, sitting proud on a small hill.

"We only allow twelve weddings a year, so we have a lottery to choose the lucky couples. We get a few thousand entries, so your friends really did get lucky."

"Thousands?" Jill looked back at the tent, now able to see how lovely the site was. "It looks better from here," she mused. "You get a better perspective."

"Yeah, you do. But people love this place from any perspective, Jill. They truly love it. If we allowed it, we could rake in truckloads of cash by just renting the place out for events."

"Why don't you?"

Lizzie gave her a gentle slap to the side of her head. "All of that traffic would screw with the animals! Damn, don't you have a soul?"

"I think I do," she said, looking down at her chest. "But I guess I've never seen it, so I can't be sure…"

"Look," Lizzie said, grasping Jill by the shoulders and turning her so they faced the broad expanse of land. "This is one of the prettiest places in Vermont. The preeminent landscape architect of his day—maybe the best American designer *ever*—laid the whole place out. This was a flat piece of unadorned land by the lake—nothing special—and now it has thousands of trees, every kind of native plant, hills, valleys, hidden paths, forested glens. It's a goddamned showplace!"

Jill laughed at her exuberance. "Sell it, girl! I'm ready to rewrite my will."

"You should," she said, clearly miffed. "It takes a lot of money to keep the place going for its intended purpose, and I'm passionate about that."

"Don't hit me," Jill said, moving away in case Lizzie didn't follow orders, "but I don't know what its purpose was."

"It's a damn model farm!" She kicked at a stone, leaving a white mark on her nice, navy blue heels. "If people who've lived here their whole adult lives don't know that… Shit," she grumbled, looking truly upset.

"I'm really unaware," Jill insisted. "I get focused on the stuff I like and don't look around. Really. I see ads for events out here all of the time, but I've never been interested in any of them." She stepped back another foot, making sure Lizzie couldn't reach her with a punch. "What's a model farm?"

"God damn it!" She grasped Jill by the shoulder of her jacket and started off, quickly, back down the path. They passed the wedding, then kept going until they reached a large, low, red brick building. "This is the dairy barn," she said. "You know that milk comes from cows, right?"

"Uhm…milk," Jill said, squinting. "That's the stuff they use to make ice cream, right?"

"Oh, you're friggin' hilarious," Lizzie said, still scowling. "Around 1900, the daughter and son-in-law of a big industrial magnate spent a shit-ton of their own money to build this place. A lot of the country was still agrarian, but more and more people were leaving farming to move to big, industrialized cities."

"I learned about that from your father," Jill agreed. "He loves to talk about the Industrial Revolution."

"Right. Well, our founders reasoned that using cutting-edge farming practices could keep the country fed, even if the number of farms continued to shrink. So they did all sorts of research to determine the best kind of cattle for milk production, the right way to graze them, the perfect feed—everything they could think of to optimize the land. We're still trying to do that," she insisted. "It's important work."

"You really care," Jill was touched by her passion.

"I do. I care much more than I did about the museum—even though I'm crazy about art. I love having this big piece of gorgeous land, right on the shores of Lake Champlain, serving as a model of animal husbandry and agriculture and landscape architecture. This place shows how you can make land beautiful, while still making it productive."

"Damn," Jill said, thoroughly impressed. "It's really cool they were so successful."

Lizzie's shoulders sank. "They kinda weren't," she admitted. "Farmers don't like to take advice from rich city people who learned everything in books. They had a hell of a time even getting people to use Swiss cows, which really are great for milk production."

"But it's still here after a hundred plus years. It's obviously been successful on some level."

Lizzie still looked a little defeated, but with the setting sun highlighting her gorgeous reddish brown hair and the light making her pale green eyes shimmer, it was hard to focus on the damn farm.

Lizzie was still locked into her reverie. When she spoke, her voice had a wistful quality to it. "The property is mostly intact because the grandchildren of the founders refused to sell to developers. They're the real heroes. They set up the foundation, which I work for, and we make some money selling cheese and knick-knacks. But we rely on government and foundation grants and individual bequests for most of our operating capital."

Jill put her index fingers up in the shape of a cross. "Don't speak of grant-writing. That's the work of the devil."

"You don't have to do that?"

"No way. I'm in charge of keeping track of money, not asking for it."

"I'm pretty good at it, but I prefer charming people into leaving us money through trusts and estates."

A gust of wind kicked up some clouds of dust, as well as Lizzie's skirt. She was clearly used to wearing dresses, because she unconsciously put her hand down by her knee, keeping her hem right where it belonged.

"You've got a very impressive job for someone your age," Jill said. "I mentor a group of young professionals at the U, and they'd kill to have that kind of responsibility."

"If I've made it sound like I'm in charge, I'm full of it. I've got a manager, and he reports to a VP who handles the big fish. I'm the one sniffing around for loose change. Like those people I was taking around today. I was trying to get them to adopt an acre of land. Small potatoes."

"Well, I would have whipped out my checkbook," Jill said, finding she meant it. "How much for an acre?"

"Ten thousand."

Nearly swallowing her tongue, Jill choked out, "Dollars?"

Lizzie laughed, then took Jill by the arm and led her over to the milking area. "Cheapskate. All talk, no action. Let's go check out the women who really keep this place going." She raised her voice and called out, "Hello, girls. I brought a friend."

A few cows mooed, but most were too busy chewing their cud as their bulging udders were being tended to by a couple of kids in big, mud-spattered boots. One of them spotted Lizzie and offered a hearty wave before she went back to work.

"I never pictured you as being the farm type," Jill said, as Lizzie waved back.

"How did you picture me?" Lizzie looked up at her and blinked coquettishly.

"Uhm…"

32

"You didn't spend two minutes of your whole life thinking of me, Jill Henry. Don't even try to lie."

"You were a kid!"

"Right. But I'm an adult now." She extended her hand and Jill took it, then Lizzie gave it a hearty shake. "If you'll think of me as a fellow adult, I'll try to stop thinking of you as the super cool big kid."

"I can hold up my end of the bargain, but don't be too quick to reduce my cult-like status." She laughed to herself at the thought of Lizzie or anyone else thinking of her as super cool. "Hey, a guy I work with wants to ask you out. What do you think?"

"Someone here today?"

"Well, yeah. Where else would he have checked out your butt?"

Lizzie took Jill by the arm and marched her back to the party. "Why didn't you tell me you had a lead in my marriage quest? I've been wasting my time talking about cows when I could be charming the pants off some prospect."

Rushing to keep up with Lizzie's pace, Jill said, "You don't mind that he was mainly interested in your butt?"

"Hell no. Why penalize a guy for being perceptive?"

❧

A couple of weeks later, Jill was sitting in her office, rushing to organize a series of reports to close the books on spring term. Scott, her friend from the budget office, walked in and dropped inelegantly into one of the chairs that faced her desk. He had a full head of dark hair that he'd obviously been running his hands through. A big hank that should have been on the left side had crossed over to the right, and was sticking up a little. "If I'm going to have any chance at a weekend, I need your numbers, stat."

Without looking up, she moved her chair a little closer to the twin monitors that took up most of the center of her substantial desk. "Working on it." He didn't get up, so she added, "The end of a semester's always a bear. What makes you think you're going to get a weekend this time?"

He didn't reply, and after a few more seconds ticked away, she turned to look at him. He was wearing his reading glasses, and he gazed at her over the tops of them. "I'm supposed to take Lizzie out tomorrow, and I don't want to have to cancel."

She scooted her chair away from the desk, then leaned back in it, studying him. "Is that right?"

"That's right. Since you set us up, you're invested."

Humming a little tune, she focused on her monitors again, a smirk in place. "First date with a woman with viable eggs. Whoop-de-do!"

"Third date," he corrected. "We got together a couple of days after we met, and again last Sunday." He held up three fingers and wiggled them. "I make it a habit to cut bait if I don't make some serious progress by date number three."

Putting her fingers into her ears, she shook her head. "Enough! I'll work through the night to make sure you've got my numbers. Just promise you'll never give me any details about whatever you're *not* going to do to that poor child."

"It's all because of you," he said, loudly enough to penetrate her rudimentary ear plugs. "When we're sitting around, years from now, telling our kids how we met, you'll be the lynchpin."

She tore her attention from the column of numbers she was double-checking. "That's actually kind of nice to think of. I hope it works out for you two."

His lecherous grin came back. "Have I mentioned how sweet her caboose is? It feels even better than it looks."

"Out!" she demanded, pointing at the door. "Keep your dirty mind out of my office or I'll have to have it cleaned!"

Chapter Three

THROUGH DEDICATED EFFORT, AND more harassment from Scott than usual, the books were properly closed by late Saturday afternoon.

Now that she was free, Jill surveyed her options for the rest of the weekend. It once again felt more like the end of winter than the beginning of summer, with a solid week of gloomy, rainy, dismal skies depressing Jill much more than they should have. She'd been sitting far too much for the last few days, and perversely decided to make her butt hurt even more by driving to Sugar Hill. This going down twice in four months was rare for her, but ever since the party, she'd longed to spend some time with Janet and Mike. This was a perfect weekend to satisfy that desire.

Just to make sure, she called the Davis house to check that she wasn't interfering with any plans. When she got the okay, she called her parents' house to keep the police from wasting a trip when she unexpectedly knocked on the door. Now that she had the all clear, she grabbed a sandwich, a bottle of water, a big box of chocolate covered mints, and took off, really looking forward to being able to savor the mints. If she played it right, they'd last the whole trip. Maybe one…no, two…for every five miles she covered. She knew it was weird to play with her food, but she loved to make the things she liked last. And she really, really liked her mints.

On Sunday morning, right after she grabbed breakfast in town, Jill drove over to the Davis'. It was almost as cold, and equally cloudy as the previous day, but her mood was buoyant, reminding her of exactly how she used to feel when she'd get on her bike and ride over to the Davis house early on Saturday morning. They never did much, but the place was always full of life—and acceptance.

Janet opened the door after Jill rapped on the door twice. "I love a girl who keeps her promises," Janet said as she threw the door open and wrapped Jill in a hug.

"I don't make them if I don't think I can keep them."

They walked inside together, but before Jill could put her bag down, Janet said, "How about a walk? Mike can't get around the neighborhood much anymore, and I prefer to walk with a friend."

"I'd love to. I've been sitting on my butt for an entire week."

"Let me get my coat, and my damned gloves," she grumbled. "Go into the den and say hi to Mike before we leave. I think he's watching the Sox."

Jill ducked into the den, the space having earned that distinction after Donna and Kristen left for college. She still recalled their outrage when they'd returned from school to find a television, an easy chair, and a sofa in place of their beds. Space was always at a premium in the Davis house, and you couldn't abandon your plot for months at a time without a land grab. She'd felt so bad for the pair, she almost asked her mother if they could stay with them during winter break. However, overnight guests were never permitted at the Henry house, that was an edict so firmly entrenched she hadn't had the nerve to pose the question.

"Mr. Davis…I mean, Mike," she said when he looked up. "How are things?"

"I'm good," he said, but he sure didn't look it. His color was much worse than it had been the night of the party, and his voice sounded thinner. "I'm better than the Sox, that's for sure. I don't think this is gonna be our year, Jilly."

She almost teared up at his use of the nickname. No one in her own family had ever referred to her as anything but Jill.

She perched on the arm of the sofa and took a look at the score. "They've barely gotten out of the starting blocks. They'll be a better warm-weather team."

He took a quick glance out the window. "Don't know when that's gonna happen. I haven't been warm since August."

"It'll come," she said, hoping she was right. "Janet and I are going for a walk. Can we get you anything while we're out?"

"It's Sunday," he said, giving her a puzzled look. "Nothing's open."

"Then I hope you don't need anything. We'll be back soon."

"Don't rush," he said, waving a hand. "They've got another eight innings to torture me."

Jill went back to the living room, and held Janet's jacket for her to slip into.

"Thanks, honey. Does Mike want anything?"

"He said nothing was open, so I suppose not."

"If the market isn't open, he's not interested. They have ice pops he likes."

They went outside, and Jill buttoned her coat and turned the collar up. Ridiculous weather for May. "I'm surprised Mike wants ice pops. He said he's been cold since August."

A troubled expression crossed Janet's face, but it disappeared quickly. "That's because his circulation's so bad. But the ice feels good on his throat. That oxygen really dries him out."

"How long has he been using the oxygen?"

"About two, no three years. It helps, that's for sure, but it limits him too. He hates to go out now, not that he was ever much of a rambler."

"No, that's not a term I'd use for him," Jill agreed, putting her hand over Janet's when she threaded it around her arm.

"I just hope he doesn't suffer." Janet was staring straight ahead when she spoke, and her voice caught a little. "I can't talk to the kids about this. They all try to act like he'll live to a hundred." She pulled Jill closer and leaned into her for a few steps. "I feel like I can talk to you as an adult."

"You can," she agreed. "I love Mike, but not the way your kids do. I'm sure it's really hard on all of them to see their dad struggle."

"Sure. Of course it is. But they can't bury their heads in the sand. He's on borrowed time, Jill, and they're going to have to come to terms with that."

"I'm sorry," Jill said softly. "I really am."

"I should have broken up with him in 1965," Janet said, a flash of anger flitting across her face.

Jill stopped abruptly. "What?"

"I'm not saying I don't love the idiot," she insisted, bumping Jill's shoulder with her own. "But if I'd broken up with him because of that stupid habit, he might have dropped it. I never liked the damn things, but smoking was what people did. It never occurred to me to lay down the law."

"Don't blame yourself. He knew it was a dangerous habit."

"Yes, but no one thinks of things like that when they're fifteen. That's how old he was when he started. Your parents don't smoke, do they, honey?"

"Not my mom. Never. But my dad's one of those people who can smoke socially. He never buys a pack, but he'll have a few if someone offers them."

"He's still a good looking man," Janet said. "I see him around, at the market or the post office. He's working, isn't he?"

"Uh-huh. He's still a sales rep for that paper company in Brattleboro. I guess he's had the job for four or five years now."

"Still on the road, huh?" She gave Jill a half-smile.

"That's what he likes. He covers all of Vermont and New Hampshire."

They walked without speaking for a while, with Jill on the lookout for spring flowers. Forsythia was out, but other than a few crocuses, the earth didn't believe the calendar. As if Janet could hear her thoughts, she said, "They're still sugaring at Green Mountain Farms. Sugaring. In May!"

"Isn't the season usually over by April?"

"Every year that I can recall. They say climate change should give us earlier springs, but the weather didn't get the message this year. Of course, some damn fools say that means there's no such thing as global warming."

"People don't want to believe," Jill said. "If they believe it exists, they have to wonder what caused it. Then they might have to admit they played a role, however small." She shrugged. "It's hard for people to admit they might have helped screw up the planet for their kids and their grandkids."

"Acting like everything's the same doesn't make it so," Janet said, not a flicker of indecision in her sharp voice. "You've got to face facts and make plans. That's the only way out of trouble."

Jill squeezed her arm, feeling her whole body warm from that slight contact. "That's one of the things I admire about you, Janet. You don't lie to yourself."

"I try not to," she admitted. "It's a pretty stupid habit, if you ask me. But most people do it, so maybe I'm the odd duck." She got quiet again as they got close to the river. "Some of my kids think I'm too harsh. Too unsentimental."

Jill let out a soft laugh. "I could show them harsh, but my mom would call the police if I brought anyone over." She snapped her mouth shut. Talking in a disparaging way about her family was not something she did. Ever.

Janet pulled her to a halt, then peered up at her for a long while. "Do you know…" She pursed her lips together and tried again. "Does your mom have emotional problems? Or is she just…"

It was strange. Really strange to be talking about this, but no one had ever asked her so directly. Maybe it was all right. She took a breath and said, "I'm honestly not sure. I've always assumed she was just odd. But I've done some reading on psychological problems and I think she might have something going on." She stopped, then added, "Not that I could bring it up at this point, but if she'd had some help when she was young…" Sighing, she finished, "I'm not sure what she was like when she was young, but she had to be different. Otherwise, why would my dad have wanted to marry her?"

"Her money," Janet said, not even flinching. "I'm sorry, honey, but that's the damn truth. She had half of your grandfather's estate."

"Everybody knew about that, huh?" She'd hoped that wasn't true. Had honestly hoped her parents had loved each other at some point, but even mild affection had never been a visitor at the Henry house.

"Yes, sweetheart," Janet said with warmth. "There were four hundred people in town when we were kids. Everyone knew everybody and everything." She let out a short laugh. "We weren't the major metropolis that we are now."

"Population six hundred and fifty, unless you have more grandchildren on the way."

"No, but if we did, everyone would know. There aren't any secrets, Jill."

"But you didn't know if my mom had emotional problems or was just odd."

They started to walk again, and when Janet spoke she sounded very thoughtful. "We knew your dad better than your mom. She lived over near Rockingham, so we knew her more from church than town." She shrugged. "We all just thought she was odd. There are a lot of people like her in New England. Flinty."

"She's flinty, all right," Jill agreed. "I can't imagine how I would have turned out if I hadn't basically lived at your house." She stopped again and gazed into Janet's eyes for a minute. "I didn't get a chance to thank you when Mark and I..."

"There's no need," Janet said, briskly. "You fit in from the start. What's one more when you've got seven hungry little mouths?"

"I always felt bad that I couldn't reciprocate. I don't think Mark ever set foot inside my house."

"Well, I think you overstate the role we played, but if we did anything to help you grow into the lovely girl you are, I'm damned pleased."

"You did a lot," Jill insisted. "You made me feel like I wasn't an imposition." She winced when that came out. It was one thing to talk in generalities, and another to reveal too much.

Janet latched onto the word and looked at Jill, unblinking. "Is that how you felt? Like you were an imposition?"

She bit at her lip to keep from crying, but warm pale eyes bore into her own, welcoming her to tell the truth. "Yes," she said, her voice breaking. "It's how I still feel. They've never called me, never written me a birthday card, never asked for any details about my life. I've always felt like a boarder, a person just passing through."

Janet wrapped her arms around her waist and Jill lost it—completely. Sobbing against Janet's shoulder, she whimpered. "I don't like to complain. I know they do their best…"

"Nonsense. They've let you down, and so have we. I let Li…other people stop me from staying in contact with you—when I knew I should have. I knew you didn't have anyone else looking out for you, and I feel like shit about it, Jill. Just like shit."

"It wasn't your job," she murmured. "You fed me most nights, checked my homework, made sure I got to all of the birthday parties, got me involved at church, taught me to drive…and we weren't even related. You did more than anyone had any right to expect."

"But you needed more," Janet said fiercely. "And I closed my mind to that." She grasped her and shook her gently. "And for that I'm deeply, deeply sorry."

Jill stood up tall and wiped her eyes with her fleece gloves. "If there was anything to forgive, I'd forgive you. But there isn't, Janet. Honestly, there isn't. I was a college graduate when we lost touch. Well able to care for myself."

Janet's eyes were still trained on hers, showing warmth and real curiosity. "We all need others. Have you had people care for you? Women who've truly loved you?"

"Yeah, I have," she said, suddenly shy. "I met a woman when I was in grad school whose family treated me like one of their own."

"But you're not with her now?"

"Oh, god no!" The mere thought of it made her head swim. "She was a lovely person, but we weren't great together. We were together for almost two years, though."

"That's not very long, Jill."

"No, but it was enough. I started to learn what I needed in a partner and almost got it a few times." With as much confidence as she could build, she said, "I've surrounded myself with friends I can rely on. And I've had some good relationships. I've been loved, Janet. I really have."

"I'm so glad," she said, grasping Jill's hand with a surprising amount of strength. "A lot of people who were raised in such a cold place would turn out to be just as withdrawn."

"I'm not," Jill insisted. "And, even if you won't accept the truth, that's because of you and Mike and your kids. You saved me."

∞

Jill tapped her foot as she waited in line for her morning coffee. She had a coffee maker at home, but much preferred buying a cup on campus, so she could enjoy it while navigating her in-box. It also didn't hurt that they had killer scones. She didn't allow herself to order one every day, but Monday mornings usually required a treat to make them more bearable.

She was on her way out when Scott came in, looking worse for wear. "Hey," she said, brightly.

"Shh!" He held a finger up to his lips. "I spent waaaay too long at a craft beer tasting yesterday."

"How was your weekend? I know you had special plans—that I don't want to hear about."

"Then you won't. I'll stop by your office when I can talk."

"Busy morning? Things are calm for me, now that the term's over."

"I'll come by when I'm *able* to talk," he clarified. "My schedule's empty."

Jill took an indirect path to her office, enjoying the early morning calm of the campus when most of the students had departed for the summer. She was in a great mood, finding the long drive to Sugar Hill rejuvenating rather than the drain on her energy it usually was. Having a pair of friendly faces welcome her was obviously the key.

She'd neglected her in-box for a week, replying only to the most urgent requests. Now she dug deep, spending most of the morning clearing it out. She was feeling quite proud of her accomplishment when Scott wandered in and dropped into a chair.

"When am I going to learn that drinking beer all afternoon is a recipe for disaster?"

Jill braced her chin in a hand and looked at him. "I have no idea. I figured that out twenty years ago, but I think we both know I'm smarter than you are."

"You really might be," he agreed. He stuck his foot out, caught the edge of her door, and closed it. "So."

"What's wrong? You look kinda...weird."

"I feel weird." He looked right at her for a few moments, then said, "I learned two lessons this weekend. One, don't drink a lot of beer in the afternoon, and two, don't let a friend hook you up."

"Oh-oh." She winced. "I know I'll regret asking, but...Lizzie didn't like your put-out or get-out rule?"

"Nice way to put it." His wry laugh made him look slightly embarrassed, but Jill knew that was a projection on her part. Scott was always frank. "And that's not a rule. It's a..." He shrugged. "Okay, it's a rule. But it's a rule that's saved me a lot of time and effort. If a woman's weird about having sex after a few dates, she'll probably be weird about it forever. No thanks."

"Huh." She sat back in her chair and assessed him. He looked funny. Not his usual joking self. Maybe it was the hangover. "I'm a little surprised by that. I don't know Lizzie well, but she seems like the kind of woman who'd be into sex. Maybe she just wasn't ready, Scott. If you like her, give her a little more time."

"No, thanks," he said quickly. "I try to be a gentleman, so I don't talk about things like this in detail. Even with my friends." He leaned forward and lowered his voice. "But I should give you fair warning. You might want to think twice about introducing Lizzie to anyone else. She's...well, she's...complicated."

"She's complicated? What in the heck does that mean?"

"I don't want to get into it, Jill. Just"—he stood and looked at her for an uncomfortably long time—"get to know her better before you try to hook her up."

"Damn, Scott, what in the hell happened?" She couldn't begin to figure out what he was inferring.

"Nothing awful. She's not a vampire or anything. She just has things she likes that..." He shook his head. "I don't want to get into it. Just think twice, okay?"

She stood as he opened the door. "No worries. I haven't hooked many people up, and I'm going to stop while I'm ahead."

"Lizzie's a lot of fun," he said, as he exited. "She's just…out of my league."

What in the hell did *that* mean?

⁂

Jill was packing up her things when her phone rang, with the display showing an outside line. "Jill Henry."

"Hi, there, Jill Henry. Lizzie Davis. Is it too early for a university administrator to have a drink?"

Jill looked at her watch. "It's five o'clock. I think that's viable. Are you close by?"

"Uh-huh. I was meeting with your director of special events about a couple of things. I'm in Waterman. I assume you're somewhere around here too."

"I am. Why don't I meet you on the front steps? I'm ready to go."

"Great. See you in a few."

Jill hustled down the stairs, blessedly free of the usual gaggle of students moving between classes. She reached the front stairs and breathed in the fresh, sweet air. *Now* it was spring. A tap on her shoulder made her turn to find Lizzie, once again looking like a fully-accredited adult. "You cut your hair," Jill said, admiring the now chin-length bob. "It looks really good."

"Thanks. I'm in the water all of the time in the summer. When it's this length, I don't *have* to blow-dry it."

"Whatever your reasons, it looks good. I'm about ready to change stylists. Do you go to someone you like?"

"Uh-huh. I'll give you her number. As soon as you buy me a drink."

"*I'm* buying?"

"Uh-huh." She put her hand on Jill's elbow and led her towards a parking lot.

"We're driving?"

"No, I'm driving. Let's head down College. There's a new place I like that's for adults."

"We could walk," Jill said. "It's not that far."

44

"I'm wearing heels," she said, sticking a foot out as a visual aid. "And why would I want to walk down, only to have to walk back to get my car? Use your head, woman!"

Jill laughed at her chiding and followed along. Lizzie pressed her key fob when they got near a cute, small car in a unique shade of blue. The lights flashed and a "thunk" indicated the doors were unlocked.

"Is this a plug-in?" Jill asked as she got in and realized something was missing. Instead of a shifter, there was a silver button between the seats.

"Yeah. But it only gets about seventy miles to a charge. Works great for driving to and from work, but I have to take the train to visit the old homestead."

"Where do you charge it?" Jill fastened her seat belt, and shifted around in the surprisingly spacious interior.

"There's a public charging station only five blocks from my apartment." She shrugged. "It would have been nice to live in Jon's house. He installed a 240 charger just for me." Sighing, she added, "His big plug just wasn't big enough."

She wore a playful smirk, and Jill would have made a suggestive comment to her other friends, but she didn't yet know Lizzie well enough to do that. "I think it's really nice that you care about your carbon footprint."

"Someone has to," she said as she pressed that silver button and a muted chime sounded. The absence of engine sound was a little odd. More like a golf cart than a car. As they pulled out, the car really zoomed, no delay for the gas to reach the engine.

They glided down College, with Lizzie on the alert for parking. When she found a spot, she maneuvered the car into the space and turned it off. "The place I'm thinking of is about four blocks away, but I hate to waste power looking for parking. Is that cool?"

"Sure. You're the one wearing heels."

They got out and started to walk down towards the lake. "You're dressed pretty casually," Lizzie commented as she turned and assessed Jill's clothing. "Can you always wear khakis?"

"No, I get dressed up sometimes. But if I don't have to, I stay casual. I ironed my shirt though. I think that counts as dressing up."

Lizzie grasped the fabric at the cuff and rubbed it between her fingers. "I like checks. I'd call this robin's egg blue. It looks great with your eyes."

"Thanks. I find myself buying a lot of blue shirts and sweaters. I wonder if I'm vain enough to try to match my eyes?"

"Probably. I chose this place because I'm in the mood for a real cocktail. How about you?"

"I can do a cocktail. I usually drink beer, but I'm versatile."

"You look it," Lizzie said, giving her a quick glance.

They were the first patrons of the quiet cocktail bar. Lots of warm brown leather and dark-stained oak surrounded them. "Always a good sign to be first," Jill teased. "Shows your dedication."

The bartender swept his hand in an "anywhere you like" sign, and Lizzie went all the way to the back. As she put her purse down, she said, "I like to be able to see who's coming in."

A waitress arrived after they'd spent a minute studying the cocktail list, and Jill went with a vodka base, while Lizzie chose bourbon.

"Ooo, dark spirits," Jill said when the server departed. "A real drink."

"Yeah, I like bourbon and rye. I'm not much for Scotch, though."

"You were drinking vodka at Mark's party. I thought that would be your drink."

"Lisa bought vodka, so I made do." She tried to flip her hair over her shoulder, probably forgetting it wasn't long enough to do that now. "Hey, did Scott talk to you today?"

She didn't look upset, or even concerned, so Jill told the partial truth. "Yeah. He said you'd decided not to see each other any more. Are you cool with that?"

"Yeah." She made a face, one Jill couldn't easily interpret. "I was disappointed, but not surprised."

Blinking, Jill said, "I got the impression you were the one who didn't want to see him any more."

Lizzie looked at her sharply. "He said that?"

Jill thought for a minute. "No, I guess he didn't. I just assumed…"

"Why?"

"Because he seemed disappointed. Or something. It was kinda hard to tell. He didn't want to talk about it."

Now Lizzie let out a laugh, a good one. She let her head fall back a few inches, showing white, even teeth. "I bet he didn't." Their drinks were delivered and they toasted, then took a sip. "Mine's good," Lizzie said. "Yours?"

"Also good." Jill put it down and waited for Lizzie to continue speaking. But she didn't. She just smiled, coyly.

"Are you going to tell me why Scott wouldn't want to talk about it?" She slapped herself on the forehead. "I will never, ever set people up again."

Laughing, Lizzie gave her a playful tap on the arm. "Don't let this scare you off. Scott's a nice guy. I could easily see most women liking him a lot. Go ahead and set him up if you run into another single woman."

"I probably won't get the chance. He's the finance department's version of George Clooney. Lots of women, most of them not lasting long."

"Clooney's married now. You're going to have to come up with a new guy."

"Scott claims he's ready to settle down too," Jill said, testing the water. "But maybe not."

Lizzie brought her glass to her lips and took a healthy sip. Then she set the glass on the table and said, "Do you want to know what happened? I'm not embarrassed to talk about it."

Wincing, Jill said, "I don't know. Do I?"

Lizzie laughed at her. Not with her. At her. "Are you always so skittish?"

"No, not really," she admitted. "It's just weird when you have friends who've dated. I'm definitely getting out of the matchmaking business. Too stressful."

"Just sit there quietly, and I'll tell you what happened." She took a breath. "Scott likes to move to the bedroom sooner than I do," she admitted. "I read a book once that said you should never sleep with anyone you wouldn't want to be."

"Wouldn't want to be? I don't get it. Why would you want to be Scott?"

"No, no," she said, frowning as she tried to explain herself. "The point is that you should only have sex with people you know well. People you respect. Admire, even. I took that advice to heart. I've never had sex with a guy I didn't know and trust."

"Ahh." Jill smiled and nodded. "I had a feeling it was something like that." She picked up her glass to take another drink.

"So I told him he could fuck me, if I could fuck him first."

The table was now covered in a fine spray of vodka, grapefruit juice and Aperol. Accompanied by Lizzie's laughter ringing out through the empty bar.

"That's about what he did," she said, still laughing hard.

"I can't...I can't imagine what went through his mind," Jill said, furiously wiping vodka from her shirt and the table. "He doesn't know your sense of humor, Lizzie."

There was stark silence from across the table, and Jill stopped her cleanup to look at her. "I wasn't kidding," she said, straight-faced. "I don't like to waste time with guys who aren't flexible."

"Flexible?" Jill knew she was staring, but couldn't help herself. "A guy who'd do that would have to be very, *very* flexible."

"You don't?" She batted her eyes, totally knocking Jill off stride.

"I don't what?"

"Allow women to fuck you," she said, as though they were having a normal conversation.

"I...I...I don't think that's something I want to talk about."

"That means you do," she announced, a sly grin blooming. "If you didn't, you'd deny it."

"For god's sake, Lizzie, I have a..." She struggled to find the right word, without sounding crass. "I'm designed for that."

"So are guys," she said blithely. "Men need to see what it feels like to be on the bottom once in a while. To know how it feels to be pushed into doing something you're nowhere near ready for."

"I am really, *really* never going to fix you up again. No wonder Scott looked like he'd seen a ghost!"

"He was a big baby," she said, waving her hand. "I don't pound away at a guy every night. I just want someone who's open to new things. The fact that Scott shut me down without a moment to think about it showed me he wasn't my type."

"Lizzie," Jill said carefully. "You wanted to fuck him in the…"

"In the ass," Lizzie supplied when it became clear Jill was a little squeamish. "Guys *always* ask for that, and my butt is no more made for it than theirs is. Turnabout is fair play."

"But Scott didn't ask for that." She swallowed nervously. "He didn't, did he?"

"No, I think he wanted standard sex. But he got all prudish when I told him what I needed in an LTR."

"LTR?"

"Long term relationship. I like to get everything out of the way up front," she said, very businesslike. "I waited too long with Jon, and now he thinks I misled him."

Jill put her head down on the table and moaned. "Oh, god. He broke up with you because he didn't want to be on the receiving end of your…"

"Dildo. I have a dildo, Jill. And a harness. Actually, I have two. Dildos. A small one for men," she added, her devilish smile making her eyes sparkle.

"Damn it, Lizzie, you're going to be single for a very long time if that's an entrance requirement."

Lizzie laughed. "*Entrance* requirement. That's funny." She shook her head. "That's not a requirement. It's something I like, but only if a guy's into it. I just brought it up because Scott was pushing me, and I wanted to push back."

Jill leaned back and looked at her for a minute. "That makes sense. Kind of." She took a sip of her drink, then nodded when the server strolled by and asked if they wanted another. She didn't usually have two cocktails by six o'clock, but this wasn't a usual day.

"It makes perfect sense. Jon wasn't into it, but he also didn't push me to do things I didn't want to do. Our relationship was very balanced."

"But he broke up with you," Jill reminded her.

"Yeah." She let out a heavy sigh, then drained the rest of her drink. "He freaked out when I told him I like to have sex with women."

Jill was very, very grateful she hadn't had another mouthful of her drink, because it would also have been sprayed everywhere. "What?"

"I'm bi," Lizzie said, smiling when the server dropped off their drinks. "She's cute, isn't she?" Her eyes followed the server, clearly checking out her ass.

"You're bi? Since when?"

"Since ever. I had sex with girls before boys." She narrowed her eyes in thought. "Do you know the Halperns?"

"Dr. Halpern? The chiropractor?"

"Yeah. His daughter Erica was the first person I had sex with. She's a big ol' dyke now. Lives in Northampton. Mecca for your people."

"Holy crap!" Jill dropped her head to the table again. "Why are you telling me all of this? I could have lived, happily, and not known any of these details."

Lizzie poked her shoulder. "I'm not embarrassed about being bi. Don't try to shame me. It won't work."

Jill sat up quickly. "I'm not trying to shame you, Lizzie. It's just…" She shook her head. "I don't know a lot of active bisexuals."

"You only know passive ones?"

"No, no, I just know women who were with guys and then figured out they were lesbians. And one guy who was married to a woman before he fell in love with a guy. But no one who goes back and forth." She took in a breath, trying to process all of this. "How does that work, anyway?"

"Sure you want to know?" Lizzie took a sip, looking over the rim of the glass with a foxy smile. "It might give you the willies."

Jill rolled her eyes. "You've already told me you like to fuck guys. How much worse can it be?"

She pointed at Jill, scowling. "You're trying to shame me again. Knock it off."

"I'm sorry. Really. I'll keep my editorial comments to myself."

"Fine. I'll answer your question." Her eyes met Jill's. "If a guy's into it, we could invite a woman to join us in bed. If he's not, I might arrange a date for myself, like with someone I met on a hook-up app."

"What does your mother think of this?"

Lizzie laughed. "Do you honestly think I've told my mother I pick up women using an app? She'd strangle me!"

"I assume she knows you're bisexual." Jill slapped herself on the head again. She was going to concuss if she kept this up. "Of course she does. You've made it clear you're not embarrassed. Nor should you be," she added, emphatically.

Lizzie didn't look so self-assured when she raised her glass for a sip of her new drink. "I'm not embarrassed," she said carefully. "I've never been in an adult relationship with a woman, so there's no reason to bring it up."

"What? Why not? I mean, if this is part of your identity…"

"I suppose it is," she said, clearly hedging. "So far it's been a sexual thing. Mostly. And I don't feel the need to tell my mother what I like to do in bed."

"I get that," Jill said. "But if it's more than that. If it's something that made you break up with a guy you really liked…"

"He broke up with *me*. He didn't believe I could be faithful if I was bi. Which is just asinine," she insisted, her cheeks coloring. "Straight people cheat all the damn time."

"You just said he broke up with you because you liked having sex with women. That implies you *asked* to have sex with women."

"I *didn't* ask. We were in bed one night, and he asked me to tell him my fantasies." She let out a sigh, looking truly sad. "After I told him I fantasized about women, he started questioning me. Once I admitted to being bi, I was out on my ear."

"Harsh," Jill said soberly. "Very harsh."

"Agreed. Especially because I'd consciously given up women to be monogamous. He was worth it," she said, the corners of her mouth turning down a few degrees.

Jill wasn't sure if she was treading on thin ice, but she asked the question anyway. "Do you think you could have been monogamous forever?"

Lizzie put her chin in her hand and sat quietly for a minute. "I *think* I could have. But given that my desire for women is really strong, it would have been hard." She sighed again, this time with a determined look making her eyes spark. "I would have focused on him and our kids. If you're going to be an adult, you don't have to scratch every itch you get."

"I think the strap-on would have come out at some point," Jill said, unable to avoid teasing her. "You would have needed some excitement."

She let a smile bloom, and it eventually lit up her face. "That's probably why he really broke up with me. He feared my big, throbbing dick."

Jill shoved her fingers in her ears and closed her eyes. "I can't hear you and I can't see you. Tap me on the arm when you've stopped trying to give me nightmares."

<hr/>

When Jill got home that night, a big box was lying on her porch. She picked it up and opened it with one of her keys, then pulled out several wads of tan paper before lifting out a lovely, graceful, wrought iron lamp, with six delicately curving arms, each wired to hold a bulb.

Pleased, she held the piece up to the light and took a good look at it. It was just the kind of thing she'd buy for herself. She'd never been crazy about the fixture she had over her dining room table, but Mark couldn't have known that. He did, however, know her, and he'd used that knowledge to make something she couldn't wait to hang up. He didn't need to offer such a generous gift, but she was really glad he had. Maybe one day they could actually sit down and have a drink together—if Lisa let him.

Chapter Four

ON A COOL, BUT CLEAR night in mid May, Jill rushed around her house, neatening up for bridge. Seven people would be there in less than an hour, and she still had a decent amount of work to do.

She'd made snacks; fresh vegetables and dip, some hummus, tabouli, pita chips, taco chips, and salsa. The taco chips would go first. They always did; but then, people would eat the vegetables once they had no other choice.

The cats knew company was coming, and had secreted themselves in a closet or under a bed. She wasn't sure how they always knew, given that she cleaned the house once or twice a week and cooked regularly, but when guests were coming, David sought shelter moments before Goliath joined him. When guests were there, not a treat in the world would entice either of them to come out. That made most of her friends semi-seriously believe she kept a litter box just for fun.

Everything was dusted, the throw pillows were fluffed, the half-bath on the first floor was spic and span, the matching glasses were washed and set out on the breakfront in the living room, dessert plates nestled next to them. Cloth napkins sat next to shining forks and spoons. Everything was ship-shape.

Just before eight, she turned on some music, choosing one of the streaming services she could access through her computer in the den. When she'd done some remodeling, she'd had speakers run into every room on the first floor, letting her fill any spot with sound. It hardly mattered which of her many channels she picked, though. Someone would change it within moments of arriving.

Jill went into the living room and peered out the window when she noticed movement on the street. Karen and Becky were, as usual, the first to arrive.

Friends filled different needs at different times, but these two had been her stalwarts for the entire time she'd been back in Burlington.

Becky was attired in her usual frumpy professor look, with her hair in need of a trim, and khakis that she'd probably owned since the nineties. Her usual Birkenstocks were a source of good-natured teasing from the whole group, but Becky wasn't the type to care if people teased her about her style. It would be quite another thing if you tried to make her feel inferior about her brain. Jill had watched the usually mild-mannered woman trounce a lecturer who'd attempted to belittle her at a party, something she hoped she never had to witness again.

Karen was always a little more stylish, but she also went more for comfort than trend. Wearing nothing to attract attention or make too much of a statement, she looked like a psychotherapist, which is exactly what she was.

Jill opened the door and, after exchanging hugs, her guests were their usual, complimentary selves. "Your place always looks so neat and orderly," Karen said, looking around wistfully as Becky took a right, heading for the den. "Our house is so filled with books and papers, it looks like an abandoned library."

"Becky's an English professor," Jill reminded her. "That's a professional liability."

"We should do better. Hey, Beck," Karen called out. The music changed to something much mellower than Jill had chosen. As expected. "Why don't we do some spring cleaning? I read you should donate all of the books you haven't looked at in the last year to the library."

Becky walked into the kitchen, and put her hand on Karen's back. "That's a great idea, honey." She rolled her eyes when only Jill could see her. That tactic seemed like a good one to employ in a long term relationship. Agree with everything, but allow yourself to quietly retain your own view. God knew most people never got around to doing the things they agreed to. Why argue about them?

Skip and Alice were next, with the porch-light shining down on Skip's growing bald spot. A guy looked so much balder when his thinning hair was very, very dark. Jill guessed he'd try a comb-over, but was equally sure Alice would put her foot down before it got out of control.

They were arguing about something, barely taking the time to offer a hug before they went into the living room to continue talking; harsh whispering floated into the kitchen. No one paid much attention. They were notorious arguers, but they seemed to have a solid marriage. Maybe the fights were the glue that held them together.

Mary Beth, Kathleen, and Gerri were the last to arrive. Mary Beth and Kathleen owned a big house not far from Jill, and Gerri was their tenant—for the last fifteen years. Jill wasn't sure how they worked the arrangement out, but she'd known lots of relationships that didn't last half as long, so they were doing something right.

Mary Beth and Kathleen had been friends for years. Kathleen was around Jill's age, and Mary Beth a few years older. Gerri was a bit of an enigma, working at home in some sort of technical support job. She didn't seem to have separate friends, and usually tagged along with Mary Beth and Kathleen for everything from bridge to holidays to family funerals. That wouldn't have worked for Jill, but they seemed perfectly content to be thought of as a group.

Of the guests, half of them worked at UVM in some capacity, but none were in Jill's exact department. She wasn't afraid to socialize with co-workers, but she preferred going out for a drink or dinner to having them over to her home. There was a line she was careful not to cross, and letting business associates know too much about you seemed a little dangerous. Maybe that was her mother's influence.

Gerri had been brewing beer for a few years, and she'd brought some of her summer ale for the group. Alice, a teetotaler, brought a case of diet soda that would most likely remain in the pantry until the next time they came. There were many junk foods Jill liked, but she'd never been able to stomach a diet anything.

They began to play, several years of experience keeping the games fast but loose. No one got particularly invested in the outcome, and they stopped for breaks more often than most groups would. That's why Jill enjoyed the evenings. Even though they were fairly good players, they didn't believe it was a life or death proposition.

"Hey, Jill, have you seen Becca lately?" Mary Beth asked when they were taking one of their three breaks. Mary Beth worked in admissions with Jill's ex, but had been very respectful of both of them, never serving as a gossip carrier.

"No," she said, realizing everyone had grown quiet, listening for her answer. "I haven't seen her since the day she moved out."

"How do you manage that?" Skip asked. "I see every person I'd rather avoid on a daily basis. Sometimes I wish I worked at Ohio State or Minnesota. It'd be nice to get lost in the crowds."

"I'm not sure why we haven't seen each other," Jill said. "I haven't gone out of my way to avoid her. We must be on different schedules."

"I only asked because she had to put Boomer down," Mary Beth said. "I know you were fond of him."

"Oh, crap," Jill said, her stomach doing a flip. "I loved that damn dog. I found a few strands of short yellow hair when I was vacuuming earlier and thought of him." She let out a sigh. "I'll send her a note. She must be devastated."

"It's been hard on her," Mary Beth agreed. "He was fourteen years old. They tell me that's old for a Lab."

"He was a good boy," Jill said, realizing she was using the playful voice she always used with Boomer.

"You should get a dog," Skip said. "You could use the company."

"I've got cats," she reminded him. "Two." Walking over to the mantle, she took down a photo. "You'll never see them, so here's a picture of them in Santa hats."

"It's time to get a girlfriend when you start dressing your cats up in costumes," Skip snickered.

"Becca was the costume arranger. Where I grew up, cats stayed outside. The thought of dressing them up or celebrating their birthdays would have made you the laughingstock of the whole town."

"All sixty of them?" Kathleen teased.

"Six hundred," Jill corrected. "I counted them all when I was there a couple of months ago."

"How'd that go?" Alice asked. "I know you were worried."

"It went well. Very well, as a matter of fact. My old friend and I will probably never be close again, but I reconnected with his parents. I'm going to stay in touch."

"That's great," Alice said. "They have a big family, right?"

"Uh-huh. Seven kids. I found out the youngest works at Hollyhock Hills. Have you guys been there?"

"Yes," they answered, almost in unison. "Who hasn't?"

Jill raised her hand. "Until the wedding, I'd never been near the place. Lizzie, my friend's little sister, works in development for them."

"They have a great restaurant," Kathleen said. "Given how you love food, I'm amazed you haven't been."

"Now you're talking," Jill said. "I thought it was just a farm. If there's a good restaurant, I'm all over it."

"That's a good place for a special date," Skip said. "I took Alice there for our tenth anniversary."

Alice looked at him like he'd lost his mind. "You did not! I went to a conference there, but you certainly weren't with me."

"I did," he insisted. "We had a great meal. The side doors were open, and it was warm…"

"Our anniversary's in January, you idiot! If you were there, you were with someone else, so you'd better think twice about reminiscing about your lovely dinner."

You could see him gulp from across the room. "Maybe I saw a photo of the place. You know how suggestible I am."

"You're a dunce," Alice muttered, heading back to her seat. "Let's play cards before I have to call my divorce attorney." She glared at Skip. "He's on speed dial."

They played until near midnight, with Kathleen and Alice coming out just ahead of Becky and Jill. She walked everyone to their cars, lingering at the last one—Karen and Becky's. Karen always zoned in on troubling emotional issues, and she asked gently, "Are you really going to write to Becca?"

"I feel like I should. Boomer was very important to her. It feels awfully cold to ignore her loss."

"She's not over you, Jill. Be careful in reaching out. You don't want to send the wrong message."

"I won't ask her to call me to reminisce," Jill promised. "But I don't want her to think I don't care at all. That's just not true."

Karen leaned forward and gave her a hug. "You're a good person. Just don't make her think there's still an ember burning if there's not."

Jill jogged back to the house, the crisp spring night chilling her in just a shirt and jeans. She started to check the doors and the windows, and by the time she'd finished, both David and Goliath were brushing against her shins. "Oh, here are my brave boys," she said, bending to scratch behind their ears. "I'd tell you two about Boomer dying, but you'd probably laugh. All you did was torture that poor guy, when he just wanted to be your friend."

They went to their food bowls and chomped on some kibble, unmoved by the loss of their former step-brother. While it was fresh in her mind, Jill went to the den and wrote a brief note about Boomer's death. It was a tough line to straddle, but she thought she'd done a good job of making clear she had empathy for Becca's loss, yet didn't want to discuss it further. Breakups truly sucked.

❦

Jill took advantage of the first sunny, warm Saturday of the spring to dust off her bike. She could have been riding for two months now, but found she always delayed until it was reliably warm. Maybe she was a wimp, but she hated to ride when her hands were freezing.

She zipped down quiet city streets, heading for the path that ran along the lake. It was in rough shape, and was supposedly being renovated, but it was still nice to just pedal hard and not have to worry about cars. Her competitive juices were flowing by the time she'd reached the end of the path, and she crushed it for as long as her lungs held out, then took a breather and turned to do the loop again. Pushing herself to her limit was the fun part of exercising. She'd never been the kind of person to take a long, slow ride to admire the scenery. Her thing was to push until she could hardly breathe, slow down to catch her breath, then crank it again. By the time she'd gone down and back and down again, sweat was dripping into her eyes, and her T-shirt stuck to her back.

It was still early, just nine, and she hadn't stopped for coffee before taking off. Coffee always made her have to pee, and searching for a restroom was a drag. After taking her phone from its waterproof case, she searched for espresso, finding a highly rated place only a few blocks away.

She'd cooled off a little by the time she arrived, but was still a sweaty mess. After hanging her helmet off the handlebars, she started to lock the bike, but noticed a guy carry his into the shop. So she followed suit, hefting it onto her shoulder as she maneuvered through the doorway.

The place was remarkably large, and she realized it was actually the lobby for the office building, with an espresso bar in one corner, window seats and small tables spread out across the space. She did a double-take when she saw Lizzie sitting on the floor in the corner, pointing and laughing at her.

Jill rolled her bike over and looked down at her. "Something funny?"

"You," she said, her sparkling eyes roaming all over Jill's body. "So butch and bedraggled. Is this your weekend look?"

"Pretty much." She grasped the hem of her shirt and fanned it away from her body. "I love to sweat."

"Where'd you ride from? Canada?"

"Just my house," she said, smiling at the question. "I did the lakefront path a few times. It's so nice early in the morning, before it's filled with kids and strollers."

Lizzie blinked up at her, the interested smile of a moment ago now gone. "Why haven't you called me?"

"Why haven't you called *me*? I gave you my number, but you didn't give me yours."

A skeptical look settled on her face. "You could have gotten my number in two seconds if you wanted it." A flicker of what looked like insecurity flashed across her face. "I thought maybe I'd freaked you out when we got together for drinks."

"Don't be silly." She leaned her bike against the wall and folded her legs to allow her to settle next to Lizzie on the floor. She'd probably need a fork-lift to get back up, but she didn't want to stand over her. "Why would you even think that?"

Lizzie's gaze shifted nervously, her attention locked onto her keyboard. "I told you some pretty personal stuff. I kinda thought you'd call to at least touch base after that. If you want to be friends, that is. Maybe I read you wrong."

"I definitely want to be friends," Jill said, adding some force to her words. "And I'm sorry I didn't give you a buzz. Now that it's warm, I've gotten into all of my spring things and haven't taken the time to follow up." She twitched her head towards the counter. "Let me buy you a cup of coffee."

A little of Lizzie's devilish side showed when she said, "I looked you up on the UVM salary chart. You can afford to buy me a cappuccino."

"I hate working at a public university," Jill grumbled. "It sucks to have everyone know exactly how much you make."

"You make almost three times what I do," Lizzie said, slapping her bare knee. "Three times! And I guarantee I work more hours."

"I could make even more if I worked at a for-profit company," Jill admitted. "But money isn't my primary motivator."

Lizzie bumped up against her shoulder. "Only people who make a lot say that. It'd be your primary motivator if you were drowning in bills."

"You've got a good point." She struggled to her feet, trying not to show how stiff her knees had gotten in just a few minutes. "I'll buy you three cappuccinos if you like."

"One will do. Make it a decaf this time." As Jill walked away she called after her, "A piece of lemon pound cake wouldn't go uneaten."

After delivering two cups, Jill went back to carry two plates, one with pound cake and one with something that looked like an apple tart, but was supposed to be a Danish. "I think this is about a thousand calories," she said, holding it up like she was weighing it. "I probably burned that much, right?"

"If you came from Canada. I wouldn't worry about it, though. Unlike my poor sisters, who fight every calorie, you must burn them efficiently."

"They're a couple of years older than I am. Maybe twenty pounds will leap onto me in a few years."

"Nah. If you're fit at forty, you're going to stay there. Your mom's thin, isn't she?"

"Uh-huh. My dad too. I lucked out."

"What are you up to today? Are you going to keep riding?"

"No. I think I'll cut my grass and plant some flowers. I'm going out tonight, so I'll try to squeeze in a nap."

"Out…with a woman?"

"Yeah, but not that kind of out. I'm going to some friends' house for dinner and some kind of board game." She almost asked Lizzie to come with her, but quickly had second thoughts. Karen and Becky shouldn't have to set another place at the table due to Jill's guilt at ignoring her social obligations. "Want to come over and help me plant?"

"I'm not in the mood to garden today." She patted her laptop. "And even if I was, I've got to finish writing a grant by Monday. I hate being a responsible adult," she groused.

"Then we'll have to get together and do something you like. What's your favorite thing to do?"

"Mmm…" She took a sip of her coffee as she half-closed her eyes. "I like to go see the Lake Monsters."

"You're a baseball fan?"

"Uh-huh. And I watch basketball a lot. Hockey too. Men and women for that. Women only for basketball."

"Really?" Jill sat back against the wall and looked at her carefully. "We should go to a game sometime. There's no problem getting into women's games, but I can get prime seats for men's hockey."

"I bet you can have whatever you want, up there in your ivory tower, rubbing elbows with the provost."

"No," she said, chuckling. "I give money to the Victory Fund. I'm allowed to buy priority season tickets to basketball and hockey, but I never do. Most of my friends are couples, and I can only buy two seats."

"So you don't go?"

"No, I still go, we just don't get the good seats."

61

"How about your girlfriend? Was she a sports fan?"

"Not a bit," Jill said, shaking her head. "We didn't have that much in common, to be honest. She liked to read and cook and putter around the house. I like to go out and socialize."

Lizzie's gaze narrowed as she let it linger on Jill, moving up and down her body for a few seconds, like she was considering her for a task and wanted to make sure she was fit for it. "Do you ever go to clubs?"

"Once in a while. But I don't have many friends who like live music, so it's rare."

"You've got one now," she said decisively. "How about First Friday?"

"The gay thing at the club in South Burlington?"

"Yeah. Sometimes the band is horrible, but it's only five bucks. And the DJ afterwards is usually good."

"It's a deal." Jill found herself shaking on it, then wondering why she'd agreed to go to a small, crowded club where she'd probably be the oldest person by decades. Oh, well, they'd still let her in. There were laws against age discrimination.

Lizzie finished her cappuccino, then easily rose, as if pulled by an invisible wire. She offered a hand when Jill struggled to follow.

"I would have gotten up eventually," she joked. "I might have had to get on my hands and knees first, but I would have gotten there."

"It's time for you to go play in the dirt, while I go finish this grant."

"You're not going out later?"

"Oh, sure. That's all in my schedule. If I'm finished by four, I can take a nap."

"Just what I was going to do," Jill said. "I love afternoon naps."

"Me too. My friends are coming to pick me up at ten, so I should have time to grab some dinner."

"Sounds like my night, but mine will start at six," Jill said. "That's the difference between thirty and forty."

Lizzie gave her a long, assessing look. "You don't look anywhere near forty. Jon was almost your age, but more than one person asked if he was my dad."

"If anyone thinks I'm your mom, we're not going to hang out. That's a promise."

They went out into the sun, with Lizzie holding the door for Jill to carry her bike out. "Hey," she said, seeming a little hesitant. "I was in a weird mood when we went out for drinks. I probably made it sound like I was some sexually obsessed whacko."

"Not a bad thing to be," Jill teased.

"No, but that's not who I am. I definitely enjoy sex, and I definitely know what I want, but I'm not out screwing all of Burlington or anything."

Jill put a hand on her arm. "I didn't think that, Lizzie. And if you did, more power to you. You're young and you're single. If you've got the energy, why not burn it off?"

"Yeah, I guess." She shrugged. "I think I was trying to shock you, and I might have been too successful."

"I wasn't shocked," Jill said, even though she had been. "I tend to think I'm the wildest person to come out of Sugar Hill. It's nice to know I have some competition."

The cocky smile was soon back in place. "Oh, you've got competition. Lots of it."

Chapter Five

JILL'S FRIENDS CARLY AND Samantha were planning a trip to Boston over Memorial Day weekend, and they were after her to go with them. "I know you love my company," Jill said at dinner one night. "But I can't help thinking you like my car as much as you do me."

"There's nothing wrong with our car," Carly insisted. "It just doesn't like to go on long trips."

"No, It doesn't like to be towed *home* from long trips," Jill said. "How much did you pay to have it dragged back from Portland?"

"That was an anomaly," Carly said. "Orville's a perfectly good car. We haven't had much trouble at all."

"How many miles does Orville have now?"

"Just over two hundred thousand," Samantha said, wincing when Carly gave her a stern look. "Well, he does."

"A Subaru can last for forty years," Carly insisted. "We want you to go with us because we like being with you. And if your car wants to come along…all the better. I know she likes to see the bright lights of big cities."

"I would," Jill said. "But I don't have anyone to watch the boys. Stephanie's back home in Rutland for the summer, and I don't want to have a stranger in my house."

"Who's Stephanie?"

"A kid from UVM. She's been house sitting for me for three years now." Jill sighed. "I'll have to replace her when she graduates. But it's hard to find a kid who's responsible and doesn't have parties when you're gone."

"You should have had kids," Samantha said. "There's always someone home at our house."

"Oh, yeah, that's the best reason to reproduce," Jill teased. "Cheap labor. So Trent and Presley aren't going to Boston?"

"They're in high school, Jill," Samantha said, speaking as if Jill were slow. "They don't go anywhere with us."

"Would either of them like to feed my boys?"

"No!" Carly said, eyes wide. "I like you too much to have either of them do something horrible. Which they might. It's a crap-shoot with those two."

"I might have one option," Jill said. "Let me make a call and see what I can come up with."

❧

Jill still hadn't remembered to ask for Lizzie's home number. So she called Hollyhock Hills and asked for the development office. "This is Lizzie Davis," she said, her voice a little lower and crisper than normal.

"Hey there, it's Jill."

"Hi. What's going on?"

"I was wondering if you were going to be around for Memorial Day weekend."

"Uh-huh. I'm totally free. What do you want to do?"

Oh, crap. She sounded so interested. "Uhm, I'm going to Boston. I thought you might want to look after my cats."

"Oh." After just a few seconds, her enthusiasm ramped back up. "I didn't know you had cats. Of course, you're a lesbian, so I should have guessed..."

"Funny. I have two, both low maintenance. They don't need medication or special diets or anything. I just need someone to feed them and clean the litter box."

"I guess I could do it."

"But you don't sound excited," Jill said. "Do you have any friends who'd like to get away from an annoying roommate?"

"All of my friends are in that boat." She laughed, sounding more like herself. "I'd love to go to your house and pick up cat poop, Jill. I can't think of a better way to spend a long weekend."

"Uhm, you could come to Boston with us. My friends Carly and Samantha are planning the trip. Samantha's a big history buff and she's never walked the Freedom Trail."

"I think I'll stick with the cat poop. When should I be there?"

"We want to avoid traffic, so we're going to leave late on Friday."

"Late? Like 6:10?"

"You're the funniest development officer in all of Burlington, Lizzie. Keep working on that act."

⸹

On the Friday in question, a knock on the back door had the cats scurrying for cover. "Chickens!" Jill called out as they soundlessly disappeared, just two gray streaks as their bellies got low to the ground and they fled upstairs.

She went to the door and opened it to find Lizzie, wearing a bike helmet, weighted down with a bulging backpack. "Where's the poop?" she asked, sliding by Jill to enter. "God damn it," she grumbled as she looked around the kitchen. "I thought maybe the outside was nice, but the inside was a dump. Your house is fantastic, you jerk!"

Jill couldn't stop herself from laughing at Lizzie's outrage. "I'm sorry?"

"I don't have many role models. You know, women who've made it on their own. But I could work until I'm a hundred and not be able to afford a place this nice."

"You're what? A coordinator?"

"No. I'm an associate. But my manager's only two years older than I am. And the director's around fifty. He's not going *any*where."

"Cheer up. You can always move to another foundation or a university to boost your salary. That's what I did."

Lizzie dropped her backpack to the floor, removed her helmet and ran her fingers through her hair, fluffing it into place. "I assumed you've always been at UVM."

"No, after I got my MPA, I worked at Middlebury for three years, and Dartmouth for two. Then I came home to UVM. I make thirty thousand more than I would have if I'd stayed the whole time. Employers are like lovers. They think more highly of you when someone else wants you."

"But I love Hollyhock Hills," Lizzie moaned. "I'd love to stay there until I retire…at a hundred."

"Talk to me when it's time for your review," Jill said, clapping her on the back. "I'll give you some tips on how to get a decent raise."

"A raise," Lizzie grumbled. "There are a hundred people who'd do my job for less."

"Talk to me," Jill insisted. "We'll come up with a strategy."

"Fine. Now show me to the poop."

An enclosed porch was located right next to the back door. The box was on a large plastic mat, currently devoid of litter. Jill had tried everything in creation to keep the clay from being tracked all over, but she'd yet to come up with a solution that the boys would use. And when they vetoed something, she was the one who paid the price. "Here's their spa bathroom," she said. "You probably won't even see them, but David is the smaller, more dominant one and Goliath is the big softie."

"You're serious? They won't be all over me like cats always are? You'd think I was made of catnip."

"No, my boys are afraid of their own shadows. I have good friends who've been coming here for years and have never seen them. I put pictures of them out just to prove they exist."

"Okay. So what are the house rules? No drug sales, no underage hookers. What else?"

"I trust you, Lizzie. Just make yourself at home." They walked into the living room. "You won't need it, but you can have a fire if you like. Just open the flue."

"Your place is sick," Lizzie said, looking around. "Old house with contemporary furniture. Just what I'd do." She moved over to a chair and rubbed her hand along the fabric. "I couldn't afford the furniture, much less the house."

"I like the house, of course, but it isn't nearly as expensive as it would be if it was in the Hills Section or Five Sisters. I've got some pretty sketchy neighbors on the next block down." She pointed across the street to the ramshackle two story. "That place has at least fifteen students packed into it. I'm not easily annoyed, but even I've called the cops on them."

"So you're saying I could snap one of these up for a hundred thousand?"

"Uhm…no," Jill admitted. "But it took me quite a few years to save enough for the downpayment. That's just how it goes."

Lizzie patted the chair again, looking down on it fondly. "I wonder if I'll be able to sit up in a chair like this when I'm a hundred and can afford it."

Jill played along with her teasing. "You're in good shape. You've got a chance."

When they entered the den, Jill said, "I'll leave my computer on. Then you can listen to one of the music streaming sites. I've got speakers in all of the rooms downstairs."

"Really sweet setup, Jill. I'm getting more jealous by the minute." She drew her fingers over the pattern on the decorative glass panels that flanked the casement windows. "What do you call these? They're very cool."

"Just a diamond pattern I guess. I love clear stained glass, and didn't even mind the dozens of hours I spent taking all of the layers of paint off."

"Was the house in bad shape?"

"Not bad, for the most part, but dated." She led the way into the kitchen. "Everything was about like this. The kitchen's my next project, but I'm dreading it."

"My brothers did my mom's kitchen in four days. Lure them up here and you'll be done before you know it."

"Don't tempt me. Now for the upstairs," she said as she moved from the kitchen to the center hallway. "You can see where I've spent my money."

"Buying the house was enough to impress me. If you'd just furnished it with boxes, I'd still think it was cool." They reached Jill's bedroom, her oasis of calm.

"Niiiiice. Do I get to sleep in here?"

"You can if you want. But I've got a guest room right next door."

Lizzie walked over to the big, padded headboard, put her hand on it, then sat on the bed. "What is this? Angel's wings?"

"Uh-huh. How'd you know?" She picked up a remote and said, "This controls the TV and the DVR and the lights. I could explain how to use it, but you'll forget. Just play around with it. It's fairly intuitive."

"I'm gonna lie in bed and watch everything on your DVR," Lizzie said, an impish look on her face. "You've probably got hours of Masterpiece Theater and costume dramas from BBC America."

"And infomercials for dentures and hearing aids." She led the way into the bathroom, and tried not to gloat.

"Oh, for Christ's sake! This place is big enough to wash my car!"

"There used to be three bedrooms and one bath up here. I reconfigured it to two beds, one small and one large bath. Guess which one this is?"

"It's crazy nice. Just crazy," she insisted, her gaze traveling over every detail. "I'd never leave if I had this."

"Oh, sure you would. But I'll admit there aren't many hotel rooms I've been to that are better. Doing something just the way I wanted it was awfully nice."

Lizzie sat on the edge of the soaking tub. "I haven't taken a bath in years, but I'm going to get back to it tonight. Think of me while you're driving down I-89."

"You're not going out?"

She stood up and started to exit the room. "Nah. Most of my friends took off for the weekend. I'm going to hang out and relax."

"Ahh, now I feel like a jerk. Did you stay just to do this?"

"No," she said, laughing. "I don't ever play the martyr. My friends weren't going anywhere I wanted to tag along. But when they get my incessant texts, they're going to wish they were here."

"Here's the control for the tub," Jill said, waiting for Lizzie to stop and look back into the room. She pointed to the twin handles mounted high on the wall. "Don't lean over when you turn them on or you'll get a surprise."

"I can figure things out. Don't worry about a thing."

"I hope you have fun, Lizzie. I bought some stuff for you to munch on. And if you see anything you want in the fridge or the pantry, feel free."

"I'm not the teenaged babysitter, Jill. You don't have to make me popcorn." She elbowed her playfully.

"I want you to have fun. Really."

"I will. Can I bring my bike in?"

"Sure. Or you can put it into the garage. Whatever's easier."

"A garage?" She looked like she was going to weep. "You have a garage?"

"You'll have one too," Jill insisted, patting her on the back. "Just give it time."

<hr>

On Monday afternoon, Jill walked into her house, expecting a pair of gray ghosts to fly down the stairs to greet her, but the place was strangely silent. She put her bag down and looked around, seeing almost no evidence of Lizzie's presence. Assuming she'd gone, she went upstairs and entered her bedroom. There, on the neatly made bed, Lizzie was lying on her side, David snuggled up behind her knees, Goliath draped across her thighs. Two little gray heads picked up somewhat listlessly, then they both began to purr while kneading their human pillow. Luckily, Lizzie was wearing jeans, or she would have had scratches all over her legs. Jill watched for a few seconds, tempted to snap a picture, but left the threesome to finish their nap in peace. Apparently, Lizzie *was* made of catnip.

<hr>

It had been a while, a long while, since Jill had gone to a club. While getting ready, she did the math, but was unable to come up with a good memory of the last time. It *might* have been since she'd returned to Burlington. If so, that was just dumb. While she didn't want to be one of those people who hung out with a much younger crowd, trying to act like she was close to college age, she truly did love live music. Indie rock was her thing, and had been since she was in high school. The bands changed frequently, but the basics remained the same. It was music that got little airplay, from bands that rarely made money, gained fame, or stuck together long, but she loved the energy, the drive of young musicians and songwriters trying to share their thoughts with the world.

She'd spent most of her life in Vermont, or nearby, but she'd traveled some for work, and conferences, and to visit friends. In New York, or Los Angeles, or San Francisco, or even Boston, she'd never be able to go to a club and not stick out like someone's mom. But she knew Vermont well, and was confident she'd be able to blend in wearing jeans and a T-shirt. That might not have cut it at a straight club, but it would work in a gay place.

She was surprised that Lizzie had even known about the event. It certainly seemed like she was mostly straight, with brief forays into the gay world for sex. And this wasn't a very well known event. But Lizzie was proving surprising in many areas, and Jill decided she'd have to just see what she came up with next.

Jill offered to drive, and as she pulled up in front of the address Lizzie had given her, she checked her phone again, sure she'd gotten it wrong. The building was in the South End, a big, old two-no, three-story home, with a mansard roof, very close to where they'd had coffee. It wasn't very well kept up, but it was certainly large. She texted, announcing she'd arrived, and a few seconds later, Lizzie came out the front door and dashed down the stairs, looking very well put together. Well, that wasn't true. Her jeans were skin tight and ripped in half a dozen places, and it looked like she was wearing three T-shirts, each strategically torn. It wasn't sleek, but her look was perfect for a club.

Jill had only seen her at work or play. Those were the only two modes that Jill had. But Lizzie had another personae, and it was on display tonight.

When Lizzie reached the car and opened the door, Jill saw that not only was she dressed to impress, she'd also taken the time to apply eye makeup to make her lashes heavy and dark. "You look a lot better than I do," Jill said, scowling. "Even though you've got holes in your clothes."

"All you have to do is let a woman see this car and you're hooked up," she said as she closed the door. "Is this a damn Audi?"

"Uh-huh." Jill knew she should be embarrassed to have spent so much on a car, but she really wasn't. She drove a lot, and it was important to her to have a car that was not only comfortable, but safe. All-wheel drive was a must, and her baby could hug the road in any weather. She patted the dash. "This is Freyja."

"You named your car?" She moved around in her seat for a moment, then fastened her seat belt. "I guess I don't blame you. The seats wrap around you like a lover."

"That's what I thought." She started to drive, commenting, "My last car was twelve when I turned her in."

"How many miles?"

"Around two hundred and fifty thousand. I expect this one to last as long."

"Well, you clearly throw your money away, but at least you don't do it often."

"I like to buy well-made things and take care of them. I only traded my last one in because they wanted many, many dollars to repair a blown head gasket." Lizzie had thrown her off-stride, and she recalled her confusion about the house. "I thought you'd be in an apartment building. You don't rent that whole house, do you?"

She let out a snort. "I don't rent a whole floor. Just half of the third floor. My father would call it a flop-house, but it's all I could find. I'm stuck till October, which leaves me off schedule for competing with students in August. I'm screwed."

"I had some sketchy places when I was renting. Maybe you should think about buying. You could probably buy a decent starter home."

"No real estate talk," she said firmly. "I want to have fun tonight."

"Suggestion withdrawn. But if you want to talk about it…"

"I'll keep you in mind." She pulled down the visor, slid a panel over and looked at her makeup in the light that shone down on her. "The light in my bathroom's so dim, I can never tell how I look. I went a little crazy with the eyeliner." She let out a giggle. "Can I use your car to get dressed from now on?"

"Sure. I'll have a key made for you."

Lizzie reached over and patted her leg. "You probably would. You're a very sweet person, Jill. I'm glad we're getting to hang out."

"Me too. Although my friends have all been making fun of me. They say I'm too old, by twenty years, to go to this club."

"No way," she said dismissively. "If they think that, they haven't been."

"You have?"

"Uh-huh. A couple of times. It's just a few blocks from here," she warned. "If you find a spot, grab it."

It took a while, but Jill finally found a parking spot she approved of. That was one of the downsides of having a nice car. You got a little careful about where you'd leave it. Lizzie had bought tickets, and the guy at the door scanned the bar code on her phone. Then they went into the crowded, dim, noisy room.

Lizzie was right in that there were a few people close to Jill's age, but Jill's friends had also been right. Lizzie was a little old for the crowd, who looked like they were college-aged. There were no seats, so they squeezed into an empty spot to listen. The band wasn't bad. A little tortured. A little earnest. But that was often the case. Lizzie disappeared and came back a while later with beers. She handed one to Jill, leaned close and shouted, "Camel's Hump lager. Jon probably sampled this very batch."

They clinked the necks of their bottles together and Jill nodded her approval after taking a drink. "He makes a nice beer."

Lizzie paid rapt attention to the band, starting to move her hips to the music. Then Jill noticed her scan the room, clearly checking out the crowd. Thinking about Lizzie's sexy cologne, rock-star eye makeup, and trendy clothes, it was clear she wasn't planning on spending the evening merely talking to Jill. But it was too crowded to roam, and they stood close to one another during the set.

The band played until ten, then Jill went to buy another round while they set up for the DJ. They changed the lighting scheme too, with a little more light falling on the crowd. When the DJ started to spin, Jill leaned against the back wall, perfectly content to watch people dance. Lizzie nodded her head in time to the music, with her body twitching like she couldn't control it. "Don't you like to dance?" she shouted over the noise.

"Sometimes. But I like to check out a place first. Go ahead if you want to."

She handed Jill her beer. "Feel free to down it if you want. I've got work to do." Her evil laugh was just barely audible, but it made Jill smile. It was a little hard to see, with a strobe flashing every couple of seconds, but Lizzie didn't seem to have any trouble finding women to dance with. And why should she? Anyone would be attracted to her big smile, the carefree, graceful way she moved around the crowded dance floor, and the way she sang along to every song she knew.

Things had changed since Jill was in college. Now people didn't really dance with one person. They just danced, with people getting close then fading away after a song or two. Lizzie danced with as many men as women, with a lot of really energetic guys urging her on. It was a surprisingly wholesome scene, with people just getting off on moving their bodies to really loud music.

Jill had let Lizzie's beer grow warm, limiting herself to two. She was dying for a bottle of water, but the bar was jammed with people crowding around it and she hated that kind of scrum.

Lizzie had found a very cute young woman to dance with, and Jill noticed she moved a little more energetically as she teased her, moving close, then flitting away to dance in front of someone else. She reminded Jill of a honeybee, hovering for a moment, then moving a little bit farther away, only to come back. The woman she was flirting with put her hands on Lizzie's hips to hold her in place, but as soon as she did that, Lizzie gave her a very friendly wave and walked back to Jill. Her hair was wet, with a few strands stuck to her forehead, and her shirts looked limp too.

"You don't hold back," Jill said. "Are you having fun?"

"Yeah. Of course. I love to dance." She reached down and picked up the beer that sat by Jill's foot. "I'm gonna hate this, but I'll pass out if I don't get some liquid in me." She shivered with distaste as she gulped down the beer. "Nasty!"

"I'll go get water. Just hang on for a minute," Jill said, raising her voice to compete with the music.

Lizzie took her by the hand. "Dance for three songs, then we can leave and go get a Big Gulp or something."

74

Jill wasn't going to drink thirty two ounces of soda at one in the morning, but she consented. Having Lizzie drag her forcibly behind her helped in the decision-making process.

The song changed to one Jill was familiar with. She was a little rusty, not having danced once in the time she was with Becca, but after a few minutes she loosened up and simply let the beat tell her hips and her feet where to go. Lizzie wasn't flitting around now. She stood very close to Jill, brushing against her every once in a while, heat radiating off her body. Lizzie really knew how to move, and if she hadn't been Mark's little sister, Jill would have put her mind to seducing her. But Jill flushed that thought out of her brain in a matter of seconds. As Lizzie said, you didn't have to act out every impulse you felt, or something like that.

Good to her word, after three songs she put her hand on Jill's back and herded her towards the exit.

The cool, fresh air hit them like a slap. A slap they both relished. "Damn, it was hot in there," Jill moaned.

"I danced for an hour longer than you did. I'm dying!" They made it to the car, with Lizzie peeling a T-shirt off, despite the fact that it couldn't have been more than sixty degrees. She wiped her face and neck with it, then threw it on the floor when she got into the car. "I need water, but I also need food. Wouldn't you love a big order of fries right now?"

"I'm not sure why, but that seems like a good idea. Where to?"

"There's a pub I like not too far away. I think the kitchen's open for another fifteen or twenty minutes. Can you get us to College that fast?"

"Freyja is at your service. Ride on, girl!" Laughing, Jill peeled out, then drove at her normal speed to reach the place right at the deadline. "Go in and order for us," she said. "I'll park."

Jill had to leave her trusty goddess five blocks away, but the walk let her cool down a little, or at least let some of the sweat evaporate. The pub wasn't nearly as crowded as the club had been, and Lizzie had secured a table. She stuck her hand up and waved Jill over.

"Weren't you wearing a white T-shirt a second ago?" The shirt was gone, with Lizzie now displaying a lot of skin. The bar was dark, but Jill was certain she'd changed.

"Yeah. I made a critical error in wearing a leotard. I can't take it off, so everything else has to go."

Laughing, Jill said, I'm not going to check to see if you still have your jeans on."

"I do. But I'm tempted…"

"I don't want any trouble. Your mother would never forgive me if you were carried away by a pack of guys."

Lizzie simply smirked at her. "I ordered a shandy, but I figured you wouldn't want any more alcohol, so I got you some sparkling water."

"Perfect." The server brought their drinks and they attacked them like they'd just emerged from a long march across the desert. "Damn, I needed that." Jill took out her phone and took a selfie, then moved over to stand next to Lizzie and take one of them together. "I want to show my friends that I not only stayed up with the youngsters, I actually danced. I think I look appropriately trashed, don't I?"

"Pretty much," Lizzie said, laughing. "Did you have fun?"

Jill moved back to her side of the high table and sat on her stool. "I had an excellent time." The server walked over with a huge plate of fries and a bowl of chili, with raw onions, cheese and sour cream lying on top. Jill looked at the food, then said, "My stomach might hate me in the morning, but tonight, I'm living large."

Lizzie started to shovel fries into her mouth like she hadn't eaten in days. "Damn, these are good." She took another big gulp of her shandy and said, "I don't do this very often, to be honest. Every month or two is enough for me, but if I don't go out once in a while, I start to feel like I'm stuck in a rut."

"I don't generally feel that way, but after dancing just a little I feel better. Looser," she said, frowning. "That doesn't seem like the right word, but it's all I can think of."

"I think it's the perfect word." Lizzie took a few fries and dunked them in the chili. As she chewed, she said, "Dancing knocks the rust off."

"Good analogy. I'm in danger of letting myself get rusty." She mimicked Lizzie and dunked some fries in the chili. "If you ever need a partner when you go dancing, give me a call."

"You're on," she agreed. "You're fun to hang out with. I don't have many lesbian friends, and I don't like to take my straight friends to gay clubs."

"No? Why?"

She shook her head as she swallowed her latest mouth-full, with a few more fries in her hand, waiting to be gulped down. "My friend-group's in flux. I don't have anyone who'd appreciate a gay club right now, and I don't want my straight friends staring at people."

With her hunger partially satisfied, Jill could slow down and eat one fry at a time, but that dipping was a good idea. She'd have to remember that. Chewing thoughtfully, she said, "What's...mmm...I'm trying to think of how to ask this properly."

"Just ask," Lizzie said, waving her hand. "You won't offend me."

"How do you identify? I mean, I know you call yourself bisexual, but are you only interested in dating both sexes at once?"

"I'm not locked into that," she said quickly. "That's actually never worked out great for me."

"But you said…"

"I know what I said. And I have brought a woman into bed when I've been with a guy. But that's never been what I really want. I'm not sure what to try next."

Jill dunked a fry, then popped it into her mouth. "Details? Or would you rather not?"

"I don't mind." She took a long drink, and set her glass down. "I've been with three guys since I've been out of school. All relationships, not hook-ups. But I always knew I was bi, so I thought it would work to bring a woman in once in a while."

"But it didn't?"

"It worked the first time I tried—but more for Nick, my boyfriend, than it did for me."

"But...you did it for yourself."

"Uh-huh." She took a big bite of chili. "Hot!"

"Spicy?"

"Yeah," she said, waving her hand in front of her mouth. "You don't notice it when you just dunk." After cooling her mouth down with a sip of her drink she said, "Nick was very open-minded about the whole thing. We were monogamous until we'd been together about a year. Then I got the urge and met someone at a conference who I thought would be up for it. Nick was all for it, and we got together with this woman. It was great," she said wistfully. "That satisfied me, but then Nick wanted to ask her over again. I would have loved to get into a long-term thing with her, but she came to work at the Gardner, and I didn't want to be that involved with a co-worker."

"That makes sense," Jill said as she took a bite of chili and fanned her mouth just as Lizzie had. "I don't want people I work closely with to come to my house, much less be involved with them."

"Yeah. But Nick wouldn't stop. For the next year, he badgered me until we hooked up with a woman we found on a dating app. That was a disaster. She'd never been with a woman and found she wasn't into the whole thing." She rolled her eyes. "No fun at all."

"Why'd you break up?"

"He loved having two women focus on him. Not that I blame him," she added, laughing softly. "But I wanted it to be a special treat. Not something we spent all week planning and working on."

"I get that. I really do," Jill said. "Too much work."

"Exactly. He just wouldn't let it go, so I had to break up with him. Two years—down the drain."

"I've been there," Jill said. "You think you're close, that you're building something, but something critical stops you cold."

"Ice cold. So, for my next boyfriend, I chose a guy who wasn't into having three-ways, but didn't mind if I slept with a woman once in a while."

They'd grown close enough that Jill felt comfortable teasing her. "And that didn't work either, since he's not here."

"Nope." She drained her drink, then let out a sigh. "He was a heck of a nice guy. An ob/gyn resident at Mass General."

"Cool. At least he knew the terrain."

"Oh, yeah. He was a good lover. And he didn't complain when I hooked up with someone from a dating app. But then he kept asking me questions, comparing what she did with what he did. All of a sudden, he had performance problems. Every time we had sex he'd check with me every two seconds. 'Is this okay? Does this feel good?' I ruined him, Jill. I inadvertently destroyed his confidence."

"Damn, who knew it would be this hard to find a guy who wanted an extra woman once in a while?"

"I sure didn't. I assumed a guy would think it was like Christmas."

"And then you met Jon."

"Yeah. I was willing to focus on him, but he just didn't believe me."

Lizzie's posture had gotten much more relaxed. Now she was leaning against the wall, too tired to hold herself up. Or maybe she was sad. "Did you really think you could go the rest of your life without a woman?"

She slumped towards the table, and dropped her chin in her hand. No doubt about it. She was sad. "I thought so. I would have given it everything I had." Shrugging, she added, "But how do I know? I might have started to crave a woman. But I wouldn't have cheated on him. I don't *do* that."

"But he probably didn't want to think of you wanting a woman, even if you didn't act on it."

Lizzie sat up, her normal energy back in place. "Like he wouldn't be attracted to other women? You don't act on those desires for the security of monogamy. It's a trade-off. For *every*one."

"I guess it is," Jill said thoughtfully. "I still had occasional fantasies about other women when I was with Becca. I just ignored them."

"Yeah. Or you can use the fantasies during sex. You can talk about them," she said, clearly frustrated. "I wanted to do that with Jon. To talk about women and what I wanted to do with them as a way to turn him on. But he wasn't into it. At *all*."

"You've had bad luck three times in a row. But there's no need to give up. A guy I know likes to be with two guys at the same time. He uses a dating website for kinky people. Have you tried that?"

She shrugged. "I'm rethinking. It might be time to turn in my active bisexual card and go into the inactive category."

Jill reached over and covered her hand. "I'd hate to have you do that just because you've had trouble finding the right guy. Give it another try."

"We'll see." She waved the server over and said, "Do I have time for another shandy?"

"Last call," the bartender yelled out from behind the bar.

"Must be my lucky day," she said, with a happy grin making her look like she'd won a prize.

While they waited for the server to return, Lizzie checked her phone. After a minute Jill snatched it from her hand and held onto it. "If you're not a trauma surgeon, you can't ignore me to text people you'd rather be with."

"I wasn't," she insisted, twitching her fingers, clearly anxious to get it back. "I was looking for a survey I read about. I thought we could do it."

"A survey?" Jill handed the phone back. "What kind of survey?"

"It's a thing a psychologist devised to let people get to know one another quickly. A bunch of questions that most people wouldn't ever ask, but probably should."

"Uhm, I guess I'm game. But don't embarrass me and ask what I do in bed. I'm not telling," she insisted, glowering playfully.

"Fine, fine," Lizzie said, still searching. "Okay. Here it is." She cleared her throat and said dramatically, "First question. Would you like to be famous? If so, for what?"

"No. Nothing," Jill said immediately. "Hey, this is easy!" She took a sip of her water. "Now you."

"Mmm…" Lizzie screwed her face up, making her look like a kid. "I wish I'd had the talent to be good at one of the arts. But I didn't. I guess I don't want to be famous either. Certainly not just for the thrill of it."

"We're in sync. Must be a Sugar Hill trait. We're not fame seekers."

"Question two. If you could change one thing about your childhood, what would it be?"

Jill could feel her lip curl up in distaste. "I should plead the fifth on this one."

"Come on," Lizzie said, taking Jill's hand as their eyes met. There was something safe in that open gaze. Nonjudgemental.

"All right." It was tough to spit out, but she forced herself. "I wish I'd had a different mother."

She closed her eyes, afraid to see the look on Lizzie's face. Her hand was tenderly stroked, then a soft, warm voice said, "I wish you had a mom just like mine. One who was always on your side. Always interested."

"Yeah," Jill agreed, her mouth dry. "It would have been nice to know I mattered."

Lizzie looked like she was about to cry, but she scanned down her list, probably ignoring all of the other questions about families. "Here's a good one. Go back and forth and tell your partner something you admire about them."

"Easy," Jill said, warming to the subject. "I like how mature you are. The first time I saw you at work I could tell you didn't have that goofy 'I'm just a dunce' thing so many young women have."

"Nice. I know just what you're talking about, and I'm damned glad it doesn't seem like I do that." She put the phone down and stared at Jill for a moment. "I admire how kind you are. And thoughtful. You don't have a mean bone in your body."

"Oh, I probably do," she teased. "They're just hidden under my skin." She thought for a moment or two. "I admire how you're planning your life. Knowing what you want and trying to get it is very mature."

"I have my mature moments. But I've made some dumb mistakes too." She pointed at Jill. "I admire you for coming out when you were young. That wasn't very common for Sugar Hill at the time."

"I like to be honest," Jill said. "Hiding something important makes me feel...bad."

"It was still a risk. And you took it."

Jill gave her a smile. "I'm gonna get a big head from all of these compliments—but I don't want to stop." She let her mind go over all of the things she liked about Lizzie. "I admire that you do a job where you don't make a lot of money—just because you believe in the organization."

"Jobs aren't that easy to get," she hedged. "I might give it up tomorrow if someone offered me a big raise to sell crack to school kids."

"Uh-huh. That sounds like you."

"Well, I admire that you work at the U. You could make more as a comptroller at a big corporation. And no one would know your salary," she teased.

"Probably true. But I like the environment. It's collegial." She found herself laughing at her silly joke. "It's a college, right?"

"You're endlessly funny," Lizzie agreed, her attention already diverted to her phone. "I like this one." She looked up at Jill. "If we were going to be very close friends, what should I know about you?"

Jill leaned back on her stool, her mouth slightly open. "Damn, that's a tough one!"

"Come on. I know you've got an answer in that pretty head."

"Uhm," Jill found herself scrambling, the answer just not coming. Then she took a cleansing breath and said the first thing that came to mind. "I'd like you to know that I'll never screw you over, or play games with you. When you need me, I'll be there, even if it's difficult. I'll be on your side, Lizzie," she said, the force of her answer catching her by surprise.

"Good answer," Lizzie said, her pretty eyes blinking slowly. "My turn." She took in a breath and let it out. "You should know that I've always tried to be the woman my parents want me to be. They were very good influences, and I know if I do what they'd like—I'll be fine."

Jill reached across the table and gripped her hand, feeling her eyes well up with tears. "We could both do that and save a lot of time worrying about things. What would Janet and Mike do?"

"I'll have T-shirts made," Lizzie said, reaching up to cuff Jill playfully on the chin. "Okay. We've skipped about thirty-five questions, but there's one final thing you're supposed to do." She leaned over, her face just inches from Jill's. "We need to stare into each other's eyes for four minutes."

"Four minutes!"

"Yep. No cheating. I'm going to set my timer."

Jill could feel the hairs on the back of her neck stand up. She tried to always look people in the eye even though it didn't come naturally to her. But to do it for four minutes? She might pass out before they were halfway done. Then Lizzie reached over to hit the damned button, and Jill set her mind to playing the game. She hated to lose—at anything.

Leaning in, she settled herself, preparing for a long slog. A sweet half smile curled Lizzie's lips, and her eyes radiated warmth. That Jon guy was a moron. Who wouldn't want to look into those beautiful eyes? And if you could be kissing her gorgeous mouth at the same time? Who cared if Lizzie dreamed about women? If she was sleeping with you—make her not want anyone else. Man up!

Jill's mind had definitely wandered. Forcefully, she concentrated on Lizzie. Just Lizzie. She seemed so smart. So quick. Like she had all sorts of talents and skills she could whip out whenever she needed them.

The phone was lying right there, but she'd have to break eye contact to see how much time was left. Of course Lizzie didn't seem anxious in the least. That little smile had departed, and now her eyes bore into Jill, making her feel utterly exposed. But this was good. It was good to be vulnerable with a friend. To show you trusted them enough to open up.

If only the time would go faster!

Okay. She could do this. The time had to be over soon.

Jill took a breath and focused again, trying to look into Lizzie's soul. What made her tick? What did she want out of life? What would make her happy? The answers were all in there. Jill just had to wait—everything would be revealed as they got to know each other better. That thought made her smile. A rich, warm smile that immediately had Lizzie smiling back. They sat there, staring into each other's eyes, big grins on their faces. Then the buzzer sounded.

"Whoa!" Jill gasped, dropping her head onto the table. "That was hard."

"Not for me," Lizzie said softly.

Jill craned her neck from her uncomfortable position, and met Lizzie's eyes.

"You looked so open. So approachable. I could have done that for another five minutes."

"Let's work up to that," Jill said, relieved it was over. "I'm glad we did it though. It was…" She didn't want to admit it, but her whole body was tingling. Like she'd been given a burst of energy. It was strangely similar to the way she felt when she'd been on a great roller coaster.

"I'm stoked," Lizzie said, getting right to the heart of the matter. "I could run home."

"You know, I could too. But Freyja gets her feelings hurt if I don't take her home and put her in her stall."

Lizzie looked at her phone one last time. "Here's an easy question I don't have to ask. Who in your life would you be most upset to lose. The answer is clearly Freyja."

⤬

They didn't get to Lizzie's building until two thirty. "My boys are going to have called the police to file a missing person's report."

"I like your cats. If I had a little more room, I'd get one."

"They don't take up much space."

Lizzie laughed. "You'll have to come up to my apartment some day. Then you'll see why I can't have a cat."

"Hey, I'm going to have a barbecue to celebrate the beginning of summer. Want to come? You can bring your friends. It's going to be big."

"Sure," she said, giving Jill a wide grin. "I love parties."

"It's two weeks from tomorrow. I'll have a couple of kegs of beer, and I'll provide burgers and dogs and sausages. So bring a side dish or a dessert. Cool?"

"You're on. And I promise to only bring my well-behaved friends."

"It's a really big party, so you can bring anyone. And if it rains on Saturday, the rain date is Sunday."

"Sounds great." Lizzie leaned over and kissed her cheek. "I had an awesome time. Thanks for chauffeuring me in your limo."

"I had a very memorable evening," Jill said, finding herself edgy about saying what was on her mind. But she gutted it up and got it out. "Your last question? About who I'd miss?"

"Yeah?" Lizzie asked, her voice soft and gentle.

"I'd miss your mom," Jill admitted, with tears coming to her eyes. "Now that I have her back in my life, it'd kill me to lose her again."

Lizzie leaned over and wrapped Jill in a gentle hug. "You won't. Promise." She kissed Jill's cheek again, her lips warm and soft. "We're never going to let you go."

"Thanks." She sat up and wiped at her eyes, feeling a little foolish. "Freyja and I enjoyed ourselves a lot. See you in two weeks."

"Bye," she said, those piercing eyes lingering on Jill for a few long seconds.

Jill watched her walk up the path to her apartment, shaking her butt to the beat that obviously still played in her head. Mark had always been her favorite Davis sibling, but he was no match for his little sister. They weren't even in the same league.

Chapter Six

THE NEXT DAY, THE weather app on her phone promised warm temps and clear skies, but not until afternoon. Jill pondered her options, certain she didn't want to waste a Saturday morning and hoping the drizzle would stop. On impulse, she called Janet. "Good morning," Jill said when Janet answered. "I was thinking about driving down. Are you up for a visitor?"

"Always, Jill. Could you tell I was thinking about you?"

"You were?"

"Uh-huh. I saw your father this morning, and you've been on my mind ever since."

"Where'd you see him? At the market?"

"No, he was driving down the road when I was at the post office. Do your folks know you're coming?"

"No." She thought about it for a moment. "I think I'll just come for the day."

"You know," Janet said, her voice growing a little softer. "You can always stay with us if you'd like. We've got three bedrooms empty most nights."

"Aww, that's really nice of you. I'm not sure I can take you up on the offer, but it's tempting."

"Your mother wouldn't need to know," Janet reminded her.

"Thanks. I'll definitely consider it. For next time. A friend's having a birthday party tomorrow at noon, so I'll probably drive home tonight. We'll see how I'm feeling."

"Great. We look forward to seeing you, Jill. It's always a treat."

"Thanks, Janet. You know I feel the same."

She had to keep her speed down, due to the rain, but Jill pulled into the Davis drive well before lunch, wedging in next to the SUV that took up most of the space.

After dashing up to the front door, she knocked, surprised when a teenaged boy opened it. "Hi," Jill said. "I'm here to see your grandparents."

"Okay," he said, turning to walk away. Jill laughed to herself and opened the door, hearing voices in the kitchen. She moved through the living and dining rooms, then pushed open the swinging door, finding Janet standing at the counter with Lisa, the monosyllabic door opener, and another kid. Jill stopped in her tracks, wishing she could turn tail and run.

"Jill," Janet said, smiling as she moved across the room to hug her. "I was hoping you'd be here in time to meet the kids. They're going to play baseball, and they stopped in to show me their new uniforms." She put her hand on the taller kid's shoulder. "This is Christian, and Joshua."

"Hi, guys," Jill said.

Neither one met her eyes, but they both muttered something.

"Hi, Lisa."

"Hello, Jill." She was trying to smile, but it seemed to take quite an effort. "What brings you down?"

"Just wanted to stop in and see Janet and Mike. This seemed like a good day."

"Your father certainly took off early this morning," Lisa said, a frown turning the corners of her mouth down. Jill noticed she'd begun to develop vertical lines along the sides of her chin, making her look uncomfortably like a marionette. "Where does he go early on a Saturday morning?"

"I have no idea," Jill said. "I don't...I don't know." She was going to say she didn't feel the need to check up on him, but didn't think that was a smart move. Poking Lisa was never going to be productive.

"He used to spend his nights at the Irish Rover in Brattleboro, but they don't see him much any more. Does he have a *friend* somewhere else?"

"He's a friendly guy," Jill said, trying to control her voice.

"Oh, everyone knows how friendly Rich Henry is," she said, a smarmy grin on her face.

"Lisa," Janet said, her tone much sharper than usual. "You'd better get going if you don't want to be late."

After checking her watch, Lisa nodded, oblivious to the fact that her mother-in-law had just basically told her to knock it off and leave. "I guess we'd better go, boys. Kiss Grandma goodbye."

They did as they were told, giving Janet the "I don't want to do this" kind of kiss that teenaged boys were so skilled at.

"You two have fun today," Janet said, as she hugged them both.

"Most of the grandparents come," Lisa said, pointedly.

"Good for them!" Janet just smiled, an expression that meant she'd heard you but wasn't going to do whatever it was you wanted. Janet had never been the type to be coerced into anything. Kind of like her youngest. Too bad Mark hadn't inherited just a bit of that trait.

"The boys would like it too," Lisa added. "Wouldn't you boys?"

They were barely listening, but when Lisa repeated her question, they managed to shrug.

"I can see how much it means to them," Janet said, smirking. "Maybe Jill and I will walk over."

Lisa got behind the kids and guided them towards the door. "Oh, don't bother. They won't do more than goof around today." As they exited, she called out, "See you."

Janet gave Jill a puzzled look as she sat down at the big kitchen table. "What went on between you two to make her so…"

"Hateful?" Jill supplied. She sat down too, and folded her hands in front of her. "I truly don't know. I can only guess it's because I'm gay and my dad's a cheater, but who cares about stuff like that?"

"Lisa does," Janet said. "I swear she thinks she's the only one stopping the moral decline of Southern Vermont."

"The summer after I graduated from college, when I was living at home before starting grad school, I ran into her one day. Mark had obviously told her I'd come out as a lesbian, and she marched up to me and said she loved me as a child of God, but detested my lifestyle."

"That's Lisa." Janet sighed. "I'm not sure if she honestly thinks she's going to change people, or if she just likes being superior."

"Hard to tell," Jill said. "But I hate to see her raising three kids to have that same mindset."

"I do too," Janet said, looking a little glum. "Grace, their sixteen-year-old, already has more of it than I'd like. She's always telling me about kids at school who don't do things the way she thinks they should."

"I was hoping Mark's good nature would rub off."

"It might, if he ever tried to push his point. But he's not going to do that." She rolled her eyes. "I love him. You know how much I love him. But he wouldn't stand up to a strong wind. And the kids know it."

"It's sad," Jill agreed. "He can't be happy."

"It's hard to tell. I know he likes having Lisa in charge, but she's probably more in charge than he wants."

"I'm surprised they have three kids," Jill said, shivering at the thought of how they got them.

Janet reached over and slapped her playfully. "Don't start! I make it a habit to never think about my kids' sex lives, but I'll admit I've often wondered if they have any kind of chemistry."

"Don't look at me. I never understood what Mark saw in Lisa, and I'd be surprised if he didn't ask himself the same thing every once in a while."

Janet stood and went to the window. After peering out for a few seconds, she turned and smiled. "As soon as Lisa left, the sun peeked out. You won't catch me saying there's a correlation."

"But I can catch you thinking it."

She looked like she was about to laugh, but she turned and headed for the door. "Let's go see the kids loaf around the ball-field. Neither of them likes to play, but all of their friends do, so they go along with the crowd."

"Sounds like they take after their dad more than their mom."

"Sounds like," Janet agreed, taking Jill's arm as they left the house.

They'd just started to walk when Jill said, "Is Mike resting?"

"No, he's riding around in a golf cart." Her smile grew as she spoke. "He's on a new inhaler and it's helped more than we'd hoped. He's still using oxygen, but just when he sleeps. His mood has improved a hundred percent."

"That's fantastic! Is he able to play golf, or just ride?"

"He's starting off slow. Today he's going to ride along. Or so he says. Knowing him, he'll be carrying his clubs and trying to get his pals to go for thirty-six."

"That's the Mike Davis I know," Jill said, smiling at the thought of the younger, very energetic history teacher. "He used to run around our classroom like crazy, demonstrating one thing or another. He made school fun."

"He was a good teacher. I know he misses it."

"I'm surprised none of the boys went into teaching. They had such a good example."

"None of them showed any interest," Janet said. "Beth…Lizzie" she said, correcting herself, "thought about becoming a professor, but she didn't want to stay on and get a Ph.D." She laughed softly. "She's such a practical kid. She said it wasn't fair to even let kids study art history, since there aren't any jobs in the field."

Jill did a stutter-step as she took in this surprising information. "I didn't know that was her major. I thought she would have gotten a business degree."

"No, she's always been into art and music. I'm not sure where she gets it, since we never took the whole brood anywhere!" She laughed. "The only museums that kid ever got to were on school trips, but she wound up working at one. A very good one." She put her arm around Jill's waist and gave her a hug. "She told me about cat-sitting for you. That was nice of you to hire her to do that. She's always looking for ways to rustle up a little cash."

"Uhm… I didn't offer to pay her." She slapped herself on the forehead. "Now I feel like a jerk!"

"Oh, please," Janet said, waving her hand dismissively. "Lizzie doesn't do a single thing she doesn't want to do. Believe me, if she'd wanted money, she would have told you what she charged. The girl's not shy."

"I was treating her like a friend," Jill admitted. "But I should have paid her, just like I do my usual cat-sitter."

"I'm sorry I brought it up, honey. But I really meant what I said. If she'd wanted money, you'd know it."

They reached the baseball field, but didn't get very close. The rain had left puddles near the benches, which were filled with parents. "Let's just make sure the kids see us, then keep going. I don't want to listen to Lisa proclaiming they're headed for the Hall of Fame."

The boys waved back when Janet put her fingers into her mouth and let out a very loud whistle. "That'll do," she said. "Let's go have lunch."

They returned to the house to find Lizzie, sitting on the counter, drinking a soda. She wore her usual T-shirt and skinny jeans, but today they were tucked into hunter green rain boots. She shook her head mournfully when she met Jill's gaze. "I could have had a ride down here?"

"I had no idea you were coming."

"Neither did I," Janet said, going over to stand between her legs and pull her down for a hug. "But I'm glad."

"There wasn't much going on, so I thought I'd come down and spread some cheer." She gave Jill a pointed look, fierce yet clearly playful. "It only took me three hours on the train. Plus the time I spent waiting for Tim to come pick me up while a certain someone was monopolizing my mother's time." Her focus shifted back to her mother. "Where's Dad?"

Janet had a very pleased look on her face when she said, "He's out with Whitey, Chet and Wayne, playing golf or riding around in a cart. Either way, he was as pleased as punch when they came to pick him up."

"Awesome!" Lizzie slid off the counter and slapped Jill on the back. "Give me a buzz next time you want to come down." Her eyes narrowed, and her voice dropped. "Unless you're trying to sneak ahead of me in the favorite daughter category."

Jill laughed. "No, I'm not trying to compete. I honestly didn't think to call you. Do you come down often?"

"*All* of the time," Janet said, as she went to the refrigerator to pull out a few items. "She keeps a closer eye on Mike than I do. You know, I was pleased to hear she was staying in Burlington over Memorial Day, hoping she was going to do something with her friends. Then I found out she was cat-sitting for you."

"It was like staying at a really nice hotel, Mom. Best vacation I've had in a couple of years."

"I haven't properly thanked you for doing it," Jill said. "Put me on your calendar for dinner."

"I've got to make you dinner too?" she asked, her mouth dropping open. Then she began to laugh. "You don't have to do that, Jill. I enjoyed myself."

"I might not have to, but I'm going to. Let's have dinner at the restaurant at Hollyhock Hills. I've heard it's great."

"That's way too expensive," Lizzie protested.

"I'd like to go. I'll come early, and you can give me a better tour."

"Okay," she said, grinning. "Maybe I can shake some dough out of you at the same time. We're trying to restore the formal gardens."

"You can give it your best shot. After a couple of glasses of wine, I might agree to anything."

<hr>

By seven o'clock, the sun was thinking about setting, but the temperatures were still warm enough to be in shirtsleeves. Mike stood about twenty feet from the 14th hole, and he flicked his wrist, letting the Frisbee sail towards the target. As Jill hung back from the basket, ready to catch an overthrow, she reflected on how damned happy she was. The first day of the year to actually feel like summer, all of her favorite Davises playing Frisbee golf, and Mike's color and energy level so much better than they'd been during the winter. Days didn't get much better than this.

Lizzie darted after the disk when it veered off in her direction. She grabbed it on the fly and flung it at Jill, not even pausing to set herself. "On your toes!" she said, laughing when it hit her in the chest.

"Give me a second!" She bent to pick up the disk, then took her turn, dropping it into the net with a degree of accuracy that surprised her.

Whipping her hands in the air, she did a joyful victory dance. "I've still got the touch!"

"Winner buys the next round," Lizzie announced, holding up an empty beer bottle. "Jill? Dad?"

"None for me," Jill said. "I'm the designated driver."

"I think I can have another," Mike said. "As soon as we're done, I'm going to plop down on my sofa. No driving until church tomorrow."

Janet walked over and put her arm around Jill's waist. "Thanks for taking our girl home. She would have had to leave already if she was taking the train."

"I'm happy to have her." She took in a breath, letting all of her favorite scents in. "Great night, isn't it?"

"There's nothing like a warm summer night," Janet agreed. She took the disk from the basket. "I'm up."

"Have at it." Jill stuck her hands in her back pockets and took in the evening. It wasn't like it had been when she was a child. Then you couldn't be outside without at least ten other kids from the neighborhood coming to join the Davis gang. But it was peaceful, welcoming, nurturing. The very definition of home.

The katydids hadn't started chirping yet, but the sun was already behind the hills to the west, and the whole place smelled of summer: rich, fragrant soil mounded around vegetables just starting to poke their heads out, fresh-mown lawns, a hint of charcoal from someone's dinner, and a pungent profusion of marigolds that ringed the patio.

Janet's throw sailed far over the basket and Jill jogged to fetch it. She bent her knees and let it fly, hitting the basket and making the metal chains sing.

"She's a natural," Mike said. "You always had a good eye, Jill. Too bad girls didn't play ball when you were a kid."

Lizzie was walking towards them when Mike said that, and she turned and jogged back into the house. When she returned, a few minutes later, she held a frame in her hand. "Speaking of the world's greatest women baseball players," she announced, then handed the frame to Jill.

"Oh, that's cute," Jill said, grinning.

Janet came over to stand by her and take a look at the photo. "She was a plucky little thing, wasn't she?"

"I didn't know she'd played," Jill said, looking fondly at the photo of Lizzie and a dozen boys, gold shirts and white pants hanging off their skinny bodies, big, gold caps atop their heads, with stylized "SH" lettering gracing the fronts.

"You don't remember that? Oh, she was so proud of herself."

"I was at the U by then," Jill said, checking the date on the photo. "I went up early that summer to get a math class out of the way."

Janet smiled at her, probably recalling that Jill had taken every opportunity to go to Burlington early and stay late. Once she'd gotten away from home, she rarely returned. "We have at least one movie of our little star playing a game. What position did you play, honey?"

"Second base. I didn't have a strong arm, but I was accurate." She jumped into the air and landed with her feet spread well apart. "And I could avoid someone trying to take me out."

"I'd love to get up to Boston to see a game this year," Mike said wistfully. "Mark promises he'll go every year, but he's always got something going on."

"I'll take you, Dad," Lizzie said. "Any time."

A sour look settled on his face. "It pisses me off that I can't just go where I want, when I want."

"You can," Janet said, putting her arm around him. "You just need someone to tag along." Turning to Lizzie, she said, "Can you try to get tickets, honey? Maybe Jill would like to come along. You're still a fan, aren't you?"

"Sure. Always."

"You two have schedules you have to work around. Just tell us when we're going, and we'll be ready."

"Great," Jill said, already working out the details in her head. They'd have to stay overnight…

"Are you ready to head back, or do you want to stay over?" Lizzie asked, interrupting her train of thought.

94

"I guess I'm ready. But I don't want to rush you. It's fine with me if we leave at ten."

"I worry about you driving so late," Janet said. She put her hands on each woman's back and led them toward the house. "Mike," she called out, "Pick some strawberries for the girls. You know how Lizzie loves them."

"Some lettuce wouldn't hurt if you've got any extra," Lizzie said. "Just a few leaves. I usually make a sandwich for dinner and I hate to have to buy a whole head."

"My thrifty girl," Janet said fondly, wrapping an arm around Lizzie's waist.

They went inside, where Lizzie packed up her computer and put her flip-flops back on. Then Mike came in and they discussed the proper way to transport fairly ripe strawberries. It was eight o'clock before they'd said their goodbyes and were in the car.

"If I could capture a day and replay it when I needed a boost"—Jill turned to smile at Lizzie—"this would be the day."

Lizzie moved her seat back and stretched out. "I can't argue with you on that. Although it would have been nice to snare some homegrown tomatoes. They're never ready before August, though, when summer's almost over."

"No such talk! It's just beginning, and I'm going to enjoy every damned minute."

On the following Saturday morning, Jill woke to a stripe of warm sun painting her body. As soon as her eyes opened, a little gray face hovered above her, then a pink tongue swiped across her lid. "I can open them myself, Goliath." She giggled. "Let's go have some breakfast, boys," she said as she swung around and set her feet on the floor. "Once I start getting ready for the party, you'll be so freaked out you won't eat a thing."

The boys usually got dry food, but when Jill knew they'd be hiding all day she gave them a treat. As she opened the can of something disgusting, they weaved around her legs so enthusiastically she had to laugh. "I'm really going to give this to you. Promise. I swear I won't forget in the middle of dishing it out."

Once they were happily gorging themselves, Jill made coffee, then had a small serving of granola. She knew she'd eat way too much throughout the day, so it made sense to start off slow. As soon as she was finished, she started to cook, confident almost everyone would bring desserts. She loved baked beans, so she put together a big batch and set them in the oven to bake. The boys had been interested, with David dancing around on the counter, despite her removing him every single time she caught him. But when someone knocked heavily on the back door, both cats hit the ground and took off—the last she'd see of them until the final guest left.

After directing the delivery guys to where she wanted the kegs set up, she went back inside and made burgers. It was cheaper and easier to buy pre-made ones, but if she was going to cook, she was going to do it right. And that meant grinding her own beef and forming it into patties. The whole process took a while, but she still had time to make a heaping bowl of cole slaw before noon—the announced starting time.

As always, Karen and Becky were the first to arrive. They knew her well enough to know she liked home-cooked food, but since neither of them had any culinary talent, they brought two nice bottles of wine for her to drink at a future date. "I know you'd prefer a quiche or something," Becky said, "but at least you won't have to throw this out when no one eats it."

"I appreciate your concern for the health and well being of my guests," she said, kissing them both. "Did you bring some chairs?"

"Already in the backyard," Karen said. "Want help?"

"Sure. I bought a few games for kids, since I know we'll have a bunch of them. You can help me set them up."

When they walked outside, Carly and Samantha were figuratively dragging Presley and Trent into the yard. Trent was going to be a senior and Presley a sophomore in high school, and had reached the age where going to a party with their moms was just short of torture.

"Just the people I wanted to see," Jill said, amping up her enthusiasm. She'd known the boys since they were small, and had a good relationship with them. She was sure they would have rather been doing just about anything else. "Will you guys check out the games I bought and set them up?" The boys glared at each other for a few seconds, then Trent nodded and moved over to the table where Jill had placed the stuff. Since Trent had gone, that let Presley follow along and not look stupid. As they walked away, Carly said quietly, "Sometimes I wish we'd stopped at cats."

Samantha put her arm around her. "She's having a bad day," she explained to the others. "Presley told her he'd skip college if he had to go to the U."

"He might," Carly whispered. "He was put on this earth to torture me."

"Oh, he's your baby," Jill insisted in the voice she always used around small kids. "Remember how happy you were when he would tell everyone his mommy was the smartest person around because she was a pofesso?"

"I got stupid when he turned thirteen," she grumbled. "I can't wait for him to grow up and find a woman who'll put up with him."

"Default heterosexuality?" Jill teased. "Are you sure a professor in the Gender, Sexuality and Women's Studies division should assume her kid's straight?"

"I've seen his browsing history," she said, looking ill. "If he's not straight, he really doesn't know how to use the internet."

Jill clapped her on the back. "Is it too early to have a beer? I'd like to forget that last comment really quickly."

By two, over fifty people were in the backyard, standing in cliques that mirrored their interests. Jill noted that people with kids always tended to talk to others in the same situation, no matter their employment. She had the barbecue going, and was just about to go inside to get the food when Lizzie pushed open the gate to enter. She looked around, then smiled when her eyes met Jill's. "Hey," she said, walking over for a quick hug. "I heard there's a good party going on around here."

"You're just in time." She noted Lizzie's tight jeans and green T-shirt with the album cover for a band from the seventies emblazoned on the front. "No shorts? We're finally having a hot day."

"Nah. I don't think I own any. Jeans work year-round." She looked over the crowd. "Big group. I thought you'd have nothing but lesbians."

97

"Not a requirement," Jill said. "Most of my friends are from the U, and, despite what some people think, lesbians haven't taken over the entire faculty and administration."

"Ooo," she said, quietly. "Scott's here. I should have asked if he was coming."

Jill winced. "I forgot to tell you." She gripped her arm. "Are you able to stay?"

Lizzie's head cocked. "We spent three evenings together. No big deal. For me, at least. Did he bring someone?"

"Uh-huh." Jill pointed at the comely young woman who was busy laughing at his jokes. "The blonde with the big…eyes."

"Yeah," Lizzie agreed. "Those are huge eyes. 34-Cs at least." She let out a soft laugh. "I'm glad he got right back in the saddle." She turned and looked expectantly at Jill. "How can I help?"

"I think I've got everything under control. Why'd you come alone? No one in town this weekend?"

"Eh." She shrugged. "I like to go to parties alone unless we all know the people. Besides, I think I told you my friend base is kinda low right now. I've got work friends, but my real buds are in Boston."

"You'll get more," Jill predicted. "You're awfully easy to like."

"I'll go mingle. Maybe my new best friend is in your backyard at this very minute."

Jill watched her head over to a group of people from admin. One thing was clear. You didn't have to coddle Lizzie Davis at a party.

An hour later, Jill sat at a table with Jason and Ben, Carly and Samantha, and Skip and Alice. Trent, Presley, and Skip and Alice's fourteen-year-old, Aaron, were all trying to impress Lizzie at the bean-bag toss game. Younger kids were impatiently waiting their turns, with Lizzie holding Olive's hand. The little three-year-old, usually very shy around strangers, looked up at her with an adoring smile.

"If your friend wants to babysit," Jason said, "she's hired. Olive never takes to people that easily."

"I'm not sure she babysits," Jill said, "but she housesits. I can attest she's great with cats."

"She wouldn't like ours," Ben said. "No one likes Carmen."

"Don't be so sure. She's one of the few people my two have ever revealed themselves to."

"You don't have cats," Skip insisted, his usual joke.

"I most certainly do, and Lizzie's my proof. Just ask her."

"Later," Skip said. "She's keeping Aaron entertained, and one thing I've learned is to never interrupt a kid who's doing something legal that isn't bad for him."

<hr/>

Jill, Ben, and Gerri were in the kitchen, parcelling out the uneaten food for people to take home. No matter how many people came to a party, the three of them ended up on kitchen detail. Why that was, Jill would never know.

Lizzie poked her head into the kitchen, and Jill saw that she was carrying Santiago, one of the youngest of the whole crowd. One of his dads was right behind her, saying, "Can we put him down in the den?"

"Sure. Let me get a blanket."

"I can handle this," Lizzie said to Tony. "You can go keep an eye on Xavier."

"Twins," he said, rolling his eyes. "Why did we think twins were a good idea? Are you sure?"

"Yeah. I'll sit down and have a beer."

"Great." He squeezed her shoulder, kissed Santiago on the head and took off.

Jill followed Lizzie to the den, grabbed a cotton throw and stretched it out on the floor. "Did I hire you to babysit today?" she asked, smirking. "Every time I look up, you're charming little boys or big boys."

"Don't forget little girls," she said, as she gently lay the baby onto his back. "In twenty years, Olive's going to be mine."

"She can be yours right now. Her dads want to hire you."

She made a face. "I appreciate that, but I'm more into housesitting. My work schedule's too unpredictable to be able to plan ahead, and a house doesn't care if I'm only there a few hours a day." Her expression morphed into a silly smile. "You can't do that with a baby. People get all pissy about it."

"Want me to watch him? You really don't need to stay inside."

"No, I'm cool. Let me go get a beer. Want one?"

"Sure. Why not?"

Lizzie was only gone a minute or two, returning with two beers, both a little fuzzy. "I didn't want to take the time to check it out, but I think your keg's warm."

"No big deal," Jill said, accepting the cup. "That's one way to get people to pack up and leave." She took a sip. "You're right. It could be a little colder."

"You can't help but learn a few tips when you live with a master brewer." She whipped off her T-shirt, with Jill purposefully averting her eyes when she caught sight of the lacy white camisole she wore.

"Aren't you hot?" Lizzie asked. "I understand why you don't have air conditioning, but it's really toasty."

"I have a unit in my bedroom." It wasn't possible to avoid looking at Lizzie in the small room. Going braless under a nearly transparent camisole must have meant she didn't mind if people saw her nipples.

Lizzie sank to the ground, plopping down right next to the adorable baby. He seemed to sense her presence, and stuck his chubby hand out to rest on her leg.

Jill had lost her train of thought, but then remembered what had caught her interest. "You talk about Jon a lot. Do you miss him?"

"A little. It's a pretty fresh wound. We just broke up in February."

"Really? You were newly broken up at Mark's party?"

"That was the week after he booted me. I was pretty down that night."

Jill nodded. "You seem much perkier since then. Now I know why."

"I was more drunk than not that night," she admitted, an impish smile settling on her face. She put her hand on Santiago's head and ran her fingers through his thick, dark hair. "If you need to do something, I'm perfectly happy to sit here with this little guy."

"I think I'm good. I've got two people in the kitchen, and a couple picking up trash in the back." She put her hands around a knee and stretched her back out. "It's nice to sit for a while."

"You throw a good party," Lizzie said. "Top quality food too. Hey, I didn't see the brownies I made on the dessert table."

Jill sat up like she'd been poked in the back. "You brought brownies?"

"Uh-huh. Made 'em from scratch. I put them in the kitchen when I first got here."

"I didn't eat dessert, since everything came from the grocery store and I'm a big snob about food." Jill got up and headed for the kitchen. "I'm gonna find them and possibly demolish the whole batch."

"Bring me one," Lizzie quietly called out after her. "Your friends brought some cheap-ass desserts. No offense."

Jill returned a minute later with the pan, a knife and two napkins. "It wouldn't be wrong to sit on the floor and gobble these down, would it? I barely had a thing to eat today. I was waiting for a burger, but people snarfed every single one down before I could snatch one."

"Now I feel bad for eating two." She gave Jill a playful poke in the ribs. "I don't really feel bad. The burgers were awesome, and you know you have to fight for food when there's a Davis around." Lizzie took the knife and cut the pan into four huge brownies. "I'm not surprised you didn't have time to eat. You were running around like crazy. Next time, invite fewer people." She eased one of the squares from the pan and handed it over. "And tell people to go to a decent bakery if they don't want to cook. Those cookies from the grocery store were sad."

"The kids like them. But if I'm going to eat something filled with calories, I want something good." She took a big bite, nodding happily. "And these are damned good."

"Glad you like them. I don't cook much, but I like to bake."

"Just like your mom." Jill laughed at the memory. "I can remember having dried out, under-seasoned meat loaf and lumpy potatoes, followed by a perfect lemon meringue pie. Even as a kid, I knew it was harder to make the damn pie, but your mom just didn't care about regular food. She was only marking time until dessert."

101

Lizzie shoved her brownie into her mouth, holding the pan under it to catch the crumbs. "I'm not much different, but I appreciate good food too. I don't bother to make it, but I appreciate it."

"That makes two of us. I'm already looking forward to going to your restaurant."

"Me too. Even though I'm totally serious that you don't have to treat. I enjoyed being here."

"My mind's made up. When are we going?"

"How about next Wednesday?"

"Great. Send me a reminder, will you?"

"Sure. I'll make a reservation for six. I know you like to go to bed early."

"How about seven? Then I can come early and take a tour."

Lizzie stuck out her hand and they shook. "Done."

Chapter Seven

IT TOOK MUCH LONGER to get to Hollyhock Hills than it should have, and Jill texted Lizzie when she was still at least fifteen minutes away. When she finally pulled up to the entry gate, she nodded to the guard. "Jill Henry. I have a reservation for dinner."

He looked at a list, then waved her through. "Have a nice time," he added.

She drove along the ambling road, concentrating only on finding a parking spot close to the house. There were two small lots, and she left the car in one, grabbed her purse and walked towards the building. When she got to the entrance of the huge, dark-shingled home, a man held the door open for her. "Welcome to Hollyhock Hills," he said. "May I direct you?"

Lizzie appeared in the entry. "I can take this joker off your hands, Pete."

"Hi, Lizzie," he said, looking at her like most twenty-something guys probably did. Like she was something delicious that was just out of reach. "Do you need a golf cart or a car?"

She put her hand on his shoulder and gave it a squeeze. "We're good, but thanks. Come on in," she added, when she turned to Jill. "We don't have time for a proper tour before dinner, but our table's ready early. Let's eat and then walk around."

"Sounds great. I'm so sorry I'm late. Traffic was *really* bad."

"It's always bad where Route 7 meets I-189. Don't worry about it. I should have warned you."

They entered the lobby, and Jill stopped to stare. "Is this still a house?" The place was magnificent. Probably around a hundred years old, with gorgeous oak paneled walls and a massive fireplace along one wall, and French doors all along the back of the room, allowing a view of the lake in the near distance. The doors were wide open, with a cool breeze making the sheer curtains flutter. Bookcases lined the back wall, with large, worn leather couches and upholstered chairs sitting in front of them, everything facing the fireplace.

"It's a hotel now, but this was the residence for the family. We're in the parlor." She took a right and led the way through another equally impressive room. "And this was where the men went after dinner to have a cigar." They stopped at a podium where a young woman was making notes in a large book. "Hi, Gretchen," Lizzie said. "We have a reservation for seven, but Rick said it wouldn't be a problem to seat us early."

"Not at all," she said, reaching down to pick up a pair of menus. "Let me show you to your table."

"This was the family dining room," Lizzie said as they walked into yet another tastefully decorated room with another oversized hearth and fireplace. The room wasn't all that big, with around twenty tables placed a respectful distance from one another, but it still had a grand, stately air to it. Jill noticed this room also bore floor to ceiling French doors, each of them open. "I thought we'd sit outside," Lizzie said. "Is that okay?"

"It's perfect," Jill agreed.

Their hostess put them at the table closest to the lake, with a long swath of verdant grass leading to what looked like a drop-off to the water. Jill met Lizzie's gaze as they settled into their chairs. "I assume the family built this to impress guests? It *works*."

Her face lit up in a pleased smile. "It's cool, isn't it? I've only eaten here once, and that was for work. You can't really enjoy your food when you're pitching." She snapped her napkin open and draped it across her lap. "Tonight, I can relax."

"You look great," Jill said. "I've gotten used to seeing you in jeans and T-shirts. A nice dress and heels is taking me a second to get used to."

"Thanks." She reached over and put her fingers on the placket of Jill's blouse. "I like that. I couldn't tell if it was knit or silk."

Jill looked down at herself. "It's some kind of nylon print. I thought I should ditch my khakis for the night, so I wore my nicest slacks."

"You look nice," Lizzie said. "You told me you wore blue a lot, and I don't see any reason to change. That shirt makes your eyes as blue as the sky."

"My goal," Jill said, grinning. "Even though no one at work ever notices what I'm wearing. I blend in like the wallpaper."

"I learned to notice details when I was in school. If you ask me in six months what you were wearing tonight, I'll be able to tell you." She opened her menu and said, "Our bartender is good. He makes five or six special drinks a night. See if any of them work for you."

Jill ran her finger down the list, thinking. "Yes, yes, no, probably not, yes and yes. I think I'll get the one with gin and blackberries and mint."

"We don't make the gin, but the mint is from the garden. It's a little early for the blackberries to be local, but they will be in August."

"I swear, you're becoming a farmer!"

"Not really. I just pay attention."

A young woman glided over and put her hands behind her back, like she was auditioning. "Welcome," she said, addressing Jill. With a quick nod to Lizzie, she said, "It's good to see you, Ms. Davis."

"I'm off duty, Lara," Lizzie said. "This is my friend Jill."

"Nice to meet you," Jill said. "I love your restaurant."

"We're glad to have you."

"Lara's in grad school at the U," Lizzie said. "As is nearly every other server." She inclined her head towards Jill. "Jill's a big deal in the administration. Be nice to her and she might knock a few hundred bucks off your tuition."

"If I could, I would," Jill said, smiling up at the young woman.

"I'll treat you well even without a kickback. Can I interest you in a drink?"

"You can," Jill said. "Maybe two."

⬲

They'd finished their main courses by seven thirty, and Lizzie said, "They're not swamped tonight. Let's see if we can sneak out for a tour, then come back for dessert."

"Sounds good if it wouldn't inconvenience them."

105

"I'll go check in the kitchen." She was up and gone before Jill could say a word, and when she returned in a couple of minutes she grasped the back of Jill's chair and pulled it out as she rose. "No problem. I said we'd be back by nine."

"That late?"

"Sure," she said, leading Jill down the lawn. "Sunset's at eight-thirty, and dusk isn't until nine. There's a lot to see."

Jill took a look down, seeing that Lizzie wore attractive slingback heels. "Do you want to put on some more comfortable shoes?"

"No need. I didn't have to talk to a single visitor today, so I was barefoot until I went downstairs to pick you up."

"I last wore heels when I was in a wedding. I think I was twenty-three," Jill said. "I have dressy flats, but that's as far as I'll go."

"Have you had your big birthday yet? Or should I not bring it up."

"Turning forty?" Jill shook her head. "I don't much care. And no, it's not until August."

Lizzie stopped near a landscaped area, planted with a wide variety of roses and summer annuals. "Mine's in August too. I'm the fourteenth."

"I'm the sixteenth," Jill said. "I don't remember your birthday being near mine."

"Why would you?" Lizzie took her arm and held it gently. "You can act like you paid the slightest bit of attention to me, but you didn't. I was just an annoying kid."

"Well, you're not annoying now." She let out a laugh. "All of my friends want you for housesitting or babysitting or whatever they can talk you into. You made quite an impression."

"I like your friends. They seem like good people." She led Jill along the neatly planted paths of flowers. "This is the garden we're trying to rebuild."

Jill spent a minute taking a good, long look at it. She was a decent gardener. Nothing like her mother, who devoted every spare hour to the hobby, but she knew a good bit about flowers. "It looks awfully nice to me."

"It does, but it's so close to the water that the ground's eroding. It needs to be moved up a little closer to the house, and, of course, we'll redo the drainage so it'll last another hundred years."

"How big a check do I need to write?"

"A pretty big one," Lizzie said. "Two and a half million. It's a bigger project than it looks."

"I bet I can pay to move a rose. Or a..." She reached down and cupped a big, pink blossom. "A peony."

"My favorite flower," Lizzie said. "We had peonies all along the garage when I was a kid. I forget why we took them out, but now there's just some boxwood that don't do very well."

"I thought you said you weren't much of a gardener."

She shrugged. "I don't remember saying that."

"Yeah, when I met you that day at coffee. I asked you to come help me plant."

"Oh, right." She nodded. "I had wicked PMS that day. I couldn't wait to get home and gulp down some drugs."

"You could have said that, Lizzie," Jill said gently. "I get PMS too."

"I guess you do. I just..." She looked thoughtful for a few moments. "I don't like to complain. Next time, I'd love to help you plant."

"Unless you have PMS," Jill teased.

"If I do, I'll admit it."

"Great. I love to have someone to talk to while I'm working in the yard, but all of my friends have their own houses. No one wants to take mine on."

"I'd be happy to help. You don't happen to know how to do electrical work, do you? I'd gladly exchange garden work for a new light fixture in my bathroom."

Jill shook her head. "I'm pretty handy, but I'm frightened of electricity. I use a guy..." She thought for a minute. "Did I show you the fixture Mark sent me?"

"No." She smiled. "I didn't know he did that."

"Yeah, I was really touched. He's ducked my calls to thank him, so we still haven't spoken since the day after his party, but I took it as a really nice token."

Lizzie shrugged. "He doesn't have the nads to stand up for himself, but I still love him."

"Nads?"

"Gonads. He's deficient."

"One area I'm happily in the dark about. Anyway, I've got a good electrician. Maybe we can work out a trade."

"I'll make that deal any day. Hook me up." Lizzie touched Jill's arm lightly, guiding her from the garden towards the lake. "Let's head over to the pasture where we've got some sheep and lambs. I love those little guys."

They walked around the back of the house, then along a path built right on the lakeshore. The sun hadn't yet set, but it was almost hidden by the Adirondacks, just across the lake in New York. "I love this view," Jill said, stopping to reflect upon the peaceful lake.

"Me too. I haven't been in the water yet this year. How about you?"

"I make it a habit to never go in before it's sixty-seven. What's your lower limit?"

"If I have to, I can do sixty-five. Much colder than that and I just shiver." She cocked her head and said, "Last year, some friends and I got a sweet boat ride on my birthday. If the guy offers again, want to double up? My birthday's on a Friday, so yours is Sunday. We could split the difference and do it on Saturday."

"Sure. Some friends are having a party for me on my actual birthday, but I don't have anything planned for Saturday." She bumped Lizzie with her shoulder. "You're having a big birthday too. Does it freak you out?"

"Yes," she said, as she gave Jill a push. "A lot more than yours does!"

"Aww..." Jill draped an arm around her shoulders as they stood on the banks of the lake and watched the sun dip behind the hills. "Why are you freaked out?"

She looked a little embarrassed, but said, "Because I feel like I've blown a lot of years and don't have much to show for it. A lot of my friends are married or partnered, and I haven't even had a date, except for Scott, since Jon dumped me."

"You haven't? Really?"

"Thanks for saying that like it's impossible to believe. I could find someone to go out with, but I'm looking for a relationship. Like I have been since I was twenty-five," she emphasized. "And I'm having zero luck. The people I'm interested in clearly aren't interested in me."

"You'll get there, Lizzie. You're pretty, you're smart, you're charming, and you've got a great job that you love. Who wouldn't want to be with you?"

"Many people," she said, pouting a little. "The list is really long."

"That makes no sense at all. If I were a guy, you'd be exactly the kind of woman I'd be looking for."

Lizzie turned and looked into her eyes for a few seconds. "Thanks," she said, finally turning away, clearly embarrassed. "That makes me feel better."

"You know what would make me feel better?" She didn't wait for an answer. "Dessert. Let's go get it."

⟐

Near the end of June, one of Jill's co-workers popped his head into her office. "Do you like baseball?" Ramon asked.

"Yeah. A lot. Why?"

"There's four tickets to the Lake Monsters floating around. I thought I'd ask you before I passed them on."

"For tonight?"

"Yeah. Want 'em?"

"Sure. I think I can scare up some people to tag along. Thanks for thinking of me, Ramon."

As he left, she pulled up her contacts list and scanned it. She could probably convince a few of her couple friends to go, but that left a spare ticket. Maybe Lizzie could take that one…

That put her on a different tack. She found the number and made the call, hoping she wasn't making a mistake. She'd find out if she was overstepping quickly enough.

Jill was driving, and she texted her arrival when pulled up at Lizzie's apartment. A minute later, Lizzie ran down the walk, looking particularly cute. As always, she wore jeans. Tight ones. Luckily, she was one of those people who looked long and lean in tight jeans. A black tank top showed under an open white man-tailored shirt, and Jill recognized the tank as the leotard she'd worn at the club. She looked more mature in a regular blouse, a little dressier than her usual T-shirt.

"My first game of the year!" she said as she threw the door open and climbed in. "And I can get hammered, since you're driving. Who's excited?"

"I'd be more excited if I could get hammered too," Jill teased, "but I'm definitely up for this. Some of my friends like to go to games, but they don't really like baseball. It's more fun to go with a real fan."

"I'm a real fan," Lizzie declared. "Ever since I was little and saw my brothers put their uniforms on." She held her hand over her heart and patted it. "They looked like gods to me. So tall and imposing in their uniforms and cleats. I always knew I'd play."

"I would have loved to have played, but a girl had never even tried out when I was the right age."

Lizzie reached over and poked her in the side. "Then you should have been the first."

"Mmm." She shook her head. Her mother would have yanked her out of school and sent her to a non-baseball playing country before she would have allowed that. "I wasn't a risk taker back then. It took me a while to get the confidence to push myself."

"You seem to have plenty now. And now's when it counts."

The team played at the UVM baseball stadium, so Jill was able to use her parking permit to glide right into a good lot. "We could probably park closer, but Freyja likes this lot," she said. "She hates it when people ding her doors."

"Yeah, Freyja seems like she's really picky about stuff. She might need a few sessions with a counselor."

They walked across campus to the stadium, chatting about the team. When they approached the gate, Jill waved to her guests. "I had four tickets," she explained, "so I invited a couple of friends."

Lizzie put a restraining hand on her shoulder to slow them down. "Co-workers?"

"No. Chase is the electrician I use, and Mason's his brother. Nice guys. You'll like them."

The Martin brothers were all cleaned up for a change. They each wore cotton shorts and plaid shirts, the first time Jill had seen either of them in anything other than T-shirts.

When they got close, Jill made the introductions, with the brothers both looking like they were glad Jill had called. She knew they were both single, with Mason, in particular, complaining about how hard it was to find a woman to date.

Lizzie's enthusiasm had waned, along with her chattiness. Jill didn't think she got shy around strangers, but maybe she was different when the strangers were single straight guys. Jill was certain the always jovial Martin brothers would soon have her under their spell.

Their seats were fantastic. Right behind home plate, just ten rows up from the field. Mason went in first, then Jill said to Lizzie, "Why don't you sit next to Mason?"

"Can't," she said, shaking her head. "I need to be on the aisle."

Jill was going to ask what made that so, but she didn't want to embarrass her if she had some phobia about being in the middle of a row. So Jill went in next, followed by Chase, then Lizzie.

They'd barely gotten settled when Lizzie jumped up. "I'll go for beers." She was backing up as she looked at each person. "Everyone?" When they all nodded, she turned and jogged up the steps, gone before anyone could follow.

"That's the woman who's really friendly and looking for a boyfriend?" Chase asked, frowning at Jill. "I've had warmer receptions from *ex-girlfriends*."

"She's friendly. I promise," Jill said. "Maybe she's nervous."

"She didn't look nervous," Mason said. "She looked pissed."

Mason was wrong. Thankfully. After Lizzie came back with the beers, she seemed a little remote, but certainly not angry. Jill was pretty sure Mason and Chase would think she'd really opened up, but she hadn't.

Still, she seemed to be having a good time, and managed to impress the guys with the depth of her baseball knowledge.

"I've never known a girl who understood that the batter can run to first if the catcher drops the third strike," Mason said.

"Then you've never been with a *woman*," she stressed, a smile showing she wasn't offended, "who understands baseball. By the way," she added, "the rule's only in effect if there's no one on first or there are two outs."

"No," Mason said, sounding hesitant. He turned to his brother. "Really?"

"Uhm…I dunno."

"Look at the logic behind the rule," Lizzie explained. "If the ball was live with a man on first, the catcher would intentionally drop the third strike, then fire it to second to start an easy double-play. It's the same thought behind the infield fly rule."

"You *do* understand baseball," Chase said soberly.

"I do," she admitted, smiling to herself as she took a drink of her beer. "Damned well."

When Jill returned from using the restroom after the seventh inning stretch, Lizzie said, "Mason lives in the South End, so I'm going to hitch a ride home with him."

"Super," Jill said. She smiled as she moved past Lizzie and Chase to settle into her seat. Maybe she was better at fixing up people than she thought.

Chapter Eight

A FEW DAYS AFTER THE ball game, Jill texted Lizzie, just to see if she'd had a good time with Mason. It was a busy day at work, and she was getting ready for her summer vacation, so she didn't notice until she went to bed that night that Lizzie hadn't replied. Tempted to send a follow-up, Jill passed it off as an oversight. Besides, she probably didn't want to know how well Lizzie and Mason had gotten along. The last time she'd gotten an update on Lizzie's dating habits, she'd nearly fainted.

❧

Everyone from the bridge group had, once again, chipped in to rent a big house on the lake for two weeks. They'd been to this particular house last year, and found it so perfect they'd all agreed to rent it again.

Four bedrooms, with a wide, enclosed porch that harbored two sofa beds, along with three bathrooms, two of them located in the bedrooms. Then a cozy guest cottage that easily slept four.

The house was at the tip of a spit of land, providing glorious views in three directions. Kayaks, canoes and a row boat were all provided, and when the water was unkind, a forested walking path stretched out for a quarter mile, providing plenty of space to stretch your legs. A couple of bikes were serviceable, especially if you wanted to cruise along at a leisurely pace.

It was the nicest place Jill had ever stayed—even though it was a little down-at-the-heels. But she didn't go for luxury. She went for the peace and tranquility of the vastness of the lake spread out before her, as well as the fun of being around all of her buddies. It was like freshman year in college, where you stayed up all night talking, with the freedom to do whatever you wanted.

Even though the bridge group had arranged for the house, other friends filled any spare beds. Skip and Alice just came up for the weekends, and Karen usually had to go back to see a few clients, keeping the musical beds game going. But Jill took two full weeks off work, always the first to arrive and the last to leave.

The changeover day was Saturday, at three, and Jill was going down early just to hang out before she picked up the keys. The night before, she'd texted Lizzie again, on the off chance that she wanted to tag along for a day to take Mary Beth's spot, who wasn't able to get away until Monday.

After waiting a few hours for Lizzie to reply, Jill shut off her phone. She'd done something nice for her—something she considered thoughtful. But Lizzie hadn't even called to acknowledge the gesture. She might have a good excuse, but Jill wasn't sure she wanted to hear it. Her feelings were hurt, and she tended to withdraw when that happened. Lizzie could make the next overture—if she cared to.

Early on Saturday morning, Jill loaded up the car, adding her bike in case the weather was more favorable for rides than dips, kissed the cats goodbye, and started off. The cabin was only about thirty miles away, a long enough ride to clear her mind of work and home and focus on the good stuff—water and sun. There was precious little of the latter today, with the forecast calling for a high of sixty-five. Not an ideal day to go swimming. But it wasn't raining, and that was good enough for her.

The coffee shop she'd met Lizzie at had become her new favorite, and she stopped in whenever she had time. Today she hoped she wouldn't run into Lizzie, which seemed like a good bet, given that it was barely eight o'clock.

Jill went in and ordered her cappuccino, then chatted with the barista while she made it. The place was nearly empty, having opened just minutes before. She pondered the baked goods covered by big, glass domes, and pointed at a scone. "What kind is that?"

"Lemon ginger," a low voice behind her stated.

Jill turned to find Lizzie, bleary-eyed and disheveled. She didn't smile, but her expression wasn't unfriendly. Actually, she looked a little like Janet did when she was disappointed in one of the kids.

"Hi," Jill said, turning back to devote her attention to paying for her coffee and getting a scone. Her instinct was to offer to buy Lizzie's coffee, but she resisted it.

"Hi, yourself." Lizzie took her phone from her pocket and shook it. "Sorry I didn't get back to you. Did you find a cat sitter?"

"Cat sitter?" Jill stared at the side of her face as she put in her breakfast order. After Lizzie had it squared away, she moved aside so the next person could approach the counter.

"Yeah." She fussed with a few bills, finally crumpling them up and shoving them into her front pocket. "That's why you called, right?"

"Nope." Jill picked up her coffee and let the first sip, the perfect ambrosia, fill her mouth for a few seconds. *Heavenly.* "First off, if I'd been looking for a cat sitter, I wouldn't let it go until the last minute."

Lizzie's pupils dilated a little as her eyes opened wide and focused on Jill's mouth. Given how she looked, she was nursing a hangover.

"Secondly," Jill continued, her voice a little sharp, "I'd never ask a friend to devote two full weeks to babysitting the boys. I found a retired couple who live in Rutland and wanted to spend some time in the big city. My usual cat sitter recommended them, so I'm only slightly freaked out." She made herself smile, but her heart wasn't in it. Lizzie was still giving her a sour look, for reasons Jill couldn't fathom.

"Oh." She reached over to pick up her coffee, then took it and moved across the big room to slide down the wall by the windows. Not a drop spilled.

Jill followed her, but didn't try to duplicate her feat. Instead, she grabbed a chair and sat like an adult. "How's your new light fixture?" she asked, knowing her gaze had gotten more pointed.

Lizzie didn't meet her eyes. Instead, she sipped at her coffee for a moment, then set it on the floor. "I don't have one," she said quietly. Then her greenish eyes shifted up to land on Jill. As soon as Lizzie spoke, Jill wished she'd stayed quiet. "You know," she said, sounding like she'd been trying to tamp down her anger, and had given up the fight. "I do all right at finding my own dates."

Stunned, Jill stared at her. "What?"

"Don't act like you weren't trying to fix me up with one—or both—of the Martin brothers. Chase thought you were dropping me onto his doorstep with a ribbon tied around my neck, and Mason texts me every other day about coming over, just to 'hang out.'" She made quote marks with her fingers, and the knowing expression on her face made it clear what she thought Mason really wanted.

"Oh, shit," Jill moaned. "I didn't…well, I did, but…" She took in a breath. "I'm sorry, Lizzie. I just wanted to do something nice for you."

"I don't need to be fixed up," she said, her volume rising.

"I meant about the light. You said you'd help me with some yard work in exchange for electrical help, so I farmed out that part to Chase." She looked away, embarrassed to admit how hurt her feelings had been at having her offer ignored. "I was looking forward to spending a Saturday afternoon working on the yard with you. I figured you'd have good ideas for planting."

"I do," she said, clearly still pouting. "I could make your backyard look like fucking Giverny."

"I'll call Chase and tell him you don't need your light fixed." She waited a few seconds, then said, "That was dumb of me to try to introduce you to guys. You just said you were having a tough time meeting people…"

Sharply, she snapped, "I don't think I said that. Actually, I'm *sure* I didn't say that."

Confused, Jill tried to recall their conversation. "I remember you saying you couldn't find anyone you wanted to be in a relationship with. I figured if you had more choices…"

"I don't want choices," she said quietly. "And if I did, I could find them for myself. I'm not a charity case, Jill."

"God damn it," she said, tempering the volume of her voice. "I tried to do something nice for you, and you act like I set you up with a serial killer."

"I'm sorry," she said, angrily wiping at a few tears that squeezed from her eyes as she closed them. "I just don't need that kind of help." Jill's stomach was doing flips at the sadness she saw in those puffy eyes. "It seems like I'm someone you call only when you need a favor."

"What have I done to make you think that?" Despite knowing she'd have a tough time getting up, Jill stood, then slid down the wall next to her. Lizzie's eyes were so full of pain, it felt like a punch to the gut to look into them, knowing that she'd somehow caused it.

"Other than the last minute invitation to the ball game, you've never called me to make plans. We just do something if we run into each other." Her eyebrow rose. "Is that how you treat your other friends?"

Shrugging, Jill said, "Kinda. I mean, we have fixed plans, so we don't need to call to set things up. Bridge night, game night, birthdays…it's just assumed."

"Well, we don't have that. It's the end of July and we've hung out like twice." She reached up and wiped at her eyes again. "I feel like I have to chase you, and I don't want to do that if you don't want to be chased. I feel like a fool," she said quietly, the tears really rolling now.

Jill put her hand on Lizzie's leg and gave it a reassuring pat. "I really do want to hang out with you. That's why I called you. I thought you'd like to come to the cabin we rented."

"Now?" she asked, her red-rimmed eyes looking up hopefully.

"Yeah. Right now. Or later today. We've got a spare bed that won't be filled until Monday."

"And you still want me to come?" she asked, her lower lip trembling. "After I acted like a big baby?"

"Yes," Jill said, giving her amazingly firm leg another squeeze. "Especially now."

"Okay." She rose, gracefully, then picked up her coffee and started to take it to the dirty dish container.

"Hey! Are you throwing that away?"

"Yeah. I just like a little."

Jill walked over and put her cup under Lizzie's, then tipped the tepid latte inside. "I like a lot." She draped her arm around Lizzie's shoulders and walked her to the door. "Let's pick up a few things and drive down together. I'll run you back up tomorrow night."

"No," she said, frowning. "That's a waste of gas. I'll drive myself down. Can you text me the address?"

"I can." Jill's smile grew. "But you have to promise not to ignore it."

It took Lizzie a while to get down to the cabin, but she still beat everyone else. Jill didn't have the keys yet, but she'd taken the two-person kayak off the rack and had it lying by the steps that allowed lake access.

When Lizzie got out of her car, she looked like a new person. Her hair was shining and bobbed around her shoulders as she walked, her eyes were awake and wide-open, her light jacket covered a striped shirt, and her jeans were freshly laundered, with not a baggy knee to be found.

"You look…" Jill bit her tongue for a moment. Some women were very prickly about being told they'd looked like hell a few hours earlier. "Great," she finished, deciding to keep it short.

"Thanks. I hadn't had a shower this morning. I'm surprised you recognized me."

"Late night?"

"Yeah. One of our board members celebrated his seventy-fifth birthday at Hollyhock last night. Big, big crowd. I worked until midnight, then helped clean up."

Jill started to walk towards the house, with Lizzie hoisting her backpack over a shoulder. "Why'd you get up so early?"

She shrugged. "I'm not very good at sleeping in. I guess I'm really a farm girl, even though I've never lived on a farm. Once the sun's up, I have a heck of a time staying asleep." She put a hand on her hip and did a slow assessment of the area. "Nice digs you've got here. Is this the kind of place I'll be able to rent one day?"

"If you ingratiate your way into the club, I'm sure you'll be invited next year." She smiled, just thinking of how warmly her friends had spoken of Lizzie. "That won't be hard."

"We'll see. I'm sure it'd cost more than I've got."

"Well, you're here now, no charge. I thought we'd go kayaking. Sound good?"

"Sounds perfect." She dropped her backpack by the front door. "I'm ready to go."

"I've got to pee," Jill said. "And it's too cold to jump into the lake to do it. I'll just sneak off around the back. Don't go away."

When she returned, Lizzie had put the kayak into the water, and was sitting in the rear opening, holding onto the stairs with a hand. "Hurry up! The chop is banging the heck out of me."

Jill ditched her shoes alongside Lizzie's, then gingerly lowered herself into the shifting, bouncing kayak. "Whew! Almost lost it there!"

"And I wouldn't have wanted to have to jump in to save you. The water's *freezing*."

"It's a balmy sixty-four, according to a fishing site I found. Of course, with the air temperature being about that…"

"I'd freeze to save you," Lizzie said. "My mom's really fond of you."

Jill started to turn around, but a wet paddle slapped at her back. "Eyes to the front," Lizzie commanded. "I'll provide the brawn, you guide us where you want to go."

"I think I like having you as a partner. Everyone else makes me be in the back."

"You call the stroke cadence, and I'll adjust. Want to practice turning?"

"Sure. I'll do a forward stroke on the left, and you do a reverse on the right. Good?"

"It's good if you can keep up," she said, letting out an evil laugh. "I'm kinda awesome strong."

Laughing at her hyperbole, Jill started her stroke. "How am I doing? Fast enough?"

"Yeah. We're good. Now switch so we turn the other way." They practiced that for a minute, then Lizzie said, "I think we're ready. Sound off."

"Stroke, stroke, stroke, stroke," Jill called out in a smooth cadence, raising her voice to compete with the brisk wind.

"Got it," Lizzie said. "I can keep going at this pace, and adjust when you start to cry."

"It'll be a cold day in…" She turned and said, "Today it feels like it'll always be cold, doesn't it?"

"No," Lizzie assured her. "Summer will be back. Guaranteed."

❧

119

They paddled around for almost an hour, until Jill's hands were chapped from the cold water running down the paddle. The wind had picked up, making it tough heading into its teeth, but that was part of the fun. Jill wasn't sure Lizzie liked testing herself against the wind and the chill, but she sure didn't complain, which was awfully nice. She hated to acknowledge it, but most of her friends were wimps. Good-hearted, kind, bright wimps, but wimps nonetheless.

Lizzie hadn't spoken in a while, probably because of the wind snapping their hair straight back off their faces. When she did break the silence, Jill was surprised at how clearly she heard her, despite the breeze. Her own body must have provided a break from the wind, letting Lizzie speak in a normal tone of voice.

"I'm sorry for being so bitchy this morning," she said. She sounded so much like her mom when she tackled a subject head-on. No beating around the bush. Just apologize and move on. "I've had something on my mind and I've been mulling it over way too much. That's not fair to you."

"Fair?" Jill tried to catch a look at her, but as soon as her shoulders turned the boat went right along with them.

"Yeah. Fair." She didn't speak for another minute, with Jill pondering her choice of words. "I don't want you to help me scrounge up dates, Jill."

"I heard you," she said, cursing under her breath when she turned and sent the kayak skittering off towards New York. She had to face forward and let Lizzie talk, even though she didn't know what the hell she was getting at.

"I know who I want." As the seconds ticked away, Jill knew exactly what the next sentence was going to be. She wasn't sure how she knew, but she could have said it for her. "I want you," Lizzie said, her voice now dropping down to a lower, softer register.

Frozen, Jill stopped stroking, her hands shaking so hard she could barely keep a grip on her paddle.

"I assume you'd make yourself heard if this was good news," she added, with Jill hearing the sadness enter her lovely voice.

Damn it to hell! She turned, not caring if they capsized. "Can we go back to shore? Like now?"

"Yeah," she said, grim-faced. Jill picked up the pace and Lizzie followed right along, stroking decisively through the chop until they finally made it a good fifteen minutes later. Now Jill's arms and chest were burning with fatigue. So badly she wasn't sure she'd be able to hoist herself out. But Lizzie got out with her usual nimble grace, then knelt down and held the kayak with both hands, pressing it hard against the dock.

Jill clung onto the ladder with all of her flagging strength and pulled herself up and out, to stand, shivering from head to toe, on the shore.

Lizzie put her hands on her shoulders, concern filling her face. "Did you get wet? You're shaking like a leaf."

"No, no." She put her hands into the pockets of her khakis and tried to stop shaking. But it was futile. She was terrified as well as exhausted, feeling like every nerve was about to snap. "I just need to...warm up...or rest...or something." She knew she was almost talking gibberish, but she couldn't form cogent sentences. Making her way to her car, she wrestled her suitcase from the trunk and opened it to find a red and black plaid wool jacket. As she put it on, she realized she was wearing a mash-up of her mother's dual season wardrobe, and she fought to dismiss the thought and get her head on straight. "That's better. Maybe we should walk. Get our blood moving."

"God," Lizzie breathed, her cheeks pale. "I had no idea you'd be so... whatever you are. I thought..." For the second time that day, tears sprang from her eyes, once again making Jill feel like an ogre.

"We need to talk about this," Jill said firmly. "You can't know how I feel because I don't. I've got to let this sink in."

With her cold, stiff hand, she grasped Lizzie's slightly warmer one and started to walk. In a few dozen yards they reached a path that meandered through the woods. As soon as they entered the lightly forested land the wind died appreciably, making it much easier to talk. But Jill couldn't think of a single word to say.

Lizzie took control and continued on with what she probably wanted to say when they were on the lake. "I thought it would take me a long, long time to get over Jon," she said quietly as notes of pitch and pine enveloped them. It was amazingly quiet after the slap of the water and the wind snapping their clothing around their bodies. That let her hear Lizzie's soft, firm declaration perfectly. "But you're the one, and I can't ignore my feelings."

"The one?" She sounded like a kid being told she was about to do something terrifying—and alluring.

"Yes." Lizzie pulled her to a halt and stared directly into her eyes. "You're the person I've been looking for. I was sure of it the night we went dancing."

"Lots of people can dance," Jill said, sounding like she was being strangled.

"This isn't about dancing," she said, her gaze unwavering.

Lizzie was still holding Jill's hand, despite it now being covered with sweat. Jill wiped her other hand on her slacks, even though that really wouldn't help. Summoning all of her thoughts, she said, "We can't get involved, Lizzie. We really can't."

"Of course we can." Then, more quietly, she added, "If you're attracted to me."

Jill looked at her as the dappled sun fell onto her shoulders. If Lizzie was a woman she'd just met that summer... She couldn't even imagine how hard she'd be working to convince her to go to bed with her—right then. Lizzie had everything Jill wanted, even if you didn't consider how she looked. But when you added her intelligence, her good heart, her sense of humor, her energy and her maturity to that gorgeous auburn hair the sun was burnishing a deep wine-red, and those lovely greenish eyes, she felt her knees grow weak. But Lizzie wasn't someone she'd just met. And that cast everything in a different light.

Jill pulled Lizzie's hand to her chest and squeezed it close. "Of course I'm attracted to you. But it took me until just this second to realize that. I don't think of you like that. I don't and I *shouldn't*."

Lizzie's hand went to her face, and Jill felt herself lean into it, just the way the cats did when they rubbed against her. "You're not my sister, Jill. You're a close family friend who's been out of our lives for almost twenty years. I was just learning to tie my shoes when you disappeared! It's not like you've been sitting next to me at the dinner table this whole time, and I just reached over and kissed you."

"But Mark's been my best friend since I was six!"

"So?" She stared at her, clearly perplexed. "If you crossed off every relative of every person you hung out with in Sugar Hill, no one would ever get married. Everyone in town's been with a friend's sister or brother or cousin. My mom almost *married* my dad's first cousin."

"She did?" That yanked Jill right off track. This was news to her.

"She did. And my mom's sister dated your dad. Seriously," she added, her emphasis indicating they were more than casual acquaintances.

Jill shook her head, trying to clear it enough to accept this new information. "I understand that people in a small town have all sorts of connections. But I have very, very strong feelings for your parents."

"You're not considering dating my mom, right? 'Cause that'd be wrong." A teasing grin settled onto her face, making her even more attractive. Jill grasped her hand again and started to walk, her shoes crunching against twigs and the thick carpet of decayed leaves.

"I can't see how this could work out," Jill insisted. "For so many reasons."

Lizzie pulled her hand close, holding it against her chest. Her warm skin and beating heart pulsed against Jill's flesh, making her feel a little light headed.

"I don't want to hear any reasons that might insult me," Lizzie warned. "Just don't go there."

Jill tried to sort out her feelings, but they were a hopeless tangle. She pulled out her phone, checked the time and said, "It's almost three. That's when the agent's going to show up with the keys."

Lizzie put a hand on her cheek and stared into her eyes for a minute. "Can I kiss you?" she asked, with her hand slipping to the back of Jill's neck, where she exerted gentle pressure.

"No!" She yanked away, wincing at the hurt she saw in Lizzie's lovely eyes. "I'm too damned confused."

"Okay," she said softly. They turned, but this time Lizzie didn't take her hand, and Jill felt the loss all the way back to the cabin.

As they got close, she decided to just lay it out there. To be completely honest, as Lizzie had been with her. "I'm really shaky."

"It's all right," she said, her voice soft and reassuring. "We'll talk about this when we're alone."

"Thanks," Jill said, giving her a tense smile. "I really do appreciate that. I don't think clearly under pressure. I need time for this to settle."

As soon as the agent left, Karen and Becky pulled up and they all spent a while going over the cabin like they were explorers. Jill almost forgot how nervous she was, but by the time everyone had arrived, and bedrooms were assigned, she recalled why she was shaking. Mary Beth wasn't down yet, and Gerri and Kathleen offered to share one of the rooms with twin beds, leaving the other one for Jill and Lizzie. That made sense, of course. Lizzie wouldn't want to share with someone she barely knew when Jill was available. But the thought of being roommates struck her with a wave of panic.

Karen and Becky had gone to the grocery store, and Alice was going to cook dinner. As Alice started to organize the pantry, Lizzie caught Jill's eye and gestured to the woods.

"We're going to take a quick walk," Jill said.

"I could stretch my legs," Kathleen said, starting to get up.

Jill used her secret weapon. "Great!" she said with enthusiasm. "We're going to see how may laps of the trail we can do before we croak."

As quickly as she'd risen, Kathleen sank back down. "Have fun," she said, waving. "You can tell us all about your adventures. Take pictures!"

Lizzie was still laughing as they left via the back door. Jill had her wool jacket on, but Lizzie seemed perfectly fine with a lime green spring windbreaker. She was clearly made of tougher stuff.

When they reached the woods, Jill decided to stick with her earlier plan of being completely frank. "I know this isn't the perfect time for this, but I call home on the last Saturday of every month. If I don't do it now, I'll obsess about it."

Lizzie looked at her, concern filling her face. "I know you have a hard time at home, but I don't know much more than that."

She looked so interested. And understanding. Jill almost never talked about home, but she was feeling particularly, fragile and the words came spilling out. "Do you know my mom?"

"I know who she is, but I've never spoken to her. I've said hello to your dad a few times, though. He seems nice."

"Yeah, he's a salesman, so he's friendly for a living." She met Lizzie's eyes. "My mom's…troubled. Or troubling. Both, usually."

"Does she have a mental illness?"

"Maybe." Jill nodded, then spit it out. "No one knows. She's just a very difficult person, and each call seems like it goes on for hours. I *hate* to call," she added, tension filling her voice. But she chose to get it over with, hitting the speed dial and waiting as the call failed time and again. "I'll have to go out later. If I can get close to Vergennes, I'll be able to connect." She dropped the phone back into her pocket and realized Lizzie was still looking at her with care and compassion.

"Does she rely on you?" Lizzie asked, her hand moving gently across Jill's shoulder.

"No, thank god, she's in very good health, and she's able to go anywhere she wants. She's…" Jill shrugged, unable to explain herself. "She's just hard to talk to."

"I'm sorry," Lizzie said gently. "I always feel better when I talk to my family. Even with my dad being sick. If I don't talk to them for a week, I start to really miss them." Her hand compressed around Jill's shoulder. "I'm sorry you don't have that."

"I *do* have that," she insisted. "Just not from my own parents." She took in a breath, trying to settle her nerves. Walking seemed like a good idea, so she headed deeper along the trail, where the trees once again enveloped them in a protective embrace. "That's why I can't consider dating you, Lizzie. I've just gotten this connection back. It'd *kill* me to lose it again."

"Do you honestly think my parents would…what? Stop talking to us if we were together? Do you really think they're that narrow-minded?"

"No, I don't think they're narrow-minded. But you can't convince me they'd *like* it. And I don't want to risk ruining what I've longed for."

Lizzie grasped the sleeve of Jill's jacket and pulled her to a halt. She stared at her for a few minutes, her eyes moving incredibly slowly as she scanned Jill's face intently. "That sounds like a convenient excuse. Be honest with me. If you're not into it, just say so."

Jill could almost see the hurt coloring her words. *Damn it!* Why did Lizzie have to do this? She focused on the path as she began to walk again, trying to corral her thoughts. "I meant what I said earlier today. If I'd just met you, you couldn't get rid of me."

"Then why are you so willing to give up something you might want? Don't you want a relationship? Are you happier single?"

"No," she admitted. "I'm happier when I'm partnered. Much happier. Becca didn't give me half of what I needed, but it was still hard to break up with her. The good things we had almost overcame the bad."

"So the only thing stopping you is worrying about my family? If so, I'll tell them I'm attracted to you and see what they say."

Jill gripped her hands into fists, her stomach in knots. She didn't want to add to her list of reasons, but she had to. "That's not the only thing that's stopping me."

Lizzie walked along silently, staring at the ground. "It's because I'm bi."

"Not exactly," Jill said. "But I'm not ever going to be okay with my girlfriend seeing other people." She shot a look at Lizzie. "I couldn't share you with a guy. Even once in a while."

Clearly exasperated, Lizzie let out a long breath. "I didn't ask you if you wanted to fool around, Jill. I want to be in a relationship. A *monogamous* relationship."

"But that's not what you had before. You told me that *very* clearly."

"I did," she agreed. "When I was with a man, I craved a woman's touch. But I don't think I'd feel that same urge if I was with a woman. With *you*," she emphasized.

Frustration bubbling up, Jill's voice rose. "But you don't know that! You've never even been in love with a woman. And I don't want to be the woman who can't give you what you need."

Lizzie's glare was so hot Jill could feel it burn her cheek. "You're holding my history against me, and that's just not fair."

They stopped and faced each other for several tense seconds. "Of course I am! Just like you'd hold mine against me if there was something that bothered you. If I'd had nothing but quick, messy breakups with people I talked shit about, I don't think you'd find me very attractive."

"How many significant relationships have you had? Total."

Jill thought for a minute, trying to be precise. This was important. "Five since I've been out of school. Two during college, but I just glommed onto the first two women who showed any interest. Those don't count."

"Five in eighteen years?" A dark auburn eyebrow rose. "That's not a great batting average for someone who wants a monogamous, long-term relationship. But I'm more than willing to give you a shot. Why can't you do the same?"

"Because your were with men!" Jill blew out a breath, furious with herself for letting that out. "I'm sorry," she murmured. "That was really shitty of me to say."

"No, it's shitty of you to *think*. But it's what I expected." She started to walk faster, leaving Jill in her dust as she grumbled, "I'm sick of all of these open-minded people, who know what it's like to be discriminated against, doing the same to me."

"I'm not discriminating against you!" Jill yelled after her.

"Then what do you call it?" Lizzie stopped and stared as she demanded hotly, "Give it whatever name you want. It's still prejudice."

They were both hot under the collar, but Jill was very relieved that Lizzie fought fair. She said what she thought, and then dropped it. If it were Becca on this trail, Jill would be lectured for the rest of the trip, with all of her faults listed in order.

"Can I have some time to think about this?" Jill asked. "I've got to sort things out."

"Sure," she said, a little snappish. "I can't *make* you care for me, Jill. But I can guarantee we could make something special out of this if you'll give it a try."

"There's not a doubt in my mind that's true," Jill said, knowing she was being completely honest. "I just have to do some thinking."

127

It wasn't as hard as Jill thought it would be to focus on her friends and their easy interaction. After dinner, everyone played Monopoly for a couple of hours, until Lizzie caught Jill's eye and pointed to where her watch would have been if she wore one. Obviously, her patience had its limits. After saying goodnight to everyone, they went into their room, one with the bath attached. Lizzie went to get ready for bed first, emerging wearing a long-sleeved T-shirt with "Sugar Hill Smithy" printed across the back. The shirt was long enough that it covered her upper thighs, leaving Jill to wonder if she was naked under all of that cotton. This was *exactly* what she didn't want to happen. She'd been hanging around with a really cute, single woman who was attracted to other women, and had managed to firmly ignore her instincts. Until now. Now all she wanted to do was pick up the edge of that long shirt and hope there wasn't another stitch hiding under it. *Shit!*

Heading into the bath to get her thoughts in order, Jill performed her usual nighttime routine, emerging with teeth brushed and flossed and moisture lotion covering her chapped face and hands.

Lizzie took a long look, then her face broke into a tender smile. "That's just what you used to wear when you slept over at our house. Flannel pajama bottoms and a T-shirt."

"It is?" Jill looked down, a little surprised to realize she had anything at all on. Her nerves were so jumpy, her body was numb.

"Yeah." Lizzie moved closer, so close Jill could see her pupils widen in the golden glow of the lamp. "You weren't paying attention to me, but I studied you like a treasure map."

"Oh, God," she moaned, dropping to the bed heavily. "That makes me feel like such a perv!"

"Why?" Lizzie sat next to her and took her hand, gently chafing it between her own. "I had a crush on you when I was little, then it went away."

"It really did?" Jill asked, begging for reassurance.

"Really. I sulked around the house for a while after you stopped coming over, and I rode my bike over to your street to see if I could spot you, but by the time I went back to school that fall I had a new obsession." She laughed wryly. "I was crushed out on both Leo DiCaprio and Kate Winslet once I saw *Titanic*."

Jill started to laugh as well. "I guess there are worse people to be thrown over for."

"For sure. So, here we are, twenty years later, and I've come to realize I was a damned perceptive kid." She put her hand on Jill's shoulder and kept eye contact for a few seconds. "I swear I haven't been obsessed with you all these years, Jill. Even when I heard you were coming to the party, I was more curious than anything. Promise." She took Jill's hand and put it over her heart. "I swear that's true. This is new."

Also new to Jill was the sensation of having her hand pressed against Lizzie's warm chest and feeling a strong heartbeat thrumming steadily beneath her fingers. She could get used to that very, very quickly. After pulling her hand away, she could think clearly enough to form a coherent sentence. "Can I have some time? Some time to figure out what I'm afraid of?"

"I think I know what you're afraid of," Lizzie said, her gaze as gentle as a caress. "And I promise you my family will think this is awesome. *Awesome*," she insisted.

There was no way she could know that. No way at all. She was guessing, the same way Jill was. They'd just come to different conclusions, and Jill's scared her to death.

⁂

Jill had, surprisingly, gotten to sleep pretty quickly. But she woke with a start at midnight, no more than fifteen minutes after she'd drifted off. She was one hundred percent awake, with her mind running in a dozen different directions.

Quiet voices seemed to be coming from the living room, and she tossed her feet to the floor to join her friends. Lying there, anxious and obsessing, wasn't her idea of fun. But as she sat on the edge of the bed, her eyes landed on a peacefully sleeping Lizzie, looking as pretty as she'd ever seen her.

Jill slapped at her face with her open hand. Now she was staring at sleeping women. Not too pervy! But she couldn't stop. If Lizzie woke up and saw her, she'd just have to fess up and take the consequences.

As long as she was going to stare, she decided to get comfortable. Lying down again, she punched her pillow into shape and propped her head up at a good angle. It was hard to see definition in the dim room, but the moonlight provided enough light to make out features. Jill sighed. She was stunningly attracted to Lizzie. From her unlined forehead, down to her well-shaped nose and sumptuous mouth, all of Lizzie's features combined to create a truly lovely woman. She'd known that since Mark's party, of course. If anyone had asked, she'd have easily said Lizzie was the prettiest woman she knew. But when you put her in a different category—shifting from forbidden to possible—Jill's whole body was able to focus on exactly how pretty she was.

It wasn't just her face that attracted Jill, of course. There was a reason she'd tried to hook Lizzie up with not one, but two friends—something she almost never did. Lizzie was so cool, and was such a lovely person, she wanted someone she liked to get a chance at hooking her. Now she had that chance, and she was stuck between amazement at her good luck and heart-stopping fear. She could hardly express how much she wanted to cross the few feet that separated them and slip into her bed. And given how Lizzie had approached her, she was damned sure she wouldn't be kicked out. How did this happen? How could you go from objective appreciation for a friend to wanting to crawl into her bed in just a few hours? Nothing like this had ever happened to her, and the dissonance in her feelings was driving her nuts.

As her gaze slid down and landed on the curve of Lizzie's hip, she found her mouth starting to water. *Enough!* Truly annoyed with herself, Jill rifled through her bag to find a fleece shirt to ward off the chilly night, then went to join her friends. She would *not* molest a sleeping Lizzie, even with just her imagination.

⁂

Sunday was a little warmer, and the wind had died down to a fairly gentle breeze from the North. Jill's arms and chest muscles were so sore she whimpered when she put her bra on. But Lizzie was ready for action as soon as they'd eaten breakfast. They took the rowboat out, with Jill sitting on the bench that faced the bow, and Lizzie butching it up to row.

The kayaks were already in the water, and Jill appreciated that Lizzie didn't laugh at Skip and Alice as they made the grievous mistake of trying to manage the tandem kayak. Luckily for Skip, cell service was a little spotty, as Jill had discovered the day before, so Alice probably couldn't reach her divorce attorney without a cooling-off period.

They skimmed past the bickering pair, with Lizzie rolling her eyes as she whistled a tune. "It's awfully tempting to offer advice, but no one really wants it," she said as she turned her head to make sure she was giving them plenty of room to maneuver.

"That's the damned truth," Jill said, struck, once again, by Lizzie's pragmatic nature. She could have easily guided Skip and Alice out of trouble, but they wanted to fight. It was their thing, and years of Jill's tactfully trying to suggest options for avoiding squabbles hadn't had the slightest effect, other than to frustrate her. But Lizzie went directly to the solution—leave them alone to figure out their own relationship. There were so many ways in which Lizzie had damned good instincts. Mature instincts. More reasoned and direct than many of Jill's. She would be a great partner. But what would Janet and Mike say? Their reaction meant everything. Absolutely everything.

After dinner, Lizzie did the opposite of Jill's fade away, spending a few minutes with each person, offering her thanks and insisting on paying for at least her share of the groceries. No one would hear of it, and Jill realized that was because they thought of her as a kid. Someone who'd have to reach into a relatively empty pocket to pay her share. Maybe Janet and Mike weren't the only people she had to worry about. Her friends might have an opinion about Lizzie as well.

After the long goodbyes, Jill walked Lizzie out to her car. "Are you sure you've got enough of a charge to make it home?"

"Positive. I keep a close eye on my little nameless car," she said, patting it. "I've got enough juice for forty-five miles, and my apartment's only thirty."

Jill moved a little closer, with Lizzie's lovely features even more striking in the silvery moonlight. "I worry about you. Will you text me when you get home?"

"Sure. And I'll wait until I'm parked," she said, rolling her eyes. "I already get the texting lecture from my mom."

"You don't need another mom," Jill insisted. "Yours is as good as they come. She got you to the cusp of your thirtieth birthday, so she must be doing something right."

Lizzie moved a little closer too, looking up into Jill's eyes. "Still want to do something on the Saturday between our birthdays? Or have I scared you off?"

"Yes, and yes," Jill said, nodding forcefully. "But I'll gut it up and be ready to go."

"We'll have to go early. Is that okay?"

"It's perfect. The earlier we go, the longer we get to be on the water."

Lizzie lifted her hand and slapped Jill's palm. "We'll have a great time," she insisted as she got into the car. "Excited!"

She closed the door and turned the motor on. As Jill watched her pull out, the thought passed through her mind that Lizzie was a damned nice combination of emotionally mature and totally playful. Who could possibly resist her?

Jill was up early on Monday morning, worrying. She was so agitated only exercise would blow off some of the stress. It was a little warmer, and the lake was much calmer today. She went to the dock and dropped one of the kayaks in, then paddled around until she spotted Karen leave the cabin and take a seat on one of the Adirondack chairs set up near the bank. Just a few long strokes had her back at the shore. She looked up and smiled when Karen came over to hold the kayak close.

"Thanks. I really overdid it on Saturday. I might have had to stay out here for hours until someone came to rescue me."

Fondly, Karen reached down and ruffled her hair. "You aren't the poster child for moderation."

"Only about exercise," Jill reminded her. "Thankfully." She sat on the bank, then got to her feet and pulled the boat from the water. After turning it over to let it dry, she flopped down on the pink chair that sat at an angle to Karen's.

"Let me get you a cup of coffee," Karen said, taking off for the cabin before Jill could complain. After she returned, they sat and quietly sipped their coffee, with Jill trying to decide how and if she should spill her secret.

Before she could make an overture, Karen looked at her for a long moment, then said, "Is everything okay? You've seemed awfully anxious ever since we got here. That's not like you."

A dozen threads unspooled in her head, but Jill caught the one that mattered the most. Getting to the heart of the issue, she let it out. "Lizzie's got a crush on me."

Karen cocked her head, waiting for more. Reluctantly, Jill finished by looking down at the ground and adding, "And I've got a crush on Lizzie."

Nodding impassively, Karen waited, obviously giving Jill time to finish. Finally, she said, "I'm more than a little surprised."

Her head snapped up. "Of course you are. I'm a thousand years older than she is, and she's my best friend's sister!"

Karen's face lit up with a smile. "I thought she was straight, Jill. And I'm pretty sure you're not."

Jill blinked, confused. Her past statements flew through her mind, but she had no memory of ever talking about Lizzie's sexual orientation. "Did I say she was straight?"

"I don't think so. She just looks it." She put a hand over her eyes, clearly embarrassed. "I can't believe I say things like that." She took a deep breath. "I should be able to see past the stereotype, which I *know* is false."

"I wasn't surprised that she's interested in women," Jill clarified. "But I was stunned that she's interested in me."

Karen's head tilted. "But you said you have a crush on her too. What's that all about?"

"I never, ever would have let myself think about her that way," Jill said, wishing she had a bible to swear on to emphasize her point. "But the minute she told me she was interested in me, I looked at her in a new way. Like she was a stranger. And..." She sucked in a breath as her head dropped back and her chin pointed up at the sky. "If she were a stranger..." Slowly, she lifted her head and managed a single word. One that made her sound like she was still in high school. "Wow."

"She's very, very cute," Karen said, unsuccessfully trying to hide a smirk. "And everyone likes her." She pursed her lips as she thought. "That doesn't always impress me. A cute woman can easily charm a bunch of lesbians. But the kids all loved her. They're a much tougher crowd."

"You and Becky like her?" She felt so stupid, begging for confirmation of her own instincts!

"Yeah, we do. I remember talking about her on the way home from your barbecue. We were both amazed at how Olive took to her. Kids sense kindness, Jill. It's really tough to fake."

"She's a very sweet person," Jill admitted. "If she was near my age and wasn't from my tiny home town, or the daughter of people I think of as second parents…" She slapped her face with both hands, letting out a growl. "I don't know what to do! Now that she's opened up to me, I can't stop thinking about her!"

"Calm down," Karen said as she leaned forward and patted Jill's knee. "You're catastrophizing this."

"What am I going to do?" Jill moaned louder, knowing she was repeating herself. "She's exactly the kind of woman I've been looking for, Karen. But she's off limits."

"I'm not sure I understand why she's forbidden fruit." She looked at her carefully. "Is that usually a thing for you? Do you find yourself attracted to unavailable women?"

"No. Not…" Grumbling to herself, she said, "I was with an unavailable woman once, but that was many years ago. I learned my lesson."

Karen gazed fondly at Jill, who felt like she was under a microscope. "So this has really knocked you for a loop."

"A big one!" She felt like she was speaking in a series of exclamation points, but didn't know how to calm down.

"Let's look at this logically. How big is the age difference? Fifteen years?"

"No!" She shook her head. "It's bad enough. She's turning thirty two days before I turn forty."

"Well, look at the bright side. For two whole days, she'll only be nine years younger."

Something about the way she said that caught Jill the right way and she laughed, feeling some of the tension release. "I can see why you're such a busy therapist. You're clearly worth whatever fee you charge."

"I'm not your therapist. I'm your friend. And I'm concerned that you're being so rigid about this."

"These are big issues, Karen. Really big!"

"No, they're not," she said gently. "You don't have a huge age difference. Ben's close to twenty years older than Jason, and no one even seems to notice any more. And don't forget Mary Beth and Kathleen have a pretty big gap."

"Only six or seven years," Jill corrected her. "This is *twice* that."

"Are you sure you should be in charge of the university's finances? Come on now. Don't be so hung up on the age thing."

"I shouldn't be," she admitted, "since that isn't the biggest issue. Her family is."

Karen took a breath and stared into her eyes for a few seconds before she spoke. "Would you feel the same if you were a man?"

"If I were a man...? I don't get it."

"If you were a man, and you were interested in a friend's sister, would you think you needed permission to pursue her?"

Karen's gaze was unrelenting, but Jill tried to clear her mind and think. Finally, she dropped her head and admitted the truth. "Probably not."

"I think you've got a little homophobia tied up in that thought process," Karen insisted. "Take a look at that. If you wouldn't think it was odd for a guy to ask a friend's sister out, it shouldn't be weird for you."

"But I don't want to risk Janet and Mike tossing me out on my ear. They're really important to me, Karen."

"I get that. I do. But look at it this way. If they'd cut their daughter off because she's gay, are they the people you want as parent figures?"

"I don't think they'd cut Lizzie off, no matter what. But they don't know she's...into women," Jill said, omitting the proper term. She wasn't ready to tell even her close friends that Lizzie was bi. That was Lizzie's secret to reveal if she felt like it.

"Then she'd better come out. Springing this on them would be a lot to process all at once."

Jill blinked at her. "You sound like it's a foregone conclusion I'm going to be with Lizzie."

Karen stood, moved over behind Jill, then bent and kissed her cheek. "I've seen you go through three relationships. And you didn't seem this excited about all of those women put together. I think you're already hooked. You just haven't acknowledged it to yourself."

"Oh, I am so screwed," she moaned. "So seriously screwed."

The day warmed up slowly, and by the time they'd had lunch a few of them were making noises about going into the water. Jill knew that would be a short excursion, since none of her friends were fond of cold water. But she was game. To get ready for the plunge, she chose to go for a walk in the woods, hoping to build up a sweat. Then the cold water would be a relief rather than torture.

The path was a good one, at least two feet wide and fairly level. She'd loved running in the woods when she was younger, and today seemed like a good day to give it another go. Starting off slow, she reached a reasonable pace and ran carefully for about a quarter mile. By then she was getting a good stride and she loosened up a bit, letting her feet kick up behind her as she picked up the pace.

It was damned nice to float along through the trees, making her feel like a kid again as she filled her lungs with the fresh, earthy scents. She kept increasing her pace, until she was running near her capacity, flying down the trail as she headed for home, her feet padding softly along the well-trod path. As she saw the road up ahead, she slowed and finally stopped, bending over to grab the hems of her shorts as she gasped for breath.

Damn, that felt good. Every part of her body working together to propel her along, effectively blowing out a little more of her lingering anxieties. She stood and stretched for a few minutes, just to keep everything loose. Then she started back down the road, where she pulled her phone out to check her e-mail. The signal wasn't good enough, and she started to put it back into her pocket, but she went to her photos and looked at the few she'd taken of Lizzie. Yes, she was acting like a twelve-year-old with a crush, but she had such a damned need to see her face that she couldn't stop herself. A couple from the barbecue, one of Lizzie with the group, which didn't give Jill enough detail to linger over, then one of her playing with the kids. That one was better, but also didn't show her face well enough. The photo that caught Jill's attention was the one she'd taken of them together, after they'd gone dancing. They both looked a little bedraggled, but that's not what she noticed. It was how happy they looked. Lizzie's head leaned towards hers, her smile so bright she seemed giddy. Jill had to admit they didn't look like a decade separated them. When she was with Lizzie she felt like she was a kid again. Not thirty. More like she'd felt when she was a teenager. When she was full of plans and dreams and an unbridled optimism for the future. As she put the phone back into her pocket, she forced herself to be honest. How often did you meet someone who helped you tap into the fountain of youth? And how stupid would it be to turn and run just because of some unsubstantiated fears? The answers appeared in her mind as though they were written in stone. Not very, and not very.

❧

Jill had a good excuse for not writing or calling or texting during her vacation. Lizzie knew cell service was spotty at best. But at the end of her two weeks, as Jill drove back to Burlington, she was out of excuses.

After she arrived home, she spent a long time trying to get back into the boys' good graces, resorting to giving them a couple of their favorite treats to hasten the process. She hadn't told the cat sitters where she kept the good stuff, reasoning that she had to reserve it for herself, giving her a god-like status. If just anyone could offer a treat, she'd lose her edge.

It was the first of August, it was warm, and the lake had been at a reliable seventy degrees for almost ten days. Maybe Lizzie would like to hang out on the water. Her hands were shaking when she texted her.

"I'm back home. Heading for the lake. Join me?"

Jill went to pull her swimsuit from her bag and get a towel and her e-reader. When she was putting her things in a tote bag, Lizzie wrote back.

"Boo! I'm working today and tomorrow. Jealous!"

Hating to admit how relieved she was, Jill texted back. "Maybe next weekend?"

"Going home. Chris' birthday."

As Jill was replying, another text appeared. "Want to go with me?"

Luckily, she had a ready excuse. "Got plans for Friday, so I can't." She let that one fly, then started to feel bad about being so unavailable. "Hate to not see you before our birthday bash. Any other time free?"

"I'll call if I get a night off—which I might not. Things are crazy!"

"Have fun and try not to think of me thoroughly enjoying myself today."

Lizzie replied with the emoji of a person sticking his tongue out. Jill put her phone in her pocket and headed out, uncomfortably relieved at not having to see Lizzie yet. She had two weeks to get this sorted out. Although why two weeks would help much was a question she couldn't answer.

Chapter Nine

ON LIZZIE'S ACTUAL BIRTHDAY, Jill sent thirty roses, six of each of the five colors the florist had in stock. She wasn't comfortable sending all red ones, not at all sure they were going to be lovers, and yellow was clearly for friendship, something she also wasn't sure would happen. If she turned her down, Lizzie might well tell her to take a hike. A colorful bouquet seemed the best way to split the difference. What she was trying to do was show she took note of Lizzie's significant birthday, without making a definite claim on her heart.

Lizzie got the flowers, and the meaning. Late that night, she texted Jill with a simple message. "My non-denominational bouquet is gorgeous!"

It was going to be tough dating a woman smarter and quicker than she was. *If* they dated.

The next morning, Lizzie texted from the driveway. Jill had been up for a while, playing with her hair until she finally made up her mind to just stick it into a ponytail. Filled with indecision, she changed her shirt a couple of times, finally settling on a print that made her eyes look super blue. Her dark blue shorts were faded from wear, but she thought that made them look kinda cool. As she primped in the mirror by the front door, the horn honked, making her flinch.

She dashed down the steps, her beach tote banging against her leg. Towel, sunblock, water, a long-sleeved T-shirt for sun protection, and a comb were all she carried. If the day went well, she wouldn't need her e-reader.

After opening the car door and tossing her bag in the back, Jill sat and put her seatbelt on. "You're looking particularly nice today," she said, eyeing Lizzie's oversized, white, man-tailored shirt and jeans that looked like they had some room to breathe. "How does it feel to be thirty?"

"You tell me," she said, a smirk firmly settled on her face. "You've been at this for ten years. I'm a newby."

"But still a smart-aleck. That hasn't changed."

"Odds are good that it won't." She put the car in reverse and backed out of the drive. "I really did love the flowers you sent. They were the nicest present I got—by a mile."

"My pleasure. I love buying flowers, even though I drive my local guy nuts. I want to see the exact stems he's going to use, which, I'm told, no one else does."

"Well, you did a good job. Each one's perfect. But there were so many of them!" Her laugh sounded relaxed and easy, making Jill loosen up a little.

"It only gets worse," she said. "So… Tell me the details. What did you do for your big day?"

"Not much," she said, blithely. "Some of my work friends took me out for a drink, but I was home by ten. I guess that's my new curfew, now that I'm old."

"No party?" Jill stared at her. She'd been sure Lizzie had something big planned.

"Nope. My mom offered to have one for me. But I was looking forward to doing this today. I kinda shared Chris' last weekend."

"Well, damn, Lizzie, I would have happily taken you out to dinner. No!" she amended. "We could have gone to…New York or Boston or something to look at museums. That's your thing, right?"

"Calm down," Lizzie teased. "I had a fine evening. Surviving for thirty years isn't much of an accomplishment."

"But you said you were kinda freaked out by this birthday. I would have done anything to make it special for you." She sounded overly earnest even to her own ears.

"That matters as much as actually going somewhere. And so much cheaper. Hey, I got tickets to the Sox two weeks from today. Are you in?"

"Sounds great. I think I'm free." She pulled her phone out and checked it. "Yep. What's the plan?"

Lizzie gave her a quick glance. "I'll get the hotel if you'll drive. We could take my dad's car, but your trunk is bigger and he's got a lot of stuff he has to carry."

"I'm happy to drive, but you don't have to get my hotel room."

"It's no big deal. I'll need two rooms anyway, so I'll just get one of them with two beds." She shot Jill a pointed look. "Are you cool with that?"

Jill gulped, but nodded. *Great.* She'd look like a prima donna if she demanded her own room. And it would look silly to Janet and Mike if she did. Everyone expected single women to share expensive hotel rooms. *Just great.* She'd already spent one sleepless night trying not to drool over Lizzie. Another one was coming right up.

They headed down Pine, with Lizzie making quick decisions about their route.

"Which marina are we heading to?" Jill asked. "We're still going out on a boat, right?"

"Wrong." As she turned onto Queen City, she seemed slightly distracted. "That fell through. But it's a gorgeous day, and we're going to be in the water. Good enough?"

"Sounds perfect. Should we stop for something to eat?"

"It's all taken care of. I'm organized." She turned to show a proud smile. "Now that I'm old, I get up super early."

There was only one possibility for their destination. "We're going to Red Rocks?"

"Yeah. I love it there."

"I do too." She'd gone to the surprisingly woodsy urban park dozens of times, and while she always enjoyed it, she'd been looking forward to something a little more exciting for their joint birthday celebration. But she wasn't about to let her disappointment show. Lizzie had planned the day, and Jill had confidence they'd make the best out of any spot she'd chosen.

They were early enough to fit into the tiny parking lot close to the beach, but Lizzie stayed outside, taking one of the spots on the street.

"They make you leave at seven if you're in there," she explained. "Sometimes I'm not ready to leave that early."

Jill smiled at the cute way she said that. Lizzie wasn't the kind to flaunt a rule, she simply figured out ways to get what she wanted without having to.

Lizzie had a season pass, and she whipped out ten bucks with a flourish to buy one for Jill. "I can't believe you haven't been here yet this summer. Now you have no excuse."

Jill had to shove her hands into her pockets to stop them from trying to pay Lizzie back. But that was just rude. "Thanks," she said. "I promise I'll come every day I can get away."

They walked along a path, leading to a very narrow stretch of beach. It wasn't very long, maybe a tenth of a mile, but it was darned beachy for a lake right on the shores of the largest city in Vermont.

"I guess I should have asked if you liked lying in the sun," Lizzie said as she dropped her bag onto the sand.

"I do. I'm surprised you do, though. Mark always said sun was the Davis family kryptonite." She unbuttoned her shirt, and started to fold it neatly. Then Lizzie did the same, slowly revealing a luscious body that made Jill's mouth gape open. It was like watching one of those commercials that pointedly tried to be incendiary, with a gorgeous model peeling off her clothes in slow motion.

"I didn't get Davis skin. Thank god. My mom's half Italian, you know."

Jill knew words were coming out of Lizzie's mouth, and that she was supposed to respond, but she just sank to her towel, trying not to stare.

She'd known Lizzie was thin from the skin-tight jeans she wore. But in her navy blue and white, polka-dot bikini, she didn't look skinny at all. Her womanly curves were rounded and soft, the kind of curves you wanted to bury your face into. But there was a solid muscular strength under that smooth flesh that made Jill see stars.

Lizzie's midsection was remarkably toned, and not just because she was young. Jill had never had abs you could see, and she'd been thin her whole life. No, Lizzie worked for those babies. Doing what? Jill had no idea, but she wanted to see her do whatever it was right that minute.

As Lizzie bent over to pick up her bag, all of her toned muscles tensed, making a few of them noticeably pop. Jill blinked, knowing she looked like she'd been hit on the head, but she was unable to make a lucid comment.

Lizzie plopped down next to her, her actions graceful and smooth.

"I sprayed sunblock on before I got dressed. Nothing worse than getting a burn here," she said, sliding a finger down the flesh at the edge of her top. There was nothing particularly lascivious about a woman touching her chest, but Jill had so thoroughly convinced herself it was wrong to look that it became much more tempting. Focusing on the lake, she tried to organize her thoughts.

In her head, Lizzie looked like a bunch of supermodels all formed together into one perfect woman. But she knew that wasn't true. It was the way she was beginning to feel about her that made her so stunningly attractive. She just had to remind herself of that. To get a little distance between her feelings and reality.

"Do you need sunblock?" Lizzie asked, shaking the tube in front of Jill's face.

She realized she still had her shorts on, and Jill got up and removed them, placing them on top of her blouse. "Uhm…" There was a question on the table, but she couldn't, for the life of her, recall what it was.

"Sunblock?" Lizzie asked, now smirking.

"Got some," she declared, proud of herself for remembering. She pulled it out and sprayed it on, after making sure she was downwind.

"Need help rubbing it in?" Lizzie's eyes were roaming up and down her body, making Jill suck in her stomach to try to look close to the perfection that was Lizzie.

"No, I'm fine. I just spray until there's no way there's any uncovered skin." She should have done this at home, but she clearly wasn't as organized as Lizzie was.

There were only four other groups of people on the beach, but as Jill sprayed away a few more families arrived. It was just nine-thirty and was already seventy-five, with the temperatures expected to climb to eighty in the afternoon. "We're going to be wedged in here like sardines pretty soon," Jill said.

"No, we won't. We'll be in the water." Lizzie lay on her side, and rested her head on her hand. "I'm only being nice in letting you warm up before I drag you in there and refuse to let you leave."

"I can hold my own. I was in the water every day it was over sixty-nine at the cabin. Although I'll confess I'm kind of a baby about getting in. I have to give myself a pep talk."

"Just gut it up and do it fast. That's my solution to everything that might be painful."

"Mine is to worry about it and then finally do it. Then I feel dumb that I spent time worrying when I could have gotten it over with sooner."

"You're young enough to retrain," Lizzie said. She stood and extended her hand, waiting for Jill to take it. Then she locked her grip around Jill's wrist and led her towards the water. "We're marching right in," she said, calmly and confidently. "It'll be cold, but only for a minute."

"Maybe we should go in a little at a time," Jill said, almost pleading.

"Nope. Do it all. Do it fast. Trust me."

They were at the edge before Jill could argue. Then the first tingles hit her toes, then the icy water covered her shivering thighs, then her belly, then her breasts. She tried to squeal, but nothing came out. Lizzie didn't have that problem, and she let out a high-pitched howl that distracted Jill from the cold.

"See?" Lizzie panted. "All better."

"All bad," Jill groused, trying to scowl but finding herself laughing at Lizzie's chattering teeth.

"One last bit," Lizzie said. She put her hands on Jill's shoulders and dunked her, dipping her own head beneath the water at the same time.

Jill pushed to the surface and yelped, loudly. Lizzie was right behind her, screaming, "Gonna die!"

But as soon as the warm sun hit her chilled head, Jill felt warmer. Much warmer. "I hate to admit it," she said, "but you were right. I'm cold, but it feels good."

"Swim with me," Lizzie said, stretching her body out and doing a lazy back stroke.

"Race you," Jill said, launching into action. All she'd done at the cabin was paddle around and lie on a raft, but she used to be a pretty good swimmer. Maybe her competitive instincts could overcome rusty technique and age.

They took off, both slapping the water with their hands as they tried to beat the other to the end of the yellow safety buoys. Lizzie won, but just by a hair. She was exulting in her victory when Jill said, "Again!" and took off.

They went back and forth until Lizzie started to slow down. This was when Jill had the advantage. She didn't care how fatigued her muscles got. She could ignore the pain in her arms and chest as she labored for breath. She just had to keep going. After beating Lizzie three times in a row, she came to a halt when Lizzie gasped, "Stop! Please!"

Jill flipped onto her back, the cold water keeping her buoyant as the hot sun warmed her body. "Now that was fun."

Lizzie splashed some icy water in her face. "That was nuts! Would you have kept going all day?"

Jill treaded water as she gave Lizzie a slow smile. "I don't remember having a gun to your head. You could have stopped any time."

"Ha! I can't let you win." She swiped her hand across the surface of the water, sending another splash at Jill's face. "You know that."

"No, I really didn't," Jill said, blinking the water from her eyes. "But I'm glad. I love someone who'll give me a run for my money."

"I don't have as much money as you do, but I'll give you a run to remember." Lizzie showed a smile that made it look like she was talking about something a lot more fun than swimming.

❧

They finally got out of the water, but with people now packed in so tightly it was hard to get back to their towels. After having to leap over one sleeping pair who'd mashed their blanket right up against Lizzie's, they finally made it.

"Some people don't understand beach etiquette," Lizzie said, glaring at the snoozing people. "You should leave a path, no matter how crowded it gets."

"I couldn't agree more. Want to move?"

"In a bit. Let's dry off first."

"Let me just knock the icicles off," Jill teased. She lay down on her side, relishing the warm sun as she stretched out. "God, I love summer. If summer were a person, I'd marry her."

"How do you know she's a woman?"

"Oh, you can just tell. She's fertile and lush and ripe." Jill could tell she was wearing a goofy grin, but she didn't feel the need to put on a mature facade with Lizzie. Lizzie had seen her with a nineties mullet and was still interested in her. That had to count for something.

Lizzie lay down, facing her. The sun felt so good, warming Jill from the outside in, with Lizzie's gorgeous body making every other part warm too.

"That's what I love about women," Lizzie said, speaking quietly so their neighbors couldn't hear. "That's what I wish for when I get the urge. To have a lush, ripe body wrapped around mine."

Jill smacked her lips together, now suddenly dry. "Tell me what you love about women. I'm fascinated."

"Mmm." Lizzie pulled a knee up, exposing the delicious curve of her hip. "I prefer almost everything about women. I love their bodies, their emotional connectedness, even their sensibilities." She took a breath, with her eyes half closed as she thought. "I think women are funnier than men, their books speak to me, even their art. I love a lot of artists, but it's the women who resonate. It's women who speak to my soul."

Jill blinked, amazed at the emotion Lizzie had such ready access to. "You've thought about this a lot. I can tell."

"A whole lot," she agreed. "I read that a lot of people make major life changes right before significant birthdays." She leaned closer, with Jill bedazzled by the drops of water slowly trailing down her cheek. "I can't change my attractions, but I'm going to change my behavior." She fixed Jill with a long, pointed look. "I'm giving men up."

"That seems like a pretty big thing to give up, Lizzie. Are you sure?"

She shook her head, dark auburn strands sticking to her body as her head moved. "I can't know until I try, but I'm not worried about it. I'm resolved."

"But you had to get something from men. You're not the type to stick with guys just because everyone else did."

A slow smile settled onto her face. "No, I'm not the kind who does what other people do." She took in a deep breath, with Jill fighting to keep her eyes off Lizzie's small but well-shaped breasts as her chest rose and fell. "There's one thing I like about men. The thing that's made me try to make it work."

"I assume that's sex," Jill said, feeling a little heartsick at the thought.

"No, not sex. Well, not exactly." A tiny line formed between her dark brows when she tried to explain herself. "There's a sexual energy that most men…well, all of the men I've been with, give off. It's a magnetic pull that the women I've been with haven't had."

"That sounds like something you wouldn't want to walk away from. Sexual chemistry is pretty important. At least it is to me."

"I'm hoping I just haven't met the right woman." Her voice dropped to a lower register, and Jill felt tingles chase up her back when Lizzie spoke again. "Or that I've met her, but we haven't tested our chemistry yet."

"Uhm," she said, tongue-tied. "How many women have you been with?"

"One in high school," she said, raising an index finger. "One in college. The two Nick and I hooked up with, and the one I met online when I was with Joel."

"The doctor?"

"Uh-huh."

"So you weren't with a woman when you and Jon were together?"

"No," she said, clearly annoyed. "I told you this already. I was one hundred percent monogamous with him. He broke up with me because I *told* him I was bi. I didn't show him."

147

"Sorry," Jill said quickly. "I've never met these guys, so it's hard for me to keep them separate."

Lizzie put a hand on her arm and gave it a brief squeeze. "No, I'm sorry. I'm a little thin-skinned about that."

Nodding, Jill said, "Five women is a pretty good number. That should give you an indication whether women can satisfy you."

"That could be true if I'd had sex hundreds of times. But three of my five were one-nighters. And I never got to spend the night with Erica Handler. Well, we spent the night together, but only on sleepovers. And there was no way I could talk her into doing anything at either of our houses."

"Really? I've always wished I'd started earlier, just to be able to go to a girl's house and do it." She laughed at how silly that sounded.

"No way. Actually, every time we had sex, I had to beg for it. And I do mean *beg*. It was humiliating, but I was so horny I got over myself and pleaded with her."

"Ouch! You really had to beg?"

"I had to beg Jenny in college too. I think I went back to guys after her just to convince myself I was desirable."

Jill stared at her. "No." When Lizzie just gazed back, she said it again. "No. You can't be serious."

"I'm totally serious. I had to seduce the hell out of both Erica and Jenny. Each time was like pulling teeth. Erica did a fantastic job of making me ashamed of my sex drive."

"But you kept going back to men," Jill said, now suspicious.

"I *loved* women. I truly did. But I could love men too, and they were a hell of a lot easier."

"So you're bi because it's easier?"

Lizzie rolled her eyes. "Let me explain this one more time. I'm bi because I'm bi. It's a sexual orientation, Jill. Not a preference. God, is this really so hard for people to understand?"

"I'm sorry," she said, putting a hand on Lizzie's hip. *Damn, that felt good. All springy and warm.* "I keep saying stupid stuff. Stuff I know not to say."

"The woman Nick and I slept with… The one I knew professionally?"

"I remember."

"She's the only one I've ever been with who wanted to be there and really loved sex. I could have been in a relationship with her."

"Why not try?"

"I told you. She came to work at the Gardner and I didn't want to be involved with a co-worker. And even if that hadn't happened, I don't think she would have been up for it. She leaned more straight than gay, while I'm pretty much the opposite."

This was all making Jill's head hurt. It just didn't add up. "I can't imagine why you didn't keep looking for women. There are plenty of women who love sex."

"I'm sure there are," she said, sounding tired. "But I haven't *met* them. I'm a relationship person, Jill. I didn't want to sleep with a dozen women just to test them out."

Jill almost said that's exactly what Lizzie and her boyfriend were doing when they tried to find a woman to share, but she feared she'd get a face full of sand for bringing that up. Instead, she focused on the message Lizzie was trying to give. "So you're saying the only thing that's kept you from being with a woman is that you've never met a woman who's really into you. Even though you live in Grrrlington."

"Yes, Jill, I know Burlington is full of lesbians, but I haven't met a single one who wants to go out with me."

"But…why?"

Lizzie scooted closer, her expression now sober. Her eyes flitted over Jill's face, then settled. "Because I'm bi. The few single lesbians I've met have been decidedly cool about it."

"But why?"

Jill clapped her mouth shut as Lizzie gave her a knowing look.

"I assume they feel like you do about it. That I'll go back to men."

"Yeah," Jill said, looking down, a little ashamed of herself. "That's probably true." Their eyes met again. "But unfair."

"I think so," Lizzie agreed. "But that's only been a couple of women, so I shouldn't generalize."

"So you haven't really tried to find a woman? You haven't used a dating app? Some of my guy friends do that constantly."

"A lot of people do," she admitted, sounding a little hesitant. "I don't think of myself as lazy, but it's just been easier to be with men. In every way. But then I get this longing that's really, really hard to resist. And that's screwed up three relationships in a row. I'm done trying to make that work."

"But you can't be *sure*," Jill said, heartsick over that fact.

"No, I can't. But if you can find a person who knows exactly how she'll feel about her relationship in a year or five or ten…" She shook her head. "That person doesn't exist. You work at relationships. They aren't one size fits all."

Jill nodded, then lay down and closed her eyes. That seemed like a very mature thing to say. But the uncertainty of the whole situation still scared her to death.

An annoying sensation crept into her dream, then she reached up to slap weakly at whatever was tickling her ear. The sounds of people laughing and children shrieking made Jill's eyes pop open. A grinning Lizzie hovered above her, then a hank of Jill's own hair came into focus. "You sleep really soundly," Lizzie said. "I've been tickling you for five minutes."

While rubbing her eyes with her fists, Jill grumbled, "Maybe that meant I wanted to stay asleep."

The hair fell and Lizzie sat up, then stared at Jill soberly. "I'm sorry. I don't like people screwing with me while I'm asleep either. I shouldn't have—"

"Teasing," Jill interrupted. "Totally. I had no intention of falling asleep, so I'm glad you woke me. Maybe I should get back into the water to knock the cobwebs out."

"I'm almost ready for lunch," Lizzie said. "But I don't want to eat here. Are you up for a walk?"

"Sure. Should I get dressed?"

"Mmm, probably. I don't want any branches to scratch those pretty legs." She gave Jill such a fond smile that she could have sworn her heart skipped a beat. She was losing it!

They put their clothes back on, but Lizzie didn't close her shirt. Everyone had things that hit their buttons, things they found surprisingly sexy. Seeing Lizzie's dark bikini peeking out from that crisp white shirt now had to be added to Jill's list. It was a day full of surprises.

They walked back towards the parking area, then turned left and started to walk up the road. In a short while they were enveloped by an entirely different climate. The temperature was a few degrees cooler, and the air held the rich scent of growing leaves mixed with decaying matter underfoot. Most people were at the beach on this warm, sun-filled day, leaving the paved surface relatively empty. After a hundred yards the road ended and Lizzie led the way up a trail.

They climbed up to the highest point on the north side of the park, a very manageable peak. They didn't run into another soul, but Jill had seen people carrying toddlers on their backs during previous visits, underscoring how gentle the pitch was.

When they reached a large, flat, red rock, Lizzie leaned over the railing someone had seen fit to install to keep people from falling. She closed her eyes and breathed in. "Doesn't it smell great up here?"

"It sure does." Jill stood next to her and looked down, noticing scrub pine and other tenacious trees holding on along the face of the nearly vertical rocks. "I wonder what 76 means?" she asked idly, looking at the number painted on the rock they stood on. "If it was the class of 1976, the paint would have worn away by now."

"That's the height." She looked at Jill speculatively for a moment. "You haven't jumped from here?"

"Jumped?"

"Yeah," she said, laughing at what Jill assumed was her own fear-filled expression. "Jumped."

"No way. No *way*. I've seen people do it, and I hope they're all resting comfortably in the orthopedics ward, but I'm not going to join them."

"Oh, come on," Lizzie said, her eyes dancing with excitement. She grasped Jill's hand and pressed it to her chest. "You're turning forty tomorrow. Don't you want to do something crazy? Something you know you shouldn't do?"

Inching away from the edge, Jill shook her head vigorously. "I went swimming in ice cold water. I think I'm good."

"Come on," Lizzie urged. "You know you want to. Doing things like this lets you keep a foothold in your swiftly fading youth."

Jill cocked her head. "Have you been reading poetry? Or inspirational books?"

"Maybe a few," she admitted. "I've been doing a lot of thinking about my life. But I honestly think it's good to do things that scare you a little."

"This scares me a lot! A whole lot!"

"Okay," she said patiently. "Let's move down to something more manageable." They picked up their bags and switched over to a different path. Lizzie veered off it after only a minute, ducking under branches as she forged her own trail, finally coming to an exposed, flat rock. "Oh, Jill," she breathed. "You have to do this one. It's got your number written right on it."

Lizzie had a point. A big, fat 40 was painted right at her feet. Almost daring her. "If I do it, will you go with me?" *Who said that?*

"I would," she said, sounding very sincere. "But I'd rather take a video. I want you to have a lasting memory you can look back on and remind yourself that taking chances can be fun."

"Or to play at my memorial service." She leaned forward and peeked out, shivering with fear. "Make sure they don't play 'Amazing Grace' on the bagpipes, okay? I truly hate that."

"You'll be fine!" Lizzie insisted. "The lake's at least seventy-five feet deep here. All you have to do is be careful to go in as straight as you can."

Jill started to take her clothes off, with her hands shaking so hard she had trouble with the buttons. Lizzie took over, concentrating on the work, then lifting her eyes to meet Jill's. She looked so deliciously playful, so full of life. It was almost impossible to restrain herself from taking her in her arms and kissing her senseless.

Now Jill stood at the edge, clad in only her red tank suit. At least the blood wouldn't show as vividly... She gulped, unable to swallow normally. "Stay straight."

"Yes," Lizzie said, all calm and collected. "People get hurt when they're flailing and land on a shoulder or their neck." She put her hands on Jill's waist and looked at her soberly. "You don't have to push off much. You'll easily clear the rocks if you just jump. Then keep your legs straight, point your toes, and you're in."

"A casket," she muttered.

"I won't make fun of you, or lose one bit of respect for you if you don't want to do this," Lizzie said, her gaze mesmerizing.

Jill sucked in a breath, gathered her courage and said, "Take my phone and make sure you get the video." She leaned close and tried to glower. "I will strangle you if you screw it up."

Lizzie scrambled to pull Jill's phone from her pants pocket. "Lock code?"

"2031," she said, her mouth so dry she could hardly spit the words out.

The camera emitted a "ping," meaning it was on. Jill looked right into the lens and said, "They say to live fast, die young, and leave a pretty corpse. Mine is going to be mangled, but at least I'll still be in my thirties. Tell everyone I did this of my own accord." She slapped her face with her hands, adding, "Even though Lizzie totally pushed me!" Then she moved back, took a big step and pushed off, free falling. The sensation was…remarkable. Time slowed as the scenery rushed by. She was so fascinated and terrified that she almost lost track of where she was. But Lizzie's words stayed with her and she grabbed her nose with one hand, tucked her elbows close to her sides, and pointed her toes. Then icy water whooshed past her and she had a moment of panic when she realized how far down she was diving. As soon as she stopped descending, she started to kick, breaking through the water in seconds— that felt like minutes. "Whoa!" she cried out, sticking an arm up in triumph.

"Swim to the rocks," Lizzie yelled. "I'll come get you!"

Jill blinked the water out of her eyes, stunned that she'd done something so dumb. So reckless! She didn't have any idea how to exit the water from this spot. Had she lost her mind?

It didn't take long to swim back to the rocks, but she had to wait for what seemed like a long time for Lizzie to arrive.

"Down here," she called, and Jill gamely swam a few dozen yards to reach the spot.

Lizzie was standing on a rock, bracing herself by holding onto a thin tree. "Take my hand," she instructed.

Jill did, surprised at how easily Lizzie lifted her from the water. She stood on the rock, every sense alive. "God damn, Lizzie," she panted. "That was friggin' awesome!"

Lizzie put her arms around her and hugged her tightly. "I *knew* you'd love it. I'm so proud of you for being so…crazy!"

"Now it's your turn," Jill said. "I assume you want the seventy-six footer?"

They'd been scrambling along the rocks, heading for the path. But Lizzie stopped and stared at her. "Are you mad? I'd never jump off a cliff!"

"But you made me!"

"No, no." A playful grin lit her face. "I encouraged you to have a mastery experience. That was all about opening yourself up to the unexpected."

Jill grabbed for her, catching only Lizzie's maniacal laughter. "You'd better open yourself up to the unexpected! Like getting your ass kicked!"

"Gotta catch me first!" She got to the path and scampered up it like a mountain goat. When Jill realized she couldn't catch her, she slowed down and let Lizzie wear herself out. Her lilting laugh carried down the hill as she ran, with Jill finding herself as happy as she'd been in years. That damned Lizzie Davis had thoroughly gotten under her skin.

Jill slowed down, reflecting on how she felt. For a change, she tried to turn off the warning messages and just let herself experience her feelings. They were good. Really good. Nearly every minute with Lizzie was pleasurable—to her mind and her body. Why was she fighting this so hard?

She'd gone past the higher jumping point, and finally found Lizzie sitting on her towel on a big rock, grinning like the cat that ate the canary. She patted the rock playfully. "You look like you need lunch."

Jill went close to the edge, saying, "Why isn't this a jumping spot?" Then she saw that the rocks jutted out just below the peak. "Oh. Well, that would sting a little."

Lizzie grasped her hand and pulled her down. "I'm amazed at how you gutted it up and jumped. I *know* you didn't want to."

"No, I didn't," Jill admitted. "But I wouldn't have let you talk me into it if I didn't have a little desire to do something crazy."

"Good. I'd feel bad if I thought you'd done it only for me." She took Jill's phone out and turned the screen towards her. "The video's awesome." When she hit the play button Jill watched, snickering at how terrified she looked.

"Yeah, that's when I almost wet myself," she said, pausing the action. "Maybe I did. I should play it in slow motion to see if there's anything flying out of me when I cleared the rocks."

"You were grace under pressure," Lizzie said, beaming a smile.

Jill started to laugh when she heard Lizzie on the video, urging her on. "Go, go, go!" she cried. Then, "Awesome!" at top volume.

"You almost blew my speaker out," Jill teased. "Am I the first person you've coached?"

"I guess so. I've been with lots of people who've jumped, but you're the first I had to talk into it."

"Boys, right?" Jill asked.

She laughed at that. "Of course. It's tough to talk a woman into jumping. Women are generally smarter…"

Jill got up and put her clothes on. "I'm smart enough to keep those pine needles from pricking my butt. Other than that, I make no guarantees. You'd better have something good to eat in that bag, though. Almost killing myself really worked up an appetite."

Lizzie reached into her tote and pulled out a couple of containers, a paper bag and a big knife, the blade wrapped in cardboard and affixed with duct tape.

"What in the hell are you planning on doing?" Jill asked. "Hunting and skinning rabbits?"

"I wanted fresh bread, so I have to slice it myself." She started to work, eventually laying out thick slices of multi-grain bread from Jill's favorite bakery, equally thick slices of tomato, and a good helping of basil. Then she took out a plastic tube, shook it and squeezed something all over the open-faced sandwiches. "Olive oil and balsamic vinegar," she explained. "I can't eat a sandwich without it."

Jill's mouth was watering as she watched Lizzie finish her preparation. As soon as she had the bread in her hand, she took a big bite, and closed her eyes in pleasure. "Mouthgasm," she purred.

"Definitely a mouthgasm," Lizzie agreed. "I'm going to steal that, by the way."

"Be my guest. I hope you brought a bushel of tomatoes. I could easily have six or seven of these."

"I can fill you up." She reached over and patted Jill's belly. "I think. The tomatoes and basil are from the old homestead. I loaded up when I was down last weekend."

"Well worth the trip." Jill shifted to be able to look across the lake to the Adirondacks. "This is the life. How do we do this every day?"

"Move to Florida?"

"Nah. I'd miss the mountains. And the snow. Summer's good because we have to wait for it. I kinda like delayed gratification."

Lizzie waited until Jill looked into her eyes to respond. "I'm learning that about you. But it's cool," she added. "There's nothing wrong with waiting for something you want." She reached into her bag and pulled out another container. "I almost forgot the wine! Wouldn't a crisp, mineral-laced Sicilian white be perfect with this?"

Jill looked at her curiously. "Do you know a lot about wine?"

"Nope." She put the bottle between her legs and unscrewed the cap. "But the guy who sold me this bottle said it would be perfect for our lunch."

Warmth spread through Jill's chest as she watched her carefully pour wine into plastic cups. "You went to a lot of trouble to make lunch. I want you to know I appreciate it."

Lizzie handed her a cup and they touched them together. "I had fun organizing the day. Here's to us and our very significant birthdays."

"Let's declare this our birthday weekend. From here on, August the fifteenth through the seventeenth is the official Lizzie and Jill weekend, no matter where it falls in the week."

"I'm in." Lizzie held the cup to her lips and took a big sip. "Fantastic," she said, nodding. "I'm going to buy all of my wine from that guy. Both bottles I'll buy this year," she added.

"I think we both prefer beer, but it's a bitch to take on a picnic."

"I'm glad I bought wine. It's just right," Lizzie said, sighing as she wrapped her arm around her raised legs. She was flexible enough to rest her chin on her knees, something Jill wouldn't even try. Instead, she lay down on the rock and carefully tilted the cup to avoid spilling it.

They didn't speak much, both of them happy to relax in the filtered light, with the cool breeze making the leaves in the surrounding trees flicker. "A damned good day," Jill said after a while.

"Let me top you off." Lizzie poured a little more wine.

"Not much. Oh, that's right," she said, brightly. "I'm not driving."

"I am, but I promise we'll stay until I'm perfectly sober." She topped off her own cup and took another drink. "See how smart I was to park outside the lot?" She tapped her temple. "Planning."

Eventually, the wine was gone, as were the tomatoes and all but one heel of the bread. Lizzie was leaning a little to one side, with her head getting closer and closer to her shoulder.

"Someone needs a nap," Jill said. "Want my lap?" She slapped at her thighs.

"Yes. But that'll put me at a funny angle. If you let me share your towel, I can turn mine into a pillow."

"My towel is your towel."

Lizzie scooted across the rock and lay on her side with her back pressed up against Jill's leg. Then she fussed with her towel until she had it just the way she liked it.

"Don't let me sleep too long," she said. "A half hour is my max."

"I'll set an alarm." Jill did, then lay down as well, linking her hands behind her head for a makeshift pillow. She hadn't felt this peaceful and relaxed in a while, even though her vacation had only been two weeks ago. Lizzie had the ability to make her feel both full of energy and completely calm. That was a damned nice combination.

Lizzie pressed harder against her body, then fell asleep in what seemed like seconds. Jill idly studied the back of Lizzie's head, fascinated by the wealth of colors in her hair. There was as much red as brown, with a little gold thrown in to make it gleam in the sun. Redheads were rare enough, but auburn had to be as unique. Just like Lizzie. Unique even in a family of redheads.

Jill must have dozed off as well, but only for a few minutes. She turned to look at her phone, seeing there were five minutes left on the alarm. Then she turned if off, deciding not to wake Lizzie with a harsh sound. She'd turned in her sleep, and was now lying on her belly, with her face turned towards Jill.

Damn, she was pretty. Pretty in a unique way. Sometimes women were conventionally attractive, with big eyes, a small nose and a wide mouth. Lizzie was a little different. Her eyes, while lovely, made her look a little crafty. Like she knew a good secret she wasn't going to tell you. Her nose was small, but well-shaped, almost delicate. But it was her lips that Jill found herself staring at when she spoke. In sleep, they were mesmerizing, with her upper lip straight and even, her fuller, curved lower lip meeting it at the corners to form a tiny bow. Like Cupid could easily use those lips to shoot an arrow right into Jill's heart.

Jill inched closer, now so close she could smell Lizzie's wine-scented breath. Part of her wanted to wake her, to make use of every minute of this glorious day. But she was so pretty when she slept, Jill was sorely tempted to spend the afternoon just watching her. Lizzie resolved the conflict by slowly batting her pale eyes. Then that beautiful mouth eased into a smile. "It's okay," she soothed, and Jill found herself responding to the request she hadn't vocalized. Her lips gently settled upon Lizzie's, so warm and welcoming that she had a brief sensation of being exactly where she was supposed to be. Like all of the many decisions she'd made in her life had led her right there. To Lizzie.

Their lips molded together as Jill breathed in, filling her lungs with Lizzie's scent, letting her brain fog with the captivating sensation. She reached out and touched her cheek, the softness astounding her. Then a hand settled into her hair, pulling her closer.

Lizzie's lips parted and Jill's tongue slid in without stopping to realize she'd wanted to—needed to do that. To taste her fully. A groan left her body as chills chased up and down her back. Then she gently pulled away and flopped down next to her. As she looked up, the bluest, clearest sky she could ever recall seeing filled her vision. Everything was bright and clean and clear and achingly vivid.

Lizzie's face came into focus, hovering above her own. "Best first kiss. Ever," she whispered.

Jill wrapped her arms around her and tugged her onto her chest, holding her tightly. "I didn't plan that. I'm pretty fuzzy, Lizzie. I'm not at all sure—"

"Shh." She put her fingers to Jill's lips. "Don't think. Just relax and enjoy the day. This winter, when it's ten below and the wind is coming through every crack in your house, think about today, and how it felt to lie in the sun and eat tomatoes from the garden."

"That's not what I'll think about," Jill said quietly. "I'll think about kissing you."

"That's good too. Maybe I'll be sitting by you, cuddling you to keep you warm."

"I hope so," Jill said, closing her eyes and wishing with all of her might. "I really hope so."

⁂

After lying on the rock for a long while, just feeling each other's heartbeats, Lizzie finally put her hands on the ground and pushed herself up. "How would you like to lie there and have me feed you slices of fresh peach?"

"Mmm," Jill closed her eyes, acting like this was a tough call. "I think that might be pleasurable." Then she nodded decisively. "I can't imagine not liking that."

Lizzie got up and went back to her bag, taking out two perfect peaches and her trusty knife. She peeled one, then sliced off a big strip and dropped it teasingly into Jill's mouth. "How about a little oil and vinegar on that?" she proposed.

"Couldn't hurt to try." The next piece had a tangy bite that Jill was darned fond of. "That's fantastic. But I like it plain too. Pure sweetness, or tangy? Tough to choose."

"We'll alternate." Lizzie lifted the knife above Jill's face and let the slice drop into her mouth. "This could be a racy version of *Little House on the Prairie*."

"Where Ma and Pa wind up naked and covered in peach juice," Jill said, laughing at the thought.

"Ma and Pa didn't do that kind of thing. Don't ruin my pure childhood memories." She dropped another slice of fruit into Jill's mouth. "I'm happy to make new memories, though." Her eyebrow lifted, seemingly in a challenge. Then she put her knife on the towel and smoothed the tension from Jill's forehead. "I'm teasing. I promise I won't push you, Jill. We'll go at your pace." Her mouth quirked up in a devilish smile. "But I can't think of anything I'd say no to today."

Images flashed across Jill's mind, each one sexier than the next. "I need to think," she said quickly, her confusion mounting by the second. "To make sure I feel comfortable before we go any further."

"That's all right," Lizzie insisted. "I'm very patient. When I have to be."

"I need time, Lizzie. I have to move slowly to make sure I don't screw this up."

"No problem. For now, we'll just go along like we have been." She leaned over and whispered in her ear, tickling the sensitive skin. "If you're a good girl, you get cake."

"Cake?" Her face lit up at the prospect. "I love cake."

Lizzie put her hand on Jill's belly and shook it. "Not much jiggle here. How do you drink beer and eat cake and stay thin?"

"I'll give you the Jill Henry keys to fitness. Never take an elevator if you can take the stairs, never drive if you can walk, and only eat high calorie things when they're really delicious."

"Words to live by." She pulled Jill up, sat very close, and turned her phone around. "I want a picture of us together. One we can show our kids when we tell them about the first time you kissed me."

Jill had a feeling her fantasy family would laugh their butts off when they looked at the photo of her, mouth agape, with Lizzie's head tilted close, grinning maniacally.

❧

They would have been locked in if they'd parked in the lot, so Lizzie's prescience paid off. The sun was almost fully set, and Jill had to fight to keep her feet under her on the walk down the darkening path, but they reached the car, their bodies intact, just as it got dark.

"We're going to have to scramble for cake," Jill said. "Don't even think I've forgotten."

"You don't need dinner?" Lizzie started her silent car as they put their seat belts on.

"I'll accept dinner if I can't have cake. But I'd rather have cake and skip the foreplay."

"Coming right up," Lizzie said, grinning at her, but not commenting on the sexual innuendo.

They drove for just a few minutes, reaching Lizzie's neighborhood to search for a spot at the charging station. "One day, in the distant future, I'd love to have a driveway," she sighed. "With a big old 240-volt charger." Luckily, they were one of the first cars to return from their travels, and Lizzie hooked the car up and patted it as they walked away.

"I think you should name her Sparky," Jill said, giving the little car some thoughtful consideration.

"Sparky, huh? I don't hate it. Let me chew that over for a while. I'm not used to naming cars." She laughed softly. "Given this is my first car, that's kind of a dumb thing to say."

Jill carried the bag while Lizzie got her keys out. The outer door didn't have a lock, and she had to jiggle the key in the second door to get it to open. It was an old door, probably original, with glass filling the upper half. As she closed it, Jill noticed the inside lock turned to open.

"What's to stop someone from breaking the glass and walking right in?" she asked.

"Thanks. I'll think of you when I'm cowering in my bed tonight." Lizzie grasped Jill by the sleeve and pulled her forward to walk in front. "I have one more door to stop the mad killer. I just have to hope he's not very strong."

They climbed the narrow, seriously out-of-plumb stairs, with room for only one of them at a time. Lizzie put her key into a lock of a door that couldn't possibly have been up to code. It was not only not a fire door, Jill was fairly certain it was a regular hollow interior one. It could have been kicked in, easily, and a child could have jimmied the lock with a credit card. They entered and Jill waited for her eyes to adjust to the dim light from the hallway.

"Remember when I said I'd had some sketchy apartments?" she asked.

"I know it's a dump. But it's cheap." Lizzie switched on an overhead light, which cast harsh, unattractive shadows over the small space. "Well, not that cheap. A third of my take-home pay."

Lizzie had a nice enough sofa, along with a biggish TV and a couple of lamps in the living room. "I could give you the provenance of everything, but to save time let's just say it's nice to have a bunch of older sibs who give you their cast-offs."

"It's nice," Jill said. "Very cozy."

"Wait… There's more," she said, with her eyebrows popping up and down. They stood at the doorway of the bedroom, a tragic sight. Half of it contained a full-sized bed, while the other half held a dorm-style, under-counter refrigerator, even though there was no counter, and a two-burner cooktop atop the sole cabinet. "Welcome to my bitchen. The bedroom/kitchen combo is perfect for the person who wants to grab a bite while lying in bed."

Jill met her eyes, but could only make herself comment about one thing. "The flowers look nice there."

Lizzie had put her birthday flowers on the shelf right over the head of the bed. If Jill had a shelf in that position, she'd hit her head every time she got up, but Lizzie must have been more careful.

"I dreamed I was out in a beautiful field, with flowers surrounding me," she admitted, smiling contentedly. "I must have been smelling them all night."

Turning slightly, they were in front of a dismal bath, with a plastic enclosure around a rusty tub, the room illuminated by a light that couldn't have had more than a twenty-five watt bulb in it. Jill met Lizzie's eyes at the end of the brief tour. "You've gotta move."

"I'm looking. My lease is up in October, and that's one of the reasons I didn't want Chase or Mason or whichever one of them knows how to do electrical work to bother putting a new light in the bathroom. Besides the fact I didn't want to have sex with him," she added, pointing at Jill menacingly. "Go sit down. I'll deliver your cake."

"You actually have cake? I thought you were teasing me."

"I don't lie about anything important, Jill," she said, letting her mouth curl into a grin. "And cake is important."

Jill went into the living room and switched on the lamps, turning off the harsh overhead light. It honestly wasn't a bad room, very small, but neat and sparingly decorated. She might have been happy there when she was Lizzie's age, but she hated to see someone she cared about in a place that seemed so easy to break into, as well as a fire hazard. With that thin wooden door, a fire could easily breach the interior, and with no fire escape…

Her concern about fire grew when Lizzie carried a cake, candles blazing, into the room. She sang "Happy Birthday" with a sweet, confident voice, leaning over to kiss Jill's cheek as she finished. "I hope you have a fantastic birthday," she said, sitting next to her on the sofa.

The cake was obviously homemade, but it was so skillfully executed, only the lettering on the top gave it away. *Nooooo!* it read. Jill laughed, nodding her head. "That's about it."

"Forty looks very good on you," Lizzie said, scooting closer.

Jill leaned over, made a wish, and blew the candles out, managing to keep the darned things from turning the whole place into an inferno. "This is one fantastic looking cake. Don't tell me you got up and made this today." She blinked. "You don't have an oven."

"My neighbor on the ground floor lets me use hers. I was a little tipsy when I was making it, so I can't guarantee how it'll taste. But I enjoyed doing it. I was singing away, really entertaining myself."

"Thanks so much," Jill said, turning to smile at her. "I really do appreciate this."

"I wanted to make sure you had good cake. Mary Beth and Kathleen sent me an invitation to your party tomorrow, but I've got an event at work I can't get out of. And even though they seem like nice people, I can't tell if they're trustworthy cake providers."

"They're trustworthy in that they don't try to cook anything complex. But they know how to go to a good bakery." She picked the candles from a quarter of the cake and cut very generous slices for each of them. Digging in with her fork, she moaned in pleasure. "I've had double chocolate, but this tastes like triple. Fantastic," she said. Jill leaned over and kissed Lizzie on the cheek. Then it dawned on her that Lizzie had been one hundred percent true to her word. She hadn't tried to convince Jill to kiss her again, or even bring up the topic of intimacy. *Really nice.* A woman who kept her word raised her attractiveness level significantly, and Lizzie's was already darned high.

Jill managed two slices, each bigger than most people would ever accept.

"I love a woman who isn't afraid to eat dessert," Lizzie said, as she curled her legs up under herself like a cat and leaned against the back of the sofa. "You're not even skittish, much less afraid."

"I love dessert. But only good ones. If this had been one of those cakes where the frosting tastes like oil…" She made a face. "I'd move it around on my plate, but I wouldn't eat more than the minimum required to be polite." She pointed at the cake, now missing a third. "That wasn't politeness."

"I didn't get any yesterday, but since this is my birthday weekend, I'm satisfied."

"I hope you're having as good a weekend as I am," Jill said, her heart swelling with tenderness. Lizzie could bring out the most surprising feelings, just by looking at Jill in a certain way. Those eyes seemed to reach inside to *see* her feelings, a sensation Jill was going to have to get used to.

"I'm having an epic weekend. If I kept a diary, today would get a couple of pages."

Jill let out a sigh. "I should get going, but I hate to have you unplug your car. Maybe I'll call a cab. Or I could walk. It's not very far."

"Don't be silly." She grasped a hank of Jill's hair and tugged on it. "I'm happy to take you."

They went down the rickety stairs, and walked along the quiet street to the car. Jill only lived about a mile away, and traffic was light since Lizzie avoided the major streets that intersected the big pedestrian mall downtown. When she pulled into the driveway, she turned to smile at Jill. "I hope you have a fantastic party tomorrow."

"How late do you have to work?"

"I'm hosting a brunch. It'll probably be over by four, but I have to stay and make sure everything's cleaned up right. I might make it home by six."

"Text me if you want to stop by. The party starts at two, but we should still be going by six."

"Will do." Lizzie didn't make a move for a kiss. She didn't even lean in. She just sat there, expectantly.

Jill couldn't stop herself. Those lips needed to be kissed again. In the blink of an eye, her hands were in Lizzie's hair, pulling her close for a long, tender kiss. As Lizzie sighed, her breasts pressed into Jill's chest, making her body tingle with sensation. Jill was in deep. So very, very deep.

Chapter Ten

IT WAS SO NICE HAVING your birthday in August. A bunch of friends huddling inside on a snowy day was fine for Thanksgiving or Christmas, but Jill loved summer so much she felt blessed to not only be able to be outdoors, but to have as big a guest list as she liked, not constrained by the number of people who'd fit inside.

Mary Beth, Kathleen, and Gerri were hosting, and they'd invited nearly everyone Jill knew. Their yard was big, but even at that, people were bunched up pretty close together.

Jill had a tough time being the guest, even on her own birthday, and she'd taken on the role of making sure everyone had something to drink. She stood on the back porch and looked out at the crowd, amazed that so many people had given up their Sunday to celebrate with her. This was her family of choice. A few were very close friends, closer than blood relatives; another circle was close, but not people she shared emotionally delicate topics with; and the last group were work friends—people she liked to socialize with, but not go much deeper. Each ring of the circle was larger, which made sense.

They were just about to eat, and she was tempted to count the guests, just for fun. But that seemed a little greedy. It was better to enjoy the event, rather than quantify it.

Briefly, she thought of her parents. Her dad wouldn't recall that this was her actual birthday. He'd know she'd been born in the summer, during a bad heat wave, but he wasn't the kind of guy who sweated the details. The next time she saw him he'd ask about her day, and that would be that.

Her mother would know the details. To the minute. Jill imagined she'd spend the day thinking, occasionally, of the ordeal, as she called it. Jill had been tempted to try and get her medical records from the hospital to see if they'd noted the circumference of her head. She had her doubts that she had the biggest one in the history of Brattleboro Memorial.

One thing she didn't doubt was that she wouldn't get a phone call from her mother. Once, when Jill had asked why she hadn't at least called on her birthday, her mom had brushed the question off, saying that Jill had so many friends she was never home. There was some truth to that, of course, but she honestly couldn't hazard a guess as to why she never heard from her parents. That was a mystery that would have to go unanswered. She just considered herself very lucky to have friends who truly cared about her. They made up for an awful lot.

Carly exited the house and came to stand next to Jill. She draped an arm around her shoulders and leaned her head close. "Nice party, huh?"

"Really nice. I'm living a pretty charmed life to have this many people show up."

"I'll admit you're charming, but people like being your friend because you're a good friend in return. Now we have to get you a girlfriend."

Jill turned to her and smiled. "Oh, we do, do we?"

"We do. Samantha and I are going to take over. You're not working hard enough."

"I appreciate that. I do," Jill said, "but I think I'm doing okay. You don't have to start hiring escorts yet."

"We weren't going to hire escorts," she said, standing tall and giving Jill a gentle push. "First, we're too cheap, and second, it's going to be easy. I was going to bring someone today, a real hottie from the gym, but Samantha talked me out of it."

Jill put a hand on her shoulder and looked into her eyes. "Check with me first. Please. I hate surprises. Especially blind dates."

"That's what Samantha said," Carly said, frowning. "I hate when she's right."

"Trust her. In this area at least, trust her."

⸎

They were down to the core group by six. The usual suspects who always stayed to clean up and put the house and yard back together. Ben and Gerri were cleaning the kitchen, and Carly had joined them after Jill's usual participation had been denied.

She was outside, picking up plastic cups and dropped napkins when her cell phone chirped. "Everyone you know is either here, or just left," Kathleen joked. "It must be a wrong number."

"Probably." Jill fished the phone from her shorts and smiled when she saw a text from Lizzie.

"I can be there in a half hour if the party's still on."

Jill's finger hovered over the keyboard for a little while, thoughts meandering through her consciousness. Finally, she replied. "We're wrapping it up, but come by anyway. We usually do a review."

"??"

"You'll see. Got the address?"

"Got it. See you."

After sliding the phone back into her pocket, Jill continued policing the area, finding she had a new bounce to her step. Karen, always attuned to changes in mood, caught up with her as she dumped the stuff she'd picked up into the proper recycling bin. "It's still early," she said. "Early enough to…oh, I don't know…maybe meet up with a friend?"

"All of my friends were here," Jill said, smirking at the obvious, though unspoken, question.

"Not all of them." She grasped Jill's earlobe and gave it a tug. "Come on and spill it. You've got a sly grin that won't quit."

"Lizzie's coming by. I said we usually do a play-by-play after a party. She can hear what happened without having to watch Skip and Alice start yelling so loudly the neighbors come over to see if they should call the cops."

"Oh, that was fun," Karen said, rolling her eyes. "I'm going to try to get one of them alone and attempt to lead them to some counseling. It's getting uncomfortable for us, so it's got to be worse for Aaron."

"Good luck with that. They seem remarkably impervious to how other people view them."

"True. But I know they don't want to screw Aaron up. I'll work on that angle."

"Thank god I only work with numbers," Jill said. "I love knowing that there's a right answer and a wrong answer. Having to deal with emotions all day would drive me loony."

"And I can't balance my checkbook. We all have different skills."

"You still have a checkbook? We're well into the twenty-first century, Karen. It's time to get with the program!"

⤬

Lizzie entered the backyard just a few minutes after the little group gathered around the big picnic table. Jill, Karen, Becky, Mary Beth, Kathleen and Gerri had just begun to dissect what had caused the increase in Skip and Alice's fighting, and if it was a temporary blip or something more serious.

Jill had been waiting anxiously, flinching each time an unexpected noise sounded. When she saw Lizzie, she jumped up and walked over to welcome her. Everyone at the party had worn typical summer backyard attire; shorts, cotton shirts or T-shirts. A few people wore running shoes, but most had gone for sandals. Lizzie definitely looked like she'd come to the wrong party. A dark blue print wrap dress showed off the curves Jill had been thinking about ever since she'd seen them the day before. Lizzie also wore sandals, but hers had three inch heels. Her nails were painted a summery pink, and Jill realized she'd never found herself staring at a woman's feet before. But the combination of the sexy shoes and the painted nails had thrown her off stride.

"You look nice," she said, not exactly the mistress of charm.

"Thanks. So do you." She plucked at the collar of the sleeveless linen shirt Jill wore. "More blue. Are you sure you're not in the Navy?"

"Pretty sure." They were standing close to the driveway, and Jill realized they'd been there long enough. With any other friend she'd just say hi and lead them over to the group. "Do you remember everyone?"

"I think so," she said quietly. "Becky, Gerri, Mary Beth, Karen and Kathleen. Right?"

"Perfect," Jill said, beaming. "You really pay attention."

"Part of my job. You look like a real dope if you can't recall names." She lowered her voice even more. "They're staring at us. Shouldn't we go over there?"

"Oh, yeah. Right." She led the way, saying, "Look who got all dressed up for my party."

Everyone spent a few minutes welcoming her and commenting on how nice she looked. Then Kathleen said, "Have you eaten, Lizzie? We've got a ton of food. Let me make you up a plate."

"I will," Jill said, jumping up like she'd been pinched.

"I guess I could eat a bite or two," Lizzie said, gazing up at Jill with a sweet smile. "But don't go to any trouble."

"You eat everything, right?"

"Uh-huh. I don't like cilantro or Brussels sprouts. Other than that, I'm up for anything."

Jill went into the house and started rooting around in the refrigerator. Some chicken, maybe some potato salad…

Suddenly, Karen was standing next to her. "You're acting like Presley and Trent and Aaron did the last time Lizzie was with the group. Chill out, girl. If you act like a teenaged boy, you'll zoom to the top of the chat list."

"Oh, crap," she said, putting a few bowls on the counter. "I was trying to be cool."

"You failed," Karen teased. "But I'm not sure anyone else noticed. Just slow down and treat her like everyone else."

"But she's not like everyone else," Jill whined. "Did you see how pretty she looks? She's been at work all day, but her lipstick's perfect, her eye makeup looks like she did it two minutes ago, and no one would believe she didn't have a stylist touching her hair up as she walked around the corner."

"She probably sat in the car and touched everything up," Karen said, as if that should be obvious. "She's trying to make a good impression, Jill. And I'd say she's succeeding."

Jill looked at her carefully. "You really think she's trying to make herself look better just for me?"

"She's not doing it for us, so…yeah. Is that so hard to believe?"

"No, I guess not. I've just never dated a woman who wore dresses, or sexy shoes or makeup. I'm not sure why, but I really like it."

Karen put a hand on her shoulder and gave it a squeeze. "You like it because it shows she's into you. You'd like it just as well if she knocked the dirt off her work boots, or wore a nice tie. You've got a major crush,

Jill. And if you don't want people to know yet—chill out. But if you do—go grin at her like you did when she walked in, and your secret will be revealed."

"No grins," Jill said. "I'll throw some food at her and go sit on the other side of the table."

"Smart tactic. You're really good at this."

"I know I'm not," she admitted. "But I don't want to screw this up."

"You won't," Karen assured her. "She looks at you in the same goofy way. Now go out there and try to be normal."

"Easier said than done," Jill groused as she put the leftovers away and tried to figure out how to deliver Lizzie's food without fawning over her. Not an easy task at all.

Jill almost took a tumble off the back steps when she gave half of her attention to Lizzie and only half to her feet. "Look out, Grace," Lizzie teased, looking up to gently touch Jill's leg as she placed the plate in front of her.

"Now that I'm old, I probably need bifocals," Jill said, moving down the table to the empty spot.

It was nice to have Lizzie drop in, knowing almost no one, and not seem bothered by Jill sitting a few seats away. Some of her previous girlfriends needed her near, even after hanging out with the group a dozen times.

They'd stopped dissecting the party, with the focus now on Lizzie and her job. No one had gotten the chance to question her much during the weekend at the cabin, and they were making up for that now.

"So you're in charge of keeping Hollyhock Hills up and running," Gerri said.

Jill had never seen Gerri with a date, or heard her express the desire for one. But she was sitting up straight, her full attention on Lizzie, lingering on her words like she'd come down from the mountaintop to deliver them. *Jesus!* You add a nice-looking newcomer to the mix, and all hell breaks loose.

"Not really," Lizzie said as she speared some potato salad with her fork. "We have a development director, then a manager, then two associates, and two assistants. I'm the senior associate, which only means I was hired before my coworker. I'm a long way down the chain."

Jill watched her talk, enthralled. She looked older, much more poised, more professional. That might have been because she was still dressed in her work attire, or maybe because she was still in work-mode. Either way, she seemed like a peer to these professional women, most of them in their fifties. That was a big relief. Jill hadn't realized she'd been worried about this, but now she understood it was important to her that Lizzie not be looked at like the kid who watched your house when you were on vacation, or the person who'd keep the children entertained while the adults had real conversations. She had to admit the truth. She wanted Lizzie to fit in, because she wanted to see her sitting at the end of the table for a while—a good, long while.

Jill and Gerri hefted the picnic table up to put it back in its usual place. It was nearly dark, and the mosquitoes had gotten too annoying to ignore any longer. Her phone buzzed, and she pulled it out to take a look. Lizzie, who was inside, had texted, "Your cake sucked. I know where you can get a good one. Meet me at my apartment?"

Smirking, Jill wrote back. "I was going to ask if you didn't. Mouth watering."

They all said their goodbyes, with Jill and Lizzie the last to take off. Jill hugged her hosts, adding kisses to their cheeks, then Lizzie shook hands. Jill could tell no one was sure how friendly to be. These women were usually the hug-and-kiss type, but they were a little more formal around Lizzie. Probably because they couldn't quite figure out where she stood with Jill. But they'd find out soon. She could feel this relationship starting to pick up momentum, and was almost sure she couldn't stop it even if she wanted to.

As they walked down the drive, Jill stopped at her car, poised near the sidewalk. "I guarantee all three of my hosts are watching."

"Let's give them something to talk about," Lizzie said, stepping forward. Jill gasped, then Lizzie stuck out her hand and shook Jill's. A hand went to her shoulder, giving it a fond, avuncular squeeze. "See you around," she said, looking surprisingly somber. Then she started to walk down the street to her car, while Jill tried not to let her gaze trail after her like a hungry dog.

❦

Lizzie was waiting on the small front porch of her apartment building. Jill jogged the last fifty feet, then leapt up to the landing, depositing herself right next to Lizzie. "I've still got some spring in my step."

"And a few screws loose." Lizzie reached out and swept Jill's hair off her shoulder, a tender touch that made her heart skip a beat. "I didn't neaten up my apartment before I left, so try not to judge."

"I'm not judgmental about neatness." She laughed. "Total lie. But I'll keep my judgment to myself. That's almost as good, isn't it?"

"I'll accept it." After they climbed the rickety stairs and went inside, Lizzie immediately went to open every window. "I have to keep the windows closed when I'm gone, so it gets stifling in here."

"Why do you have to close them?"

"The guys downstairs are always out in the back, smoking something, and it comes right inside. When I'm home, I can put a fan in the window, but I'm not going to let one run while I'm gone. I paid attention when the Sugar Hill Fire Department came to school to lecture us about fire safety."

"Do you want to change clothes? I can get the cake."

"Yeah, if you don't mind." She started for her self-proclaimed bitchen, then said, "Is it okay if I put my pajamas on?"

"Uhm…" She felt a zing start at her hands and work its way up her arms and down her body. "Sure. Whatever. Be comfortable."

"It's too hot to put jeans on, and I don't own a pair of shorts." She was still talking when she took some clothes from what should have been a pantry, then moved to the bathroom and partially closed the door. "I should get some shorts, but I hate to spend my money on play clothes. I've got to have a lot of stuff for work—nice stuff. People don't want to give you money if you look like you need it."

Jill ignored the cereal bowl and glass sitting in the sink, having to exert extra energy to banish from her mind the fact that the glass had soda in it. What kind of animal drank soda for breakfast? But all of her dark thoughts vanished when Lizzie walked back into the bitchen, put a hand on Jill's back, leaned around her, stuck a finger into the frosting and popped it into her mouth. "I thought your friends knew how to find a good bakery."

"They do, but I think they reconsidered when they realized how many cakes they'd have to buy to feed that crowd. Not that I blame them. A couple of big sheet cakes from the grocery store costs a quarter of what a fancy one would."

"They should have made cookies," Lizzie said. "Or brownies. There's no excuse for bad cake."

Jill turned to present her with a plate, almost dropping it when she saw her "pajamas." Sexy underwear was a much better term for it, and Jill was pretty sure she was now ready to move to Florida, dragging Lizzie along with her. This woman should never live anywhere that required flannel or wool. She was made for a silky camisole and some kind of clingy shorts that probably had a name. Other than smoking hot.

"Nice pajamas," she said, managing what she hoped was a normal smile.

"Oh," she said, grasping the hem of the camisole and tugging on it. "I don't have summer pajamas. I had to put on some of my regular underwear."

There was nothing regular about that underwear. Jill wanted to get to the living room, but she was afraid her knees would buckle. She thought she had a better chance of making it if she went quickly, so she dashed across the tiny bitchen, seeking the stability of the sofa. Dropping onto the piece without a hint of grace, she moaned in dismay when Lizzie leaned over to pick up a roll of foil. Jill had noticed before how she bent like a dancer, from the waist, with her trailing leg kicking out behind her for balance. The peach-colored garment outlined her delectable ass so clearly, Jill had to look away. It just wasn't right to ogle a woman like she desperately wanted to.

Lizzie walked over to the sofa, carrying her cake. She folded herself into a yoga-like pose as she settled close to Jill, facing her.

"Did you take a lot of dance lessons?" Jill managed. "You move like a ballerina."

"Uh-huh," she said, separating a large portion of the slice and spearing it with her fork. She eased the bite into her small mouth, then gave Jill a satisfied smile. "Don't you love taking a *huge* first bite of something scrumptious? If I could get away with it, I'd eat with my hands and tear off a piece big enough to fill my mouth."

"I won't tell," Jill said, suddenly needing to see Lizzie pick up the cake, ease it into her mouth and suck the frosting from her fingers. Where was this crazy stuff coming from? She hated bad table manners!

"I can behave," she insisted. "But it's more fun not to."

"Dancing," Jill said, feeling like she needed a punch to get her brain to track well enough to have a conversation. "When did you take lessons?"

"For a long time. Grade school. High school. College. A few things here and there since." She took another bite, this one much more moderate. "When I and all of my artsy friends were deciding whether we'd be great novelists or poets or painters, I thought dance was my ticket to fame." She let out a laugh. "Nearly every one of us is stuck in a cubicle somewhere."

"You danced in college?"

"Uh-huh. Just fooling around. Nothing too serious."

"But you took classes?"

"Uh-huh." She slipped another bite of cake into her mouth. "I minored in it."

Jill's mouth dropped open. "That's more than fooling around!"

"No, it's not," she said, shaking her head. "Minors are for subjects you like, but know you can't do much with." A laugh bubbled up. "Of course, that's true of my art history major too."

"I had no idea you were so artsy," Jill said, having trouble imagining the Lizzie she knew with the woman she'd become.

"That's because you didn't know me," she said, blithely. "But you have your chance now." She took the last bite, turned her fork around and placed it in Jill's mouth when she opened it. "An extra present for your birthday."

Jill leaned forward. "Know what I'd really like as a present?"

"Uh-huh." Lizzie's breath was warm and chocolaty sweet, and a slight smile curled her beautiful lips. "You're embarrassingly transparent."

Jill took the plate from her hands and placed it on the floor. Then she put a hand behind her waist and pulled her close. Not as close as she would have liked. If she'd had Lizzie's almost bare body pressed against her she knew she'd lose her mind. Instead, she pulled her just close enough to be able to merge their lips, sucking in a breath as they did.

Lizzie's hands were soon tangled in her hair, fingers roaming up and down Jill's scalp, sending a riot of tingles through her body. Sensation flooded her; every sense sharing in the pleasure. Pure, unadulterated pleasure. The best of all birthday gifts.

They slowly broke apart, with Lizzie swaying slightly, eyes closed, clearly wanting more.

Jill's breath was ragged as she forced herself to keep her distance. "When can I see you again?" she whispered.

Those pretty eyes blinked slowly. "Any time you want," she said, her voice so sexy Jill had to wrestle with her conscience to keep her hands to herself.

"I've got…something…" She stopped and took in a long, calming breath. "I can't remember my schedule." She took out her phone and looked at her calendar. "Wednesday?"

"Perfect. Come here? Go out?"

"Come to my house. The boys miss you." She wrapped her in a hug, then realized she'd done just what she'd been avoiding. Lizzie's nearly bare body was so unbelievably alluring she moved away in a second, unwilling to let herself get carried away.

"I hope you had a very happy birthday," Lizzie said, placing one more brief kiss on Jill's lips. "I think the Jill and Lizzie Weekend was a very big success."

"I do too." She got to her feet, shakily. "See you Wednesday." She reached the door before Lizzie got up and scampered down the stairs. It felt like Lizzie was a great big magnet, and she was a sliver of metal, unable to resist her powerful pull. She had to keep a little distance until she got comfortable with the whole thing. She laughed to herself as she walked towards her car. It was only a matter of time until she gave up the fight and was pulled right into her magnetic embrace.

On Wednesday, Jill was in the backyard, tending the grill, when Lizzie appeared on the driveway.

"Hey there," she called out as she opened the gate and came across the grass.

Once again, she was dressed for work. She'd obviously expended a lot of time finding dresses that made her look professional, sophisticated, yet still a little playful. A very nice combination.

Jill stuck an arm out, and Lizzie moved right into her embrace.

"I could get used to this," she said, tilting her chin to kiss Jill's cheek. "Coming home from work, having a gorgeous woman cooking for me." She turned her head to look at the grill. "Mmm, I love barbecued chicken."

"I cook outside every night it's not raining or snowing," Jill said, only partially teasing. "The saddest day of the year for me is when I cover the grill and store it in the garage."

"You don't like anything about winter?" Lizzie patted her side as she pulled away.

"Oh, yeah, I like winter a lot. But I *love* summer."

"We'll have to think of something to do to make winter more appealing. I've got a few ideas…" She gave Jill a frankly sexual look, then walked to the back porch. "Mind if I get myself a drink?"

"Go for it. I've got three or four kinds of beer, and some wine."

"Beer and barbecue's the perfect combo. Be right back."

Jill watched her go, so intent on her musings she missed the hot spot that had developed and had to rush to move things around.

Lizzie came back out and stood by her. "You look like you know what you're doing."

"I do. I spent a lot of time with your dad, watching his technique."

177

A delighted smile curled her lips. "My dad? Really?"

"Yeah. He was always willing to teach—even outside of school."

"He's a good guy," Lizzie said. "A really good guy." Her expression darkened. "I'd give anything to go back in time and have him choose not to smoke."

"Me too. I wish there was a way to cure him."

"There's not," Lizzie said, sounding as pragmatic as her mother. "We just have to enjoy having him with us for as long as he stays."

They stood together for a few minutes, each lost in her own private thoughts. Finally, Jill said, "I'm very glad you invited me to go to the baseball game. He probably doesn't remember this, but your dad was one of the chaperones at the first Sox game I ever went to."

"When you were in grade school?"

"I think it was eighth grade. Some school-sponsored thing. If you made straight A's in fall term you got to go to a game. It was cool," she said, remembering the singing and goofing around on the long bus trip.

"He was with you at your first," Lizzie said quietly. "I hope we're not taking him to his last."

Her chin quivered as tears started to roll down her cheeks. Jill wrapped her in a hug, offering what comfort she could. "He's got a lot of life in him yet. It won't be the last. Promise."

Lizzie's body shivered, then she pulled away and went into the house. She emerged a minute later, dabbing at her eyes with a tissue. Her voice trembled as she spoke. "I wish you could promise that and have it be true. But no one knows how much time he's got left. A bad infection could cut him down with no warning."

"I know," Jill said, grasping her hand and pulling her close for another hug. "All we have is hope, and I've got a lot of it."

Lizzie's body shivered again, and she pulled away to head back to the porch. "Can I set the table?"

"Sure. I'd like to eat out here, if that's good for you."

"It is. Be right back."

Jill concentrated on her cooking, but was unable to stop thinking of Mike, and how attached Lizzie was to him. Sometimes she had to admit there was a benefit to having a distant relationship with her parents. It wasn't much, but it was the only one she could think of.

❧

The mosquitoes came out in force by the time they were finishing dinner, so they picked up their plates and dashed into the house, just missing being dive-bombed by an intrepid one on a mission.

"Mosquitoes are the only thing I don't like about summer," Jill said.

"They don't bite me often. If there's no one else around, one will force himself to take a hit, but I'm always the last choice."

"Lucky devil." Jill stood at the sink, rinsing plates and bowls, while Lizzie quickly loaded them into the dishwasher. She didn't do it like Jill would, but having her jump in to help like she was part of the team was really nice. Jill could use the practice in letting go of details.

Once the kitchen was clean, they went into the den. Lizzie brought a pair of fresh beers, while Jill turned on the television and found the Sox playing the Angels. She sat next to Lizzie and her arm naturally draped itself around her shoulders.

"Now you're talking," Lizzie said, moving even closer. "Barbecue, beer, baseball and a...butch babe." She snickered at Jill's surprised expression. "No, you're not very butch, but I was going for alliteration."

"I could butch it up for you," Jill said. "I think."

"I'm very happy with you just the way you are. You're butcher than the women I've been with, but that's probably because most of them were trying to appeal to guys." She turned and took a long look. "I'd say you're the perfect proportion of butch. Just enough for lesbians to guess you were gay, but not enough for strangers on the street to call you out."

"That's never happened," Jill admitted. "I don't think I'd handle that well."

"How about me? Am I butch enough for you?" She batted her eyes. Jill noticed her understated eye makeup and what was probably blush on her cheeks.

"You're the least butch woman I've ever been attracted to," Jill said. "But, given how attracted I am, maybe I've been barking up the wrong tree."

"I'm not sure how I'd look if I didn't have to dress up for work. If I worked in Mark's blacksmith shop, I might turn into the butchiest woman you've ever been with."

"I think I'd still like you," Jill said, narrowing her eyes as she tried to imagine Lizzie in flannel and jeans with hammer loops. Still cute.

Lizzie took Jill's hand, placed it on her lap, and played with it, drawing her finger down the tendons and veins. She seemed to be pondering something. Finally, she said, "I don't feel one way or the other inside. I like some really girly things—"

"Like those so-called pajamas," Jill supplied.

"Yeah," she agreed, smirking. "But I like to put on long underwear and a flannel shirt and jeans and chop wood too. I *love* work boots," she added. "Don't know why, but I find them super sexy."

"Come work on the yard with me this weekend, and I'll wear mine." Jill laughed. "Quite a come-on, huh?"

"It is for me. Saturday morning?"

"Perfect."

"I'll bring Danish."

"Even more perfect. I hate apricot and prune."

"Everyone does," she said, laughing.

"It feels like we're dating," Jill said. "What did I do with all of my anxieties?"

"You know you can trust me."

Lizzie looked into her eyes, and Jill found herself agreeing completely. That was it. She knew she could trust her. "Yeah," she said, softly. "This might not work out, but not because you were a jerk or you tried to screw with me."

"I never would," she said solemnly. "And I think this is going to work out just fine. I'm brimming with confidence."

"I'm…" She tried to think of the right word. "Cautiously confident. If you hadn't been so into guys, I'd be brimming too. But I'm just not sure you're going to be able to give them up."

There. She said it. It had been banging around in her head, and Lizzie deserved to know what was stopping her from jumping in with both feet.

"Mmm." She nodded, but didn't speak for a long time. "I guess it will all come down to whether or not you believe I know my own mind."

"That's it? Really? You think this is something you can know right now?"

"Uh-huh." She nodded, her innocent gaze hitting Jill right in the gut. "I'm really, really into you, Jill. You're just what I've been looking for. Why would I long for a man if I had everything I needed?"

"I don't know, Lizzie. But you needed a woman when you were happy with a man. What's the difference?"

She sat up straight, knocking Jill's arm from her shoulders. "Were you listening to me?"

"I heard you say—"

"I'll say it again," she said slowly, her eyes flashing with anger. "I'm *primarily* attracted to women, but I can easily be with the right guy. I've found, through trial and error, that even the best guy isn't quite enough. I could be faithful, but I'd still long for a woman's touch. I don't think the opposite's going to happen," she said, her voice growing stronger. Suddenly, she sank down in her seat, all of the fire snuffed out. "But I need a good physical connection. I'm not going to lie. Sex is important to me."

"It is to me too, Lizzie. I like having a partner, but giving up my freedom isn't worth it if I don't get that extra boost that I get from sex."

"Yeah," she said, nodding. "That's it. Being in a relationship can be a pain in the butt."

"Especially the way you do it," Jill said, deadpan.

It took Lizzie a second, then she laughed and slapped at her. "I'm never going to live that down, am I?"

"I don't think so," she admitted. "My jaw almost hit the floor. I dread the thought of telling Scott if we get together. He's going to assume…"

"He's going to assume you're having a very good time in bed. And he's going to be right. Nothing you've done has made me doubt my instinct. And that's that we're going to be a very, very good pair."

"I'm willing to move forward," Jill said, wincing at how businesslike that sounded. "But I want you to come out to your parents first. They need to know you like women too."

"Hmm. I've been trying to figure out how to finesse this. I was thinking I'd just tell them I'm a lesbian. I think it's easier for people to see things in black and white."

"But you're not," Jill said. "They know you've been with men. I can't believe your mom will think you did that just to waste time."

Lizzie moved away and leaned against the opposite arm of the sofa. She took a drink of her beer, then glanced at the game. "We're getting our butts kicked," she groused. Finally, taking in a deep breath, she said, "I'll think of how to do it. But I'm leaning towards the lesbian angle. Trust me," she said soberly. "People don't get the concept of bisexuality."

"That was true for gay people for a zillion years, Lizzie. People don't like difference. But if every bisexual came out…"

"Yeah, yeah, I know. But that's not going to happen, and I can't wait for society to catch up." She reached out and took Jill's hand. "But one way or the other, I'll talk to my family. They'll either know I like men and women, or just women. Either way, I won't talk about you—yet."

"All right. Do whatever you think is best. And until then, we'll just take things slow. Cool?"

"No. But I'm not going to press you. I can be patient when I'm after something I want"—she moved over until they were nose to nose—"and I want you."

Chapter Eleven

ON FRIDAY NIGHT, JILL was scheduled to host bridge, having switched places with Skip and Alice, who were having their living room painted.

She rushed home from work to make dinner for herself, and snacks for her friends. One of the smartest things they'd done was not make dinner part of the deal. It was hard enough to have enough snacks for eight, without resorting to potato chips and pre-made dip. Not that there was anything wrong with taking the easy way out. Almost everyone else did. But Jill didn't like to have junk food around the house. It was too tempting to finish it off after her guests left.

Tonight she made hummus and tabouli, and set it out in colorful bowls with some strips of pita bread. The boys were not interested in either snack, so she didn't have to watch it carefully. They knew company was coming, and were appropriately skittish, but they hung around until the very last minute—hoping she'd have a bout of memory loss and would put out patè like she did the night that would live on in infamy. Tonight, she kept her wits about her and the boys disappeared when the bell rang.

Becky and Karen were right on time, with Skip and Alice flashing their lights as they pulled into the driveway. They were just getting drinks lined up when there was a quick knock at the door. Jill yelled out, "Come on in," and Kathleen and Mary Beth entered, accompanied by...not Gerri.

Jill walked to the front door to greet them, slowing down and staring when she saw an attractive blonde woman smiling at her. "Hi," Jill said, knowing she looked puzzled.

"Gerri couldn't make it," Kathleen said, "so we invited Elizabeth. Have you two met?"

"No, should we have?" Jill felt like she was missing something.

"Elizabeth's at the U," Kathleen said. "I thought maybe you'd run into each other."

"You're not in admin, are you?" Jill asked.

"I'm at the medical center," she said, giving Kathleen a funny look. "You don't visit the pediatrics department very often, do you?"

"It's been a while," Jill said. "Well, even though I'll probably never run into you at work, I'm glad you're able to join us. Come on in, and I'll introduce you to the gang."

Elizabeth started down the hall, and as Jill turned, she caught sight of Kathleen, giving her a big grin and a thumb's up sign. *Oh, brother! No one had mentioned an eligible candidate until Lizzie appeared. Now everyone had someone they wanted to push on her?*

Through Kathleen's conniving, Jill was paired with Elizabeth. Jill wasn't angry—exactly. But she certainly wasn't happy. Her friends knew she wasn't a fan of surprises. And bringing a woman to her house for their card game wasn't playing fair. But Jill had to be kind to poor Elizabeth. She might not have even known she was being fixed up.

Elizabeth was a good player, better than Gerri, actually. But winning wasn't the big goal for this group, and Jill would have much rather been getting slammed with Gerri as her partner than winning with a stranger. Especially this particular stranger who Skip kept trying to impress. At least there was one benefit to having Elizabeth join them. Skip was more focused on being charming than he was on picking at his wife.

After another rubber, Jill went to freshen the dip, and found Elizabeth entering the kitchen right behind her. Mmm, she knew she was being fixed up. No doubt. She leaned against the counter, watching Jill work. "Do you ever get over to the medical center?" she asked. "I'm usually swamped, but I try to make time for lunch."

"Not really," Jill said, honestly. "You know how it is, you hate to waste a lot of time walking across campus. I bet you never come over to my neck of the woods."

"Hardly ever," she agreed. "So…maybe we should meet for a drink some night."

Oh, lord. "Uhm…I've got a lot going on right now. But…let me take your number. If I can make time, I'll give you a call." Damn, she hated to screw around like this, but she wasn't ready to tell her friends about Lizzie yet, and if she turned Elizabeth down flat…

"Okay. No pressure." She shrugged. "Call me if you have time."

"Will do." They went out with the bowls refilled, and Jill gave Kathleen a narrow-eyed glance, already preparing the lecture she was going to give her after the party.

They had a few good hands in a row, finishing up winning the night. It was eleven, their usual stop time. Jill got up and went to put the rest of the tabouli into a container for Skip, who was a big fan. A soft knock at the back door caught her attention, and Jill flipped on the light. Lizzie was probably the person behind a big bunch of peonies and roses, but since only the top of her head showed, Jill couldn't be sure.

She threw the door open and laughed when Lizzie pushed the flowers up higher, completely obscuring herself. "I was clearing off a bunch of tables after an event, and decided I couldn't let these beauties go to waste. I saw that all of your buddies were still here, and thought they might like to share the wealth."

Touched, Jill helped her into the house. Lizzie's apartment and Hollyhock Hills were South of Jill's home, meaning she'd gone out of her way at the end of a very long day just to be nice. "Who'd refuse such pretty flowers?" Quickly, she leaned over the profusion of blooms and placed a peck on Lizzie's cheek. "Come on in. We were just breaking up." She stopped dead in her tracks. She'd have to explain Elizabeth. "Uhm… Gerri couldn't make it, so someone new took her place."

"Cool. It's smart to have a backup for when someone's sick or out of town."

"Yeah. I guess that's true."

They went into the living room, with Lizzie calling out, "Flower delivery. Get your flowers right here."

"Lizzie?" Becky asked. "Are you back there?"

"Yeah." She lowered the flowers, and beamed a grin. "They were going to throw all of these out. I knew you guys were playing tonight, and I thought you might want to have a few—dozen."

"They're gorgeous," Mary Beth said, walking over to sniff them. "Do you normally throw flowers out? I'd think a hospital would want them."

"That's what we usually do, but someone dropped the ball. So…?"

"Load me up," Alice said. "I love fresh flowers."

"There's enough for everyone to take two dozen," Lizzie said. As the bouquet got smaller, she looked to her left. "Hi," she said. "I'm Lizzie."

"Elizabeth." She shrugged. "It was a popular name in the eighties. Are you…a neighbor?"

"No. I'm Jill's friend. From Sugar Hill."

"Sugar Hill is a…?"

"Town. We're from the same town."

"Oh, that's nice." She nodded, then focused her attention back on Jill. She spoke quietly, but still loud enough for everyone to hear. "Let me put my number in your phone."

Jill's hand went numb as she tried to pull the phone from her pocket. Lizzie was looking at her questioningly, one eyebrow raised. Jill handed Elizabeth the phone, then waited for her to return it.

"Call me when you're free. I know a nice, quiet bar on College where you can get a great cocktail."

"I think I've been there," Jill said, smiling tightly.

"Don't forget to call," she said. "You promised."

"Uhm…" There was no way to dispute that without sounding dumb or rude. Jill could only shrug. "Maybe I'll see you," she said.

"I'll be waiting." Elizabeth, Mary Beth and Kathleen departed, carrying armfuls of flowers.

"What are you waiting for?" Skip demanded, giving Jill a playful punch in the arm. "I think she would have stayed for a nightcap if you'd offered to drive her home."

Alice gave him a lethal look, but that didn't stop him.

"Are you that out of dating shape?" he continued. "A good-looking woman tells you to call, and you say 'maybe?'"

Karen's look was sympathetic, Becky's gaze avidly switched between Skip and Jill, Alice was glaring at her husband, and Lizzie's head was cocked, clearly confused.

"I don't need dating advice, Skip. But thanks for caring." She put an arm around his shoulders and gave him a rough hug. "Take some of these flowers from Lizzie. She's about to topple over."

They divided the remaining flowers into three roughly equal bunches, leaving the last and biggest bunch for Lizzie. Then, Jill saw everyone out, while Lizzie went into the kitchen to put Jill's portion into vases. A few minutes later, Jill poked her head into the kitchen, ready for, at best, a thorough questioning.

Instead, she found both boys, dancing on the counter, walking by the vase and jumping up on their hind legs to rub their faces on the blooms, purring like mad as they did. Lizzie was talking to them, petting both as they sauntered around the vase. "Who was your mommy flirting with, huh, boys? Does she have pretty ladies over here all the time? Is this booty-call central? Huh? Who's here when I'm not watching her?"

"I've never met that woman in my life," Jill said, her voice high and strained. "Kathleen brought her over here with—"

Gentle fingers covered her lips, then Lizzie stood up and snuggled into Jill's embrace. "You don't owe me any explanations."

"Yes, I do! I wouldn't like it if you had some woman over right when we're trying to figure out if we can—"

Those fingers pressed her lips together, this time holding them tightly. "You don't owe me an explanation because I trust you. You're not the type of woman to be juggling a bunch of babes when I'm not watching you. Chill," she urged.

Jill tightened her hold and rested her chin on Lizzie's shoulder. "Damn, that's a relief."

"Have other women kept you on a tight leash?"

Jill straightened up and took Lizzie's hand, leading her to the den. They sat down, but not before Jill ran a hand down her skirt. "Pretty dress. You look fantastic in white."

187

"Thanks. I think you've seen just about all of my summer clothes. You'll have to wait for a month to see the fall and winter stuff. At least I hope I can hold out for a month. I hate to wear wool until at least mid-September."

Jill leaned back against the sofa, resting her head. "Becca wasn't very jealous, but the woman I dated before her was too insecure for my tastes. She thought I was checking out every woman on the street, everybody at the U, and was sure I was going to find someone I liked better. Of course, I *did*," she said, looking disgusted. "Anyone who'd give me an ounce of oxygen would have been better."

"I think it takes a lot of oxygen to make an ounce," Lizzie said, giving Jill a playful elbow. "You're in trouble when an art history major knows more real world facts than you do."

"I didn't take much science," Jill said. "But I'm never surprised when you know more than I do. You're super, super smart," she murmured, leaning against Lizzie and draping her arms around her. "And mature. And worldly. And confident. That's really sexy."

"I *am* confident. If you didn't want to be with me, you'd tell me. You'd feel really shitty about it, but you'd tell me."

"I would," Jill agreed, sitting up straight. "But I'm nowhere near wanting to stop seeing you. I want to see more and more and more of you." She let out a heavy sigh. "As soon as you come out to your parents, I'm ready to take the leap."

"Really?" Her brow rose again. That was so cute. It made her look like she could see right through Jill, and get into her head. "I wanted to go down this weekend to talk to them, but Donna's there with her seventy kids. There won't be a minute for me to have time alone with my folks."

"I guess it's not the kind of conversation you want to have on the phone, huh?"

"No. We never have important conversations on the phone. They'd think it was weird, and I want this to be a super normal conversation."

"Are we heading down to Boston next Friday or waiting for Saturday morning?"

"It's a Saturday afternoon game, so I thought we could drive down on Friday and save a couple of bucks by staying outside of town. We'll wander around until the game, then come back Saturday night. Is that cool?"

"Sure. How far out of town are we staying?"

She made a face. "I was trying to get the price below a hundred, so we're a ways out. I'm paying for everything, so I'm really trying to cut corners. Are you okay with that?"

"Absolutely. But if you'd rather I chipped in…"

"I've got this," Lizzie said. "I've been putting away a hundred bucks a month since spring. I wanted to take my dad somewhere, and, luckily, he doesn't want to go to Australia. The air fare would murder me!"

Jill pulled her close and tucked an arm around her. They were getting so comfortable with each other, this was starting to seem normal. It wasn't, but her body thought this was all just super.

Lizzie looked into her eyes, her grin thoroughly charming. "Wanna make out?"

"Uh-huh," Jill said, nuzzling her nose against Lizzie's. "But I'd rather wait a little bit. I'll feel much, much better about this after you talk to your parents."

Lizzie pulled away so she could get a good look at Jill's face. "What's going to change then? Do you think they're going to say, 'Oh, wow, you like women? Why not grab Jill and marry her?'"

"I'm not delusional. I just think it's wise to do this in stages. If they know you're into women, it won't be as big a surprise when you say you're into me."

Lizzie put a hand on her chest, gazing into her eyes for a minute. "I think you want to make sure I'm committed to this."

"That's part of it," she admitted. "But only a small part. I trust you," she said, holding Lizzie's hand. "I truly do."

"Okay. We'll do it your way." She leaned forward and gave her a tiny kiss. "But once we're together, we'll do everything my way. Fair warning."

She stood, fluffed her skirt out and started for the kitchen. Jill watched her walk, her eyes widening when the light caught her dress and filtered right through it. Lizzie turned to find her staring. She walked back over and said, "Now you know why I wear tap pants." She took her skirt and started to lift it, making Jill's eyes go wide. When it was dangerously high, she put Jill's hand on her thigh, where her fingers brushed the lacy hem. "See? They give me some coverage when I wear a thin skirt, without being hot like Spanx. They keep me cool."

"Cool," Jill parroted. "Really cool."

"I think you like my undies," Lizzie said, leaning over for a quick kiss.

"I do. And I'm so glad you came by tonight. My whole house smells good now. Peonies are my new favorite flower."

"I'll be back in the morning for yard work. Maybe not nine on the button, but I won't be too late."

"I'll be waiting. Patiently." Jill stood, grasped her and placed a long, gentle kiss to her lips, then stayed right there, the need to be close almost overpowering. "I wish you didn't have to go."

Lizzie didn't reply. She just gazed at Jill with that foxy look, then patted her on the cheek and started for the back door. "See you in the morning," she said, waving as she exited.

"Can't wait. I want to see some work boots, buddy."

"They will make their first appearance. And the Danish will be prune and apricot free."

Jill stood on the porch, watching until Lizzie walked behind some parked cars and disappeared from view. As she went back inside, the boys wound themselves around her ankles, crying like they were waiting for dinner. "I know. I wanted her to stay too."

⁂

Jill heard gravel crunching on the driveway at nine-fifteen, the only noise Lizzie's electric car made. Jill put her cereal bowl away, unwilling to reveal her doubts about the Danish delivery.

Heading out to stand on the front porch, Jill saw that the work boots were in the house—with Lizzie's tight jeans rolled up until they just skimmed the boots. The black tank top she wore showed lots of skin— skin that Jill knew would distract her all day. Lizzie walked across the grass, and offered up a square white box. "Your breakfast is served."

Jill placed a kiss on her cheek. "Coffee?"

"Sure. Milk and sugar. Use a heavy hand."

190

They entered the house and headed for the kitchen. "Your thank-you present's right there," Jill said, indicating a shopping bag on the counter.

"I get a thank you present? How do you know I'm going to do anything?" Two cats appeared, both crying for attention.

Lizzie squatted down to lavish attention on the boys. "Did you miss me?" she murmured. "I missed you too. Such good boys you are."

Jill handed her a mug, very pale and very sweet. "Need a hand up?"

Lizzie tilted her chin to look up at her. "I can handle it." She made a sweeping gesture with her hands as she rose, effortlessly. "Ta da!"

"You look really cute in your work boots."

Lizzie looked down pointedly. "So do you. You're a damned sexy landscaper." She grasped the pockets of Jill's cargo shorts and twitched them around, making the shorts glide around her waist. "I like roomy shorts on a woman."

Jill took the bag and snapped her wrist, making a crinkling noise when the contents shifted around. "Open your present. I think you'll like it."

Smiling, Lizzie reached inside and pulled out four pairs of shorts, one navy, one chalk, and two leaf green. "Are you trying to tell me something?" she asked, smirking.

"I am. August is no time for jeans." Jill picked up the green ones and held them up to Lizzie's face. "I knew that color would match your eyes. That's why I bought them in two sizes."

Lizzie took a peek at the labels. "Four pairs, but only two sizes."

"I thought you needed two pair, but wasn't sure what size you wore. So I bought a variety to show you the colors. I'll exchange them for the right size. If you like them, that is. No problem if you don't."

Lizzie moved to stand in front of her, snuggling close when Jill's arms naturally slid around her body. "No one's ever bought me shorts. I think I'll put a pair on right now."

"Okay. I'll plate our breakfast."

Lizzie started to unlace her boots. Then she twitched her hips as she peeled the jeans off, with Jill staring at her, unblinking.

"You don't mind, do you?" Lizzie asked. "I'm wearing underwear."

"No. Please." She moved—or shuffled—over to where she stored her plates, and took down a couple of small ones. Lizzie's jeans were so tight she had to remove them like they were an adhesive film. Gone were the silky tap pants, replaced by gray boy shorts, also skin tight. Jill couldn't imagine wearing underwear that fit that snugly, but she was really glad Lizzie did.

After checking the labels for size, Lizzie slipped a green pair on. Once they were zipped, she put her hands in the pockets and rocked back on her heels. "I think these work. What do you think?"

Before Jill could reply, Lizzie was in the bathroom, where her voice called out, "Yeah, these are good. Not too short, and not too long."

When she returned, Jill was gazing at her vacantly. "I like your undies," she said, not even caring that she looked like a dunce.

Lizzie reached down and tugged on her waistband. "What am I wearing? Oh, yeah. My boxers. Wedgie protection for when I'm going to be bending over a lot."

"You look really cute," Jill said, still staring.

"Thanks to you." Lizzie moved to her and gave her a long hug. "It was very sweet of you to buy me something to keep me cool while we worked."

Jill dropped a kiss to her cheek. "I bought you something so I could stare at your legs. Full disclosure."

"I don't mind your reasons. You're still very sweet to think of me." She cuddled against her, with neither of them in any hurry to drink their coffee, eat their Danish, or cut the grass. Why ruin a perfect moment?

⌘

On Friday afternoon, Jill drove to Lizzie's apartment just after lunch. It was easy for her to get away on a summer Friday, but she knew this weekend trip had required a lot of juggling and trading with co-workers for Lizzie.

She came bounding down the steps a few seconds after Jill texted her arrival. Cute as a pinch and always prompt. That alone made her the perfect choice for a girlfriend.

Lizzie tossed open the door and slid in. "Hello, Freyja." She patted the dash, then turned and nodded soberly. "Jill."

Jill could see the playfulness hidden behind those pale eyes. "That's all I get?"

"I'm practicing for how I'm going to behave around my parents." She slid her hand onto Jill's thigh, a habit they'd have to break that afternoon. "This is going to be really hard."

"I know." Jill didn't want to admit how worried she'd been about that, but Lizzie could probably tell. "Our timing sucks. Ideally, you'd talk to them about us this weekend, then we'd go to a game in September."

"I had to pull out all the stops to get these tickets," she said. "September was out of the question."

"We'll just have to act like friends. They know we do stuff together, right?"

"Uh-huh. I've told my mom about almost every time we've been together." She rolled her eyes. "Not about my coming by after a late night at work, just to kiss you goodnight, but all of the times that don't make me sound like a stalker. Oh! I almost forgot. Will you go by my charging station? I don't want to leave my car plugged in all weekend. They only have two ports."

Jill did a U-turn and went back towards Lizzie's apartment, finding the car patiently sipping electricity. "Be right back," Lizzie said, getting out to jog over to it and move it.

Jill watched her go, daydreaming about the day they could be open—with everyone—about their relationship. She was so crazy about Lizzie, she wanted to shout it from the rooftops. But her patient, careful nature just couldn't let go. This was too important to screw up because of impatience.

It took Lizzie a while to find a spot, and she was out of breath when she ran back to the car. "Lots of people around today. We're good to go."

As they headed out again, Jill said, "One of the things I like best about you is how thoughtful you are. Most people wouldn't move their car just so others could get a charge."

"Most people are kinda jerks. There aren't that many of us who use this station, so I know most of the cars. It irks me when one's there for a few days, so I make sure I don't do the thing that I find selfish, right?"

"Right." Jill put her hand on her leg, then pulled it away. "Gotta stop that! It's become a habit."

"We're sliding into all sorts of girlfriend habits," Lizzie agreed. "I love that."

"I do too. But we need to put them on hold for just a couple of days. Then we can indulge to our hearts' content."

"I love that expression," Lizzie said, wistfully. "You make my heart content."

"You do the same for me." Jill gave her a fond look. "You're the girliest, most romantic woman I've ever dated. Clearly, I didn't know what I wanted in a woman until I met you."

⌒⌒

That night, they carried their bags into a nondescript motel room about a half hour from Fenway. It was one of the lower-ranked chains, but there were two queen-sized beds and the place was clean.

They'd carried all of Janet and Mike's stuff up to their room, despite both of them complaining that they could handle their own luggage perfectly fine.

Jill stood in the bathroom, neatly arranging her toiletries, while pushing aside a plastic bag full of Lizzie's stuff, and another, bigger nylon bag with god knew what in it. Maybe there were some downsides to dating girly girls. They sure had a lot of toiletries. She changed into a T-shirt and cotton pajama bottoms, brushed and flossed her teeth, then took the band off her ponytail and brushed her hair.

When Jill walked back into the bedroom, her negative thoughts towards femmes immediately quelled. Lizzie had stripped her jeans off and was now wearing yet another camisole, this one cream-colored, and matching silky tap pants. "Once we start to sleep together, I can wear my normal summer pajamas—nothing at all," she said, adding a racy smile.

"I"—Jill sat down on her bed heavily—"I was going to say I really like what you have on, but I might like the alternative better." She made her hands into fists and rubbed her tired eyes with them. "Whose dumb idea was it to share a room?"

"Mine." Lizzie sat by her and leaned into her body. "When I made the reservations, I didn't think we'd be at this point."

"This I'd-love-to-tear-your-clothes-off point?" Jill smirked.

"Yeah," Lizzie said, sighing. "You send off some pretty sexual vibes for a girl. I don't think we're going to have any problems once we go"— she made a wide-eyed face and pointed to the bed—"there."

"I'm pretty sure we're going to be able to figure that out. You're going to have to wrestle me into submission before you whip your big, throbbing cock out, but I assume that won't be a problem for you."

Laughing, Lizzie maneuvered around until she was stretched out with her head on Jill's lap. "That's the very first thing I'm going to do. No foreplay, either. You've got to be tough to hook up with Lizzie Davis."

Looking down at her, Jill idly played with her hair, then began to run her fingers over her features. "You're so pretty. I love looking at your face."

Lizzie looked up at her, with such a tender expression Jill got chills. "I've always thought you were beautiful, but every time I see you, you get better looking. Is that my endorphins messing with my mind, or are you just some ever-evolving hunk of awesomeness?"

"The latter. By the time I'm fifty, people will have to shield their eyes so they aren't blinded by my beauty."

"That's just what I thought," Lizzie said, nodding sagely. "Sleepy," she murmured, a big yawn making her jaw pop audibly.

"Me too." Jill wanted to urge Lizzie to get up and go to her own bed, but it felt so nice to have her lying in her lap. They could just rest their eyes for a few minutes. She grasped all of the pillows and put two under her as she lay down, crosswise, on the bed. When she pushed one down her body, Lizzie grasped it and hugged it to herself, then made some soft noises and was out.

⸙

Something partially woke Jill. A knock? No, the sound was coming from behind her, not the door across the room. Lizzie had migrated, probably for warmth, and was now curled up against her, both of them lying crosswise on the bed. The light was on, but it seemed so far away. And she'd have to disturb Lizzie to get it. If she closed her eyes…

The door behind her opened; brighter light, the sound of a TV, then a gasp. The door closed as Jill levitated, panic roaring through her body. Lizzie grumbled and tried to curl up again.

Now the knock was unmistakable. Lizzie flew into a sitting position, her eyes remarkably wide. "What the fuck?"

The door opened a crack. "Lizzie, you must've taken your dad's toiletries. I hate to wake you, but his inhaler's in there."

"I'm up," she said, sounding fully awake. She was already in the bathroom while Jill was still trying to get her heart started again. Then she was at the door, opening it and passing the nylon bag to Janet. "Is Dad okay?" she asked.

"He's fine. Go back to sleep, honey. I'm sorry I woke you."

"It's okay, Mom." She opened the door a little wider and poked her head in. "G'night, Dad."

"Sorry to wake you kids." Mike's deep voice carried into the room. "I thought you two'd be up late."

"No, not tonight. See you in the morning."

"Okay, sweetheart," he said. "You girls sleep well."

"We will."

The door was open enough for Jill to turn and see Janet's grim expression, with those narrowed eyes locked on her. *Oh, fuck!*

Lizzie closed the door, then dropped, face-first, onto the bed. "Kill me. Kill me now."

"I think I'm the one who'll be killed." Jill swallowed, sick to her stomach. "I've never seen that expression on your mom's face."

"It wasn't good." Lizzie rolled over, then got up and went into the bathroom. Jill heard her brushing her teeth, then she came back into the room. "Screw it," she said, pulling the covers down and getting in the proper way. "There's no reason to sleep apart now."

"I'm about to have a stroke," Jill managed. "Everything I was worried about just happened!"

Lizzie grasped her firmly and tugged until they were lying down, facing each other. "Listen to me," she said, staring into Jill's eyes. "She might be upset. She might give us a hard time. But she'll come around. And my dad will parrot whatever her reaction is."

"They *saw* us," Jill moaned.

"My mother saw us sleeping close to each other. We weren't naked. We weren't having sex. If I tried hard enough, I could talk my way out of this."

Jill's eyes opened wide, and she stared at her, astounded.

"I could," she insisted. "I've slithered out of worse situations. But I don't want to do that. I'm going to tell them the whole truth. Tomorrow."

"No," Jill said, her head shaking fast. "Let them lead. If your mom tells your dad, and they want to talk about it, we will. If she wants to let it go—we do."

"My mom *never* lets things go. She tells you exactly what she thinks, as soon as she thinks it."

"I'm not sure she's going to do that this time," Jill said, not certain why she felt that way. "Let them take the lead, Lizzie. Please."

"Okay. Okay."

She moved up a little on the bed and tucked Jill up against her body. Even though she was shaking like a leaf in a bad storm, Jill allowed Lizzie to comfort her. To make her hope that, somehow, this would work out.

"I'm so sorry I screwed up," Lizzie murmured. "I opened the adjoining door to check that they had everything they needed, and I forgot to lock it. I'm really, really sorry."

"It's okay," Jill said, at least now understanding how the hell Janet had gotten in. "I never should have allowed myself to fall asleep."

"You were in the bathroom when I opened the door. You couldn't have known I did that. I should have been more careful."

"It's all right, Lizzie. Really. Let's just…try to sleep." Soon they were fully entwined, facing each other. What a rotten night. Their first time lying in bed together, with both of them so anxious Jill wanted nothing more than for dawn to come. At least then she'd know what kind of mess they were in, and if it could be fixed.

Jill wasn't sure when she'd fallen asleep, but it had taken a very, very long time. When Mike banged on the door, calling out, "Breakfast time, girls!" she levitated once again, her heart racing.

Lizzie disentangled herself, got up and went to the door. She poked her head into her parents' room and said, "If you're ready, go on downstairs. We'll get ready and meet you down there."

"Should we pack up?" Mike asked.

"Yeah. We're taking off right after breakfast."

"Got it. Shake a leg, Bethie. We've got a big day ahead of us!"

Lizzie closed the door, and gave Jill a level look. "My mom obviously didn't say anything to him. I'm not sure what his reaction will be, but he'll have one."

"Great." Jill got up, feeling like she'd been pacing up and down the hall all night. In her dreams, she had been. "Do you want to use the shower first?"

"Doesn't matter." She put her arms around Jill and gave her a long, firm hug. "Buck up. The fact that my mom didn't say anything means she's thinking about this before she speaks. That's probably good news."

"Or really bad," Jill grumbled, heading into the bathroom. She desperately needed some water hitting her in the face to have any chance at fully waking up.

⟶⟵

Mike was his usual self. Cheerful, gabby, a little loud. He had a big plate full of everything the buffet offered. But Janet had only a cup of coffee in front of her, and she stirred it idly, not looking up.

"Your mother didn't sleep well," Mike explained. "She hates a strange bed." His upbeat attitude made him seem just like the Mike Davis Jill had grown up around. His new medicine was really giving him another bite of the apple, and Jill could hardly have been happier for him.

She didn't have much of an appetite, managing just some corn flakes and a cup of coffee. The stress obviously hadn't hurt Lizzie's appetite, and Jill watched her put down two waffles and four slices of bacon, then wash it all down with a couple of glasses of juice.

198

"What should we do?" Mike asked, turning to Lizzie. "This is your city."

"We haven't done the Freedom Trail in twenty years," she said. "Wanna take a loop?"

His mood seemed to deflate as he considered the idea. "I don't know, kiddo. I'm not sure I can walk that far."

"That won't be a problem," she said, grinning. "I know you don't need one, but I rented you a wheelchair. We'll push you all over Boston."

"You did?" He started to shake his head, and Jill could see his hard-headedness come to the fore. "Wheelchairs are for people who can't walk. I don't need that."

"I know you don't need it," Lizzie said, "but it'll make the day easier. Trust me on this, Daddy."

She grasped his hand and gazed into his eyes, refusing to look away. Jill could see him soften, then he rolled his eyes and laughed.

"Have I ever won an argument with you? You've had me wrapped around your little finger for thirty years."

"Beth has a good point," Janet said. "You'll have more fun if you don't have to walk."

"I give up. But who's going to push me?"

"We'll take turns, Dad," Lizzie said. "And if you get tired of sitting, you can push me."

"You've got a deal, kiddo. Let's get going. I've got some history to explain."

⚬

They'd arranged for the chair in Burlington, so they were ready when they drove along the Freedom Trail, with Mike directing. "Here's a good spot," he said. "Can we get out here?"

"Sure," Jill said. She and Lizzie got the wheelchair out of the trunk, moving overnight bags, an oxygen tank and backpacks to extract it. Mike sat down and Lizzie started to push him, clearly testing to figure out how much force she had to use. "I'm good," she said, meeting Jill's look. "Will you park the car?"

199

"Got it." Jill got back in, glad to have a few minutes alone. Janet wasn't acting totally out of character, but she was off enough to make both Jill and Lizzie anxious. Jill was almost disappointed when she found on-street parking just a few blocks away. When she jogged back, Lizzie was pushing her dad up a gentle incline, but she was panting from the effort.

"My turn," Jill said, sliding her hands onto the grips as Lizzie let go.

"That hill's higher than it looks," Lizzie complained.

Jill watched as Janet grasped Lizzie's hand and pulled her to a stop. Then she met Jill's gaze and gave her the hand signal for "Go ahead." *Oh, fuck.* Lizzie was going to get her butt kicked. And Jill couldn't do a thing about it.

She put her legs into it, and started to push Mike faster, giving Janet the space she demanded. "Remember seeing the Old North Church for the first time when you were a kid, Beth?" He turned his head. "Where'd she go?"

"Oh, she and Janet are right behind us. They're looking at something. I remember the church," Jill said. "I was telling Lizzie that the first time I recall coming to Boston was when Mark and I were in eighth grade. You were one of our chaperones. Even though we were here for the game, you made sure to take us around for some history."

"You remember that, huh?" he said, sounding delighted. "That teacher you had thought her job was to keep you kids in your seats. She didn't know the first thing about teaching."

"I remember thinking that at the time," Jill agreed. "But no one takes kids seriously when they complain about a teacher."

"You were never a complainer," Mike insisted. "You were the kind of kid I used as a bellwether. If you said something was so, I knew I could count on it."

Jill put her hand on his shoulder and gave it a squeeze. "Thanks. And I knew you were one of the few adults I could talk to and not be ignored."

He reached back and gripped her hand. "I'm sorry we lost touch for so many years, Jill. We really dropped the ball."

"It's all right, Mike. We built a good foundation all those years ago. We can add to it now."

"I'm glad you're back," he said, sounding a little misty. "And I'm especially glad you're keeping an eye on Beth…Lizzie, I mean. I worry about her up there in Burlington, so far away from her family."

"We… I'm… It's good for both of us to be close," Jill said, desperately trying to figure out a way to state that without it sounding weird. But when your girlfriend was being lectured by her mother just a few feet behind you, it was hard to put coherent sentences together. What in the hell was Janet saying? Jill had no option but to wait and see. And it was driving her crazy!

≈∾

Jill had to use every bit of her leverage and leg strength to push Mike up to Copp's Hill Burial Ground. He was able to climb some stairs and walk around the site, after Janet called out that she and Lizzie would watch the chair.

Jill caught a glimpse of Lizzie, eyes downcast, her hands clasped behind her back. She looked like a kid being chided for playing ball in the house, something that the young Lizzie could have easily gotten away with. Every one of her older siblings complained that the rules never applied to the baby of the family, but it looked like she was finally getting the lecture she'd deferred for so long. Jill was filled with empathy for her, but it was awful to not know exactly what was going on.

Mike was blissfully ignorant, huffing and puffing his way up the stairs to stand at the top and look out at the old tombstones. "I can just see it," he said, his face flushed from exertion. "Back when the colonists thought this would be a perfect place for a windmill." He looked out at the view, able to take in much of Boston and the harbor. "It's hard to imagine what this country looked like before our ancestors got here."

"Fewer skyscrapers," Jill joked.

"It's a damn shame we couldn't figure out a way to share the land," he said, thoughtfully. "But I guess that's not what people do."

"No, I don't think that's the human instinct. Can you imagine a world where sharing was the default?"

201

"No, but I'd like to." He turned to look at the grave site, with weather-beaten tombstones listing to one side, some nearly tumbled over. "Maybe we'll all be at peace one day." He put his hand on her shoulder as they meandered around the irregular rows. "That's a nice dream too." He squeezed Jill's shoulder. "Don't tell Janet I said that. She's convinced heaven's real."

"Maybe it is," Jill said. "I can think of worse things to believe in."

"Good point. Damned good point, Jilly. It doesn't cost a thing to believe, so why not?"

Jill put her arm around Mike's waist, partly to stabilize him, but mostly because she felt so damned close to him. He was the dad she'd always wanted, and if Janet was convincing Lizzie to sever their tie—she wasn't sure how she'd ever get over the loss.

⟡

They spent a long time at the grave site, with Mike pointing out every notable preacher, soldier, and colonist he knew. As they walked back down the stairs, Lizzie was looking up at her, but Jill couldn't read her expression. It wasn't happy. That was certain, but Jill couldn't tell much more. Lizzie had hold of the wheelchair, and she pushed it back and forth a few inches. "I get the downhill portion," she said, her voice relatively close to normal. That was a good sign, right? Then a hand clamped onto Jill's upper arm, stopping her.

"Walk with me for a while," Janet said. She used a tone that left no room for dissent.

"Sure. Great."

They stood in place, waiting for Lizzie to push her father's chair out of earshot. Then Janet took a step, her hand still locked around Jill's arm. She must have been doing hand-strengthening exercises!

"Do you know what Beth said on the day you graduated from college?"

Jill blinked in surprise. "No. How would I know…?"

"She told me when she grew up she was going to marry you."

Jill stopped on a dime, her arm now at an awkward angle when Janet didn't release her hold. "She what?"

"She had a schoolgirl crush on you, Jill. I thought it was just that. A little girl's desire to *be* the older girl."

"But you don't think that now?"

"I don't know what to think," she said, staring at the ground. "But I know one thing." Her gaze shifted to lock onto Jill's. "If you're playing with her… Or taking advantage of the way she feels about you…"

"I would never, ever do that. Never," she said, hotly. "And Lizzie's not that little girl anymore. She's a mature adult who knows her own mind."

"And her own mind is leading her to get involved with you. After being perfectly happy with men since she was sixteen."

"What are you implying, Janet? Do you think I swooped into your house, determined to snatch your daughter away?"

Janet's cheeks began to flush, putting color into what had been an abnormally pale complexion. "No, of course I don't think that. But I don't think you understand what you meant to her when she was young. She *idolized* you, Jill. And you and the older kids just ignored her."

"She was a little kid—"

"I know that. You were adolescents. You shouldn't have been interested in her back then. But I think she might be confused. Or trying to make those childhood fantasies come true."

Given that Jill had no idea what Lizzie had told her mother, she was stuck. She wasn't about to reveal that Lizzie had been interested in girls all of her life, but she couldn't let that strange comment just lie there.

They were heading east again, back past the Old North Church. Jill assumed they'd go south, back to the center of the historical buildings. She normally really enjoyed walks like this, and wished she was with Mike, getting his perspective, but she was stuck. Literally.

"I've only been getting to know Lizzie since May, and I'll admit that's not very long. But I've never, not for a second, felt that she was living in the past with me. Or trying to fulfill some old fantasy. She's not that kind of woman, Janet. Come on. You know that."

"I don't know what I know," she said, her mouth set in a hard line. "My girl's telling me something about herself that's important. Very important. And I didn't have the slightest inkling about it." She stared at

Jill, eyes flashing. "How am I supposed to feel? Have we been close all of these years? What else don't I know?"

"I'm sorry this is catching you so off guard. I wish Lizzie would have talked to you sooner. I really do."

Janet's gaze sharpened. "Did you seek her out before Mark's party? Did you ever try to get in touch with her?"

"God damn it," Jill said, her voice rising. "What are you implying?"

"You're carrying on with my youngest child. Behind my back!"

Jill took a breath, unwilling to let her temper make her say something she'd regret. Quietly, she said, "I'm sure it's hard to be confronted with your child's sexuality. And I truly regret you were. But we're not doing something to you, Janet. We're figuring things out for ourselves."

"How long were you going to wait to tell us? You looked like you had everything figured out last night."

"That's not true. We're working things out. But even though this is a work in progress, Lizzie was going to come down and talk to you next weekend."

"And say what?"

"She was going to tell you that she was…attracted to women."

Janet stared at her for a long time. Quietly, she enunciated each word. "She wasn't going to tell us about you?"

"No. We…I thought it would be easier for you to get used to if she just told you she was attracted to women. Later on, she was going to tell you about us."

"I know you Jill, and I know my daughter. Neither of you would be hiding something you were proud of!"

Jill's body ached from stress, making her feel like they'd run the Freedom Trail a few times. She desperately wanted to reassure Janet, but that wasn't her place. It was Lizzie's.

"I can't speak for Lizzie, but I'm proud of the way I've handled this. I'm trying hard to take it slow and make sure she knows this is what she wants." She dropped her head, closed her eyes and said what was in her heart. "I'm trying to protect her, Janet. I'd do anything not to hurt her."

"This is going to be a tough pill for the other kids to swallow, Jill. It won't be easy for them to accept."

"I...I don't know what to say about that. I'm very attracted to your daughter, and she feels the same about me. If her brothers and sisters have issues with homosexuality—they'll have to get over them."

"It's not that easy. It's just not." She blew out a frustrated breath, then said, "Mike's going to know something's up. Let's catch up."

"You're not going to tell him?"

"No," she said immediately. "That's for Beth to do."

"She prefers Lizzie," Jill said, wishing she could pull that back in before it reached Janet's ears.

"Good for her." Still gripping Jill's arm, she picked up the pace and they were soon right behind Lizzie and Mike. Lizzie turned and gave Jill a wistful look. One that Jill took to mean "Who's the idiot who suggested going on a trip with my parents?"

⌖

Lizzie's careful foresight became even more evident when an usher escorted them to seats down the first base line, three traditional and one a big space with the seat number painted on the ground. Lizzie pushed the levers to secure the wheelchair, and sat next to her father. "Pretty sweet, huh?"

Jill was furthest down the row, stuck next to the nearly silent Janet. She didn't mind though. Lizzie was proud of herself for figuring out a way to get her father to a game, and the fact that she got great seats while letting him get around easily just made Jill's respect for her grow. This was not a woman who was vying for her affections simply because of a long-ago schoolgirl crush. Lizzie was young, for sure, but she was mature. More mature than many people Jill's age. With any luck, Janet would eventually see that.

⌖

On the way back to Sugar Hill, Mike sat in the back and provided an almost play-by-play of the Sox's dismal game. It was not their year. At this rate, they'd finish last in their division, but that didn't hamper Mike's interest. He was a true fan, loyal whether his team was first or last.

They were driving up Route 12, just a few dozen miles from home, when Lizzie asked, "Who wants to skip dinner and have a maple creemee?"

"Me," Janet said immediately.

"I could go for a creemee," Mike said, making the Davis vote unanimous.

Jill turned to look at Lizzie's happy smile. "I assume you know where there's a stand?"

"Next exit," she said, pointing. "A good place. They don't bother with regular food. Just the sweet stuff."

Jill turned off and let Lizzie direct her down the small town's main street to where a line of people were lingering outside an ice cream shop. "You're not the first to notice this place," Jill said.

"Thankfully. In a town this small, they need to lure a bunch of travelers to stay open. I'll wait in line," she said, jumping out.

Jill flipped her door open, but Janet exited first. "I'll help."

As Jill watched mother and daughter stand in the slow moving line, she realized that Janet didn't want her and Lizzie to have time alone. She was acting just like a cop investigating a crime. Never let the co-conspirators have a private conversation until you've squeezed a confession out of them.

❦

Even though he'd spent most of the day in a wheelchair, Mike was drained by the time they got home. Janet got his oxygen tank arranged next to his easy chair in the den, switched the TV on and said, "We're going to go for a walk to work some of that ice cream off."

"I guess I can be happy here," he said, looking around like he'd just seen the spot for the first time. "If Lizzie would get me a beer, all will be right with the world."

"Coming right up, Dad," she said, delivering one a minute later.

"Are you girls staying overnight?" he asked.

"Not sure. We'll see how we feel after our walk."

If our legs haven't been broken, Jill thought, for once in her life dreading an August evening stroll.

They went out the back door, cutting across the yard to go down the gravel road that led to the river. As soon as they were on level ground,

Janet threaded her arms through both Lizzie and Jill's. That was nice. Unless she was just holding on so she could kick them.

"So…" she began. "Where do we go from here?"

"I think you owe Jill an apology," Lizzie said, hurt coloring her voice. "The thought that she might be trying to…" She growled, sounding supremely frustrated. "I don't even know what you were implying. But I *know* it was an insult."

"It's okay," Jill said. "I know you're upset, Janet. I don't blame you for grasping at straws to try to figure this out."

"It's not that hard," Lizzie jumped in, her voice filled with frustration and anger. "I like women. You in particular. For the record, I didn't know I liked you until we met up again." Her cheeks got pinker by the second, until they were cherry red. "I have not been longing for you since I was in diapers!"

"I apologize," Janet said, squeezing Jill's arm. "You're right. I was grasping for an explanation, and I let my mind veer off into some crazy spot." She turned to Lizzie. "But I can't ignore your history, honey. You seemed so happy with your boyfriends. Especially Adam and Ben. And you were awfully close to marrying Jon. Don't act like that isn't true."

"It was, Mom, but…"

Jill gave her a pointed look, and Lizzie sighed and told the truth. "I *was* happy dating men. I didn't tell you the whole truth this morning."

"Now what?" Janet demanded.

"I'm not exactly a lesbian. I'm bisexual."

Janet's attention switched to Jill. "Is that true for you, too?"

"No. I'm gay. Lizzie's much more open-minded than I am." She smiled, but doused it quickly when she saw that Janet didn't see the humor in the situation.

"So before today you were straight," Janet said. "This morning you were a lesbian. Now, tonight, you're bisexual. Are there any more categories you're going to join? Or can I try to get used to this one?"

"There are other categories," Lizzie said. "But they don't apply to me. I'm attracted to both men and women. But over the last few years I've realized I can't be happy with men alone. I need…more."

Jill fervently hoped Janet didn't ask too many questions. There was no way in hell she'd easily accept her baby getting into three-ways with women she'd picked up online.

"Why on earth should Jill take a chance on you not needing more?"

Jill blinked in surprise. Now *she* was the one Janet was looking out for?

"I can't imagine Jill would like it if you decide you miss men. Would you?" she demanded, staring into Jill's eyes.

She was very, very glad they hadn't agreed on an open relationship. It was *so* much easier to defend monogamy. "No, I wouldn't like it. But I trust Lizzie to know what she needs. If we…go forward, we'll both agree to being exclusive."

"What do you mean, 'if you go forward?'"

"We haven't had sex," Lizzie piped up. Jill shot her a look, but Lizzie didn't notice. "We've kissed, but that's it. I've had to work my butt off to convince Jill I can be faithful." Scowling, she added, "Now I guess I have to convince you, and probably every other member of the family."

Indignantly, Janet's head snapped to the left. "What makes you think Beth would cheat on you?"

"I *don't* think that," Jill insisted. "But she's never been in a committed relationship with a woman. I've been worried about just what you said earlier. That she'll realize I'm not enough for her. That she'll miss men too much."

"This is giving me a headache," Janet said, reaching up to massage her temple. They'd made it down to the covered bridge, and she stood in front of one of the openings that focused your attention on the slow moving stream.

These openings had always reminded Jill of animated paintings, with their rough wooden frames, and constantly changing scenes.

Lizzie put her arm around her mother and said, "Jill's been on me to talk to you and Dad since the day I told her I was interested in her. Don't give her a hard time, Mom. She's gone so far out of her way to make sure

I'm doing what's right for me—and the family." She let go of her mother and moved over to slide an arm around Jill's waist.

Janet's expression soured again and she said, "Could you give me a little more time before you start with that? I'm not ready."

You could see the hurt on Lizzie's face from downriver, but she dropped her arm and moved away. "Okay. I don't want to upset you."

"It's too new," Janet insisted. "I don't have anything against homosexuality, but…"

"It's going to take some time to get used to this," Jill jumped in. "It took me weeks to get comfortable with the thought of being with Lizzie."

Janet took a long look at her daughter. Jill stood back and did the same, watching the last rays of a lovely sunset stream through the opening to paint Lizzie's skin a gorgeous, warm hue, with her hair shimmering like red-tinted gold. How could it have taken her weeks to let herself start to fall?

"So this was all your idea?" Janet asked.

"One hundred percent. Jill didn't give me a second look." She let out a fiendish chuckle. "Even though I was flirting like mad. She set me up with a guy she works with, then tricked me into going to a baseball game with two guys—hoping I'd like one of them enough to date."

"And you'd already decided you wanted to be with her?"

"I had a feeling the night of Mark's party," Lizzie admitted, casting a quick glance at a startled Jill.

"I had no idea!"

"Well, now you do. When you told me you were single, I knew right then and there that I'd worm my way into your heart."

"You hadn't seen me for almost twenty years! What if I'd turned out to be a huge jerk?"

"No way," Lizzie said, the voice of confidence. "Your sweetness and thoughtfulness and intelligence come out with every word. You're the same girl you were when you left Sugar Hill, but now you're a confident adult."

Janet put her arm around Jill, and gave her a tender hug. "That's all true. I'm sorry for giving you such a hard time earlier."

"It's truly all right. I'd have a lot of questions if I were in your shoes."

She nodded, then pulled away and addressed Lizzie. "When are you going to tell your father?"

"How do you think he'll take it?"

"I'm not sure, sweetie," she said, thoughtfully. "But I hope he'll have an easier time with it than I am."

⁂

They got back to the house at nine-thirty, to find Mike sound asleep in his easy chair. Lizzie tiptoed out of the room, whispering, "Dodged a bullet. I can put this off for another week."

Jill didn't think that made any sense at all, but she wasn't going to push her. "Do you want to stay over, or go back to Burlington?"

"I'd rather go back," she said. "I want to go swimming tomorrow if it's as nice as it's supposed to be."

"We have a perfectly lovely town pool," Janet reminded her.

"I can hit the town pool next weekend," Lizzie said, "after Dad chases me out of the house."

⁂

Lizzie hooked her phone up to the car stereo, choosing a playlist that was classic jazz and blues standards, then pushed the button that let her seat recline. Soon, both bare feet were up on the dash, as she lay, nearly supine, in her seat. "Well, that went well," she said, her wry laugh sounding tired and weak.

"Yeah. If by 'well' you mean no bones were broken."

"I think she handled it fine, given that it shocked the holy hell out of her."

"I do too. I think she'll be on our side." Jill reached over and took her hand. "I guess I've got to go through with this now. We'd look pretty stupid if I said I'd lost interest."

Lizzie gave her a love-filled look. "You're not the type. If you let me take a nap, I can drive for the last half."

"Go right ahead. I'll let all of the scenarios that stormed through my mind last night replay. That'll keep me up—for days."

They were home not long after midnight. Lizzie had been so groggy that Jill didn't take her up on her offer to drive, but that was fine. She could get by with little sleep for a couple of days and function pretty well. That was obviously not true for Lizzie. They pulled into the driveway, and Lizzie blinked at her sleepily. "Do I get to sleep with you?"

"Want to?"

"Uh-huh." She rubbed her eyes with her fists. "But I don't think I'll be able to manage more than sleep."

"That's all I want—tonight," Jill said, unable to keep a sexy grin off her face. "We'll get to the fun stuff soon."

"Promise?"

"Take it to the bank."

Jill dashed over to Lizzie's side to take her hand and lead her into the house. She seemed so groggy, Jill didn't want her to take a header.

The boys were joyous, but tempered their elation with a little snootiness at having Jill gone overnight. It didn't matter that Stephanie, their favorite cat-sitter, had come back to Burlington early to get ready for her last year at the U and had been with them every moment. They could be happy and furious at the same time.

Lizzie sat on the stairs and let them rub against her as she spoke softly. "Yes, we missed you. Of course we did. You don't think we have fun when you're not with us, do you?" She looked up at Jill, who was fondly gazing at her. "This time that's the truth."

Jill offered a hand up, and Lizzie took it, letting herself be hauled to her feet.

"Oh, I wouldn't say we didn't have any fun," Jill said. "Parts of the weekend were good. You certainly got us great seats to the game. I've never sat that close."

Lizzie's eyes almost closed while her mouth stretched into a silly grin. "I did a good job, didn't I. Took a dozen phone calls. I had to resort to calling someone in the front office who I worked with when I was at the Gardner. But I got it done."

"Your dad really appreciated it." Jill walked over to check on the litter box, finding it perfect. "I'm going to give the boys a snack. Then they might let us sleep in."

"See you upstairs. I'm going to dive into that bed in two seconds flat."

Jill had to laugh at the happy expression Lizzie wore as she turned to climb the stairs. The woman clearly loved her sleep. A few minutes later, Jill went into her bathroom to get ready for bed, but paused while she tried to decide what to wear. Lizzie looked so darned good in her sexy undies/pajamas, she hated to wear her usual mashup of sweats, T-shirts, pajama bottoms and boxers. But that's about all she had, so she grabbed the shirt and pants hanging from the back of the door and slipped them on.

When she exited, she realized her planning had been a waste of time. Lizzie was on her side, an arm wrapped around one of the pillows, a gentle smile curling her lips. Her deep, rhythmic breathing showed she was sound asleep.

Jill slid into bed behind her, and growled with pleasure as Lizzie reached back, grabbed blindly for something she could tuck around herself, and settled for Jill's arm. She could easily, happily, willingly, spend every night just like this. Safe and secure in her home, with Lizzie in her arms.

Chapter Twelve

THE RINGING DOORBELL SENT the cats flying for cover, with Lizzie grasping a pillow and holding it over her head. You quickly learned things about a new bed partner's sleep habits, and Jill had already learned Lizzie was clearly not easy to startle, or even wake, meaning she would not be the one to investigate strange noises.

Jill crawled out of bed, while glancing at the clock on her night-table. Nine a.m. Not ridiculously early, but not a great time for visitors. She walked downstairs, peered out through the glass sidelight and spied Gerri, who caught her eye and waved.

While opening the door, Jill tried to suppress a yawn. "Hi," she said. "What's up?"

"Ooo. You weren't," she said, looking a little sheepish. "I thought you were always up by nine."

"Usually. But I was up late last night." She stood there, hoping Gerri would get to the reason for her visit in the very near future.

"Well, I wanted to catch you before you made breakfast, but I didn't want to wake you. That's a fine line." She extended a white box. "Mary Beth had some kind of get-together with her department this morning and she went to the bakery and loaded up. She left some for Kathleen and me, but way too many. I hate to see them go to waste, and I know you like them…"

"Oh, that's really nice of you." Jill took the box, then opened it slightly to sniff and make appreciative noises. "You know my weakness."

"I'll make you some coffee if you want to go get dressed," she said, a big smile making her look like a forty-something Girl Scout.

"Aww, that's nice of you, but you don't need to do that. I'll get around to it." She hadn't moved from her position right in front of the door. Gerri wasn't the most perceptive person in their group, but she could usually pick up a clue this big. When the person you've surprised doesn't invite you past the entryway—leave!

"I was wondering," she said, fumbling a little. "You know your friend Lizzie?"

"Yeah, I know Lizzie."

"I assume she's straight, but it's hard to tell sometimes."

Jill just stared at her, not having any idea what to say.

"Is she?"

Damn, was Gerri always this dogged? Jill was much closer to Mary Beth and Kathleen, but she spent a decent amount of time with Gerri. Obviously not enough to realize she wasn't very subtle.

"Uhm…why do you want to know?"

"If she's gay, I'd like to ask her out." She laughed nervously. "If people her age even go out. I know that's not a big thing for…what is she? Twenty-five?"

Lizzie's feet hit the floor and Jill could hear her pad across the bedroom to the bathroom. Then the door closed. Jill ostentatiously looked up, staring at the spot where the noise had come from.

"Shit!" Gerri started to back away from the door. "I had no idea you had company."

"I do," Jill said, giving her a sly smile. "And you've saved us from having to go get breakfast. Thanks again," she said, as she raised the box.

"You're welcome." She stumbled a little on the first step, then held onto the railing for the next two. "You should have told me I was interrupting!"

"No problem. I wouldn't have come downstairs if I was really… involved." She waggled her eyebrows and tried to make her grin rakish. It was kind of mean to taunt the poor woman, but word would fly around their core group in the next five minutes. Might as well give them something to talk about. "Ta-ta."

Gerri stuck a hand up as she scampered down the path, hurrying back to her nearby home.

"Jill?"

"Come on down. Breakfast was just delivered."

Lizzie started down the stairs, both boys rubbing against her legs as she moved. "Did you say breakfast was delivered?"

She looked so adorably disheveled with her hair partially falling into her eyes, the strap of her camisole sliding down one arm, eyes not even half open. Jill went to the stairs and caught her when she got to the bottom step. She was only about two inches shorter than Jill, and the step put her at the perfect height for a hug. Jill nuzzled against her neck, murmuring, "You look so sexy when you've just woken."

"I do?" she purred, running her hands all across Jill's back and shoulders.

"Uh-huh. If we were at the point of…you know…I'd be guiding you right back upstairs."

Lizzie pulled away and looked at her, puzzled. "We're not at the point of…you know?"

"We're close, but I need for you to settle this with your parents."

"But I can't do that for another week!"

"Hey," she said, grasping her chin and looking into her eyes. "You're the one who skipped out last night. You could have woken your dad, or stayed over and done it today. Then it'd be over."

"Great." She pushed past Jill and headed for the kitchen.

Jill watched her go, almost drooling as her magnificent ass flexed beneath her silky shorts. Maybe they didn't have to be such sticklers for self-imposed rules…

She followed Lizzie into the kitchen and watched her move around, clearly annoyed, as she started to make coffee—noisily. They hadn't had many disagreements, so they didn't have a fighting style yet. One thing she knew was that she'd never again tolerate a woman lecturing her like Becca did. She didn't mind an argument, but only her mother was allowed to lecture her. And that was only because you couldn't change mothers.

Once the coffee-maker was working, Lizzie crossed her arms over her chest and leaned against the counter. "Why are you being so hard-headed about this?"

Jill was going to approach her, but Lizzie's body language didn't welcome that. So she jumped onto the counter and let her legs dangle off the edge. In a flash, David was at her side. She used to shoo him, but she'd finally learned that you could only train a cat to stay off the counter when you were actively watching it.

"I don't think it's fair to call it being hard-headed," Jill said. "I told you it was important to me that you spoke to your parents before we went any further." She held up a finger. "One request. Is that really asking too much?"

A dark scowl settled on Lizzie's face. "Now you're trying to make it sound like I'm being unreasonable."

"No, I'm not, because I don't think you are." Jill slid off the counter and went over to stand in front of Lizzie. "Put your arms around me," she urged.

After rolling her eyes dramatically, Lizzie did. They stood, looking into each other's eyes for a minute. "I want two things. One, to make sure you've given this a lot of thought and have faced any hurdles your family throws up. Two, I want to make love to you. A lot." She smiled, feeling a warmth in her chest when Lizzie's smile matched hers. "I mean in how much I want to, and how often I want to. I just want step one to come before step two." She leaned over, put her face up against Lizzie's sweet-smelling neck and nuzzled against it. "Is that really asking too much?"

"No," Lizzie admitted, starting to giggle when Jill began to kiss all along her neck and delightfully bare shoulders. She finally pushed her away, a little breathless. "I just like impulsive gestures. I like feeling that you can't resist me, even when you know you should."

Jill lifted her hand to tenderly arrange Lizzie's auburn locks, thinking, as she worked, that this was one area where Lizzie acted like a thirty-year-old. But that was fine. Touching, actually. It would suck if she'd already had all of the impetuousness beaten out of her.

"I can be romantic. And impulsive. I just need to get past this first barrier. Can you be patient?"

"You're worth the wait," she conceded. Then she laughed a little. "At least you say you are."

The coffee was ready, and Jill went to pull out cups. "You want some, right?"

"Uhm, yeah." She opened the refrigerator, then closed it. "I guess so."

"For someone who hangs out at a coffee shop, you don't seem to like it much."

"Yeah, I don't. But I like the space, and I like their free wi-fi, so I buy some just to pay for renting a place on their floor for an hour or two."

"I…uhm…noticed something when I was at your apartment." Their eyes met. "Would you like me to have some soda in the refrigerator?"

"Would you?" Her eyes lit up like a delighted kid. "Pepsi, please."

"That's a disgusting habit, but I'll enable it because I…" She almost said she loved her! *Jesus!*

Lizzie took the mug and added a ridiculous amount of milk, then scooped two heaping teaspoons of sugar into the mess. Jill watched her, then said, "Pepsi might have fewer calories and less sugar. I'll make sure to have some around."

"And cookies," she said, her voice taking on an excited tone. "Anything mint. And I really like potato chips with my lunch. No flavoring. None of that barbecue bullshit or vinegar or anything weird. Just plain."

Jill leaned on the counter, loving to listen to her babble away. "Anything else?"

"No, that'll do it. What can I have in my apartment for you?"

She seemed so sincere. It would have been churlish to say Jill hoped never to sleep in that fire-trap. But she tried to be polite. "I can't think of a thing. As long as you're there, I'll be happy."

"Oh, now you're being all superior." Lizzie wrapped her in a tight hug and tried to pick her up, managing to get her feet at least an inch off the ground. "Making it sound like I need soda and chips and cookies to be happy, but you're above that kind of thing." She dropped her. "You're heavier than you look."

"All muscle," she lied. "Wanna do something to get our blood flowing?"

"Sure." She poked at the box. "What's for breakfast?"

"My favorite Danish." Jill opened the box and laughed. "Wrong! Prune and apricot. The rats!"

217

Lizzie picked one up and started to eat around it, going in a neat circle. When she reached the center, she tossed it back into the box. "Not bad at all." She picked up another and held it to Jill's lips, twirling it as she ate. "You're fun to play with. Don't you think play is important?"

"Vitally," she said, meaning it. "Let's polish off the rest of these sad things and go do just that."

"I need to be in the water," Lizzie said.

"Done deal. I do too."

❦

They didn't have to drive far to get to a rental place near the lake. Jill went in while Lizzie was still slathering herself in sunblock. When she came out of the shop she held two lightweight vests and a pair of paddles. "What's sup?" she said, laughing at her own joke. "It's a stand up paddle board. Get it? S-U-P."

"Supb," Lizzie logically retorted. "Otherwise it's just stand up paddle, which isn't really the same thing." She planted a kiss on Jill's lips. "But I'll allow it because you looked cute when you said it."

"Have you done this before?" They went over to where the boards stood, all lined up neatly.

"Nope. But I'm game." She stood next to a huge one. "How tall is this? Thirty feet?"

"Just eleven. Ideally, I think we'd do better on a slightly smaller one, but they've only got the big boys left."

"I'm giving up big boys, but I'll make an exception." She put her hands on the board and tried to lift it, but the top started to go past vertical. Jill stopped it right before it toppled over on her.

"Hold on there, sparky. Carry it a little closer to your body."

"I got it," she groused, hefting it over to the tiny beach.

Jill followed behind, then put hers down on the sand. "All we've got to do is balance, bend our knees and paddle with our legs and torso."

"Sounds like dance, except for the paddling part. Very little paddling in dance."

"I think I'll just wear my suit. How about you?"

"Yeah. That'll work. Good thing I keep my beach stuff in my car, huh?" She whipped off Jill's baggy shorts and T-shirt she'd borrowed, then took all of their clothes and their flip-flops and tossed them back into the car.

They shoved the boards into the water, then sat astride them and paddled along for a moment until they were in deep water. "Ready? You should be great at this, since it's all about balance." Jill got to her hands and knees, then shakily stood, holding her arms out for balance. "So far, so good."

"How many times have you done this?"

"Once. Counting today."

"What? I thought you did this all the time!"

"Maybe I will," she said, smiling goofily. "But I've got to see if I like it."

Lizzie pushed herself up to her feet, then gracefully stood, with not even a wobble. "Not bad, if I do say so myself."

"Now we just paddle." Jill bent her knees and tried to get her whole body into the stroke. She almost toppled over, but righted herself by holding her paddle in the air like a tightrope walker. "Whoa! I hope you took lifesaving!"

"I'd definitely save you," Lizzie declared. "You're precious."

Lizzie was able to bend deep and get her whole core into the stroke. She glided past Jill on the surprisingly smooth lake, stuck a hand down by her butt and waved, making her look like she had a duck's tail.

"I'll catch you!" She was a little taller, a little stronger and a little stockier. Surely those attributes would let her storm past the elegantly gliding Lizzie.

Jill mashed down on her paddle, with her balance still a little wonky. As they got farther away from the shore, a nice wind picked up and gently pushed them along. Slowly, Jill got her footing and her balance followed along. Then she was able to make some progress. Lizzie saw her coming, and started taking long, powerful strokes that let her skim across the cold water, really making Jill work to keep up.

Her arms were turning to noodles after they'd been paddling hard for fifteen minutes, but Lizzie slowed down first. She folded herself into a yoga position and sat down on her board. "Who's toast?" she asked, holding up a hand.

"I am!" It was harder for her to sit, but she got down without going headfirst into the drink. "But this is fun, right?"

"Absolutely right." Lizzie lifted her paddle and sent a gentle splash of sixty-eight degree water onto Jill's legs.

A bigger splash came right back at her, and in two seconds they were furiously hurling water at each other, cursing when a splash caught them in the face.

"I'm gonna kick your ass," Lizzie declared when a tsunami of icy water hit her. She took a wide stroke and propelled most of it onto Jill, who shivered in the downpour.

"I give! Damn! I'm not sure we should be together. We might kill each other!"

"Nah. I'm not usually very competitive. And once you realize I'm superior in every way, you'll give up and worship me." A frown settled onto her face as she turned to look at both shores. "Are we closer to New York than Vermont?"

"Uhm…yep. I guess we'd better head back."

"How long did you rent these for?"

"Until closing. We've got plenty of time. I bet a half hour hasn't passed."

"Think we can make it to New York and back?"

"Mmm. I think it's possible," she allowed. "But we'll be demolished if we do."

"We're well over halfway there," Lizzie reasoned. "Why not give it a try?"

Jill wouldn't have done it if she'd been alone, but Lizzie made her actually want to do things that were past her comfort level. "What the hell? We can rest on the New York side for an hour or two and then head back."

They got to their feet and started paddling again, ultimately getting a good rhythm going. They easily skimmed along, reaching the other shore while they still had some gas in their tanks.

When they slid up onto the sand, Jill had a moment where she almost tumbled, but she righted herself again. "Whoo. I'm going to land on my noggin at some point, but this is a lot of fun. You're on the water, but it's not as freezing as actually being in it—unless you're being pelted by water, that is. And you can see everything. I like the perspective better than a kayak."

"But you can carry more in a kayak." Lizzie tugged on the long strap on the waterproof case she'd slung over a shoulder. "All I've got is my phone and a couple of candy bars."

"One of which I bet you're going to share." Jill sat down on the sand, letting the warm August sun take the chill from her feet.

"Okay. But only because you look so cute in that red suit." She sat right next to Jill, opened the waterproof bag and held two candy bars in the air. "You get first choice."

"Mmm, good quality chocolate." She leaned against Lizzie, enjoying the delicious caramel-filled milk chocolate, the sun, and Lizzie's presence. "I'm having a damned nice day. I'm kinda glad we came home last night."

"Me too. But I'm really not looking forward to going back to Sugar Hill next week."

Jill let out a sigh. "I'd guess not. Hey, your mom talked about a boyfriend you've never mentioned. Alex? Alan?"

"Adam. My first boyfriend. Serious boyfriend," she amended. "We were together until I decided I had to give the ladies another chance."

"Ouch," Jill said, wincing at the thought of having the same thing happen to her. "That must've been a blow to his ego."

Blithely, Lizzie tossed her hair over a shoulder, seemingly unsympathetic. "I didn't tell him the truth. We were going to college, and I convinced him we should spread our wings a little."

"That's all you said?"

"Uh-huh. My desire to be with women had nothing to do with him, so there was no reason to get into it."

That hit her like a punch to the gut. "Do I have to worry about the secret life of Lizzie Davis?"

Lizzie turned to face her dead on. Her expression was so open, so frank. Her hand went to Jill's leg as she tenderly rubbed it. "I've learned my lesson. I hide nothing from you, Jill. Nothing at all."

Swallowing her relief, Jill spent a moment just gazing into Lizzie's clear, open eyes. "I believe you. I promise I'll try to be as forthcoming as you've been. It's important."

"I'll tell you anything you want to know," Lizzie promised.

"Tell me about the people you've dated. I'm not sure what I want to know, but I'm awfully interested."

Lizzie gave her a slow, sweet smile. "I'll give you a synopsis." Turning serious, she sat up a little straighter. "I've always tried to be in relationships. Men or women. Doesn't matter. I'm looking for permanence. For something solid to built my life around." Leaning close, she placed her lips to Jill's, then moved forward, increasing the pressure. As they broke apart, she spoke quietly. "We're going to build a life together from the ground up. Sturdy. Safe. Permanent."

"Damn, that sounds nice," Jill whispered, breathing in Lizzie's alluring scent.

"It will be. Promise." She brushed the hair from Jill's face, whisking away the strays that had fallen from her ponytail. "I'm interested in you too. Fascinated," she added, looking it. "Want to tell me about the bevy of beauties who chased you all over Burlington?"

"Nothing too exciting. I dated guys in high school, switched to women when I got to UVM, and never turned back."

"I used to spy on you and Mark. I've seen you kiss guys. On my porch!" she added, giving Jill a playful punch.

"I couldn't do that on my porch," Jill said, laughing at the thought, "so I had to use yours."

A frown flashed across Lizzie's face. "Did you have sex with guys?"

"Not *real* sex. Just some fooling around."

Lizzie's eyes danced with interest. "What kind of fooling around? I want to fantasize about you doing all sorts of dirty things."

"You do?" She stared, surprised. "I haven't given this much thought, but I don't think I'd want to imagine you with other people."

"Why not? Knowing people find you hot just confirms my good judgment."

Jill laughed at her. "Your perspective is odd, but somehow complimentary."

Lizzie bumped against her playfully. "Come on... Tell me your dirty secrets."

Jill cleared her throat, as if preparing to make an announcement. "I have," she said solemnly, "had my hands around a penis. But never my mouth." She made a face, just thinking about it. "I was *way* too gay for that."

"But you let boys touch you?" She still looked like she was listening to one of the most fascinating things she'd ever heard.

"All they wanted," Jill agreed, laughing at her hyperbole. "I figured one of them would find the key to making me want to go further." She shrugged. "Never happened."

"Enter the fairer sex," Lizzie said dramatically.

"Yep. Two girlfriends in college, each an awful mismatch. But I was so clueless I didn't realize we weren't adding a thing to each other's lives."

"But you were confident enough to come out?"

"Yeah," she said, thinking of those days. "I finally realized I was going to be with women—even if I hadn't found the right one. That's when I told Mark. Right before graduation."

"Then he told his lovely stalker, and... There you have it."

"Kinda." She sat up and did some lazy stretches, trying to get her muscles loose for the return trip. The wind was blowing her hair back, but it was so cooling she welcomed it. "We'd better head back."

Lizzie stood, her supple muscles clearly not needing any convincing to start working again. "I want to know about every relationship you've had. Especially the adult ones."

"I'll tell you all about them. I'll dole out the information a little bit at a time, so you don't get sick of me." She snaked an arm around Lizzie

223

and pulled her close. "I'm surprised at how few boyfriends you've had. No quickies you slipped in just to keep things interesting?"

"Never. I have to know someone well before sleeping with them, then I stick with them until it's clear it's not gonna work."

Jill hated to be a stickler, but she reminded her of a couple of exceptions to that rule. "Unless you're just looking for an escape valve to relieve the pressure."

She waved a hand in the air. "Those women weren't in the same category as the people I was in a relationship with. When I'm committed, the rules are different."

"Then we're in good shape," Jill said as she buried her face in Lizzie's hair and rubbed it back and forth. "Because this is gonna work."

"How confident are you that we're going to make it back to Vermont? The wind is blowing right in our faces." Her arm was draped around Jill's shoulders as they surveyed the lake, watching the wind send ripples across the surface. "Hey, wanna go on a boat ride for Labor Day?"

"A make-up for the one that got canceled for our birthdays?"

"It wasn't cancelled," Lizzie said, pinching her cheek. "I wanted to be alone with you."

Feigning outrage, she said, "What if I really wanted to go on that boat?"

Lizzie grasped her and pulled her in for a kiss. "You couldn't have had a better day. Don't pout."

"I'm not pouting at all. Actually, I'm damned glad you manipulate me. Clearly, you know what I want."

"I do. I'm not sure how we're going to accomplish the next thing you want, which is to get back home, but we'll give it a go."

They started off, with the paddles feeling small and ineffective compared to the outbound trip. Tiny waves broke over the tips of their boards, further impeding them. Lizzie was in front, and she dug deep, flexing her knees and stretching to pull herself along. They were making progress, but not much, with every stroke only moving them a foot or two.

"How wide is the lake here?" Lizzie asked, her voice muffled by the headwind.

"Feels like a hundred miles. New York was so close! Did they move Vermont when we weren't looking?"

Lizzie stopped paddling and turned to face Jill. "We'll never make it." In the few seconds since she'd stopped paddling, she drew even with Jill, then fell behind. "I just lost two yards!"

"Sit down," Jill said. "You're acting like a sail." Jill squatted, then sat. "Ideas? I've got car keys, which don't help much. I locked my wallet in the car, and I don't have shoes."

"Or pants."

"Right." She took a look at Lizzie. "With that bikini, you could stick your thumb out and get us a ride to just about anywhere, but that's probably not smart."

"No, I don't like to hitchhike barefoot, in a bikini. That's asking for a perv to pick us up."

"Are you ready to tell some of my friends we're dating?"

"All of them," Lizzie agreed, smiling brightly.

"Then let's go back to New York and call around to see if there's anyone who likes me well enough to leave the state to pick us up."

❧

"Good thing we loaded up on the sunblock," Jill said as they used their paddle boards as beach blankets while waiting for Karen, who'd agreed to pick them up.

"Wish I would have brought my sunglasses. But I was afraid I'd fall off and lose them."

"Not you. You're like a cat on that board. I can't imagine how good you'd be if you practiced."

"I wouldn't mind having one of these," Lizzie said, giving the board a slap. "But I'm still at the point where I've got to budget to buy shorts."

"You can start saving for your board. I'll buy your shorts."

Lizzie reached over and took Jill's hand. "You don't… You don't think I expect you to pay for me, or buy me things, do you? The guy who owns the boat is always complaining that women expect him to pull them up to his level." She looked at Jill very soberly. "I'm not like that."

"No, Lizzie, I don't think that," Jill said, gentling her voice. "But I hope you'll let me pay for dinner once in a while. Like tonight," she said, rolling her eyes. "We've got to take Karen out to thank her for rescuing us. We should go someplace good."

"Two-dollar-signs good?"

"I was thinking three. I really like that place on Cherry. Right across from the Episcopal cathedral. Know it?"

"I know of it, but I haven't been there. If we're going out to dinner, I need to stop by my house. I'll look like a dope if I wear your clothes."

"My clothes are dopey?"

Lizzie shifted to sit on Jill's board, then leaned over and hovered just above her face for a moment. "Your clothes look lovely—on you. On me? They look like I went through a laundromat and grabbed stuff at random." She placed a soft kiss on Jill's lips. "I plan on spending a lot of time getting your clothes off, but I don't need to put them on."

Jill put her hands on Lizzie's shoulders and held her in place, loving the way her body felt when it pressed against hers. Lying in the sun, on a warm August day, with a woman you were falling for was about as good as it got.

A quick "beep" made her turn her head to see Karen's SUV pulling up alongside the road. "Good thing we decided to tell Karen we're together." She patted Lizzie's butt, urging her to stand. "This would be hard to explain, unless you were giving me mouth-to-mouth resuscitation."

❦

The three of them stood at the rail of the ferry as it puttered back across the lake. "I'm glad you didn't do this a month from now," Karen said as she raised her hand to keep the glaring sun from her eyes. "Once the ferry stops, it's a long way to New York."

"If we buy boards, we'll be sure to stay close to our side of the lake," Jill said. She looked out at the boats pulling wake-boarders, sailboats gliding along with their sails full, and jet skis zipping past, their passengers whooping with delight or terror. "It's hard to believe the lake will be mostly empty after next weekend."

226

"She loves summer," Lizzie said, sticking her lower lip out in sympathy.

"Of everyone I know, she loves it the most," Karen agreed. "She's got the soul of a warm-weather person."

"No, I don't," Jill maintained. "I like winter too. But I *love* summer."

They were meeting Karen and Becky at the restaurant at eight, which was late for Jill. But after taking the ferry back, going by Lizzie's for clothes and heading home for showers, it took every minute they had to spare.

Jill found a parking spot on Bank, then decided to cut across Church, even though the pedestrian-only street was sometimes choked with crowds. It wasn't bad tonight, probably because it was a little late.

Jill spotted her friends just ahead, and she called out. "Becky! Karen!"

They stopped, turned, and waited for them to catch up. "Good timing," Becky said, giving both of them a sly smile.

Deciding to get any discomfort out of the way, Jill said, "May I introduce my girlfriend? The divine Lizzie Davis."

Becky laughed and extended her hand to shake Lizzie's. "I'm very glad to know Jill's found someone, and even more glad that it's you."

"Thanks," Lizzie said, blushing slightly. "I assume this is going to be weird until we both meet all of each other's friends, but you guys have all been very welcoming."

"We're usually pretty laid-back," Karen said. "You'll fit right in."

They started to walk again, with the crowds making it tough to be four-abreast. Lizzie was holding Jill's hand, trailing behind Karen and Becky, and as Jill was about to greet a co-worker, her hand was dropped. She took a quick look at Lizzie, who seemed flustered.

"Hi, Celia," Jill said.

"Lizzie," the man Celia was with said, looking more uncomfortable than Lizzie did.

"Hi, Jon," she said quietly.

Jill focused on Lizzie's ex, surprised by his size. Somehow she pictured Lizzie with thin, artsy guys. But Jon looked like an urban lumberjack, black hair, thick, bushy beard, broad shoulders, plaid shirt with the sleeves rolled up to expose muscled, hairy arms.

"Do you two know each other?" Celia asked.

"Yeah. We…" He looked like he wanted to disappear. "Lizzie and I worked together on some projects when we both lived in Boston."

Jill stuck her hand out, just wanting to get the formalities out of the way so they could skedaddle. "Jill Henry," she said. "Celia and I work together."

"Good to meet you," he said, not looking directly at her. "Jon Andrews."

"We're with friends who've gotten ahead of us," Jill said. "I hate to have to rush off…" She was already starting to walk backwards, with Lizzie right at her side.

"See you at work," Celia called out, waving.

Karen and Becky were waiting for them. "Was that someone from Admin?" Becky asked.

"Yeah." Jill knew she looked like she'd seen a ghost, but it was Lizzie who anyone could tell was upset. Jill was skittish about saying anything, but Lizzie stepped up to the plate.

"My ex is dating her," she said, her eyes shifting nervously.

"Your ex?" Becky blinked. "That guy?"

"Uh-huh." She looked like she was in pain, but told the whole truth. "Jill's my first real girlfriend."

"Oh!" Becky said, obviously trying not to look surprised. "That's always awkward, isn't it? Running into an ex."

"Yeah. Awkward," Lizzie agreed.

"Uhm, do you two want a minute alone? We can go claim our table."

"Good idea," Jill said, guiding Lizzie close to one of the stores. "Are you all right?" she asked, placing her hands on her shoulders and looking her over.

"Yeah. Fine," she said, seeming anything but. "Damned small town. You can't get away from people here."

"Was that…?"

228

"The first time I've seen him? Yeah."

"We don't have to rush. Actually, we can cancel if you're not up to being with people."

Nodding, Lizzie took a deep breath, clearly knocked off her stride. "I don't know why that bothered me."

Jill watched her carefully, seeing a mix of hurt and anger.

"Maybe because he tried to act like he didn't really know you? I would have cried if Becca did that to me."

"You would have?" She looked up at Jill, seeming very brittle.

"Yeah, of course." She took Lizzie in her arms and tightened her hold when she felt her body start to shake. "Shh. It's okay. He's hiding something from her, but that's his problem. It has nothing to do with you, baby."

"Baby?" Lizzie looked up, a smile beginning to form. "Are you sure about that one?"

"No good?"

"I like it," Lizzie said, clearly considering the term. "But I wouldn't use that around my family—for a while at least. My dad calls me that sometimes and that could just get weird."

"I don't think I'll ever have the urge again. Actually, I might start calling you Ms. Davis."

"That won't be weird." She took Jill's hand and started to walk again. "I'm okay. Can you tell I've been crying?"

"Mmm, just a little." She reached into her pocket and took out a handkerchief, then dabbed at Lizzie's eyes.

"A handkerchief?"

"I have allergies. Usually just in the fall, but I like to be prepared."

"One of the many things I like about you. You're prepared."

"Yeah. That's why my friend had to take a ferry across the lake to fetch us. No wallet, no shoes…"

"No pants. Don't forget the pants."

"Oh, I won't. Neither will Karen. Expect to be teased about this for many years to come."

Lizzie pulled her to a stop and kissed her, surprising a number of people who had to veer around them. "I love thinking about being with you for many years to come. I absolutely love it."

Jill looked into her glittering eyes, so full of excitement. Of promise. "Me too, you delightful adult woman who's not, in any way, an infant or small child."

"Perfect," Lizzie said, snaking an arm around her waist as they started to walk. "Make sure you use that tonight. Can't wait."

⌘

Jill waved across the bustling dining room when Karen stood. "Are you sure you're okay to talk about this?" she asked as they moved through the restaurant. "Neither Karen nor Becky will bring it up. They're very respectful of people's privacy." They slipped by the hostess as Jill pointed to her friends.

"Yeah. I'm fine. Might as well get it over with."

They sat down and ordered drinks when the server bustled over. Lizzie took a sip of her water, with Jill noting her hands were a little shaky. "I…uhm…I've always identified as bisexual."

Both Karen and Becky were giving her their full attention, but neither one pressed for more information, which made Jill love them all the more.

"I honestly wish I were lesbian," she said quietly. "It would be easier in a lot of ways."

"I think that's true," Karen said. "I work with a lot of people who identify as bi, and many of them feel like they're caught between two worlds, neither of which understands them well."

"Right," Lizzie said, nodding. "But my real mistake has been never coming out as bi. My family doesn't know," she added, giving Jill a quick glance. "Well, my mom knows now, but I still have to tell my dad and six siblings." She rolled her eyes. "And my grandparents, four aunts, three uncles and about a dozen cousins." She put her head down on the table for a few seconds, moaning, "Why did I wait until now?"

Jill put her hand on her back and gave it a gentle scratch. When she looked up, both of her friends were giving her sympathetic looks. That helped. It really did. But it didn't make Lizzie's task a bit easier.

⌗

When they reached Lizzie's apartment, Jill put the car in park and turned it off. "Are you busy this week?"

"Uh-huh. Very. We stop having outdoor events soon, so every day in August is booked. But I'll be able to go to Sugar Hill next weekend." She bit at her lower lip. "I'll probably have to go on Sunday, though. No way I can get the whole weekend off."

Jill stroked her cheek. "It's okay, Lizzie. Wait for another week if you need to."

"No," she said, shaking her head quickly. "I've made up my mind. I'll go on Sunday, and be back for our boat ride on Monday." She took Jill's hand, with her expression sunny and bright once again. "We'll have fun on our boat ride."

"I won't see you until then?"

"Mmm. If you really want me to, I could come over after work one night, but it'll be late."

"No, don't come just to sleep. That just makes your commute worse."

"Let's see how my week goes. I assume you start to get busy right after Labor Day?"

"Pretty much." She thought of not seeing Lizzie for a week, deciding that wasn't acceptable. "Let me go to Sugar Hill with you on Sunday. Then you don't have to take the train."

"Uhm… You know I'd love to have you, but I should talk to my dad alone."

"I'll drop you off, then go to my parents'." She leaned over and put her arm around Lizzie's shoulders, pulling her close. "I want to be there for you. I know you'll need to talk."

"Okay. I normally wouldn't let you drive that far just to keep me company, but I have no idea how this is going to turn out. I'd like the support."

"You've got it. Call me if you have any free time this week. And if not, I'll see you on Sunday morning."

Lizzie kissed her cheek, then pulled back a little. "Why don't I come to your house on Saturday night? Sleeping with you will calm me down."

"My bed is yours. Any time, Lizzie."

"That's a nice thought." She put her hand behind Jill's neck and pressed gently. Their lips met for a long time, with Lizzie slowly pulling away. "I like you. A whole lot."

"I like you too," Jill murmured, her voice taking on a husky tone. "See you on Saturday."

Chapter Thirteen

JILL COULDN'T GET RID of a low-level anxiety that nipped at her all week. By Saturday she was a bundle of nerves, having gotten herself worked into a lather worrying about Lizzie. Exercise hadn't helped. Even as she rode her bike to near exhaustion, images of Mike reacting badly kept popping up.

Her legs were quivering with fatigue when she finished cutting the grass, so she sat on the front porch and read for a couple of hours, managing to transport herself to another world—one where the lesbians in question had issues that made hers pale in comparison. Regrettably, she'd read too fast, finishing the book as the sun started to drop behind the house, leaving her hours to kill before Lizzie would arrive. But now a nice breeze dried her T-shirt and gave her the boost she needed to fetch her half-moon edger and tackle the errant grass trying to climb the walk.

Edging was always slow going, but she had to concentrate to keep the line nice and straight. And focusing on something—anything other than Lizzie—was a good idea. Feeling a little nostalgic, went to her favorite music streaming app, selected a band she'd liked in high school, then let her headphones encase her in sound.

She'd started at the porch, and by the time she'd gotten to the street it was getting too dark to see. All of her focus was on the last bit she had to finish, and when something wet and soft licked a swipe across the back of her knee, she yelped in surprise. The edger fell and she whirled around to find an adorable strawberry blonde puppy excitedly leaping into the air. Right behind the puppy, laughing silently, was Becca.

"Hey," she said, before realizing her headphones were still on. She yanked them off, then squatted down to pet the puppy. "What do we have here?" The dog joyfully licked her cheeks and neck.

"This is Daisy," Becca said, bending over to pet the dog and pull her from Jill.

"She's adorable. Really, really cute." Jill stood and dusted some of the grass trimmings from her sweaty legs. "Boomer liked nothing better than to lick my legs after I cut the grass. I thought that was one of his particular quirks."

Becca laughed, the melodic sound bringing back nice memories. "I told you every dog likes that. You thought Boomer was really unique, but he was just a typical dog."

Their eyes met, and Jill's stomach fluttered, thinking about how the three of them had been the closest thing to a family she'd had since she'd left Sugar Hill. "But he was a great one. You'll never convince me otherwise."

"I'd never try." Becca bent and picked the puppy up, letting out a grunt as she stood. "I'm not going to be able to do this for long, but I love holding her."

Jill stepped closer and scratched Daisy's belly. A wide pink tongue fell from her mouth and dangled limply as she squirmed with delight. "How old is she?"

"Six months this week." The sweet, calm expression that had first attracted Jill faded into the stern, chiding one that had become far too common over the time they were together. "Some idiots bought her and wouldn't train her or cage her when they weren't home. Then, when she chewed up their stuff and wet the carpet, they gave her to Golden Retriever Rescue. Broke their kids' hearts, and Daisy's too."

"I think she'll bounce back," Jill said, leaning over to let the puppy lick her cheek again. "Actually, I bet she hasn't thought about them since you showed up."

Becca bent and put the dog back onto the ground, where she immediately started to lick Jill's sweaty legs, so enthusiastic that her wagging tail created a breeze.

"I think she'd like it if I left her here." Becca reached down and petted the dog, trying to calm her down. "Animals can't resist you."

Jill almost made a joke, about wishing women liked her as much as animals did, but she slammed her mouth shut just in time. Becca would *not* find that funny. "Did you come by just to introduce me to your new family member?"

"Yeah. We're going on long walks to drain some of her energy, and we found ourselves not too far away."

That couldn't be true. Jill didn't know Becca's exact address, but knew she lived fairly close to the airport. That had to be three miles away, too far to walk with a puppy. But she hadn't heard a car drive up so... "You guys must be thirsty. Come in for a drink."

"We've stopped a few times already," Becca said. "But Daisy will always accept a bowl of water, even if just to play in it."

They went around to the back, Jill's usual entry. The boys had been coming to the front door and peering out the glass every once in a while, just to make sure she'd return to feed them soon, but they were nowhere to be found when Jill opened the back door. "Let me find a bowl that won't break," she said as she went to the cabinet where she kept mismatched pieces.

"Still haven't done the kitchen, I see," Becca said.

"Nope. It'll take me another year to save up enough to pay for what I want."

"Hey, do you mind if I go say hello to the fellas?"

Jill pulled out Boomer's metal water bowl, a burst of shame hitting her when she realized that was the only thing she'd hung onto from three years with Becca. Warm brown eyes went to the bowl, then they met Jill's and they shared a sad smile. "I'm glad you kept that," Becca said.

"I thought he might come by and visit," Jill said, revealing more than she'd planned. She wasn't sure how she'd thought the dog would get to her house, but she had a fantasy that Becca might grant her visitation rights. Given that they hadn't spoken since the day Becca and Boomer moved out, that was a crazy wish.

"He would have liked to," Becca admitted. "He really missed you."

"Yeah." Jill stared at the floor for a few seconds. She wanted to say the same about the cats, but she was fairly sure they wouldn't miss even her so long as someone else let them sleep on them and fed them equally well.

"I'm going to go find those little monkeys," Becca said, her voice strained with emotion. "I'll close the door so Daisy doesn't follow."

Jill watched her go, then filled the bowl and slid down the wall to get down to Daisy's level. "No pressure," she said quietly. "But you've got some pretty big paw prints to fill. I hope you make your new mommy as happy as Boomer did."

The puppy stood on her crossed legs and licked her face in a frenzy, making her laugh so hard her sides hurt. She knew it wasn't smart to let a dog do that, but Becca had always been the disciplinarian. She could easily fix any bad habits Jill would instill.

They went outside and walked around the backyard, with Daisy sniffing every interesting spot, which were many. It was fully dark, and Jill had to strain to keep an eye on the energetic pup as it nosed around the backyard on this moonless night.

Becca had been upstairs for what felt like a very long time, but Jill didn't want to leave Daisy alone in the kitchen. She didn't think the puppy would do any harm, but didn't want to upset her. This was the biggest reason she hadn't gotten a dog of her own. She didn't have it in her to discipline a puppy and set rules, yet she hated to be around badly behaved dogs. She'd solved that dilemma by remaining dog-less, but knew she was missing out. You couldn't maintain an office-induced bad mood when a happy, frisky dog practically did cartwheels to welcome you home.

Daisy was bored, and had decided it was time to see her mommy. She sat by the back door, whining softly and giving Jill a yearning look. "Okay. We'll go check on her. She must have fallen asleep or something." She scratched under the puppy's chin as she put her leash on. "Maybe you did walk over here, huh? Did you wear your mommy out?"

They went up to the second floor tentatively. Daisy was a little clumsy, but her desire to see her mommy was greater than her fear of the stairs, which she clearly did not have much practice with. When they reached the bedroom, the dog stopped abruptly, sat down with a thump and stared.

Becca was sitting on the bed, with two very alert cats now standing stock-still as they stared back at this unwelcome visitor. Jill expected them to hurl themselves over the dog's head and escape to the kitchen, but they must not have been sure they could make it. Oddly, the puppy didn't make a sound. Daisy just tilted her head and stared, puzzled.

236

"I'm afraid to move a muscle," Becca whispered.

Jill tore her focus from the rigid cats to look at Becca, who Jill now saw had been crying. "If Daisy stays quiet, they might just slink away."

"Maybe they could be friends," Becca said, sounding so wistful that Jill was taken aback.

"I don't think they want friends," she said, then winced when Becca's chin started to quiver.

She reached for Goliath, who backed away from her touch, his eyes so wide it was comical. He truly looked like he was facing a legion of fearsome animals, and had mere moments to figure out the best way to defend himself. He obviously thought he had to make a move, for he got down low and a nanosecond later he and David were gone. They touched down soundlessly, then must have gotten under the bed. That was Daisy's cue and she yanked away from Jill's weak hold and tried to wedge herself under the bed as well. Luckily, the space was too small for the big-boned puppy to fit, and she only managed to stick her face under, with a paw swiping ineffectively at the now hissing cats.

Daisy whined and barked, then Becca stood and gathered her leash. With a sharp tug, she had the dog at her side. "Quiet," she said with calm authority. "Quiet," she repeated, then pressed down on the puppy's hip until she sat, gazing up at her, while still whining in frustration at the very tempting playmates she desperately wanted to engage. "Good dog," Becca said, her voice now warm and encouraging. "You're a good dog."

"Damn, I wish I could do that," Jill said.

"You'll never be good at training a dog. You're too soft a touch." She smiled, but there was a clear measure of sadness behind her dark eyes. "But I bet we could make things work this time."

Jill just stared at her, at a complete loss.

"Boomer was almost ten when we moved in. With Daisy being so young, I'm sure the cats wouldn't see her as a threat."

"We didn't break up because of the animals," Jill said, trying to be as diplomatic as possible.

"I know. I know." Becca closed her eyes and shivered. She was about to cry again. Jill could see it coming. "We broke up because I was so controlling. But I've been in therapy, Jill. I'm *changing*."

"That's good," she said, sick to her stomach with the knowledge that she was going to have to lower the boom. "That's really good, Becca."

She moved a little closer, close enough so Jill could look right into her warm brown eyes, now streaked with evidence of her tears. "I'm changing for you. So you'll give me another chance."

Oh, shit! "I don't think—"

The back door slammed, sending the dog into a frenzy of barking. The cats, their bellies almost touching the floor, slithered out from their hiding places and shot past Daisy, who dashed after them, a mass of golden and gray fur flying across the room and down the stairs.

Jill ran behind, and was just halfway down when the kitchen door opened and Lizzie stood there, holding Daisy in her arms as the dog licked her face. "You bought me a puppy!"

"No!" Jill stopped abruptly. "It's not mine." She looked up the stairs and pointed. "It's Becca's."

Lizzie's gaze traveled up the stairs and landed on the door to Jill's bedroom. "Becca's in your room?"

Jill had never so desperately wanted a woman to emerge from her bedroom—to clearly show she was fully dressed and literally just passing by. But Becca was obviously not in the mood to come out.

"Uh-huh." Jill had no idea what else to add. She knew she looked like an idiot, but she couldn't get her feet to move her in either direction.

"Okaaaaay," Lizzie said, with much more grace under pressure than Jill possessed. "Then I guess I'll take off."

"No! Don't leave. Just…" She had no idea what she wanted her to do —other than fix this mess.

"I'll take the dog out into the yard." Before Jill could agree that was a good idea, both Lizzie and Daisy were gone.

Trudging up the stairs, Jill tried to figure out how this had all transpired. A simple afternoon of cutting the grass had turned into a noisy, emotional mess. One she was certain she hadn't asked for.

Becca was standing by the window, looking out. She couldn't have seen much, but as Jill got closer, she saw that her gaze was unfocused. "Hey," Jill said, as she put her hand on Becca's shoulder.

"I can't decide who to be more embarrassed in front of," Becca said, her voice flat and lifeless. "You or my replacement."

"That's not fair," Jill said quietly. "You haven't been replaced. It's not like buying a new car."

Becca turned and regarded her coldly. "It's not? How's it different? Once you get rid of the old one, it's out of your life forever."

Stung, Jill tried to hold back, but her mouth started talking before she could stop it. "I've never had a car refuse to see me, or talk to me or veer across a path to avoid me on campus. A car's never told my friends to never talk about it with me. A car's never taken a dog I loved away and refused to let me see it."

"That's because you never broke up with a car with no warning!" Her eyes slammed shut and she let out a frustrated breath. "Can we stop talking about cars for God's sake!"

"Yes. We can." Jill moved away, going to the far side of the room to lean against a tall chest. "I'm sorry I hurt you, Becca. I really am. But things weren't working for me, and I had no reason to think they'd improve."

"How can things improve when you don't give anyone a chance? People can change, Jill. But not when they don't see the ax falling."

This discussion was a huge waste of time and energy. She'd never convince Becca she'd expressed her unhappiness for well over a year. And Becca would never convince her that Jill had killed the relationship with no warning. "I'm sorry," she said, not entirely sure what she was apologizing for. "I wish I hadn't hurt you."

"Well, you did. Now you can make things worse by forcing me to meet your new girlfriend."

"You don't have to do that. I'll go get Daisy and meet you on the front porch."

Becca brushed past her on the way to the door. "That's even more embarrassing. I'm not going to run out of here like a thief." She strode down the stairs, chin held high. "This is just like you," she grumbled, her scolding like nails on a chalkboard. "Sneaking around and…" Jill stopped just short of the kitchen doorway when Becca came to a halt.

Jill hadn't noticed much about Lizzie when she'd come in. Now that she was sitting on the floor, legs spread wide, with Daisy lying between them, head resting on Lizzie's thigh, Jill took her in. She was dressed in her usual play clothes: tight jeans and a white ribbed tank top. This one was snug, making it clear she didn't have a bra on. Lots of thirty-something women dressed like this, but lots of college freshmen did too, and Jill had to admit Lizzie looked like she could have easily been starting her first week at the U.

Daisy jumped up when Becca entered, ran to her and climbed her leg for a scratch. "Down," Becca said, probably more harshly than she'd intended.

The puppy had learned a lot in a short time, and she sat down, wagging her tail fiercely while she waited for praise. "Good dog," Becca said, giving her a much needed scratch under her chin.

Lizzie got to her feet and walked over with her hand extended. "Lizzie Davis," she said, acting like this was just one of Jill's coworkers who'd dropped by. The woman was remarkably composed for someone her age.

"Becca Hartley," she said as they shook. "Good to meet you."

"Same here. Your dog's adorable."

Daisy dashed across the tile floor, her big paws slipping as she ran back to jump on Lizzie, begging for attention.

"Down," Becca chided her. Again, the dog put all four feet on the ground, but couldn't control that feathered tail. It whipped back and forth so fast it made a whooshing sound. "Thank you," Becca said. "She's going to be a good dog." She patted her thigh and Daisy bounded back to her, then sat at her feet and grinned up at her. It was probably just the way their mouths were formed, but Jill was sure that goldens could actually smile. "Are you ready to head home, little girl?"

"Let me give you a ride," Jill said. "You don't want to walk home in the dark."

"We're fine," Becca said briskly. She took Daisy's leash in her hand and led her to the front door. Jill and Lizzie followed behind, and they paused in the entryway. "Good to meet you, Lizzie. Goodbye, Jill." Then Becca was out the door, Daisy gamboling down the sidewalk at her side.

"Awk. Ward," Lizzie grumbled. She headed back to the kitchen, and by the time Jill entered was popping the top off a beer. "How many more times might that happen?" Her gaze moved around Jill's face as she surveyed her critically. "You've surprised me with strange women in your house twice in a couple of weeks. What's the final tally going to be?"

Jill wasn't sure what she'd done wrong, but something was stuck in Lizzie's craw. It seemed like a good idea to give her a minute to herself, so Jill made for the back door. "I bought an extra-long extension cord today. I'll go plug your car in."

"We're taking your car tomorrow. No rush." She took a long slug of beer. "I'm not the type to tell you who to see, but it might be a good idea to have your ex-lovers over when you know you're going to be alone. That was really strange, Jill. I didn't like it."

"I didn't invite her!" She knew her cheeks were turning pink, only making her look guilty. "I was out cutting the grass and they showed up."

"They've been here all day?" Now Lizzie's eyebrows shot up as high as they could go.

"No. Just since dusk. It was almost dark when a dog ran up and started licking my legs."

"Why'd she come? Does she live close?"

"Not very." Jill went to the refrigerator and got a beer for herself. After opening it, she took a long drink. "Sure you want to know?"

Lizzie moved to her, gripped her arm and led her to the den, saying, "I want to know a lot. Tonight's a great time to start." They sat down, Jill in an upholstered chair, Lizzie on the sofa. "Tell me about the whole roster. I want to know about every woman I might find when I drag my ass over here to *relax* after a long day at work."

Nervously, Jill took another sip, then put her beer onto the table that separated them. "I can see how annoyed you are, but that's not really fair. I didn't invite Becca to come over, but I could hardly turn my back and slam the door in her face. We both have exes, Lizzie. This could easily happen the other way around."

"Doubtful," she said, taking another sip, then tucking the beer up against her leg.

Lizzie'd stretched out along the sofa, diverting Jill's attention as she considered that Lizzie and the boys had a lot in common. They all managed to look long, languid, and collected, even in the most ordinary situations.

"Only Jon lives in Vermont, and he doesn't know my address"—she frowned crossly—"or want to acknowledge me."

"You get my point," Jill said, annoyed at Lizzie's literal take on the issue.

"I do. But my exes are really exey. I have a feeling yours aren't." Her look grew more pointed. "So tell me about them."

"Fine." Jill shifted around in the chair, jealous of Lizzie's ability to get comfortable just about anywhere. "I already told you I dated two women in college."

"You did. It didn't sound like you were serious about either of them though."

Jill shook her head. "That's not really true, but we don't need to talk about them. I don't even know where either of them lives."

"Tell me about the ones who matter," Lizzie said, her eyes fixing Jill in place.

"Okay. The first was Jennifer." Jill thought hard, trying to get the details right. "She was about fifteen years older than me."

Lizzie blinked in surprise. "Fifteen? And you act like I'm a teenager and you're a senior citizen because there's ten years between us?"

"I guess I have a double standard."

"I'd say so," she agreed, scowling. Jill hadn't often seen what she'd characterize as an angry sip, but that's what Lizzie gave her poor beer.

"I was working on my master's and she was a physician. We met when we were both volunteering at a women's health clinic."

"And what was Jennifer's lure?" Lizzie asked, still looking at Jill like she was assessing every word.

242

Shrugging, Jill said, "She was just cool. Even though I'd been sure I was gay for a few years, I was still floundering. Meeting Jennifer showed me how grownups behaved. I really liked being with someone who wasn't filled with angst about who she was and what she wanted to do with her life."

"That makes sense. So why am I here?"

Jill smiled at the way she'd put that. "Jennifer's not here because she needed to be in charge. Of pretty much everything."

"Which you didn't like?"

Unable to get comfortable, Jill shifted again, now sitting sideways in the chair, with her legs dangling over one arm. "I liked it in some things. But…not everything."

"Examples, please."

Jill nodded. "Big one. She was a golf nut. She'd bought a condo in North Carolina so she could play all year. Within three months of meeting me, I had an excellent set of clubs, was taking lessons twice a week and playing every weekend."

"So? What's wrong with golf?"

"I don't like it," Jill said, unable to get the look of distaste off her face. "I don't like anything about it. But Jennifer couldn't take no for an answer. She was sure I'd like it if I played often enough."

"No such luck?"

"I devoted two years of my breaks and summer vacations to playing golf. And I'd have to say I liked it less at the end than I had at the beginning."

"So you broke up because of golf?" Lizzie asked dubiously.

"No, but when I got an offer to go to Middlebury to be an adjunct, I jumped at it. She didn't want a long distance relationship, so we broke up."

"Middlebury's only an hour from here! Lots of people commute every day."

"Yeah." Jill nodded. "Gives you an idea of how bonded we were."

"She just let you go," Lizzie said, her brows drawn together in thought.

"Well, yes and no. I think she assumed I'd turn down the job if she told me to. She was…surprised when I took it."

"So she laid down the line and you jumped over it."

"Kinda. She wasn't happy with me, I'll admit to that. And I should also admit to being a wuss. I should have told her more consistently that I needed some space. But I let her run things until I couldn't take it anymore. That wasn't fair of me."

"No, it wasn't," Lizzie agreed. "But I'll give you the benefit of the doubt because you were young. We all screw up when we're inexperienced. Did you live with her?"

"Not technically. But I was over at her house nearly every night. She probably thought we were more committed to each other than I did."

"Not good," Lizzie said, her gaze growing darker.

"No. It wasn't good. And you're not going to like the next one, either."

Lizzie took a drink, then set her bottle down. "Hit me."

"I didn't get serious about anyone at Middlebury, but I was far from celibate."

"Do you think I care about how many people you've slept with? Because I don't. I'm much more concerned about how you treated the people you were with than how many it was."

"Good," she said nodding, hoping Lizzie didn't ask for a number, because she truly didn't have one—other than kind of a lot. "I stayed at Middlebury for two years, then took a job at Dartmouth."

"Got it. Still teaching?"

"Uh-huh. Still an adjunct. But they promised the opportunity to move to tenure track when one of the tenured professors retired or left."

"Okay. You're at Dartmouth. Who caught your eye? Given that I won't like it, I assume it was a freshman."

"No," Jill said. "I was never into students, but dating one would have been a better idea than what I did." Her mouth was bone dry. Not even a sip of beer helped. But she had to spit this out. "I fell in love with a married woman."

"Oh, fuck," Lizzie grumbled. "That's bad. Really bad."

"I know. Believe me. I know. We were friends for months. Just friends. Then her husband left for a tour of duty in Afghanistan and we started spending all of our free time together. Things got…out of control."

Lizzie sat up, no longer calm and serene. "Her husband was fighting for his country while you were screwing her?"

"That's not…" She swallowed. "Yes. That sounds horrible, but I guess it's accurate. He came home after eighteen months and she couldn't tell him the truth. So when I heard about the job in Burlington, I jumped at the chance to get out of town. I guess it was a combination of guilt and anger at Jess for leading me on—but I couldn't leave fast enough."

Lizzie held up two fingers. "Two relationships. Two escapes. And you were how old?"

"Almost thirty when I came back to Burlington."

"That's too old for that kind of bullshit, Jill. About five years too old."

"I was immature," she admitted. "But I was in love with Jess. Really in love. We were a great pair—"

"She was already part of a pair," Lizzie snapped.

"I know that. Cheating sucks in a big way. I'll *never* do it again."

"Did she ever leave her husband?"

"The last time I checked, which has been a few years, they were still together, and they had two kids."

Lizzie lay back down, contorting her body into the kind of loose, elegant pose Goliath often made, all graceful angles and curves. "At least you didn't screw things up for her husband. Maybe she got cheating out of her system."

"I hope so," Jill said. "That's much better than thinking she's unhappy with him."

"You're over her?" Lizzie asked, her chin tilting as she gave Jill a skeptical look.

"Yeah. I have been for a long, long time. I feel mostly guilt and regret when I think of her."

"Good. You should feel guilty when you screw around behind someone's back."

"I tried to learn from my mistakes, Lizzie. I went out of my way to avoid even a friendship with women who were committed to someone else. Hell, I avoided women much older than me, too, just to not have another Jennifer fiasco. I was super careful."

"Next on the list?"

"Katrina. A drummer in an indie rock band that toured around the northeast."

Lizzie finally laughed, the first hint of lightness since she'd come in the door, what seemed like hours earlier. "You don't stick to the same type, I'll give you that."

"No," Jill admitted, smiling at the memory. "She was much cooler than I was used to. And clearly much cooler than I was. We dated for about two years, and I finally called it quits when I couldn't get her to make a commitment to be monogamous."

"Wow. You gave her two years?"

"Yeah. We never saw each other on the weekends, and she was gone for a couple of months when they opened for a more famous band. I thought it was better to give her space than be mad when she cheated."

"But you broke it off?"

"Yeah." She nodded. "Katrina liked having someone to come home to, but that's about all she wanted. I wanted security. Some commitment."

"You didn't move away, did you?" Lizzie asked, eyes narrowing.

"Kinda. I bought the house just to change things up. I doubt she'll ever show up, in case you're worried. She moved to Portland a few years ago. She manages a club now."

"There's one mystery woman left. Give it to me."

"I've never had to plow through my history like this. It's unsettling."

Lizzie gave what she probably intended as an encouraging smile, but it came off with a little bit of menace to it. "Get it over with, and you won't be unsettled for long."

Tackling things head on was clearly going to be the new normal. Probably for the best. "I met Hannah when I was shopping for furniture. She was an interior designer, and a hell of a nice woman."

Lizzie looked around ostentatiously. "But she's not here either."

"No, she's not. She lived with me for two and a half years though."

"Long time. For you," she added, pointedly.

"Uh-huh. Hannah was just what I thought I wanted. Creative, inspired, able to commit, not bossy, not obsessed with anything. Actually," she said thoughtfully, "she was the easiest person in the world to get along with—except for her jealousy."

"And that was the kiss of death?"

"Kinda. Plus, I didn't feel challenged by her. I guess… I guess it was more that she didn't feel passionately about anything. She liked her job, but if I told her to quit, she would have. She liked Burlington, but if I said we were moving to Saigon, she would have gone to pack." She shook her head. "I know it sounds awful, but she bored me."

"That's not awful," Lizzie said. "You can't stay with someone if they don't give you any spark."

"I know. But she was stunned when I broke up with her. I never told her the whole truth."

"Why not?"

Jill looked at her for a few seconds. "How do you tell someone they bore you? Especially someone so nice, so kind, so eager to please. Damn, she would have run to take assertiveness training."

"I don't think you can change your personality," Lizzie said.

"No, you can't. And I couldn't change my need to have some spark in my life. So I made up a bunch of excuses. All of them lame. I felt like a louse, but I had to do it."

"How'd it work out for her?"

"Excellent," Jill said, starting to chuckle. "She's with Jennifer—I assume playing golf until their hands bleed."

"You're shitting me!"

"Nope. Burlington's not that big a town. We had some mutual friends who knew Jennifer, and they hooked them up. They're an ideal pair, to be honest. Jennifer just wants someone to go along and let her be the boss, and Hannah wants someone to lead her. I bet they're together until the end."

"And if they're ever bored, they can talk about you and what a shit you are."

"That's probably happened more than I care to think about."

"Then Becca showed up."

"No, first I got the boys. If Becca had come into my life just a little bit earlier, I would have been happy with just her dog. But I was lonely, and a pair of cats seemed ideal."

On cue, they sauntered into the den, looked at each person before deciding on Lizzie. As she smiled smugly, they climbed on top of her, David on a hip, Goliath pressed against her chest. "Don't mind me. I'm just over here, alienating their affections."

"I think you're more than halfway there." Jill drained her beer, then went to get fresh ones. When she came back, she put Lizzie's on the table, then bent to kiss her head. David let out an unhappy mew when Lizzie shifted to receive her kiss. "Knock it off," Jill grumbled. "You get to lie on her. The least I can have is a kiss." She sat down and took a drink. "I thought I had it all figured out with Becca. Not controlling, not boring, not obsessive, not married. We even got along really well in bed. But over time, she started lecturing me when I did something wrong. Wrong meant not how she'd do it, by the way. In retrospect, I wonder if she might have been going through early menopause. Her moods were *so* unpredictable."

"And you broke up with her for being moody? Remind me to keep my distance when I have PMS."

"No," she said, annoyed. "This was a longstanding problem. We fought about everything and nothing. She wanted Boomer to have the run of the house, but that meant locking the boys up in the spare bedroom. That fight lasted the entire time we were together. She wanted me to redo the kitchen rather than the bath. But it was my house, and I wanted a nice bath more than a new kitchen."

"Oh, come on! You broke up over a kitchen?"

"No, Lizzie. I'm just telling you some of the big, longstanding things we fought over. The point is that we fought. The only way to avoid having a fight was for me to give in and let her lecture me like a child. But being treated like a child made me not want to sleep with her any more. You can't get hot when you feel like you're in trouble."

"So you stood up for yourself over the bathroom."

"Not really," she admitted. "I hired a contractor and had the old bathroom ripped out while she was at work. Not the most mature thing I've ever done, but I was at the end of my rope."

"Damn, Jill," she said, shaking her head. "You've got a lot of strikes against you here. I'm not sure I'd be jumping in with both feet if I'd heard all of this before."

"What?" Jill jumped to her feet. "That's ridiculous! Every couple breaks up for reasons that don't necessarily make sense to an outsider. Damn, do you think I like having you break up with a guy because you couldn't agree on having three-ways just *once* in a while?"

"That's not fair," she said quietly. "I was trying to make our relationship work."

Hotly, she snapped, "Well, I'm sorry. But I was trying to find someone I wanted to spend my life with. I made some bad choices, but I tried to be honorable."

"You broke up with every one of them," Lizzie stressed. "And for reasons that should have been obvious from the start. No one starts lecturing you and demanding things be done her way after three years. And you can tell if someone's jealous in a couple of weeks! You just didn't see it."

"That's probably true," Jill admitted.

"It sounds like you're not able to judge your own needs and desires until you've been beaten over the head by something you don't like. What will it be with me? Clearly, you don't know!" Her voice had risen and cats came flying off her when she sat up. Beside herself, she started to pace across the den. "Maybe you'll think I'm too controlling, or too argumentative. Or I'll bore you."

Jill got to her feet and tried to calm her, but Lizzie shrugged her off. She stopped and glared at Jill, eyes filled with anger. "I've told my mom about you and I can't take that back! For the rest of my life, even if I leave right this minute and never see you again, my mom's always going to know I'm bi." She gave Jill a push to clear the way. "I wasn't ready to tell her, god damn it! And if we can't make this work, it will screw up everything! Why did you have to be so damned rigid about telling everyone? It's wrong to make someone come out before they're ready. You're as controlling as Jennifer and Becca put together!"

"God damn it, Lizzie. I'm so fucking sorry."

That broke the tension and Lizzie let herself be enfolded in Jill's embrace, her body losing its stiffness to become loose and pliable. Then her arms tightened around Jill, holding on as if someone was trying to pull them apart. "I wasn't ready," she sobbed, her tears breaking Jill's heart.

"I'm so sorry," she whispered. "It was wrong of me to push things. It was wrong to go to Boston together. We should have kept our distance from your family and worked on our relationship at our own pace. I screwed up."

"I'm the one who wanted you to go with us. And I'm the idiot who left the door unlocked. But"—she sucked in a gasp of air—"I can't tell my dad yet. I'm just not ready."

"It's okay," Jill soothed, kissing her forehead and her cheeks. They held each other for a long time, until Jill felt Lizzie let out a big yawn. "Let's go to bed."

They walked up the stairs together, hand in hand, but Jill paused at the landing. "I don't think we should sleep together tonight."

Lizzie stepped back and glared at her, immediately angry. "So you're the soul of understanding, but you're still going to get your way. I tell my family, or we don't sleep together."

"I'm not trying to just get my way," Jill insisted. "I want to take this slowly, Lizzie. I want to avoid the pitfalls."

"How is sleeping together a pitfall?"

"It is for me. I'm not going to have sex with you until you're sure you're committed to making this work."

"I *am*. Why won't you believe me?"

"Because you aren't ready to tell your parents the truth about your identity."

Lizzie grasped Jill by the shoulders and squeezed. "They know me better than any two people on this earth." With a rough shake, she added, "My *identity* doesn't change when I have sex with someone new."

"This isn't about sex, Lizzie. It's just not."

"It is," she insisted. "And I don't want to have to tell my dad we're having sex." Her voice rose as the color in her cheeks did. "What if we don't have any chemistry? Then I'm supposed to go back and say, 'Hey, you know what? I couldn't get Jill off, Dad, so we're not doing it any more.' My sex life is none of his business!"

"Fine." Jill was developing a headache from hell. She peeled Lizzie's fingers from her arms and turned for her bedroom. "We can talk about this later. I'm just not into arguing about it anymore."

"Don't leave!"

The tone in her voice was one Jill had never heard from her. Fear, definitely, maybe even panic. Turning, she looked to see Lizzie holding herself, arms wrapped around her body as her eyes closed against the tears that fell down her cheeks.

"Don't give up on me," she whimpered plaintively.

"I'm not." Jill rushed to take Lizzie in her arms and gently stroke her back. "That's never crossed my mind. I just want to get this right."

"By not making love? *That's* how to do it right?"

"No, no," Jill murmured as she caressed her angel-soft cheek. "I know myself, Lizzie. Once we're intimate I won't be able to back off. And if you're not able to commit to being a full time lesbian…"

"How is telling my dad going to convince you of that? It makes no sense."

"Maybe you're right. But if you're willing to risk a little, that'll give me some assurance that you're committed. You'll have some skin in the game."

"I'll have *all* of my skin in the game," she insisted, her gaze now heated. "Given how you feel about my family, and how they feel about you—once we tell them, we're as good as married. And we haven't touched each other!"

"That's not true. It's just not. If we don't get along well…" She sucked in a breath, not having any idea of how to finish that sentence. "I guess it'll be pretty sticky."

"I want to go home," Lizzie said, her voice shaky and thin. "I don't want to sleep in your damn guest room."

251

"If you want to go home, I'll pay for a cab. I don't want you driving after you've had a couple of drinks."

"Great. Just great." She stormed off, stomping down the stairs like she was going to break through the boards. A few seconds later, she was back, with her backpack in her hand. "I'll be the hostage in the guest room." She brushed past Jill and must have hurled her bag onto the bed, given the sound it made.

Shaking her head in frustration, Jill went into her room to get ready for bed. A few minutes later, she went to the switch by the door to turn off the overhead light. The door of the guest room was open, the light blazing. Not wanting to go to bed on such a sour note, Jill went to stand in the doorway. Lizzie was in her tank top and a pair of gray boy-shorts. Her heels were resting on the bed frame, elbows on her knees, chin in her hands, looking as sad and lost as Jill felt. Her gaze traveled slowly up Jill's body, and when their eyes met she said, "I'm afraid."

Jill sat next to her and put an arm around her waist. "Talk to me," she said gently. "Tell me."

She took in a deep breath and let it out slowly, like she was giving herself time to clear her head. "Look. I know it's only been two weeks, and that probably doesn't seem like much in lesbian time. But in straight time, that's like a year. I'm terrified that our sex drives aren't going to match. That I'm going to be chasing you like I had to chase Erica and Jenny. And if I have to do that…" Her hands gripped into fists and she pounded them hard against her knees. "It makes me feel so…small," she finally said. "So needy. Like I'm obsessed with sex." She sat up a little straighter and met Jill's eyes. "I'm not. I'm really not. But it's important to me, Jill. And I need to know it's important to you too."

"There's nothing to be afraid of," Jill said, tightening her hold and pulling her close. "Nothing. We'll be great together, Lizzie. I promise you."

Lizzie tilted her chin, her eyes so full of doubt Jill's heart skipped a beat. "A guy would have been begging me for sex by now. *Begging*. But I don't feel any urgency from you at all. You kiss me once or twice and then just walk away. Like you can take it or leave it. And if you're like that now…"

Jill put a hand on her shoulder and pulled it forward, so they faced each other. Softly, she said, "I'm not good at doing things halfway. I'm in or I'm out. So I've tried to keep it casual, but not because I don't want you." She took her hand and put it on Lizzie's cheek, closing her eyes as she stroked it. "I'm so attracted to you, I don't even have words to express it. I want to make love to you, Lizzie. I want it *so* badly." She moved towards her and captured her lips. Jill's hand went to the back of her head and pulled her close, pressing into her hard. Lizzie's mouth opened and Jill's tongue slid inside, then gently explored, probing the silky soft warmth until Lizzie let out a low, raspy moan.

Then they were on their sides, holding onto each other tightly as they traded hot, wet kisses that left them both panting. "I want you," Jill murmured. "More than I've ever wanted another woman." Her hand slid down along Lizzie's side and stopped abruptly. Gripping her hip, she grit her teeth. "You have to risk to love someone. I'll take the leap if you want me to. Right now," she pledged.

"But you're not ready," Lizzie said, a furrow forming between her brows.

"It's more important to reassure you. To show you how much I want you." She kissed her again, letting all of her desire pour from her body. "I want you to *crave* me for the rest of your life. I'll do anything to satisfy you in every way. That's a promise."

"Kiss me," she whispered, her eyes tightly closed. "Just kiss me."

Jill gripped her firmly and easily pushed her onto her back, then lay on top of her, letting Lizzie feel the weight of her body. She lifted up slightly, and gazed at her lovely face for a few heartbeats. Her pulse was thrumming, making her a little weak, and her desire had grown to such a height, she knew she couldn't turn back. Jill lavished those trembling lips with kisses, pushing against her squirming body until they were both purring with need.

They kissed for so long, Jill's lips felt swollen and hot. Lizzie lay limp in her arms, looking up at her quizzically. "Are you ready to make love?" she asked.

"That can't be a serious question."

"Emotionally," Lizzie clarified. She ran her hand down Jill's back, wet with perspiration, then let her fingers tickle across her side to touch an achingly hard nipple. "I can see your body's ready."

She couldn't begin to think clearly. All of her blood was rushing to her breasts and the throbbing pulse that beat between her legs. She had just enough mental acuity left to say, "I only want to make you happy. That's my only priority."

Lizzie reached up and ran her fingers along Jill's hairline, wiping away a bead of sweat. Then she settled her hair against her shoulders, clearly wasting time as she thought. "I don't understand why it's so important to you that I talk to my dad."

"I'm not sure either," she admitted. "I know it doesn't make sense. It just feels important."

"Okay." She patted Jill's side as she turned, dislodging her. "I want you to be a hundred percent into this." She placed a gentle kiss on her lips. "Like I am."

"I'm into *you*," Jill said fiercely. "I'm one hundred percent into you."

"We'll get there. I'll try to be a little more patient."

"Not too much," Jill said. "I'm patient enough for both of us most of the time. I just need a little bit from you."

"That's all I have. A little bit." She pulled Jill close for a final kiss. "And you can have it."

Chapter Fourteen

THE BOYS, EVEN THOUGH they were besotted by Lizzie, slept with Jill. She didn't like to admit the truth—that they probably chose her simply because they were more confident of her skills in feeding them. Still, it was nice to have them cuddled up next to her as she worried and puzzled through the night, analyzing her entire dating history. Sleep, when it came, was fitful, and she was happy to get up when the boys started making their demands.

Lizzie wasn't going to bound out of bed today, that much was clear. But when she was still asleep at nine, Jill went upstairs to wake her.

It was already warm, with high temperatures predicted in the eighties. Lizzie had thrown off the sheet, and was lying, spread-out, across the bed. She'd turned so that she was almost on her belly, with her arms flat on the bed, like she was being robbed.

Jill sat on the edge of the bed and ran a finger down her back, starting at the top of her spine. The thought of doing this every day—finding new ways to wake her, gave Jill a thrill that made her shiver. Lizzie clearly had doubts about Jill's desire and drive, but those doubts would be short-lived. She had no worries about keeping up in either area, even with a much younger woman.

It took quite a few seconds for Lizzie's brain to register the light touch, but she finally made a little whimper of complaint and stretched her legs out. Another teasing touch had her shaking her shoulders, like she was trying to dislodge whatever annoying thing was bothering her.

Jill shifted around and lay on her side, then started to stroke Lizzie's body. It took a while, but she finally gained the ability to speak. "Leave me alone," she grumbled.

Chuckling at her grouchiness, Jill tucked an arm around her and pulled her close, then peppered her neck and shoulders with kisses.

"Don't leave me alone," Lizzie mumbled, finally laughing a little.

"It's after nine," Jill said. "If you still want to go to Sugar Hill, we've got to get moving."

She sat up abruptly. "Nine?" Swiping the hair from her eyes she blinked a few times, trying to focus. "Why am I asleep at nine?"

"Was I supposed to wake you up? You didn't ask me to."

"I thought I'd hear you. Or that the cats would wake me. God knows they did when I watched your house over Memorial Day."

"We were all on good behavior."

"Bad behavior," Lizzie insisted as she got to her feet. Her tank top was twisted around, the top of a breast peeking out of an arm hole. Frowning, she straightened her shirt, then did the same for her shorts. "Were we wrestling or something? I'm exhausted."

"Nope. But I feel like I slept for ten minutes. I guess we're just anxious."

Lizzie walked around the bed and stood in front of Jill, who opened her arms to relish the comfort and security of holding Lizzie close.

"Do you have any Pepsi?"

"No, but we can stop and get some on the way."

"Give me ten minutes. I'll let my hair dry on its own."

"I'll be waiting." As Jill got up to leave, Lizzie grasped her hand and whirled her around. "Next time I spend the night, we're showering together. Among other things."

"Can't wait," Jill said, grinning happily as she went downstairs to get ready.

It took Lizzie a few more than ten minutes, but they were on the road by nine-thirty. Jill dutifully stopped at the first convenience store they passed and got Lizzie a huge Pepsi with ice. Then one more stop for two donuts, one glazed and one vanilla with multi-colored sprinkles. Jill glanced at Lizzie as she ate her breakfast with gusto, thinking of the plain yogurt with fresh berries she'd consumed. There were definitely benefits to being thirty.

"Guess what I did while I was lying awake for hours?" Jill asked after they were on the freeway.

Lizzie gave her a look so filled with sexual innuendo Jill nearly drifted off the road.

"Something you won't have to do for yourself when you get off this chastity kick."

"Not that," she scoffed, even though she had, in fact, had an orgasm fewer than five minutes after returning to her own bed. "I spent the whole night assessing what I've learned from my past relationships."

Lizzie's eyebrow rose dubiously. "You waited until *now* to do that?"

"No, I've done it a lot. But I felt clearer about some things after I talked about the whole string. It was like seeing a highlight reel."

"Don't keep me waiting," Lizzie said while poking Jill in the ribs. "I'm definitely interested."

"Well," Jill said, clearing her throat. "I realized that all of my relationships had something critical missing. Something that I didn't notice, or didn't want to notice. I can complain all I want about my partners, but I'm the one who accepted less than I needed. My fault," she insisted, patting herself on the chest.

"I think that's true," Lizzie said thoughtfully. "That's one reason I'm vaguely glad we're going slowly. I want you to have room to pull the plug if there's something you need that I can't give you."

"Nothing," Jill said, totally confident in her belief. "You're the right woman for me. I'm sure of it."

Lizzie gazed at the side of her face for a long time, her focus so intent Jill felt it as a touch.

"Once we tell my whole family, we're locked in. Are you sure that's what you want?"

Jill turned and met her gaze. "I'm positive. No doubts."

"Okay." She gripped her leg tightly and gave it a shake. "After today you're truly a member of the family." She leaned all the way over and managed to reach far enough to kiss Jill's cheek. "The thought of having you by my side at Christmas dinner is really, really appealing." She started to rub the muscles in Jill's shoulder. "How are you going to handle your family? Are you going to tell them today?"

"No. That wouldn't be a good idea."

"You're waiting for…what?"

"They don't know I'm gay." She flinched, assuming Lizzie would, at best, slug her. But when she turned to take a look at her expression, it was simply one of puzzlement.

"Why not?'

"We don't have that kind of relationship," Jill said, unable to think of a better way to explain it. "We just don't."

"You're forty years old," Lizzie said, now moving her hand up and down Jill's arm. "You've been with women your whole adult life. Neither of your parents have asked about that?"

"Not a word. They don't ask personal questions. Heck, I'm not sure they know what I do for a living."

"What?" Lizzie's voice echoed in the confines of the coupe.

"They know I work for the U. I think," she added, having to give that a moment's thought.

"God damn, Jill. What… I don't even know how to follow that up with a question."

"We're not close. I don't have any better way to explain it."

Lizzie let her hand slide down until it rested on Jill's leg. For the next hour, she stroked it, patted it and massaged it, but she didn't say another word.

Jill thought about her situation as Lizzie was clearly doing the same thing. They were about an hour away from Sugar Hill when Lizzie asked, "Do you want to have a better relationship with your parents? Or have you given up?"

"I…" She took a moment to consider her answer. "I like to believe that one day we'll grow closer. But I think that's wishful thinking."

"Then we'll just share my family. God knows there are enough of us to go around."

Jill grasped her hand, brought it to her lips, and kissed it tenderly. "I'd really like that."

"And if you change your mind, and want to tell your family about us —I'll support you in any way you want. Promise."

"I don't think I will, but it's nice to know you're behind me."

"I am," Lizzie said, her voice full of concern. "I want your parents to realize what they're missing by not knowing you better, but I trust you to know whether or not they're able to change."

"Thanks." A lump formed in her throat. "I'll think about it some more. It might be a good idea to talk to them, even if it's not something they want to know."

"No rush. We've got time," Lizzie said as she leaned over to place a soft kiss on Jill's cheek.

⁂

They sat in the driveway of the Davis house for a few minutes, with Lizzie giving every indication she was about to vomit. Jill had nothing but sympathy for her, but there was truly nothing she could do or say to make it better. This was Lizzie's dilemma.

That thought must have hit her at the same time, for she reached for the door handle, flipped it open and stepped onto the drive. "I'll call you," she said, then marched right up to the house.

As Jill drove away, she thought about Lizzie and her courage. As anxious as she was, she just got it over with. That was a fantastic trait that Jill could stand to copy. Maybe being an honorary Davis would rub off on her.

The drive to her parents' house only took four minutes. It was so close she should have walked, but she didn't want Lisa, the town crier, to see her car at the Davis house.

When her mom didn't answer the door, Jill walked around to the back. Wearing her summer uniform of khakis and a cotton shirt, her mom was on her knees in front of a bed full of dahlias. "Those look great," Jill called out across the yard, twitching when her mom started visibly.

"I hate to have someone sneak up on me," she said, her shoulders hunching in anger. She hadn't even turned around, but Jill knew the exact expression on her face. Her brows were drawn together, mouth pursed tight. Like she'd just eaten something unexpectedly sour.

Speaking as softly and gently as she did after startling the cats, she said, "I'm sorry, Mom. I thought you were expecting me."

"I'm busy, Jill. Do you think I'm sitting here watching the clock?"

"No, of course not. I just…" Trying to explain herself was a waste of time and energy. She walked closer. "Can I help?"

Her mother finally looked up. Jill had asked this question at least a thousand times, and for the entirety of her youth the answer had always been an unqualified "no." In the last few years, however, she'd proven herself competent enough to assist in a few things.

"Your father's supposed to keep the front yard up, but he does a terrible job. Why don't you cut the grass and edge the walk and the drive? Then I don't have to supervise him."

Jill's shoulders dropped and, without comment, she went to the garage to get the mower. She'd driven two and a half hours to cut the grass—a half acre away from her mother. Typical family time for the Henrys.

After finishing the yard, Jill went into the house to get a cold drink. Her mother was sitting close to the house, drinking what looked like lemonade. She held up the glass. "I was going to offer you some, but I never know what you can have with your allergies."

Blinking in surprise, Jill started to say a mild ragweed allergy didn't have much bearing on her diet, then a dim memory hit her. "Do you mean the egg allergy I had when I was really young?"

"People die from those every day of the week, you know. You'd better be careful."

"Yeah. Okay." She went inside, took a glass from the perfectly organized cabinet and filled it with water. Gazing out at the lovingly manicured yard, she thought about her mother's comment. Her egg allergy had been really mild, and it had disappeared by the time she'd started school. But she did remember her mom focusing on it much more than she should have. Was she just frightened of things she couldn't control? Jill had no idea. She went out and pulled a chair over close to the house to keep it in shade. As soon as she sat down, her mother got up.

"I think I'll run over to the garden center." She started for the house, then stopped. "Will you be here when I get back?"

The garden center she liked was almost in Brattleboro. She'd be gone for two hours—at least. The lack of an invitation to join her wasn't an oversight. She didn't like passengers in the car. "No, I'll probably be gone by then."

Her mom gazed at her for a minute, like she was going to say something important. Jill maintained eye contact, only to hear, "Can you drive a screw straight?"

"Yeah. What do you need?"

"I've got those frames I put around the evergreens along the front of the house. Could you put them together for me? They'll fill the garage, but I'd like to have them ready just in case we get an early snow."

It was August the thirtieth. And her mother wanted to fill the garage with big, plywood covers that looked like sidewalk advertisements. Jill knew whose car was going to be sitting outside until those covers were put over the plants. Her father was treated like an unwelcome houseguest.

"Do you have a drill?"

"Of course. You know where everything is."

Well, that much was true. Everything was neatly boxed and labeled. If you couldn't find something in that garage, you just weren't trying very hard.

While Jill finished her water, her mother had gathered her things, then come back outside. "You don't need to go inside, right?"

"I guess not. I'll just close the garage door when I'm done."

"Good. Now if you're not *sure* you can do it right…"

"I'm pretty sure, Mom," she said, strangely pleased at having essentially been given a promotion. She'd never been asked to do anything that required decision making.

"Oh. I have a birthday card for you." After looking through her purse for a moment, she pulled it out. "I would have mailed it, but I don't trust the mailmen not to steal anything that looks like it might have money in it."

Jill started to open it, but her mother was already walking to the car.

"Drive safe," she called out. "Half of the people on the road are crazy, and the other half don't care what they hit."

"Bye," Jill said, the all too familiar feeling of abandonment hitting her in the gut. Each time it was a sucker punch, but she'd learned to ride it out, to reassure herself the feeling wouldn't last long and that she had friends and love in her life. Still, it was so hard to maintain that perspective when she'd always felt like she was bothering her mother. Like her mere presence was an inconvenience that her mom would really rather be without.

As the car backed out of the long drive, Jill waited, hoping for a final glance. Or a smile. Even a wave to show they'd had some sort of connection. But her mother stared at the rearview mirror as she backed out quickly and precisely. The way she did everything—with a robotic lack of emotion.

⸙

After finishing her tasks, Jill spent most of the afternoon cooling her legs in one of the most charming spots in her very charming home town. The town pool was tiny, barely big enough for twenty people standing shoulder to shoulder. Actually, it was more of a pond than a pool, with a stone edge and black water that looked like it might be any depth you could imagine, but it was just four feet deep, and always chilly. Jill assumed it was fed by a nearby stream, but she'd never bothered to ask. All she knew was that it was a little piece of heaven to sit on the edge and smile at the kids who came by to tentatively poke a toe in, then run back to their moms, insisting it was freezing cold and deeper than the sea.

Her smile grew much bigger when a hand settled on her shoulder. She looked up to see Lizzie staring down at her. "I tracked you on your phone."

Jill started at her feet and let her eyes travel up what seemed like yards of shapely, muscular legs. "Where did you get those shorts?"

"High school. Or maybe college. When I saw you were over here, I figured you might be in the pool." She plucked at the tiny shorts, so brief they wouldn't have covered her regular underwear. "These were all I could find." She kicked off her flip-flops and stood on the single step. "You're staring," she teased, reaching down to shut Jill's mouth. Then she sat right next to Jill and leaned against her. "I have a great father," she said, sighing.

"I know that." Jill pressed back against her. "Wanna tell me how great he was this particular day?"

"Nothing unexpected. He asked me a few questions, then said he was surprised. No judgment at all. Just surprise."

"That makes sense. I think that was true for your mom too."

"He wants to talk to you," Lizzie said, her eyes dancing with devilish pleasure. "I think he wants to know your intentions."

"Now?"

Still smirking, Lizzie nodded. "He's waiting."

Immediately, Jill scrambled to her feet, picked up her running shoes and waited for Lizzie to join her. "Why aren't you moving?"

"I've already talked to him. He wants to see you. Alone."

Jill could feel the blood drain from her face. "Oh, shit. Am I in trouble?"

"Maybe," she said, singing the word like a kid.

"You're getting way too much enjoyment out of this."

"Look at the bright side," Lizzie called after her as she started to walk. "He'd never hit a woman."

The Davis house was two minutes from the pool, and Jill's legs were still cool and damp when she got there. Mike was sitting outside in the backyard, a beer in his hand when he looked up and waved Jill over.

Awkwardly, she leaned over and kissed his cheek. "Hi," she said, unable to think of another word.

"Did Lizzie tell you she could have knocked me over with a feather?"

"Uhm, yeah," she said, finding herself nearly nonverbal.

"I had no idea she was attracted to girls. But to you?" He took a long drink of his beer, then looked her up and down. "You probably want a beer too. You don't mind getting it yourself, do you?"

"No, not at all." She got up and made for the house, but he redirected her.

"Right there by the porch. In the cooler." She opened the battered cooler, recognizing it from her childhood. The Davises didn't throw things away while they still had useful life in them. She loved that about them. Jill grabbed a beer, twisted off the cap and put it into her pocket. Then she went back and sat down next to Mike.

"I didn't say this to Beth...Lizzie," he corrected himself. "I've got to get better at calling her what she wants to be called."

"She appreciates that," Jill admitted. "But she knows it's a big change for you and Janet."

"She likes to keep everyone on their toes." He elbowed Jill playfully. "Don't think you're going to escape that."

"Oh, I know I won't. Not a doubt in my mind."

"Right. Well, I didn't say this to Lizzie, but I always hated it when she brought a guy over. That last one—Jon, especially."

"Really? I thought he was a good guy."

"He was a big lunk." He stuck his hand out a few inches from his chin. "Bushy black beard. Broad shoulders. Looked like he could wrestle a bear and give it a run for its money."

"And you didn't like that..."

He made a face. "I didn't like to see a *man* put his hand on my little girl. I know that's stupid," he added, "but it gave me the willies."

Laughing at the way he said that, Jill asked, "It won't give you the willies to think of Lizzie with me?"

He clapped her on the back. "I'm not going to give one minute's thought to what you two do behind closed doors. What I don't know won't hurt me." His teasing smile faded as his voice took on a sober tone. "I know you'll treat her well. You won't hurt her like some of those jerks did." His hand moved until it settled on her shoulder, where he gave it gentle pressure. "You're a hell of a nice girl, Jilly. I couldn't ask for better for my baby."

The tears were filling her eyes before she had a chance to stop them. She wiped at her eyes with the backs of her hands. "I'd give anything to have a talk like this with my own dad." *Damn it!* She hated to let things like that out.

Mike reached over and pulled her close. Jill rested her cheek on his shoulder, sniffling for a few seconds.

"I've always thought of you as the daughter I got to pick. When you think of it, that's much better than a blood relation. Sometimes the only thing you share with a relative is DNA." He released her and she sat up and wiped her eyes again. "We chose you because we love you, Jill." He patted her gently on the cheek. "I'm just a little worried."

"About me?"

"Naw," he said, shaking his head. "I'm afraid Lizzie might run you ragged. She can be a handful, you know."

"I know," she admitted, laughing. "I had a girlfriend who I broke up with because she never challenged me, never argued or stood up for herself."

"That's not my...Lizzie," he said, obviously catching himself on the name.

"No, it's not. We've already had more arguments than I ever had with the woman I'm referring to. But I think that's good. I know I'll have to jog to keep up, but I think I'm up to it." She swallowed and said what was in her heart. "I just want to make her as happy as she makes me."

He slapped her on the leg. "She's happy. Happier than she was the whole time she was with that ox who called himself a brewmaster. She seems more settled, Jill. Like she's got something figured out."

"I think that's true," she said, realizing that was exactly what it seemed like. Jill wasn't sure why, but Lizzie had been afraid of committing to a woman. She prayed with all of her heart that was a hurdle she'd cleared.

"Is she still talking about having a dozen kids?"

"A dozen?" Jill said, ripped from her thoughts.

Mike let out a bark of a laugh. "Last time she talked about it, she was down to just a few. But kids are important to her, Jill. Always have been."

Nodding, Jill said, "We haven't talked about it yet, but we'll figure it out. If she needs kids to be happy, we'll have some or adopt some." She felt a smile build. "Having kids with Lizzie sounds like a heck of a lot of fun, to be honest."

"That's the spirit," he said, grinning at her. "Might as well give in and let her lead. That's the secret to a happy marriage."

Mike had a radio next to his chair, and he turned it on. "How about a little baseball? Sox are down in New York tonight."

A dog barked, loudly. Then a fluffy gray thing raced around the house and stood a few feet away, barking like he wanted Jill and Mike to get up and follow him.

Then a girl, probably high-school aged, came running around the corner. She stopped as abruptly as the dog had, and stared with the same perplexed expression.

"Hello, Grace," Mike said. "Do you know Jill Henry?"

Jill stood, expecting the girl to offer to shake hands, but she didn't make any indication she was going to do that.

"I know who she is." This was clearly Mark's daughter. Jill could pick out pieces of Mark and Lisa, all combined to form a pretty, sober-looking kid. Her hair was brown like Lisa's, but she had Mark's coloring, along with his freckles.

"It's good to meet you," Jill said, deciding to sit if the kid wasn't going to shake her hand.

"Why are you here?" she asked. The words were ruder than her tone, which simply made her sound genuinely puzzled. "Don't your parents live in town?"

"Yeah, they do. I visited them earlier, but right now I'm having a beer with Mike."

"I thought Lizzie was here."

"She's over at the pool. Wanted to cool off."

"Why aren't you over there?"

The kid was a regular detective. No nonsense.

"Because I'm here," Jill said, tired of being interrogated. "I can't be two places at once, and sitting here, listening to the Sox makes me perfectly happy."

"Where's Gramma?" Grace asked, clearly needing to know everyone's location.

Mike made a vague gesture towards the road. "She's visiting Tim and his gang."

266

The girl stared at him for a few long seconds, looking more like her mother by the moment. "Why would she go see Uncle Tim when Lizzie's here?"

Mike started to laugh. "You'll have to ask her that, honey. Come by tomorrow. We'll have a cookout."

"Will Lizzie be here?" She turned to Jill, her eyes narrowing slightly. "Will you?"

"No. We're driving back tonight."

Grace nodded soberly. "I'm gonna go find Lizzie." She left with the dog following closely behind.

"Just like Lisa at that age," Jill said when the kid was out of earshot.

"I wish that was a compliment," Mike grumbled. "She'd be a nicer person if she took after her father more." He took a drink of his beer, then shook it, indicating it was empty. "How about getting an old man another?"

Jill got up and fetched a fresh beer and handed it to him. "Forget what I said about Grace," Mike said. "She's a good kid. And wishing she was something else is just dumb on my part. You get what you get."

"All true," Jill agreed. "Think I should go get Lizzie?"

"Nah. She'll come back if Grace bugs her. Lizzie doesn't put up with much. You'll learn," he predicted, then laughed again, slightly devilishly.

The Sox were having a good night, scoring at will against a Yankee team that had been equally tepid that year. It was remarkably calming, even zen-like, just sitting in the backyard listening to Joe Castiglione take over the play-by-play duties in the third inning.

The fireflies were gliding around the yard, a few katydids were revving up, and the mosquitos had barely made their presence felt. This was what home was. Being with people who knew you well enough that you could be perfectly content to just sit. Conversation was fine, but certainly not required.

It had been fully dark for a while, and Jill decided it was time to find Lizzie. She pulled out her phone and searched for Lizzie's, seeing it move, in fits and starts, down the street.

Then Lizzie walked around the side of the house, calling out, "What are you two doing sitting in the dark? The mosquitos are gonna eat you alive."

"They must be busy somewhere else," Jill said. "I thought maybe they'd gone over to the pool and bitten you so badly you'd passed out."

She came over and stood slightly behind Jill, then put her hand on her head and ruffled her hair. "They don't like me. But Grace hasn't gotten the Davis skeeter immunity. She was slapping them away every two seconds."

"You were over there forever," Jill said. Her head snapped around and she stared at Lizzie. "You didn't tell her about us, did you?"

"Silly thing." Lizzie leaned over and kissed Jill's cheek.

It was dark, so Mike couldn't see how flushed Jill got. She just hoped they really eased into being affectionate with each other. It was going to take a while to normalize that.

"I pick my spots, and Grace is not the person to start with."

Jill stood and stretched. "If you want to get back tonight, we'd better get going. What time do we have to get up in the morning?"

"We're meeting at the dock at nine, so eight should do it." She moved over to her father and bent to kiss his cheek. "We're going on a boat ride to hold onto the last bit of summer."

"Then you'd better get moving. If your mom comes home, you'll be here another hour, telling her how our conversation went."

"It went great," Lizzie said. She leaned over and wrapped her arms around her dad, holding on for a long while. "I love you, Daddy."

He patted her arms as she stood up. "And I love you. Both of you," he added pointedly.

Jill bent to hug Mike as well. "Thanks for being so understanding. I knew you would be—eventually. But I was worried it'd take you a while."

"You know what?" he asked as she stood and brushed her hair back over a shoulder. "When your body starts to fail you, you stop worrying about little stuff. And who your kids date is *very* little stuff." He grasped Lizzie's hand and pulled her down for a kiss. "But it's big stuff to you two, and I'm glad you told me. Now scoot."

"See you soon," Lizzie said as she took Jill's hand and started to walk.

"Tell Janet I said 'hi,'" Jill added.

"I will. Listen to the Sox on the way home," he advised. "They're playing like they should have done in May. If they'd gotten off to a better start, we'd be listening to a game that might mean something."

Jill didn't say what she was thinking. That listening to the game with Mike had meant a great deal to her, whether the Sox won, lost, or tied.

❦

They got into the car, and as Jill guided them down the silent, empty street, Lizzie reached over and picked up the card that was lying on the dash. "What's this?"

Jill took a quick look. "Oh. My birthday card from my mother. You can open it if you want."

She placed it back on the dash. "I don't need to pry into your personal things. I just noticed it because it wasn't here before."

"It's not personal. Trust me."

Lizzie shrugged and pulled the card from the envelope. Something fell out and she picked it up and held it in front of Jill. "Two twenties."

"Yeah. I get whatever age I am."

Lizzie didn't comment, but she read the card in silence. "One question. Why does she put 'Mom' in quotes?"

"She does?"

"Yeah. That's a little…"

"Odd?"

"Yeah. It seems odd. Like she's using a title that isn't hers. Or a nickname or something."

"That sounds about right." Jill took in a breath, then said, "I'd decided I was going to tell her about us. I didn't expect to get anything in return, but I felt like a jerk insisting you talk to your family while I skated by."

Lizzie briskly rubbed her hand across Jill's thigh. "You're a long way from being a jerk."

"I didn't do it. As soon as I got there, my mom asked me to cut the grass, then I was allowed to put together some ugly frames she puts around her favorite evergreens. While I was doing that, she went to the garden center—after locking me out of the house, of course. We didn't say more than twenty words to each other."

She must have sounded sad about that, because Lizzie leaned over and nuzzled against her cheek for a few seconds. "I wish she knew how lucky she was to have you."

Shrugging, Jill said, "I'm not sure she feels that way. I don't think she dislikes me or anything. But I'm also not sure it would bother her if I never stopped by again."

Lizzie didn't reply verbally. She just kept her hand on Jill's leg, idly touching her for a long time.

Once they were on the highway, Jill said, "Are you and Grace pretty close?"

"Yeah, not as tight as we were when she was young, but still close. I ran over there every day after school to help out when she was a baby. But... You know how it is. As they grow up, they only need you in fits and spurts."

"What was today's fit? She seemed very intent on talking to you."

"She wanted to talk about choosing a college."

"Is she a junior this year?"

"Yeah. It's decision time for her." Lizzie clearly had some unspent energy, and she recounted, in detail, the advice she'd given the kid. As they got closer to home, she started to wind down, with her comments coming less frequently and her voice getting softer. Jill took a look at her when they passed Williston, finding her seat back, with her head slumped to one side. Luckily, they were about twenty minutes from home, so her neck wouldn't be too stiff.

Home, Jill thought. She wasn't sure if Lizzie had everything she needed for the boat ride, but they could run by her apartment in the morning if they needed to. Jill needed to sleep with her, so she headed for her own home, smiling at the thought of cuddling up next to her... girlfriend. Now that Mike and Janet knew, they were on much more solid ground—at least in her view. She put her hand on Lizzie's leg, feeling the baby-soft skin of her thigh. The shorts Jill had bought for her had been about a foot too long. These were perfect. Simply perfect.

Chapter Fifteen

JILL WOKE TO ONE of the cats delicately licking her cheek. It was too early. She put up a hand to push him away when she encountered something much bigger than a sleek little cat. Lizzie started to laugh.

"You're already pushing me away? Damn, give me a chance first!"

"More sleep," Jill murmured, nuzzling her face against Lizzie's nearly bare chest. The sensory message finally reached her brain and she lifted her head and blinked. Jill's face had been pressed against warm, soft skin covered by only a tank top and she wanted to sleep? Maybe she *was* too old for Lizzie.

"What time is it?"

"Almost eight."

"It's cloudy?" she asked, her voice so plaintive it made Lizzie laugh.

She got out of bed and opened the blinds, letting in bright, warm sunlight. "It's a beautiful day, and we're going to have fun. Let's get going!"

Jill crooked a finger, while trying to adopt a sexy expression. "I've finally gotten over my skittishness, and you want to go out? Shouldn't we spend the day in bed?"

Lizzie walked back to her and stood by the bed, then pressed her hand to the back of Jill's head, cradling it against her hip. "If you want to cancel, you won't hear a complaint out of me." As Jill turned her face to look up at Lizzie, she added, "But I don't want to hear any crying about how you didn't get to go out on a boat on a lovely, warm Labor Day. Maybe our last chance for the year..."

"I'm up, I'm up," Jill said as she tried to get everything moving in the same direction. "Do you have to go by your apartment?"

"Yeah," she said, making a face. "Unless you want to lend me a swimsuit."

"We'll stop by your place," Jill said. "I only have one piece suits, and I can't wait to see you in that bikini again."

"Someone's libido is waking up," Lizzie teased, giving Jill a pat on the butt. "Finally."

"It's awake. More awake than the rest of me, that's for sure. Can we stop for coffee?"

"Sure can. As long as we can stop for Pepsi too."

"Let's hit it."

❧

They were dutifully waiting on the dock at nine a.m. sharp, with Jill nursing a giant cappuccino, while Lizzie still worked on her equally large Pepsi.

"You haven't told me a thing about the guy who owns the boat," Jill said. "Is he a co-worker?"

She made a face. "Kinda, but not really. His dad's on the board of directors. Jeffrey's a spoiled rich kid, but he's also pretty committed to Hollyhock Hills, so I try to ignore his faults."

"Those are…?"

"Lizzie!" A man called out.

Jill turned towards the voice and almost laughed. The guy walking down the dock was a caricature of a young, wealthy, show-off. Aviator sunglasses covered his eyes, and his longish brown hair tumbled across his forehead as he walked, despite his snapping his head to the left to urge it back. His golf shirt had the words "Stiff Ripples" embroidered on the breast. The shirt was loosely tucked into Madras plaid shorts and his feet were in very old Topsiders. As he got close, Jill noted the heavy stainless steel watch and a bracelet woven into nautical knots. Given his tan, he spent a heck of a lot more time on the water than he did behind a desk.

"Hi, Jeffrey," Lizzie said, her usual relatively laid-back personality amped up a little. "Ready for a fun day on the lake?"

"I am. Have you seen Madison and Alexis?"

"I don't…" She paused as she narrowed her eyes in thought. "The girls who just started working at the restaurant?"

272

"Yeah. They're coming with us. Do you know anyone else who wants to come? I can take six, and I've got enough beer, tequila and vodka for an army." He moved close and extended his hand. "Jeffrey Collins."

"Jill Henry," she said. Now that he was right next to her, she saw that Jeffrey was at least her age. He just gave the impression he was a kid.

"I can't think of anyone off the top of my head," Lizzie said. "But let me know in advance next time, and I'll be able to fill any available spots."

"Do you work at Hollyhock?" Jeffrey asked Jill as he lifted his glasses to get a better look. It had been a while since she'd felt like she was on display before a man, but Jeffrey's gaze started at her head and moved very slowly down her body. Had no woman ever told him to knock that crap off? She didn't want to make things tough for Lizzie at work, but she was going to be the first to disabuse Jeffrey of the habit if he didn't look her in the eyes. Given that he didn't seem to be interested in her answer, she didn't bother replying.

"Jill works at UVM," Lizzie supplied, obviously fine with putting up with a leering dude in exchange for a boat ride.

"Good old UVM," he said, letting out a low chuckle. "I wouldn't have minded staying close to home, but we're Yale people." Jill swore he'd adopted a weird preppy accent somewhere in the middle of that sentence. His attention shifted, and he turned and waved when a couple of very young women called out his name.

"Here's our girls," he said, gazing at them like they were the latest additions to his meat rack. "It's gonna be a good day. Four pretty girls and a fast boat. What could be better?"

Lizzie introduced herself and then Jill to the newcomers, both students at the U. Given how old they looked, they were still undergrads. Great. Just what Jill needed. A senior administrator getting caught by the harbor patrol for serving minors liquor. What in the hell had Lizzie been thinking to accept an invitation from this sleezeball? As much as Jill loved the water, it would have been nicer to have stayed in bed to start their relationship off with a bang. But it would be unconscionably rude to leave at this point, so she bit her tongue and followed along.

They trooped down the dock to stop before a thirty-seven foot monster with a gleaming stainless tower sticking up, already holding two wakeboards and a pair of massive speakers. Black, white and red graphics splashed along the sides, giving it a menacing look. Jill stared at the boat for a moment, having never been on one that big or that powerful looking.

"Nice, isn't it?" Jeffrey asked, his tone making it clear that was a rhetorical question.

"Yeah. Really nice. The fuel must kill you though."

"Not an issue." He started to unsnap the snug, black cockpit cover. "You can't worry about stuff like that when you're having fun."

Well, that was one way to look at things. Jill pitched in and helped, while Lizzie stowed all of their gear in cubbyholes under the seats. Then Jeffrey sat in the captain's chair, let the blower run for a minute, and started the engine, the low throaty roar making Jill's skin prickle. She really did like to go fast… Maybe putting up with a leering jerk would be worth it.

Madison and Alexis settled down on a curved bench in the rear of the boat, clearly labeling themselves passengers rather than crew. So Jill and Lizzie helped cast off, letting the dock lines fall, then standing at the ready with aluminum poles just in case they were pushed around unexpectedly. Once they were clear of the marina, Jill headed for the bow, with Lizzie right behind her.

One of the many benefits of living on Lake Champlain was the fact that you rarely had to go far to be in deep water. Moments after leaving the dock, Jeffrey hit the throttle, snapping their heads back. Then they were flying, zooming past slower craft as they moved away from Burlington.

"Nice," Jill said as the wind blew her hair straight back and made her sunglasses shimmy.

Lizzie leaned over and spoke just loud enough for Jill to hear. "Jeffrey's kind of a prick, but his boat's nice enough to make up for it."

"So far," Jill agreed. She wasn't sure that would be true when the alcohol started flowing, but for now the boat was tilting the balance in his favor.

After they'd whipped past everything Jill recognized, the lake widened a bit. Jeffrey slowed down, stood up and said, "Who wants to go first?"

Madison and Alexis were game, but neither of them had been on a wakeboard before. Clearly it was not Lizzie's first time at this rodeo, for she proved to be a very adept instructor when each of them tried to get up. It was slow going, with Jill acting as lookout, sitting next to Jeffrey, telling him when to cut the engine, which was about four seconds after he started off. Both of the young women seemed vaguely athletic, but it took lots of patient explanation from Lizzie, and lots of dunks in the cold water to get each of them up for rides of about a minute.

Then it was Lizzie's turn. Jill couldn't stop smiling at the confident grin that settled on her face as she got her feet locked onto the board and gave Jeffrey the signal to take off.

She rose like one of the osprey that lurked about the lake at dusk, graceful, elegant and effortless. In seconds, she was leaning back, carving the hell out of the wake that the big, fast boat kicked up. Jill wouldn't have been surprised if she'd done a 360 degree flip, but Lizzie seemed content to just glide across the water, jump the wake with a "whoop", then glide back across to do it again. She stayed up for a good five minutes, until Jeffrey made a very sharp turn, nearly sending her into the bank.

"Fuck you!" Lizzie shouted as her head popped out of the water. Luckily, she was laughing, allowing Jill to stay out of jail. Strangling a board member's child would have been a faux pas, but she wouldn't have been able to stop herself if his antics had hurt her brand new girlfriend.

"I was just trying to give you a thrill," he called out when they got close to pick her up.

"I want another ride," she yelled back. "This time, don't screw with me!"

"She's a spitfire, isn't she?" he asked Jill, grinning lecherously.

"She is." *My spitfire*, she wanted to declare, but they hadn't talked about how open they could be. They'd have that conversation as soon as Lizzie was back in the boat.

⌘

Jill wasn't as graceful or able to balance as well as Lizzie, but she could get up and stay up. Jeffrey didn't try any tricks with her, allowing her to luxuriate in the cool water, with the wind blowing in her face, her thighs tensing as the board sent her flying over a wake. Life didn't get any better than this. Speed, exhilaration, power, and a calm that she felt deep in her soul. But the thing that made it magic was seeing Lizzie in the boat, clapping her hands and shouting encouragement. Every time Jill would fly over the wake, Lizzie's hands went up like Jill had scored a touchdown. She couldn't hear her, but she knew she was letting out a loud cry of pleasure, just like Jill had done for her. Her thighs were going to complain in the morning, but this was a perfect capstone to the end of a perfect summer. The summer she fell for Lizzie.

⌘

Jill had to give credit where it was due. Jeffrey was a damned good host. He'd brought a big basket full of sandwiches which he'd had made at Jill's favorite deli, along with all sorts of side salads and chips. Lizzie, in keeping with her endless appetite, gobbled down two sandwiches, her own bag of chips, and seventy-five percent of Jill's. Then she started eyeing the brownies and cookies lying on the little table in front of the curved aft bench.

"Are you going into the water again?" Jill asked. "'Cause you'll sink like a stone if you keep eating."

"Ha!" She grabbed a huge chocolate chip cookie and took a big bite. "I'm not afraid of a stinkin' cookie."

"I don't know where you put it all," Jill said, unable to stop staring at her ridiculously toned belly. The thought of licking her way across that savory flesh was too damned distracting, so she got up and fetched them both a beer. They hadn't yet succumbed, but it was hot and why the hell not?

Lizzie took three big gulps. "Why does being in the water make you so thirsty?"

"Dunno. Maybe…" Jill shrugged. "Dunno."

Jeffrey had been paying rapt attention to Madison and Alexis, but he came to stand in the bow, where Jill and Lizzie had stretched out, letting the sun dry them.

"Good day, huh?" he asked.

As Jill regarded him, she had to acknowledge that he wasn't such a bad guy. He probably just wanted to be liked. Undoubtedly, he also wanted to screw all of them—at the same time—but he wasn't a bad guy. He'd probably been bullied a little in school. Something about him gave off that air, and now he was using his money—probably family money—to buy friends. Jill felt a moment's guilt, then decided he'd gotten his money's worth. A full tank of gas for a day of looking at scantily clad women who wanted him to like them. At least three of them wanted that. Jill was fine either way.

"We're having a great day," Lizzie said, beaming up at him. "I wasn't happy when you tried to kill me, but other than that…"

"Oh, I wasn't trying to kill you. You're just so damned good that I have to knock you off or we'd be out there all day."

"I'm not that good," Lizzie said, even though you could tell she knew just how competent she was.

"I go out with a lot of people, Liz, and you're the best." Jill didn't like the "Liz" comment, but if Lizzie didn't mind, it wasn't any of her business. "You've got those incredible legs." His gaze went to her thighs and stayed there longer than Jill was happy with. "I bet you could crack walnuts with those babies."

"Never tried," she said, sloughing off the comment. "Can I get you something to drink? The guy who owns this place has it *stocked*."

He held up his glass, still half full of vodka and tonic. "I'm set. Speaking of legs, are you still dancing?"

She shrugged that question off too. "A little. I'll have more free time now that summer's over."

"Have you seen her?" Jeffrey asked Jill.

"Seen her dance? No. Where would I see that?"

"She was in something… Where was that?"

Lizzie sighed. "When I'm not swamped at work, I'm in a group that performs around the area. Nothing big," she insisted. "Just amateurs who like to play around."

"She's excellent," he insisted. "You put one of those black, clingy things…" He gave Lizzie a quizzical look. "What do you call those things?"

"A leotard?"

"Yeah. Put a leotard on this girl and I swear to god, you'd bet she was the model for a Greek sculpture." His gaze grew a little more familiar. "If you ever need some cash, you could make a fortune dancing in a club."

Jill had a very good idea of what kind of club he was talking about. And she didn't like it. At all.

"I don't think my boss would like to see me shaking my ass for twenties," Lizzie said, clearly not bothered by his obvious leering.

"Your boss doesn't have an ass like you do." He took a big sip of his drink, laughing at his joke. Jill tried to determine if she could hit the cup with the heel of her hand and drive it up into his brain, but she stopped herself. If Lizzie didn't mind this jerk, she had to keep her jealousy to herself. He hadn't said one suggestive word to Jill—probably because she was too old for him. Still, Lizzie had chosen to come, knowing Jeffrey was a letch, and Jill didn't have the right to tell her how to spend her free time.

"After we dock," Jeffrey said, "we should go out. There's a new place on College I like."

"Been there," Lizzie said. "But we can't go tonight. It's a school night, you know."

"Oh, come on," he said, his smile getting a little insistent. "Don't tell me you don't go out on a weeknight."

"I really don't," Lizzie said.

"Are you dating someone? Is that the problem?"

"There's no problem," she said, still smiling calmly. "But I'm going home when we get back to the dock."

He obviously didn't get turned down often, because he didn't have any idea how to gracefully let it go. His brow furrowed as he leaned towards her. "That means you're dating someone, doesn't it."

"Uh-huh." Lizzie got up and plopped down onto a stunned Jill's lap. "I'm dating this gorgeous thing." She draped an arm around Jill's neck, grinning up at Jeffrey.

His mouth dropped open, then he started to laugh. "Yeah. Sure you are."

Lizzie didn't say another word, content to just smile up at him.

"You are?"

"We are," Jill said, trying to look menacing.

"Okay." He finished the rest of his drink in one gulp. "I'm not selfish. I don't mind sharing."

"I do," Jill said sharply.

"Hey, don't get all bent out of shape. I'm just being friendly."

"I'm friendly too," Jill said, knowing she didn't sound it. "But we're going home—alone."

"Fine. Fine." His hands rose in surrender, then he turned and headed back to Alexis and Madison, grumbling, "You try to show people a good time and they act like they're going to punch you in the face."

Lizzie leaned close and whispered, "You did look like you were going to punch him in the face."

"I was close," Jill admitted. "I've never hit anyone in anger, but today was going to be a first."

"Come on," Lizzie said, playfully jumping around on Jill's lap. "You can't take guys like him seriously. They're always on the hunt. You just have to make it clear you're not catchable."

That last little interplay had rubbed Jill the wrong way. Big time. Her mouth started moving before she was sure what was going to come out of it. "If you want to go on a boat next year, we'll rent one. If we can't find a place to rent one, I'll save up and buy one. If you can't wait for that, you can go play with Jeffrey any time you want." She could feel her anger growing with each word. "But this was my last time on Stiff Fucking Ripples."

"Okay then…" Lizzie stood and looked at Jill for a few seconds, then turned and moved back to join the others. Jill saw her take another beer from the cooler, then perch on the side of the boat, immediately joining in whatever stupid conversation stupid Jeffrey was cracking himself up about. Jill turned and stared out at the water, trying to get her temper under control. She knew she was pouting, but she couldn't help it. Still steaming, she dropped the bow ladder and stood on the seat. "Going swimming," she announced before she launched herself into the lake via a shallow racing dive. The water had never felt so refreshing.

⌘

Lizzie spent more time with Madison and Alexis on the way back than she did with Jill. When the boat was going slow, she was gone, but when it was flying at speeds too loud to consider talking, she came back. Clever.

They returned to the dock about eight, with the sun already dropping behind the trees. There was a decent amount of work to do to rinse the boat and get the cover on, and they all pitched in, with Lizzie directing the project. As soon as the last snap snugged the cockpit cover up tight, Jill and Lizzie said their goodbyes, leaving Jeffrey trying to convince Madison and Alexis into accompanying him to whatever club he could get them into. He probably had a handy supply of fake IDs for the underage girls his daddy's money reeled in.

Lizzie took Jill's hand as they walked to the car, but she didn't try to engage. After starting the car, Jill put it into drive and went towards Lizzie's apartment, going south rather than north. After a few minutes, Lizzie spoke quietly. "Are you really mad at me?"

"I'm not mad."

"Then why are you taking me home?"

Jill shot her a look, seeing that she looked like she might cry.

Reaching out, she took Lizzie's hand and kissed it. "I'm taking you home so you can get some clothes and your car. If you leave from my house in the morning, you'll save time."

Her frown disappeared in an instant. "I get to sleep with you?"

280

Jill tried to look serious, but couldn't keep it up. A sly smile settled onto her lips. "If we run out of steam, yeah. If not, we'll sleep some other time."

"Really? We're really going to...you know." She took her fists and rubbed them together, then put a finger inside a fist and pulled it in and out.

As she was trying to make yet another rude gesture, Jill laughed and said, "Yes, Lizzie. We're going to do exactly what that asshole Jeffrey is fantasizing about us doing. That was the last time I want to utter his name, by the way. Are you good with that?"

"Perfectly good." She leaned over and kissed Jill's cheek. "Excited!"

"Me too." She pulled up in front of the apartment and gave Lizzie a gentle push. "So shake a leg. I'll be waiting for you."

Lizzie struggled into the back door with a garment bag in one hand, and her backpack filled to the brim in the other. It didn't help that two cats were winding their way around her ankles, but Jill found it too funny to step in.

"Help me!" Lizzie demanded, laughing.

"Don't you like it that the boys are so happy to see you?"

"I'm thrilled. Now take something so I don't step on one of them."

As Jill grabbed the backpack and put it on the counter, Lizzie draped her garment bag over a chair, then stooped and grasped a cat in each hand. She held them close and each one nuzzled against her chin as she giggled. Jill whipped out her phone and snapped pictures until the whole group tired of it. "I think they know your status is changing," Jill said. "You've become a member of the pack."

"I'm beat," Lizzie said, placing the cats back onto the floor and moving over to Jill, where she dramatically draped herself along her body. "I ran around my apartment like a maniac, trying to make sure I had everything I need for work. I hope I've got a pair of matching shoes, because I have a meeting with some bigwigs at nine."

"Then we should go to bed early." Jill let her fingers glide across Lizzie's face, sliding some errant hanks of hair away from her forehead.

"Not a bad idea," Lizzie said, smirking. "I like to be in bed by eight forty-five most nights."

Jill placed a short, soft kiss to her lips. "I used to stay up until midnight, but I think eight forty-five is my new bedtime." Jill took her hand and led her over to the pantry. "First, I have some welcome presents for you." With a flourish, she held her hand out, pointing at two kinds of mint cookies, and two styles of potato chips, one with ridges and one without.

"You're a goddess," Lizzie said, sliding an arm around Jill's waist and hugging her. "For the record, I like regular chips. Any brand. Whatever's on sale."

"That's not all." Jill guided her to the refrigerator, opened the door and revealed plenty of Pepsi; a six pack of cans and a liter bottle. "I didn't know your preferred delivery system."

"I'm easy to please. Whatever's cheaper."

"Two more things." She reached in and pulled out a white box, then opened it to reveal six big chocolate covered strawberries and six potato chips, each half covered in chocolate.

"Where did you get these?" Lizzie asked, bubbling with delight as she snagged one of the chips and gobbled it down. "They're delicious!" She stopped and gazed at Jill speculatively. "When did you have time to get any of this?"

"Yesterday, while I was waiting to see if your father came for me with a gun, I called that little store near downtown where the guy makes his own candy. He agreed to hold these for me. Karen picked everything up for me, then I zipped by her house on the way home from the boat. One more quick stop at the grocery store let me beat you by about five minutes." She opened the fridge one more time and pulled out a big bottle. "I've been saving this for a special occasion. I think tonight qualifies."

Lizzie took the black bottle and read the label. "This is beer?"

"Uh-huh. Cask aged like wine. Since we both prefer beer to wine, I thought this would be better than Champagne."

Lizzie clasped her hands behind Jill's back and gazed at her, her vivid green eyes assessing Jill's face like a work of art. "You're a fantastic blend of utter pragmatism and total romance. I think I could fall for you, you sweet thing."

"You *think?*" Jill leaned in and kissed all around her face, tickling the sensitive skin with her lips. "You'd damn well have better already fallen."

"I fell way before you did," Lizzie said, playfully tweaking Jill's nose. "You're damned irresistible."

"That's what I've been telling you." She took the beer, then put it into a plastic bucket and filled it with ice. Then she tucked two beer glasses against her chest, ready to go upstairs. "Not the most elegant presentation, but I know you like your beer cold."

"I do. Let me carry the goodies," she said, taking the box.

"You want all of that?" Jill asked. "At once?"

"Yeah." She started to laugh as she popped another chip into her mouth. "Duh."

They walked upstairs, with the gray ghosts running up before them. "Are we going to be covered with cats?" Lizzie asked. "Not that I mind, but they might have their tender psyches tarnished when they see what I'm going to do to you."

"They don't stick around if there's too much movement." Jill couldn't stop herself from letting out an innuendo-laden chuckle. "And I plan on moving a whole big lot."

They went into the bedroom, and Jill set the bucket on the dresser, placed the glasses next to it, removed the foil and popped the cork. It made a funny sound, almost like a Champagne cork, but more muted. Then she filled both glasses and handed one to Lizzie. "To us," she said, touching the rims of their glasses together.

"I like the sound of 'us,'" Lizzie said, tinking their glasses once again. They each took a sip. "This is kinda weird, but I like it."

"Just like me. Kinda weird, but…"

"You're not weird at all," Lizzie said, taking Jill's glass and putting it on the dresser, "but I do like you. A whole lot." They were standing very close, so close Jill could feel the warmth of Lizzie's breath.

"I'm"—she closed her eyes briefly—"nervous."

Jill took her in her arms and gave her a long, tender hug. "We probably should have just gone with the flow the other night. Lovemaking's usually better when it's spur of the moment."

"No, that's not it." She reached for her glass and took a long drink. "It's bigger than that."

Jill put an arm around her and pulled her close. "Tell me what you're worried about."

She made a face. "All kinds of things. Mostly I'm worried that we're not going to be in sync. The stakes are a lot higher now that I've told my family about us. Plus, everyone at work will be talking about it the second Madison and Alexis come in." She rolled her eyes. "Coming out at work and home before we've barely touched each other is really new for me." She searched Jill's eyes for understanding. "I feel a lot of pressure."

Jill put her hands on Lizzie's shoulders and gently massaged them, feeling a good bit of tension in the muscles. "There's no pressure, because there's nothing to worry about. We're really attracted to each other, and we'll figure everything else out. Simple. Really simple."

"Are you sure?" Lizzie looked into Jill's eyes, clearly seeking reassurance.

"I am. We're going to be good together, Lizzie. I *know* it." She put her arms around her and pulled her close. "Maybe it's time to stop talking and start doing."

"Yeah. That sounds like a great—"

Jill dipped her head and captured Lizzie's pink lips, placing a long, soft kiss upon them. "I'm not nervous," she murmured. "Because I know everything's going to be great. But I'm...I can't think of the word."

"Anticipatory?"

"I think that's the perfect word."

"So I'm nervous and you're full of anticipation. Maybe we should whip off our clothes and dive in. Just like I do when I jump into the lake."

"And you say I'm romantic," Jill teased. "Come with me." She took her by the hand and led her to the bathroom. "The first time you saw my tub, you said you were going to jump right in. Did you?"

"No, I never got the chance."

"Good. We can start our relationship off with our first shared bath." She leaned over, closed the drain and turned the water on.

"Your ceiling's raining!"

The cats flew into the room, and perched upon opposite ends of the rim, where it was widest. Then they each stretched a paw out, trying to catch the water as it fell, not seeming to mind that they were a good six inches short of their goal.

Jill pointed at the wall, where the handles were mounted two feet higher than the rim. "I wanted to be able to have two people in the tub, with neither of them getting the faucet or the handles in the back. Filling the tub from the ceiling was an idea I'd never considered, but it works great."

"You're a genius. A true genius." Lizzie moved close and joined the cats in staring at the water as it cascaded loudly into the tub. "I could stand here all day and watch this, and I *hate* to waste water."

"I've got one more little romantic touch." A box lay on the window sill, and Jill opened it, then shook the contents into the tub. "I called my favorite florist and had him find every peony he could get his hands on." Beautiful blush pink petals floated atop the water as Lizzie's eyes filled with tears.

"You're so sweet," she murmured, taking Jill into her arms and kissing her with a burst of enthusiasm. "You remembered my favorite flower."

"I remember nearly everything you've ever told me," she said, placing soft, sweet kisses on her lips. "Everything you say is important." She picked up a bottle from the ledge that surrounded the tub. "Milk bath? It won't overpower the smell of the peonies."

Lizzie took her hand and tipped it, quickly making the water opaque. "Nice," she said as they watched the tub fill. "Now we have to get naked. Wanna start?"

"No," Jill said, laughing nervously. "I'm really confident when it's dark, but I've seen you in a bikini. You've got an Ivy League body, while I'm a safety school—at best."

"Big baby," she teased. "Let's close our eyes, strip and get into the tub. Then we'll drink the rest of that huge beer and get a little tipsy. You won't even notice all of my horrible flaws."

"Yeah," Jill said, nodding. "It's your thirty-year-old dancer's body that I'm worried about."

"Close your eyes and get naked," Lizzie insisted, squeezing her eyes shut.

Jill watched her whip her tank top off, grinning at the first sight of Lizzie's adorable breasts, so cute she couldn't stop staring at them.

"Why don't I hear your clothes dropping to the floor?"

"Uhm…busy," she said, leaning over to turn off the water. Then she unbuttoned her shirt and threw it forcefully to the floor. "Better?"

Lizzie was starting to snake out of her tight jeans, and Jill closed her eyes, playing along with the game and giving her some privacy.

"I'm not sure I'm going to be able to do this and not kill myself," Lizzie said as the sound of a tiny splash reached Jill's ears.

"No fair! Now I'm going to have to climb in while you're already there. That'll be lots harder!"

"You snooze, you lose. Ahh. This is perfect. Make sure the food's close, 'cause I'm not getting out for hours."

"I've got to open my eyes to do that, but I won't look."

"I'm submerged, you silly thing. You can open your eyes, but I'll keep mine closed. Damn, I'm starting to second guess myself here. You're kinda slow."

"Not the best seduction line I've ever heard," Jill said, returning with the snacks and the beer. Lizzie was, as promised, submerged. The last couple of inches of her hair were floating on the water, and Jill went to twist her own up and put a clip in it to avoid that. "Okay," she said, clapping her hands. "Strawberries and chips nearby, beer right on the floor. Ready for action."

Lizzie stuck her hands up, moving them around, trying to grab whatever part of Jill she could reach.

"Keep those hands to yourself. For a minute or two. I don't want to step on you." She had to figure it out as she went, but she finally slid into the water, and settled back against the tub. "This is kinda weird," she said. "We've never seen each other naked, but we're in very vulnerable positions."

"I like it. It's a little mysterious. Can I open my eyes?"

"Yep. I'm as covered as I'm gonna get."

Lizzie opened her eyes, her gaze immediately going to Jill's breasts, which didn't quite float, but the tops of them peeked out from the cloudy water. "I like those," she said, a lecherous look on her face. "I knew they were going to be pretty, but they're actually Rubenesque."

"The art history degree pays off," Jill teased.

"I love all of the parts of a woman," Lizzie said, completely serious now. "But it's always breasts I long for." She smiled at Jill, her expression so sweet and content Jill's heart skipped a beat. "I'm so happy I'm here with you."

"Me too. Really happy."

Lizzie reached down and grasped Jill's glass firmly before handing it to her. "Don't drop this. That's one ER visit I don't want to have to make."

"These are plastic," Jill said. "It only took one glass breaking when the cats were young to convince me to switch. Never again. It felt like I had a dozen cats. Why are they so fascinated with broken glass?"

"Their curiosity isn't always in their best interests." She moved her foot, letting it slide across Jill's belly. Then it skimmed along a breast, catching a nipple as it moved past. "I'm curious about you. I haven't seen you in a bikini, but your swimsuit doesn't hide much." She leaned forward and captured Jill's lips in a long, hungry kiss. "I'm not nervous any more," she said. "I'm ready to satisfy my curiosity."

"And I'm not very anticipatory. A warm bath was just the ticket."

Lizzie scooped a handful of peony petals and held them up to her nose, sniffing delicately. "It's going to take a while to peel these off our

287

skin, but I really appreciate the gesture. One thing I know about you," she said, gazing into Jill's eyes, "is how thoughtful you are. That's a trait that's worth an awful lot to me."

"I wanted tonight to be special. I think about you every damned minute. I might as well put all of that focus into action."

Lizzie relaxed against the tub and let her head rest on the rim. The warm water was obviously calming her, as her voice got softer and her words came out more slowly. "No one at work's going to be surprised when Alexis and Madison tell everyone I've got a girlfriend. I zone out all day long, just thinking about you."

"Tomorrow you can think about how nice it was to lie in a big tub, having your girlfriend feed you chocolate covered strawberries." She held one up in front of Lizzie, smiling when she caught it in her teeth and sucked it into her mouth.

Lizzie pulled the stem out and dropped it into the water. "Why not?" she asked. "A little more vegetation can't hurt." Then she leaned forward, put her hand behind Jill's neck and pulled her close for a long, gentle kiss. "I'm not going to be thinking about strawberries tomorrow," she murmured huskily. "I'm going to be thinking about how you move when I'm making love to you."

Jill stayed right where she was, an inch from Lizzie's lips. "I think I'm clean enough. Why don't we go make some memories?"

"Give me a minute to actually wash the lake water off. And have a little more beer."

Jill handed her a filled glass, then took a bar of soap and rubbed it briskly in her hands, creating a nice lather. "Let me help." Her hands slid along Lizzie's arms, as she leaned back and took long drinks of her beer, then each leg lifted straight up into the air, with Jill almost swooning at the graceful way those legs rose from the water, so elegant and powerful. Jill was all in, and she was going to continue to wash all of the parts she'd been dreaming about, but Lizzie gave her a playful grin and slipped the soap from her hand, then let her hand dip below the water line for a few seconds.

"Now it's your turn." Lizzie returned the favor, washing Jill's arms and shoulders and legs, then handed the soap off for Jill to wash her more hidden parts. Then Lizzie stood, rising elegantly as the water sluiced down her body. Quickly exiting, she held a hand out to steady Jill, who settled against her body, wrapped in a warm embrace.

"I like this," Jill said, moving her shoulders to make their breasts gently touch.

"Me too. You're just how I thought you'd be. Kind and gentle and thoughtful."

Jill grabbed a bath sheet and unfurled it to wrap around both of their bodies. Hugging Lizzie tightly, she murmured, "That's a lot of me. But there are pieces of me you haven't seen yet. Let's go explore those." With the towel caught between them, she placed her hands on Lizzie's face and held it still as she lavished kisses on her lips. "I love the feel of your lips," she murmured.

"Mmm. Kissing is my favorite thing." She grasped the ends of the big towel and patted Jill dry, flicking off stray peony petals as she did.

Jill took the towel and wrapped it around their shoulders as they walked towards the bed.

"I was going to sleep here when I stayed over on Memorial Day," Lizzie said. "But I couldn't do it. I already had such a big crush on you that I didn't want to drive myself crazy by smelling you all night."

Jill stroked her face, gazing into the warmth of her eyes. "I caught you napping here when I came back. You looked so cute I almost took your picture. This didn't register at the time, but you honestly looked like you belonged here."

"I think I do." Lizzie grasped the sheet and pulled it down, then sat on the bed and maneuvered Jill until she was right in front of her. "I'm sure I belong with you."

Jill pressed Lizzie's head against her hip, idly playing with her damp hair. "I'm sure too." She sat next to her, then guided her down, where they snuggled against each other. "I've never been so certain about anyone, Lizzie. I know this is going to work. I can feel it in my bones."

"Kiss me," Lizzie murmured, pulling Jill close.

They were soon wrapped around each other, Jill's leg resting on Lizzie's hip as their mouths remained locked together. It was like being lost in a sea of kisses, floating along on a warm, gentle current.

Then Lizzie's lips were on her neck, making Jill's toes curl as teasing kisses fluttered along her skin. Warm lips hovered above her ear, whispering, "I knew one day we'd be right here. I'm so glad I waited for you."

Jill shifted her hips, maneuvering Lizzie onto her back. Then she leaned over her, memorizing the way her eyes flashed in the warm, dim light, the flush that covered her cheeks, her beauty catching Jill by surprise. She blinked, trying to understand. She'd known how pretty Lizzie was from the first moment she'd seen her at Mark's party. Seeing her here, though, so unguarded, so open to Jill's touch, made that beauty bloom like a gorgeous flower at its peak. "You're the most beautiful woman I've ever seen," she whispered, meaning that with every bit of her heart. "My hands are shaking at the thought of touching you."

Lizzie gave her a lazy, indulgent smile. Then she took Jill's hand and put it on her breast. "I'll help you."

Lizzie might have thought Jill was just being complimentary. But she wasn't. She was truly stunned by her. Something about Lizzie touched a part of her that no one else had ever reached. She was desperate to explain herself, to make Lizzie understand what this meant to her, but she didn't have a single word at her disposal. All she could do was touch her—reverently, and hope that her feelings could travel through that touch.

She moved down Lizzie's body and captured her breast, laving the perfectly formed nipple until it grew rigid in her mouth. Lizzie squirmed under her, breathing heavily as her fingers slowly slid along Jill's scalp, making a riot of goosebumps break out along her arms.

In just a few minutes, Lizzie was pushing herself into Jill's open mouth, moaning louder as Jill sucked more forcefully. It seemed like Lizzie's hands were everywhere, grasping, holding onto any part of Jill she could reach.

As Jill's mouth left one flushed breast, she latched onto the other, with Lizzie purring her satisfaction. Jill grasped the breast she'd just abandoned, feeling its heat in her hand as she squeezed it. "More," Lizzie whimpered as Jill pulled her entire breast into her mouth and sucked hard. Suddenly, a pair of legs were wrapped around her waist, squeezing her in rhythm as Jill devoured her.

Breathless, Jill moved up, with Lizzie's legs letting her go. They kissed again, deeper, hotter, until she was once again barely able to take in a breath. Then Lizzie's hands were on her shoulders, pushing her down. Jill smiled at her forcefulness, and started to make her way down her body. Those strong legs captured her again and held her in place as Lizzie took her breast in her hand and fed it into Jill's open mouth. The groan she let out made Jill's nipples harden, and she sucked the flesh into her mouth with a force she'd rarely used. But Lizzie wanted this. Without question.

Those long, lean legs squeezed hard, with a bit of moisture swiping across Jill's chest as Lizzie thrust her hips. "More," she begged, with Jill responding immediately, her head swimming with lust.

Lizzie's hands went to her head, pulling her in as hard as she could. Her hips thrust hard, panting out nonsense as she began to shake. Jill held on, squeezing, sucking, mouthing her quivering flesh as Lizzie shuddered and moaned.

A cat jumped onto the bed, levitated, then disappeared so quickly Jill thought she'd imagined it. Suddenly, she was on her back, with Lizzie's flushed face smiling down at her.

"You almost killed me," she panted, out of breath. Then she leaned down and kissed Jill with such fervor she was breathless as well. Lizzie finally moved an inch away. "That has never happened to me. How did you know exactly what I needed?"

"I'm psychic," Jill teased. "And you locking me in place with your legs gave me a tiny clue."

Lizzie collapsed next to her, gazing at her profile. "Nope. You're gifted. That's the only answer."

Smiling at her, Jill said, "Do you think I'm going to argue with that?" She stroked her cheek, and flipped away a few beads of moisture. "You're stunningly hot. Has anyone ever told you that?"

"A few," she said, clearly trying to look cocky. "But I only care if you think so."

"I do. And if you don't start touching me, I'm going to have to touch myself. Then you're going to look like you're just lazy and—"

Lizzie cut her off with a long kiss. Then her hand slid down Jill's body, gently, teasingly touching her here and there. No real destination. No hurry whatsoever. Whenever she reached a place that felt particularly good, Jill would encourage her, pressing her hand down or growling with delight. Then Lizzie sat up slightly and stared at her body—boldly. "I'm never going to get tired of looking at you. Thank god my imagination isn't good enough to picture exactly what you look like, or I never would have held out this long. I would have dived right in when we were at Red Rocks."

"We'd had one kiss!"

"I know." She laughed softly. "I'm not saying it would have been appropriate. Just that I would have done it."

"Thank goodness love is blind." She put her hand on her belly and shook it. "No more flat stomach for me. You're going to have to look in the mirror to see any abs around here."

"Oh, I like this," Lizzie said, moving close to murmur into Jill's ear as her hand caressed her belly. "You're soft and smooth and womanly. Everything I missed when I was with men. I can't tell you how many times I ran my hand over a hairy chest and wished I could feel a soft breast."

"I'm not as tough as you are," Jill said, pulling Lizzie's head down to her breast. "But I'd love to feel your mouth on me."

The erotic purr that rumbled in Lizzie's chest was nearly enough to send Jill over the edge, but she got control and opened herself up to the gentle touch. Lizzie kissed her like she was made of spun-sugar, just the way Jill liked it. Teasing, soft, butterfly kisses, with the perfect amount of pressure to send tingles down her spine.

When Lizzie had her in such a state that she couldn't possibly remain still, she moved down her body, kissing and licking Jill's belly, then pausing between her legs. With aching tenderness, she opened her with her thumbs, and gazed at her, reverently, for a moment. "This is where I belong," she whispered so softly that Jill had to strain to hear. There were tears in those vivid green eyes, and Jill felt like they were experiencing something deep—something profound—together. Then Lizzie dipped her head, took in a deep breath and let her tongue bathe Jill in a whirlwind of sensation. Desire, passion, drive, need, all rolled into one as Lizzie's delicate tongue probed her tender flesh.

Jill was so painfully aroused she could hardly stay still. Lizzie worked with a slow, patient focus, clearly determined to make Jill lose her mind. Finally, her moaned entreaties made her pick up her speed, and she responded when Jill stretched her legs wide open and pulled Lizzie against her body until she quickened the pace. "Perfect," Jill gasped, throwing her head back as the waves of sensation washed over her and her body jerked and twitched as her climax rolled through her, making every muscle tense and relax until she was limp, barely able to breathe.

Lizzie was cuddled up next to her, kissing her neck and along her chest, her hand never stopping its gentle caress of Jill's overheated body.

"What's going to happen when we really know each other well?" Jill asked lazily.

"I can't wait to find out."

Jill turned her head to see her avid gaze, with her lovely mouth curled into a sated grin. Every part of her wanted to show Lizzie how one climax was just the start. Hannah used to call her Supergirl, with each subsequent orgasm just making her want another. But she'd learned that Lizzie needed her sleep. It was eleven o'clock and she had a big meeting in the morning. "You know what I'd like?" Jill asked.

"No, but if you tell me, it's yours."

Jill got to her feet, feeling a little weak in the knees. But she made it to the bathroom and grasped one of the strawberries by the stem. Then she came back to bed and fed it to Lizzie, watching as her eyes closed when the chocolate hit her tongue. "I want to make you happy," Jill whispered. "That's my goal in life."

Lizzie's eyes opened and were immediately filled with tears. "That's what I want too. My new number one goal."

"Come lie next to me," Jill urged. "Let me cuddle you to sleep."

Lizzie blinked, then stared at Jill for a few seconds. "Sleep? Really?"

"Don't you have to get up early? I was trying to be thoughtful."

Lizzie pushed her to her back, then slid onto her hips, looking down at her. "I do get up early. But how many times are we going to make love for the first time?" Her soft laugh was like a caress. "Probably not more than a few dozen."

With one powerful thrust of her hips, Jill now looked down on Lizzie, a playful smile tugging at her lips.

"I don't ever want you to go to sleep unsatisfied. Especially not tonight."

"Then get back to work. You've barely touched me!" She started to laugh as she grasped Jill's hands and moved them all over her body. "Look at all of this skin you haven't even begun to explore."

Jill met her eyes, loving to watch the playfulness so vividly reflected in them. Having a lover who knew how to play was going to be epic!

"There's one spot I've been eyeing ever since our birthday weekend." Ostentatiously, she focused on the bedside clock. "I guess I've got time to poke around a little bit."

"Poke around a *lot*," Lizzie urged. "I've got all night."

Jill rolled onto her side, and propped her head up with her hand. Slowly, she let her gaze travel up and down Lizzie's body, then her hand went right for the prize, Lizzie's sculpted belly. When she spoke, her voice was low and soft, nearly reverent. "That day at Red Rocks I was so tempted to lick my way across these ridiculous muscles." Her gaze slid up until their eyes met. "I didn't know I was into bellies until I saw yours." A finger teasingly followed the dips that traveled down her body, bracketing a flat band of muscle right in the center. "Every time I've fantasized about you since that day I've spent a long time thinking about this exact spot."

Lizzie clearly wasn't embarrassed about being complimented. A sly cat-like smile covered her face. "I can give you more to work with if I sit up a little." She started to rise, then held her position, with definition popping out across her belly.

"Can you hold that for about ten minutes?" Jill asked, her tongue thick in her mouth, her sex tingling with feeling. Leaning in, she swiped her tongue across every muscle, lavishing attention on each hard-earned bit of flesh. "So sexy," she murmured.

As Lizzie lay back down, Jill stayed right where she was, poking the muscles with her tongue. Now the horizontal dips were gone, just the two long vertical lines highlighting her belly. "When you're on your back, you drop down to a two-pack." She looked up again. "Not that I'm complaining. You're still as sexy as hell."

Lizzie's hand went to her head, then gentle fingers removed the clip that held her hair back. "You can play with my two-pack and I'll play with your hair. Fair trade?" Her fingers slid along Jill's scalp, sending waves of sensation down her spine.

"Very fair," she said, her voice cracking. "That's an erogenous zone."

"I could tell," Lizzie murmured. "I can feel your nipples harden against my leg." A hand slipped down and gently twisted a firm nipple.

"Another erogenous zone," Jill squeaked.

"I think you have a lot of them." She gripped Jill's shoulders and urged her to move up. As Jill hovered over her, Lizzie slipped both hands behind her neck and exerted gentle pressure. Their lips met again, soft and warm. Tender kisses slowly turned into hot, needy ones, with Lizzie forcefully sucking Jill's tongue into her mouth as she let out a low growl.

Breaking away to catch her breath, Jill paused over her, taking in her lovely face and glittering eyes. "I've never been happier," she said, a burst of emotion making her feel like she might cry.

"You can cry any time you feel like it," Lizzie whispered, apparently able to read minds. "You're safe with me."

"That's it," Jill murmured, her heart fluttering in her chest. "I feel safe with you. Safe to show you how I feel, how I think. That means... everything," she admitted, a few tears springing to her eyes.

Lizzie's gentle fingers flicked them from her lashes, then a soft kiss brushed over each eye. A warm embrace enfolded her and she nuzzled against Lizzie's body, certain she could lie there for years and not tire of it.

"I've only been with people I trusted," Lizzie said quietly, her voice having grown thoughtful. "But this is different. I always felt like I had to hold back a little. Like I might be laughed at if I got too close too fast."

Jill tilted her head so their eyes met. A full smile bloomed on her lips as she said, "You can't be too close. I'm ready for every bit of Lizzie Davis to open herself up to me."

Lizzie smiled down at her. "I've made love before, but it's always taken a while to turn from sex to love." She ran her fingers all over Jill's face, like she was touching something sacred. "But not with you." She moved down to wrap Jill in a tight embrace, then kiss her with abandon. They moved against each other as their lips met, skin sliding against skin, until Jill was throbbing with sensation.

"I have to taste you," Jill managed, nearly unable to speak. "Right now." She slipped from Lizzie's weak embrace and moved down her body, pausing to place a reverent kiss on her belly. Then she found herself bedazzled by the heat radiating from Lizzie's beautiful body. Her skin glistened in the lamplight, every part of her aroused and ready to be touched.

Jill's mouth watered as she nuzzled between her legs, taking in her distinctive scent, the scent she was going to memorize down to the individual molecules. The thought of spending hours nestled between Lizzie's firm thighs was enough to make her climax without being touched. But she forced her focus from her own body to Lizzie's and swiped her tongue up the length of her, smiling when Lizzie let out a low, pleasured groan.

Each sound she made urged Jill on, but she forced herself to take her time, to make this a long, slow first exploration of a place she was going to return to again and again.

Lizzie's heels trailed up and down Jill's back as she twisted and thrust her body just where she needed attention. Strong hands gripped Jill's shoulders, guiding and holding firm. All the while, Lizzie purred like a cat, a low, satisfied hum, more expressive than a thousand words would have been.

After a long while, Lizzie began to squirm under Jill's ministrations, and her breathing grew ragged as her legs opened wider, clearly begging for more. Jill pressed into her, focusing her attention on the trembling flesh that pulsed under her tongue. Hands flew to her head as Lizzie's body became rigid for a few heartbeats, clearly on a precipice. Then a low, rumbling moan made her shiver from head to toe. Suddenly, she collapsed onto the bed, arms and legs splayed out in all directions. "Good god," she murmured. "I have never, ever had an orgasm the first time I had sex with someone." She grasped a grinning Jill by the arm and pulled her up. "Come up here and kiss me, you luscious thing."

Jill curled up next to her, and wrapped her in her arms. "Happy?" she asked.

"Terminally." She gave her a long, gentle kiss then neatened Jill's hair, pushing it off her face. "Now I know why you didn't have a care in the world about how we'd get along. You knew how awesome you are in bed!"

A sharp slap to the butt made Jill wince. "I get a slap for being good in bed?"

"No, for holding out on me. You should have told me you have three or four tongues in that pretty mouth."

"Well, I normally try to act like a human. I don't want people to know I'm a super-evolved alien from an all-lesbian planet."

"I'd believe it," Lizzie insisted. "Now you just have to deliver the goods exactly like that twice a day and everything will be perfect." As Jill's eyebrows went up, Lizzie started to laugh. "I wouldn't be able to walk!"

"I'm more than willing to try. We'll do it until you're on the verge of limping, then cut back a little."

"We can think about cutting back later," Lizzie said, sliding her hand down between their bodies to gently begin to probe between Jill's legs. "I'm sure I could make you tingle again right now."

"You definitely could," Jill agreed. "But then I'll want to return the favor and…" She twirled her index finger in a circle. "You'll stumble into your morning meeting looking like…I'm not sure what you'd look like if we stayed up all night making love."

"It wouldn't be good, but it might be worth it," she said, her smile adorably devilish.

"Let's save some for tomorrow. I don't want to wear you out on our first night."

"Mmm," she snuggled up against Jill's body, her talented hand skimming along her side. "Sure?"

"Yeah, I think so. I could clearly go on, but I don't want you dragging tomorrow."

"I won't argue," she said, stretching out and sticking her arms up over her head as she yawned loudly. "I do have to be sharp."

"Come on. Let me cuddle you to sleep."

"You're not just phenomenal in bed… You truly like to cuddle?"

"Truly."

Lizzie rolled onto her side, and Jill pressed herself against her back. "Secret?"

"Sure. Your secret's safe with me."

"I wasn't much of a cuddler before. But I'd glue myself to you if I could."

"That might be the sweetest thing you've ever said to me." Jill grasped Lizzie's arm and tucked it against her chest. "Got your alarm set?"

Abruptly, she sat up, then got to her feet and headed towards the bath. When she returned, she was pressing buttons on her phone. "Gotta get up early."

"That's why we're going to sleep now." When Lizzie lay back down, Jill stroked along her arm, then let her hand trail down to her leg, where she kept up a gentle massage. In a few minutes, Lizzie had totally relaxed. Jill felt her jerk once, then settle down again. When she started to breathe heavily, Jill buried her face in her hair and whispered, "I love you."

Lizzie started, then turned, her eyes wet with tears again. They gazed at each other for long seconds, then she searched Jill's eyes. "You do?"

"I do," Jill said, full of confidence.

"Are you sure? Absolutely sure?"

"I am. I love you, Lizzie. I truly do."

"I love you too," she whispered, tears sliding down her face to land on her pillow. "You make me so happy."

"We'll make each other happy. Promise," she murmured, then graced her lips with a final kiss. "Now close those beautiful eyes and go to sleep. We've both got big days ahead of us tomorrow."

"Together," Lizzie said, her eyes still brimming with tears. "We'll share our big days together."

"There's no one on earth I'd rather share them with." Jill tucked an arm around Lizzie's waist, smiling when she nestled her face against Jill's chest and slowly drifted off to sleep.

Chapter Sixteen

AN ANNOYING BUZZING PULLED Jill halfway out of a lovely dream. The volume grew, then a weird voice said, "Pound the alarm." Music played for a few seconds, something very techno, then the voice commanded again, "Pound the alarm." Now the bed shook, and a muttered curse preceded a warm softness disappearing. Cats whined for attention, then…silence. Utter silence. Nice.

⌘

The alarm gently woke Jill at seven thirty. Immediately, she reached out to find the spot next to her cold. And entirely without cats. She sat up, wincing at her sore abs and thighs, courtesy of wake boarding, then looked around. No sign of Lizzie or the boys. They'd never failed to start their antics a few minutes after sunrise. Had Lizzie locked them out? No. The door was wide open. Jill got up and opened the blinds to see a low, gray sky, with a clear threat of rain.

Her curiosity wasn't as great as her need to have some warm water help her wake, so she went to shower. The glass doors were dry, abandoned clothes were still lying in front of the tub, along with the box of berries and chips. It had been moved a few feet, probably by a feline checking it out, but neither one of them liked chocolate, thankfully, so it was otherwise unmolested.

After standing in the pounding water much longer than usual, Jill blew her hair dry and got dressed. When she went into the living room, the boys were in their favorite morning spot, along the back of the sofa, in front of the big picture window, waiting for the sun to come out and warm them. They regarded her with lazy detachment, with David closing his eyes to manage a soft "meow" of acknowledgment.

The kitchen showed only one bit of evidence of Lizzie's presence. An empty Pepsi can with a sticky note lying on top of it. Little hearts and a stream of X's and O's covered the yellow square, and Jill smiled like she'd received a sonnet. After folding it, she put it in her pocket, just so she could take a look at it later.

The cats' bowls had fresh food in them, their water was filled, and their litter box clean. Jill took out her phone and texted Lizzie. "You're quieter than a cat! How'd you sneak out without a sound?"

In a few seconds, a reply came back. "You sleep like the dead. Busy!" That was punctuated by a smiley face giving a kiss.

Well, that wasn't terribly romantic given they'd made love for the first time just hours earlier, but, all things considered, Jill decided having a quiet lover who cleaned the litter box was a lot more valuable than hearts and flowers.

❧

The first day of fall semester was always crazy on campus. Besides a ton of new students not quite knowing where they were going, it was a day for everyone to greet old friends, usually by loitering on the central staircase of her building, blocking the way for harried administrators.

Jill made it back to her office after meeting with her boss, the VP for finance, and spent a moment reminding herself that the newness would wear off in a day or two and people would remember how to walk in a straight line. She checked her phone, a little disappointed not to have heard from Lizzie. Rather than mope, she texted her. "If you come over for dinner, I'll make your favorite dish. What *is* your favorite dish?"

It took a half hour for Lizzie to respond, but the phone finally buzzed. Jill took a look at the message. "Too many favorites to pick one. I'm incredibly easy to please. But I've got a class tonight. How about tomorrow?"

Jill stared at the phone for a minute. They'd made love. They'd jumped off the cliff and *declared* their love. Something that had taken her six months to do with Becca. And after that, Lizzie was too busy to come by?

She stood and dug her wallet out of her briefcase, heading out in search of a cappuccino. It took a few minutes to get out of the building, but once she was out in the drizzle, she felt better. While walking to the Davis Center, she reminded herself that they were going to have to be

301

attentive to each other's needs—especially at first. Lizzie was a very independent woman, and Jill had to give her the space to live her life. That meant no whining when Lizzie wasn't willing to trash her plans to spend the evening together.

After ordering her coffee, Jill sipped at it as she walked back across the campus. She had to grow up and not be so damned clingy. This was a good day to start. Texting while she walked, she wrote, "Tomorrow's great. Stay over?"

"Great. Miss you! XOXO."

"I miss you too." Then she used the same emoji Lizzie had, adding a big kiss to the end of her text.

By five-thirty Jill had answered every critical e-mail, fought every minor fire that had broken out, and calmed down at least a dozen people. Now she was looking forward to going home and getting some exercise, even if she had to ride her bike in the rain. Someone stood in her doorway; it was her friend Scott.

"How was your day?" Jill asked. "Did it suck as much as mine?"

"Yeah, I'd say it did." He entered and sat on one of her guest chairs. "Doing anything tonight?"

"Nope. Well, I was going to ride my bike. I thought some exercise would let me vent a little of the agitation this sucky day has built up. Boy, people act dumb on the first day of a term."

"That's the brutal truth. Let's go have a drink. I'll buy."

She thought about it for a second, then nodded. "Good idea. We've barely seen each other this summer."

"Yeah. What's up with that?"

"Oh, you know me. I love summer so much I can't wait to run out of here at the end of the day."

"I thought maybe you'd finally found a girlfriend." He gave her a sly smile. "Holding out on me?"

She blinked, then decided this was a discussion better suited for a bar. "I'll tell you over a drink. Walk or drive?"

"Let's walk. It's been drizzling on and off, but I think it's clearing up."

She picked up her briefcase and walked around her desk. As they stood in front of her door, he said, "Hmm… You're all dressed up. I'll drive so you don't ruin your shoes."

"Thanks. That's a better idea." She turned her key in the lock, then started to walk towards the stairs. Just as they hit the landing, an auburn head popped up and Lizzie was grinning at her.

Jill stopped and stared. There was no way Lizzie had gone to work looking like this. Hair pulled back into a haphazard ponytail, a black scoop-neck leotard top and tight yoga pants that stopped at her shins, along with flip flops. "What are you doing here?"

"Nice greeting," Lizzie said cheerily. She turned to Scott. "Good to see you again."

"You too. How've you been?"

"Excellent," she said, grinning so happily she looked like she was auditioning for a toothpaste ad. "I thought I'd come by and catch you before you left for the day." Her gaze settled on Jill, her expression so filled with pleasure a total dunce would have known there was something going on between them. "You look fantastic, by the way."

"Uhm…thanks." They were totally blocking the stairs, with people having to work their way around them as they left for the day. "Scott and I were going out for a drink. Want to come?"

"No, I've got my class at six. I guess I'll walk you down." She started back down, carrying her usual backpack and another, bigger bag over the other shoulder. She descended the stairs like she was walking on air, almost dancing as her feet kicked out in front of her, barely hitting each worn marble step. Jill and Scott were fifteen steps behind her by the time they got to the bottom and exited the building.

"Pays to be young," Scott said, looking at Lizzie with a little more interest than Jill was comfortable with.

"It's temporary," Lizzie said. "I don't bounce out of bed the way I did when I was twenty-five."

Jill resisted the urge to take Lizzie in her arms and give her all the kisses she'd been daydreaming about. Instead, she stuck to business. "Where's your class?"

"Patrick Gymnasium."

"You're taking a *class* class? Like for credit?"

"One degree's enough for me. I'm getting back into a troupe I dance with when I have time. The guy who runs it is on the faculty. Ben Barnes. Do you know him?"

"We don't get out to meet the faculty much. It's all numbers for us."

"You'll meet him," she said, still smiling at Jill like she was about as happy as a human being could be. She was also basically ignoring Scott, which Jill didn't mind a bit. Lizzie hoisted her bag and said, "I'd better go. Just thought I'd drop by."

"I'm glad you did," Jill said.

Lizzie put a hand out and put it on Jill's waist. Then she pulled her close and gave her a brief, chaste kiss. Almost like you'd give your sister. "See you." Then she started to walk backwards, waving as she went. "Bye, Scott," she said, but her gaze never left Jill.

"See you around, Lizzie," he said as she turned and nearly skipped down the path. Then he turned to Jill, whose cheeks were undoubtedly pink. "You're fucking her!"

Her hackles rose in a nanosecond. "That's a very impolite thing to say."

"What?" He held his hands up. "What'd I say?"

"We're *dating*. Let's keep it clean, okay?"

He took her by the arm and turned towards the path that would lead them downtown. "We're walking," he said. "I want to hear the whole sordid story." His laugh held an evil tone. "I always imagined you as a pitcher. Now I know better."

She gave him a look, but didn't reply. How could you possibly respond to that jibe without explaining way, way too much? *Thanks Lizzie. Thanks a lot for trying to make a point about being dominated!*

⁂

Jill was sitting outside on her patio, both cats standing at the screen door, crying to join her. She'd never let them, given that they were indoor cats for a reason, but that didn't stop them from wanting to explore the great outdoors and guilt-trip her for preventing their travel plans.

It had stopped raining in the afternoon, and even though it still looked threatening, it didn't smell like rain. That wasn't very scientific, but she could usually tell when a downpour was about to begin.

She'd had a vodka and tonic with Scott, and was now nursing another, while also reading the newspaper on her tablet computer. It was surprisingly warm out, but the mosquitos were few and far between, thankfully.

"Hey there," a warm voice said.

Jill looked up to see a bedraggled Lizzie, still wearing the same outfit she'd had on earlier, but with her hair hanging in big hanks, obviously wet.

"Really nice surprise," Jill said, standing to hug her. "I didn't think I'd get to see you."

"I didn't want to promise anything, just in case I was too tired to move, but I've got a little fuel left in my tank."

As Jill reached for her, Lizzie warned, "Keep your distance. There was some problem in the women's locker room, so I didn't get to shower or change."

"That's sweat?" Jill assumed she'd rushed over after showering and hadn't bothered to dry off properly.

"Yup. Ben worked my *ass* off!"

"What in the hell do you do to work up that kind of sweat?" It was fairly dark in the yard, but now that she looked she could see that Lizzie was wet all over. Soaking wet.

"Haven't you ever watched a dancer work out?"

Jill laughed as she shook her head. "I don't dance, so I'd have to lurk around dance...places...to see that."

"Studios," Lizzie said, tapping her on the chin. "We work in studios. You'll have to come watch."

"I could do that?"

"Uh-huh. But you should probably wait until we're really working on a program. At this point, Ben's just torturing me and that's not much fun to see."

"You're working up to something?"

"Uh-huh. If we can get a space, we're going to do something for First Night."

Jill squealed with delight. "I can spend New Year's Eve watching my girlfriend dance?"

Grinning, Lizzie patted her side. "That's the kind of enthusiasm every dancer wants to hear. It's still up in the air, but Ben's working on it." She grasped the hem of her T-shirt and fanned herself with it. "Can I take a shower?"

"Sure. Of course."

Lizzie picked up the vodka and tonic Jill had placed on the counter and drained it in one gulp. Then she let her gaze wander up and down Jill's body so frankly Jill nearly felt naked. "You look pretty dirty to me. You'd better come along."

"Best two sentences I've heard all day." Jill took her hand and they went up the stairs together.

"Did Scott ask if we were dating?"

"Yeah. In his own clever way."

"Are you cool with that?" She winced. "After I kissed you, I thought maybe I shouldn't have. But I couldn't help myself." She put her hand on Jill's butt and patted it. "You looked so cute. Like a big, important banker or something."

"I had a meeting with our outside auditors. I have to dress like an adult because they do."

"One of these days I'm going to have to figure out what it is you do," Lizzie said. "I get the impression you're a big deal."

"No rush." They went into the bathroom together and Jill proceeded to remove the clammy garments that clung to Lizzie's body. She was still hot, her skin warm to the touch. "It's fine with me if you come to my office every day and plant a big, wet kiss on me. I'm sure Scott will tell everyone about us by the time I get in tomorrow, so it won't be a secret."

Now that Lizzie was naked, Jill whipped off her own T-shirt and flannel boxers, leaving them on the floor as she stuck her hand into the shower stall to turn on the water.

"Everyone at my office started whispering around three, which is when the servers get in. I assume our boating buddies spilled the beans. So I guess we're out, huh?"

"I guess so. That was simple, wasn't it? Tell someone who likes to gossip."

"I'm going to go tell my sibs this weekend."

"All of them?"

"Yep. I think I'll start in Portland, then work my way down. I'll take Friday off so I can spend a little time with my sisters."

Jill opened the door and stepped in. "Perfect," she said as Lizzie joined her. "I guess you want to go alone?"

"Yeah. I think I should." Now that the warm water was pounding down on them, she stood right in front of Jill and wrapped her arms around her. With her head pressed against Jill's shoulder, she said, "I'd rather spend the weekend with you, but I don't want them to find out by mistake. That would really be hard for them."

"Mmm. They won't be hurt that you've been having sex with women for half of your life without telling them?"

"I'm not sure I'm going to talk about my history." She shrugged. "We'll see how it goes. No matter what, Kristen will be hurt. She's the sibling I'm closest to, and..." Lizzie let out a long sigh. "She'll feel betrayed. But not as badly as if she heard about us from someone else."

"And you feel okay omitting the other women you've been with?"

"Yep," she said decisively. "This is a relationship. That was sex. To me, there's a big difference."

"To me too." Jill squeezed her tightly. "But when I was thinking about you dancing, I wasn't thinking about our relationship."

Lizzie looked up at her, grinning. "What were you thinking about?"

"Sex. Just sex. Lots of sex. Sex with you." She knew she looked a little vacant, but the blood that should have been going to her brain was being diverted to a lower altitude.

"Lather me up and I'm yours." Lizzie pulled Jill close and kissed her, while letting her hands glide all over her body. "So," she murmured,

"Does Scott think I chase you around the house trying to do to you what I threatened to do to him?"

"Definitely," Jill said, laughing wryly. "I let him think what he wants. I couldn't come up with a way of setting him straight that didn't require a whole lot more detail than I wanted to give."

"At this point, you could say you have no idea what he's talking about." Lizzie slapped Jill hard on the butt. "At *this* point."

Jill threw her head back and laughed. "This point is going to last for a while. A good, *long* while."

❧

It was just dawn when that annoying voice said, "Pound the alarm. Pound the alarm." Jill wanted her eyes to open, but Lizzie soundlessly slid from bed and padded across the room, two little cat voices fading away as she left.

It was unbelievably hard to force her eyes open, then demand that her feet hit the floor. She had a hard-wired aversion to getting up one minute before she absolutely had to, and this was a good forty-five minutes before her alarm was scheduled to go off. But if Lizzie could drag her butt out of bed so stoically, so could Jill.

Lizzie took a very fast shower, and was already blowing her hair dry when Jill shuffled into the bathroom and let herself be enfolded in a hug.

"Oh, my little sleepy-head got out of bed."

"I wanted to see you before you left for work, and I knew I'd never make it if I didn't get up right away."

"You didn't have to do that," Lizzie said, patting Jill's sleep-lined cheek. "I could come in and kiss you before I leave if you want me to. Would that work?"

"Yeah, I guess." She shrugged. "I just wanted to see you." She sat on the edge of the tub and grasped the boys when they jumped up alongside her. "Do you boys want to sit with me and see what girls do to get ready for work?"

Lizzie got very close to the mirror, assessing her face. "Haven't they seen you? You're a girl."

"You're a different kind of girl. We're all going to learn something."

"I have no secrets," Lizzie declared. She grasped the edge of her quart-sized food storage bag and dumped the contents out onto the counter. "First some foundation." She took a sponge of some sort, dampened it, then put a little tinted liquid on it. With smooth, practiced strokes, she swept over her whole face. The color matched her skin tone, but it evened it out to make her skin look flawless.

"I had no idea women did that," Jill said, staring at her. "I thought foundation was that really heavy powder my grandmother used to wear."

"Nope. Liquid's better." She unscrewed the top of some shimmery powder. "Now a little highlighter." Carefully, she brushed the powder under her brow, then right at the edge of her eyes, then quickly across her cheeks.

"Should I be watching this?" Jill asked, fascinated. "I feel like I'm in the inner sanctum, where only initiates get to enter."

"I'll put makeup on you any time you like. But you don't need it. I just got in the habit when I worked at the Gardner and now I feel like I looked unfinished when I don't wear it."

As Lizzie took a black pencil and ran it over her upper lid, Jill thought about that. She wasn't sure what she preferred—fresh-faced Lizzie or sophisticated Lizzie. But she was sure they were both awfully pretty.

Now mascara, just on the upper lashes, darkened and thickened them. A quick brush of pink on her cheekbones made them pop. Then Lizzie turned and said, "How about a kiss?"

"Sure." Jill stood and placed a gentle one on her lips. "I like the way all of this stuff smells. It's really girly." She giggled at her use of the word. "I sound like I'm watching my older sister get ready for the prom."

"Just work," Lizzie said as she carefully applied a judicious amount of lipstick that made her pouty lips shine. "Ready to go shake money out of pockets."

"Uhm…" Jill discretely pointed at her naked body. "You might want to add a few things."

"Just a few."

They went into the guest bedroom, where Lizzie took out the dress she'd brought. As she dug into her bag for fresh underwear Jill said, "Where are your tattoos? I meant to ask the other night, but you kept distracting me."

"Tattoos?" She ostentatiously looked down at her body. "Do I have tattoos?"

"Not that I can see, but I thought everyone under forty had a few."

"Certainly not everybody, since I don't have any." She put on a bra that was just for show, so insubstantial it was barely there. "Almost everyone I knew was getting them left and right, but I kept holding off." She put her dress over her head and shimmied into it. "I'm so particular about art, I kept changing my mind about what I wanted. I dropped the idea when I realized I'd want a different one all the time."

"I'm glad you don't have any," Jill admitted. "I don't hate them, but I like you just the way you are."

"You were never tempted?"

"Not really. They were pretty popular when I was in college, but it was still the edgier kids who got them, and I was never edgy."

Lizzie slipped into a pair of bone-colored heels, took one last look at herself in the mirror and picked up her tote bag. "I'm ready to go slay dragons."

"You look really, really good," Jill said, knowing she probably looked like a love-struck dope.

"Thanks. I hope I look good enough to talk people into handing me every bit of their liquid assets."

"You do to me. If I've got it, you can have it."

Lizzie leaned over and whispered into Jill's ear as she put a hand on her breast and gave it a gentle squeeze. "I'll just take your heart. That's all I'll ever need."

⁂

On Friday morning, when Jill's alarm went off at seven-thirty, she lay perfectly still, waiting for the boys to start whining. Curiosity got the best of her after a few seconds of silence and she cautiously opened her eyes. The bed was empty, but when she put her hand on the spot where Lizzie should be, the lingering warmth from her body made her smile.

"Lizzie?"

"Give me a second," she called up.

"Just checking to see if you were still here."

"I am. Take your shower."

Jill didn't mind being told what to do, so she followed orders. When her hair was almost dry, the bathroom door opened and Lizzie entered, carrying a mug and a plate. She was wearing one of Jill's T-shirts, which just covered her butt. It was a little big on her, which was strangely sexy. It was amazing what attracted you when you were falling in love.

"I like your shirt."

"You don't mind my Donald Ducking it in your kitchen?"

"Donald Ducking…?"

"He wore a shirt but no pants," she explained. "I don't want to show my butt to your neighbors, but I was pretty sure no one could see in."

"You may shake your cute little ass all over my house. We've got plenty of privacy."

Lizzie placed the plate on the vanity table, then bent and kissed Jill's cheek. "For you. I felt like playing housewife today."

Jill grasped her by the hips and tumbled her into her lap, with the small stool she sat on squeaking under their combined weight. "What a nice way to wake up. If you ever want to quit your job, I could think of a hundred things to keep you busy."

"Check with me after I've paid off my student loans." She took the fork and cut a bite of pancake, then moved it around while making airplane noises. "Here it comes. Open the hangar."

Jill opened her mouth and the bite slid inside. "Mmm… You don't have to play tricks to get me to eat pancakes. Perfect amount of syrup, by the way. Full coverage, but not oversaturated."

"I like to make you happy." She cut another bite, readying it for when Jill had swallowed.

"You do," Jill said soberly. "You really do. When are you leaving?"

"When you do. I'll drop you off at work, then keep going." She placed a soft kiss on Jill's cheek. "Are you sure you don't mind my taking Freyja? I'm going to put a lot of miles on her."

"I don't want you going with some guy you found on Craigslist, Lizzie. I'll feel much better knowing my trusty Freyja will be with you."

"I've been all over New England with people I found on Craigslist." She started to poke all around Jill's belly and sides. "You're not going to get all maternal on me, are you?"

"No," she said, giggling under the assault, "but you hadn't found a ride back from Portland to Massachusetts. You've got enough things to worry about this weekend. The last thing you want is to be online every minute, trying to hitch a ride."

Lizzie held her tightly and placed a long, soft kiss on her lips. "I like that you worry about me. But I'm not going to stop hitching rides with strangers. I don't like to waste fuel when I don't have to."

"I get that. I do. And I wouldn't have insisted if you weren't trying to hit four cities in three states in three days."

She made a face. "It doesn't sound like much fun when you put it that way. I wish Donna hadn't moved all the way to Portland. That's the leg of the trip that's gonna take the most time."

"I haven't been there in years. How long will it take you?"

"About four hours. Donna's gonna take the afternoon off work so we can have some alone time."

"Sounds good. Then you're going to see Kristen tomorrow?"

"Uh-huh." She put the next bite in, then kissed Jill's cheek again. "That'll take about three hours from Donna's house. I'll stay over at Kristen's on Saturday night, then do all four boys on Sunday. I'm gonna have to start early to get 'em all in."

"Are they expecting you?"

"The boys aren't. But Chris and Tim and Adam all live within a half hour of each other. If one's not home, I'll move to the next. I'll catch them all at some point. It's not like any of them ever go anywhere."

"Nervous?"

"Not really. I love all of my siblings, but if they can't accept me as I am, I'll make do. When you've got six brothers and sisters, the stakes aren't as high to make each of them like you."

Jill had been unable to get a nagging worry to leave her alone, and it flared up again. "But you don't seriously think they'll give you a hard time, do you?"

"Nah. Mark won't like it, but he won't say so. Lisa will hate it, so I'm not going to tell her at all. Mark can handle that mess."

"The other boys won't mind?"

She seemed to think for a minute, even though Jill knew she'd been mulling this over in her mind for quite some time. "They might be shocked, and my being with you will knock them for a loop, but they'll be fine. They've all been around plenty of gay people, and none of them are particularly narrow-minded."

"Good. I don't want to have to worry every minute you're gone."

"Aww…" She tickled under Jill's chin. "You don't have to worry even one minute. I'm a big girl."

"You're *my* girl," Jill said, looking into her eyes, "and I'm protective of you."

Lizzie took a bite of the pancake, and chewed thoughtfully. "I didn't like it when my boyfriends said I was theirs. But it's fine when you do it." She kissed Jill's cheek, then wiped a dot of syrup from it. "Apparently I don't mind having double standards."

"I can't help it. Even though I know you can take care of yourself, I want to watch out for you."

"That's part of being in love." She tilted her head and they shared a long, sweet kiss. "You *do* still love me, don't you?"

"I do," Jill said, grinning. "Four days and counting."

Lizzie put the last bite of the pancake into Jill's mouth. "Let's get going. I don't want you to be late. Meet you downstairs."

Jill watched her leave, wishing she hadn't wanted to go alone. Only four days in and she could hardly stand the thought of not seeing her all weekend. Being in love was *harder than it looked*.

A few minutes later, Jill hefted Lizzie's backpack onto her shoulder and followed her out to the car. Lizzie was wearing her crisp white shirt over her favorite black leotard, black leggings, with knee-high black leather boots. Jill thanked her lucky stars that Lizzie wasn't going to get into a car with a strange guy from Craigslist. Not that Lizzie wasn't attractive every day, but today she was off the charts. And if Jill had been forced to spend the day thinking of how some stranger would be gazing at that stupendous ass, perfectly highlighted by those leggings…she wouldn't have been worth a thing at work.

⚜

Jill was walking home that afternoon when her phone rang. She pulled it from her pocket, not bothering to see who it was. "Hello?"

"Jill?"

The voice was completely familiar, even though she'd only heard it a couple of times in twenty years. "Hi, Mark."

"Hey. I'm in Burlington and thought I'd wait for traffic to die down before I went home. How about dinner?"

"Uhm, I've got something at eight, but I'm free until then. Does that work?"

"Sure. I'll come by your house. Is that good?"

"Okay. I should be there by five-thirty. You've got the address, right?"

"Yeah, I do. My GPS can find it."

"Great. See you soon." She picked up her pace, a thread of anxiety stirring in her gut. Lizzie had been sure Donna wouldn't call the other kids to tell them her news, but you never knew…

Jill had barely gotten the front door open when she heard Mark's truck pull into the driveway. She was going to cut through the house and tell him to come in the back, but her eyes scanned the kitchen first. Damned good thing. Lizzie had left a note on the refrigerator. "Don't fall in love with anyone else while I'm gone." That wasn't too bad, but she'd added drawings of stick-figure women kissing and lying on top of one another. Her attempt at showing the figures with their heads between each other's stick legs was funny—to Jill. She was pretty sure Mark wouldn't like to see that the figure on the bottom was named Lizzie and the one on top Jill.

The front bell rang and she stumbled over the annoyed, frantically fleeing cats getting to it. "Hi," she said as she opened the door. "I'm about to have an uprising here. My cats were headed for dinner when the bell rang, but now they're hiding like little chickens."

He walked in, looking a little sheepish. "Is it okay that I surprised you? I didn't think I'd be in town long, so I didn't call to set something up."

"Of course it is. Come on into the kitchen."

He followed her, commenting, "Your house is awesome, Jill. Damn, don't ever let Lisa see this. She'd kill me for not making enough to buy a nice place."

Jill thought about that while she portioned out a snack for the boys. Mark had been a very good student, always trying his best to please his teachers at every level. His hard work got him to summa cum laude, no surprise to Jill. His mind had always shown him to be a cut above.

"All that matters is that you do something you love," she said, while filling up the water bowl.

"I like what I do," he said thoughtfully. "But I'd like it a lot more if I didn't have to worry about money."

"Lisa doesn't work, right?"

"No, she never has." He corrected himself immediately. "I mean, she works constantly. Just not for money."

"I'm sure it was nice for her to be home when your kids were young."

"Yeah." He nodded, then stuck his hands in his pockets and looked around the kitchen idly. "But they're not young any more. I have no idea how I'm going to pay for them to go to college."

"No savings?" she asked, even though that was an indelicate question.

"Not much. Hell, I couldn't reliably pay the rent on the apartment we live in. Saving money's pretty much impossible."

She stopped, stunned by that comment. "You can't pay the rent…?"

"Got any beer?" he asked.

"Sure. But I'm ready to go if you are."

"I like to have a beer or two before I go out. Saves ten bucks."

"Right. That makes sense." She took two beers from the fridge and they went outside to drink them. A very annoying cool wind had been blowing all day, reminding her that summer was on the way out, but it was still warm enough to sit outside for a while.

He started to play with the label on his beer, cutting a stripe down it with his thumbnail. She'd almost forgotten she'd asked a question, but when he began to talk it came back to her. "You know The Foundation owns the shop, right?"

"Oh, sure. I mean, I didn't know that, but it makes sense."

"In exchange for the apartment, I open the shop to the public and do free tours on the weekends. Then everything I earn is mine to keep."

"Wow. That's…nice," she said, frankly amazed that he'd gotten such a sweetheart deal.

"I know how lucky I was to fall into this," he said. "But there are a lot of weeks where I don't make a cent. What I make in the summer and fall has to carry me all year."

"How'd…" She wanted to make sure she framed the question sensitively. "How'd you wind up being a blacksmith? I never knew you were the creative type."

He shrugged, then took a drink. "I'm not, really. For a few years I worked in Brattleboro, at a small accounting firm. But the lead guy retired and sold his client list to a bigger place in Bellows Falls. They promised we'd get a chance at a job, but that was just a promise." He let out a heavy sigh, his slumped posture showing just how badly he'd been beaten down. "I was going to look for work in a bigger town, but Lisa had her mind set on staying in Sugar Hill." He shrugged. "You know how it is. She's really close to her parents, and she's comfortable there."

"I understand that. It's a great place for your kids to grow up, and being close to all of their grandparents is really nice."

"Yeah, it is. So I looked for work for a long time, trying to find anything close. Then old Mr. Rooney said he was thinking about retiring, and he asked me if I'd like to take over for him."

Jill blinked in surprise. "Just like that? You hadn't worked for him?"

"Nope. He knew I wanted to stay in town, and that I didn't have a job. So he taught me the basics and I took over. I'm still learning, fifteen years later." He shrugged. "I'm not a natural. I can copy things I see, but I've never created anything on my own. I just don't have that kind of eye."

"But you like it?"

He smiled, shrugged and said, "It's a job. Does anybody *like* having to work?"

As he said that, it hit Jill that this was Mark in a nutshell. He'd worked hard in school, but just to please his parents and his teachers. His efforts were never based on true intellectual curiosity. Now he was working for himself, and didn't have that same carrot of approval dangling in front of him. He wasn't a lazy guy, but he didn't have the drive, that need to be successful that all prosperous business owners had. He was just getting by, and always would be.

Luckily, his sister was nothing like him. Mark needed to please others. Lizzie needed to please herself. Years ago, Jill would have preferred Mark. Her battered psyche was drawn to kind souls who demanded little from her. But now? She smiled to herself. Now she loved the feistiest member of the whole clan. The one who was going to keep her on her toes for the rest of her life.

⌘

Jill was running late, but not too late, managing to reach Skip and Alice's house only ten minutes behind schedule. She'd tried to get Mark back on the road as soon as they'd eaten their burgers, but he dawdled and wasted so much time it was clear he just didn't want to go home. Finally, she got up and paid the bill, then stood at the door until he followed her out to the street. One quick hug and she took off, walking as quickly as she could to reach Skip and Alice's, which was only about a half mile away. Normally she would have driven, given the tight schedule, but she couldn't afford to have Mark see Lizzie's distinctive car.

She was panting when she knocked and entered. Everyone was already seated, and they all gave her a hard time for being late—a real rarity for her. She sat at the empty seat, next to Karen, who leaned over and said, "Everything all right?"

"Yeah. I had dinner with a friend, and had a hard time getting away. But I'm ready to play some cards," she said, slightly louder. "Let's do this."

⌘

She'd decided she was going to tell the group about Lizzie, but shoehorning in that kind of information wasn't all that easy. She couldn't

317

do it while they were playing, so she waited until they took their first break. Cornering Karen, she quietly said, "Ask me what's new."

"What?"

"Ask me. I need an intro."

"Oh," she said, nodding. "Gotcha."

They went back to the group, getting involved in some small talk about the U. Karen went into the kitchen to get a fresh drink, and when she came back she said, with studied casualness, "What's new, Jill? We haven't seen much of you for the last few weeks."

"Mmm." She popped a chip in her mouth while nodding. "I've been really busy."

"With what?"

"With Lizzie," she said, waiting for someone to notice and comment.

Gerri picked up on the remark. "Are you working on something together?"

"I guess you could say that." She hadn't planned on how to dive in and now felt awkward. But she was in this far, and couldn't turn back. "We've been spending a lot of time together."

Skip stopped his side conversation with Gerri and gave her a sharp look. "What kind of time?"

Now she knew her cheeks were flushed with embarrassment. She could never hide it. "Quality time," she said, then made a face at how stupid that sounded.

Now Alice diverted her attention to Jill. "The girl who watches your house?"

"She's not a girl," Jill said, already on the defense. "And yes, that's who I'm talking about."

"You're…?" Skip took his hands and placed them together, then raised his eyebrow.

"Yep. We're together."

"I could have sworn she was straight," Skip said, his frown showing he was disappointed that she wasn't. "Did you turn her?"

Six lesbians gave him a chiding look in unison.

"Hey! You're the ones always joking about getting toaster ovens for new recruits. I didn't make that up!"

"I didn't trick her into anything," Jill said, trying not to show her annoyance. "And even though it isn't really anyone's business, Lizzie has been with women before. She's not a new recruit."

"How old *is* she?" Kathleen asked, before Mary Beth elbowed her sharply.

"She's thirty," Jill said, deciding to just get it out of the way. "Yes, she's much younger than I am, but we really like each other. We're a good fit."

"Well, I can't fault your taste," Skip said, slapping her on the back. "Isn't she from your home town?"

"Yeah. Her older brother and I were best friends through college."

"How does he feel about this?" Alice asked. "My brother would have strangled any of his friends who tried to date me."

Jill started to feel a little sick. "We'll find out. She's telling her brothers and sisters this weekend."

"Do they know your address?" Alice asked. Jill stared at her. Sometimes Alice could be annoyingly blunt.

"I don't think they'll form a posse and hunt me down, if that's what you're asking." She took a drink of her beer with shaking hands. "I hope."

⌘

The people at her table kept tossing questions at her for the rest of the evening, but once their surprise had worn off everyone seemed happy for her. They were on their last hand when Jill's phone buzzed. Taking a look, she saw it was a text from Lizzie.

"Love notes?" Skip asked.

"Probably. I'll call her back when we're finished."

Her attention was so split, Jill missed taking an easy trick. Gerri, her partner, gave her a sour look when they lost the contract by one trick, but she didn't complain. As they helped put the chairs away, Jill quietly said, "Sorry about screwing up. I'm thinking about Lizzie more than my game."

"Don't worry about it. We're not playing for money." She stacked a couple of chairs in the corner and gave Jill a long look. "Of course, if we had been, you'd probably win the whole pot. Your luck's been very, very good."

⌘

As soon as she was in her car, Jill made the call.

"Hey," Lizzie said when she answered. "Did it take you that long to throw the other women out of your house?"

"Yeah," Jill agreed. "You know how irresistible I am. The poor things were heartsick."

"Did you play bridge?"

"Uh-huh. And had dinner with your brother."

"My brother? Mark?"

"Yep. He was in town buying some supplies. He said he was trying to avoid traffic, but I think he just wanted to hang out."

Lizzie sighed audibly. "Poor Mark. He's kind of a sad-sack, isn't he?"

"I hate to use that term, but it's apt. I think he's let his life get away from him."

"Marrying the wrong woman can screw things up for you. Thank god that's not going to happen to you," she said, laughing at her own joke.

"I'm not going to argue with you on that. As Gerri told me tonight, I'm a very lucky woman to have you."

"She said that?"

Jill could hear the delight in Lizzie's voice. "Uh-huh. And she's right. I'm very, very lucky."

"Me too. And my luck is holding with my sister. I didn't know this until today, but she knew about Erica. Turns out she saw us in the park late one night."

"When you were a kid?"

"Yep."

"Damn, Lizzie, what in the heck were you two doing?"

"I thought you didn't like to imagine me being with other people."

"I don't. But…how old were you?"

320

"Mmm. Fifteen, I guess. And we were just making out...I think. It was hard to get Erica to do more than that even when we were hiding in the garage."

"The garage?" Jill laughed, imagining Lizzie's tenaciousness at finding places to be alone.

"My mom had a big old minivan. The back seat was perfect, at least to me. Erica wanted to be in a cave in the mountains."

"My poor little Lizzie. All she wanted was a horny girlfriend."

"Kinda true," she admitted, laughing. "My whole life would have been different. So, ever since Donna saw us, she's been wondering if I'd ever swing back around to the ladies. She wasn't surprised at all about my being interested in a woman."

"That's great! I always thought Donna was pretty perceptive."

"Oh, not so fast, slugger," she said, her laughter sounding slightly evil. "She's not at all sure I should be with someone so..."

"Intelligent? Attractive? Cultured?"

"Yeah," Lizzie said. "Either one of those or...ancient."

Stunned, Jill managed to say, "She honestly thinks I'm too old for you?"

"Kinda. But I think I convinced her that you're really immature."

"That's my girl," Jill said, laughing. "Always going to bat for me."

"She'll be fine. She was just giving me advice, not expressing any real concern."

"I'm surprised by that. I mean, ten years isn't insignificant, but we're from the same generation."

"Yeah, but she has friends who're married to guys eight or nine years older and they're always complaining that their husbands really hold them back. I think she's worried that might happen to me."

"It might," Jill admitted. "But not because I get lazy or voluntarily stop being active. I can't guarantee something won't knock me down in my prime of course."

"Cheerful thought! Do you have any other depressing concepts to share?"

"No, that's about it. Oh. I miss you. Is that depressing?"

"Nope. You're supposed to miss the woman you love. You still love me, right?"

"Right. Going on five days and I'm not bored with you yet."

Lizzie's voice grew softer and Jill could just picture her. Head tilted to one side, a sweet smile turning up the corners of her mouth.

"I really do miss you. You make the day a lot more fun."

"That's true for me too. I'll especially miss having you in my bed. Do you have a nice place to sleep?"

"With four kids still at home? I get the lower bunk in my youngest niece's room. Luckily, she's in high school and doesn't wet the bed anymore."

"Gosh, I wish I'd been able to go with you," Jill teased. "We'd get to share it!"

"Maybe next time. Play your cards right and I'll have you sleeping in bunk beds all over New England."

"If you're snuggled up beside me, I'd be just fine with that." She finally started her car and put her seat belt on. "I'll give the boys a kiss for you."

"Thanks. Tell them I'll be back on Sunday. Do they know the days of the week?"

"Sure. And they can count to fifty and do simple arithmetic. They're really advanced."

"I'll test them on Sunday."

"It's a deal. I love you, Lizzie."

"Love you too. I'll call tomorrow."

"G'night." Jill clicked the phone off and sat there for a while. It had only been a few days, but she already could feel a part of her world wasn't quite right. Lizzie was the missing piece.

⁂

On Saturday night, Lizzie didn't call until almost midnight. Jill had been pacing around for an hour, waiting. When the phone rang, she answered on the first ring. "I thought I'd never hear from you!"

"Argh! This day got screwed up so many times I can't even count."

"What happened?"

"Nothing huge. I left late because my youngest niece wanted me to help her with a report she had to do, then Kristen got stuck ferrying her kids to different sports. Her husband was supposed to do it, but he had to go in to work… It was all just screwed up. So we didn't have any time alone until the kids were occupied or in bed, which was only like an hour ago."

"I guess it went okay, if it only took an hour."

"Yeah," she said, sounding a little deflated. "It went okay."

"What really happened?"

Lizzie let out a long sigh. "Kristen wasn't as understanding as I thought she'd be. She was kinda…pissy about it."

"Oh, Lizzie, I'm sorry."

"Yeah, me too. If I wasn't tired, I'd take off right now. But that would just make her mad and I don't want to do that."

"Can I help? Want me to come down there? I could meet you at a nice hotel."

"Aww, you really would do that, wouldn't you?"

"You bet. I'd do anything to take the sadness from your voice."

"That helps. Knowing I'm coming home to you helps a lot."

"I was going to talk to you about that. Isn't your lease up in October?"

"Uh-huh. What about it?"

"Move in with me. I really want you to."

"Jill! We've been together six days!"

"I know. But I love you, Lizzie, and I want to spend as much time as I can with you. What better way than to live together?"

"I don't know," she said, clearly skittish. "What if you get sick of me?"

"I won't. But if you get sick of me, you can always move. Not that you're going to, of course. I'm really pretty awesome."

"I love you, you silly thing. And I'll think about it."

"Which way are you leaning? Not that I'm pushing you or anything."

"I'm leaning towards you. Of course. But I'll have to do some budgeting to see if I can afford it. I run a very lean operation."

"Don't worry about it. I can handle all of the housing costs. You can concentrate on paying down your student loans."

"That won't work. I have to contribute or I won't feel like I belong there."

"But the house is in my name. I get the tax deduction, and I'll get the appreciation if I ever sell. So the mortgage and real estate taxes are mine. That's fair."

"Utilities? Could I afford them?"

"How about half? That's fair."

"I think you've already talked me into this, roomie. When do you want me?"

"Tomorrow. As soon as you get back, we'll go pack up your work clothes. I want you sleeping with me from here on out. So do the boys, but they pay nothing, so their vote doesn't really count."

"You've got yourself a deal. Excited!" she said, all of her disappointment with her sister seemingly forgotten. Jill felt like she'd done a good day's work, given that making Lizzie happy was her new life's goal.

Chapter Seventeen

THE NEXT DAY, JILL was just about to toss a kayak into Lake Champlain when her phone rang. "I've got to get this," she told Carly. "If you want to put in and catch up with Samantha, I'm good."

"Okay. Yell if you need help."

She answered the phone. "Hey, Lizzie, what's up?"

"Mark," she said, her voice strained and clipped. "He's furious with me and with you. I've never seen him so angry, Jill. I'm going over to my parents' house for a while, hoping to wait him out so he calms down and can talk some more without screaming at me."

"I can be there in three hours," she said, her heart hammering in her chest. "I'll borrow a car and—"

"No, you don't need to come. I'll be okay, but I needed to tell you. I'm"—she started to sniffle—"I'm so hurt."

"Oh, sweetheart," Jill soothed. She tried to calm down and think of Lizzie, rather than her own anxiety. "It'll be all right. If Mark wants to have a relationship with you, he'll come around. I bet this is more about his general unhappiness. He's just taking it out on you."

"Maybe." The background noise stopped completely. "I just got to my parents' house. I'll call you later, okay?"

"Yeah. And don't forget about my offer. I'm happy to come down."

"I know. I'll call you if I need you." She sniffled again, and said, "I always need you. I'll call if I need you quickly."

"Take care of yourself, Lizzie. You're precious to me."

"Thanks," she said, her voice still shaky. "You too."

Jill hung up, got into her kayak, pushed off and paddled furiously to vent some of her anxiety. She mused that she'd been sure having six brothers and sisters would have made things easier for Lizzie. Her instincts had been bad.

❦

It was almost impossible to relax and enjoy the day while she was anxiously waiting for a phone call. Even a warm, sunny September Sunday on the water, her favorite place. Thankfully, the next call was much better. Janet and Mike had successfully reassured Lizzie that Mark was going through his own troubles right now, and would surely come around in time. Lizzie sounded much more like herself as she drove up to Bellows Falls, where her other brothers all lived. Hopefully, they'd make this less about them, and more about Lizzie.

Now that Jill was more at ease, she tried to clear her mind of distressing thoughts and concentrate on her paddling. It was just the first week of September, but the lake was already noticeably colder than it had been last Monday when they'd gone out on "Stiff Ripples."

Jill put all of her energies into paddling hard, working her body to its capacity while she enjoyed what might be her last time on the lake this season. The summer had all gone by too quickly, but next summer she'd have Lizzie with her the whole time. That would make it a great one, no matter what the weather held in store.

By the time they'd paddled back to the shore, Jill's arms were like wet noodles. Her abs had finally calmed down from wake boarding, and here she was stressing them again. When her girlfriend could twist herself into a pretzel without even breathing hard, she was going to have to fight to stay in shape.

They went to a juice bar and had smoothies, then Samantha and Carly had to get home to their kids. Assuming Lizzie would be home late and would need to talk, Jill headed home for a nap.

As she approached her house, her whole body tingled with sensation when she caught sight of Mark's truck filling her driveway. Something about the way the big, black truck took up her access and blocked the way to the garage felt like a violation.

She pulled over and turned off the car, then spied him sitting on the front steps. There were two perfectly comfortable chairs on the porch, but he'd plunked down on the middle of the top stair, his hands on his knees, looking more like a statue than a man. That was the posture of a guy who was furious. As she got out, she thought of his heavy muscles, perfect for knocking her halfway down the street.

She walked up the sidewalk, tentative, anxious, and angry all at the same time. By the time she stood in front of him, he still hadn't lifted his head. A ball cap was pulled down low, covering his eyes, and the red flannel shirt he had on stretched across his back, the seams straining.

Without meeting her eyes, he spoke, cold fury staining his words. "How long have you been after her?" A second passed, with the question barely registering in Jill's puzzled mind. "How *long*?" he said, tilting his chin so his rage-filled eyes locked on her.

For the first time in her life, she was afraid of him, but her fear wasn't as strong as her anger. Words started to tumble out before she had a moment to let her fear temper them. "I don't have to explain myself to you. This is between me and Lizzie." She turned to go back to the car, but before she could blink he was right next to her. His incredibly powerful hand locked onto her forearm, stopping her like she was a child.

Heart beating wildly, she forced her voice to remain calm and level. "Let me go."

"How long have you been after her?" he demanded, his volume rising again.

She was tempted to scream. Her neighbor across the street was the kind of person who loved to call the police at any and all violations of the penal code—even though she imagined most of them. And she was almost always home.

Jill tried to put this into perspective. She'd known Mark her whole life. There was no way he would hurt her. But when she tried to move forward to get some distance, his hold tightened. She wasn't sure if he'd pressed on a nerve or what, but her arm started to tingle, then she was on her knees, holding her arm as she stared up at him.

"What in the fuck do you think you're doing?" she cried.

"I didn't do anything!"

He looked at his own hand, like it had snuck away and done something he couldn't possibly be responsible for.

Jill got to her feet, her arm stinging like it did when you hit your funny bone. They faced off, with Jill moving back towards Lizzie's car.

Then Mark advanced on her again, clearly as angry as he'd been when she pulled up.

"I asked you a question, and I want to know the answer."

She studied him carefully, looking for the slightest indication he was going to touch her again. When he stopped a few feet away, her pounding heart slowed enough for her to decide to answer.

"I've never been after her, Mark. I thought your sister was straight, and I was perfectly happy to be her friend."

"Nice," he spat. "Blame it on her."

"I'm not *blaming* anything on her. I'm telling you how it was."

"Bullshit!"

He said that so loudly, she was almost certain Mrs. Higgins was already on the phone to the cops. Normally, she would have taken him around to the back so they could talk in peace. That was no longer an option. She wasn't going to put herself into a vulnerable position. Staying out in the front would provide more witnesses if he lost control.

Just so Mrs. Higgins could see she was there by choice, Jill carved a wide path to walk up to the porch and sit down. Mark followed, standing in front of her, glaring.

"Listen," she snapped. "I've got a neighbor who thinks this street is a hotbed of crime. She might have already called the cops, but if you touch me again, I guarantee a patrol car will be here in a flash. So sit down and stop being such a jackass."

"*I'm* a jackass," he fumed, jerking a thumb towards himself as he fell into a chair. "You've had your eye on my little sister since she was a kid. You're a fucking pedophile!"

Stunned, Jill stared at him. "Listen to yourself! I haven't seen Lizzie for eighteen years! Pedophiles don't wait for their victims to turn thirty, you idiot. That's Lisa talking." She almost bit her tongue at that last comment, but it was too late to take it back.

"I think for myself," he growled. "But Lisa was right about you. One hundred percent right. You're a god-damned pervert. And I mean that literally. You're gonna burn in hell for what you've done to my sister."

She couldn't stop herself from rolling her eyes. With all of the evil in the world, how could a reasonable person believe God was obsessed with adults being in loving relationships? "Things are changing, Mark. The Pope doesn't even believe that any more. Come on into the twenty-first century. It's nice here."

"Go fuck yourself," he grumbled. "Of course, you'd rather be fucking my sister."

"I love your sister," she said, her anger ready to boil over again. "And I don't appreciate you talking about our relationship like that. Have some fucking respect. For her, if not for me." Her phone rang, and she almost ignored it. But if it was Lizzie, she didn't want her to worry. She pulled it from her jeans pocket and looked at the display, then swiped across the screen and lifted it to her ear. "Hi, Janet," she said, trying hard to sound calm.

"Is Mark there? Christian said he took off hours ago, and won't answer his phone." She was almost panting with fear.

"He's here."

"Let me talk to him, Jill."

She extended the phone. "Your mom wants to talk to you."

He grabbed the phone and said, "This is between me and Jill." Then he stabbed at the "end" button and tossed the phone back, with Jill fumbling to stop it from falling.

"What are you going to do? Beat me up?" she demanded, then realized how foolish she was being. She didn't know this guy at all. Her old friend was a twenty-two year old who was gone—a ghost from her past. And acting like that gentle soul was the same person as this hulk glaring at her might get her into a whole hell of a lot of trouble.

As she feared, he didn't take the taunt well. "I might. I just might kick your ass," he spat. "Something your family should have done when you started this crap. If they'd beaten this out of you when you were a kid, you might have straightened out."

She jumped up and stood behind the chair, just to have something to slow him down if he made a move towards her. "What in the fuck are you talking about? Jesus Christ! Who've you been listening to?"

"Nobody tells me what to think. I know what you've been up to. You've fucked your way all across Vermont and New Hampshire, and now you're trying to screw my sister up. To make her like *you*."

"She *is* like me," Jill said clearly. "And neither of us needs your permission to love one another."

"What do you know about love? You had it staring you in the face for…" He screwed his eyes closed, then shouted, "Years! But you had to throw it right back in my face." He was so angry, so filled with hate that she feared he'd strangle her. She was sweating, even though it was cool and windy on the porch. Images of his hands closing around her neck made her jump off the side of the porch and start for the street. But he got up at the same time and tried to cut her angle off. "I'm not gonna let you break Lizzie's heart too."

A car roared down the street, and from the corner of her eye she saw red lights flashing. Thank God for Mrs. Higgins! Doors opened and slammed, then a pair of cops were striding quickly up her sidewalk. "Step away from each other," one of them said, and Jill gladly moved back, well out of reach.

"We're fine, officers," she said, surprised by how weak and tremulous her voice was. "My friend was just leaving."

Having the police right in front of him brought the eager-to-please Mark back. "Yeah," he said, now mumbling in a low, quiet tone. "I was just leaving."

One of the officers approached Jill and guided her over to the driveway, out of earshot. "What's going on?" he asked, gazing at her with penetrating eyes.

"Nothing. He's an old friend who just found out I'm dating someone he doesn't think I should be with."

"Has he hit you before, ma'am?"

"No! We're just friends. We've never been involved."

"Did he have his hands on you?"

She almost lied. Almost let the good years give him a pass. But this guy, this angry, bitter guy didn't deserve one. "He grabbed my arm to try to make me stay and listen to him. I…" She pulled her sleeve up, saying,

"I don't think it left a mark." But there were now dark red fingerprints across her forearm, and a purple mark on the pale skin underneath. "I didn't realize he held me that tightly," she admitted.

"We'll take him in," the officer said. "That'll give him a while to cool off."

She closed her eyes, thinking of the repercussions that would have. "Please don't," she said. "I'll leave and go to a friend's house."

"He'll come back," the officer said. "You should consider getting a restraining order, ma'am."

Immediately, her protective instincts roared to life. Having Mark arrested would upset Lizzie. And Janet. And Mike. She couldn't do that to them. "That's not necessary," she said quickly. "If I leave, he'll leave. I'm sure of it."

The cop started to speak again, but Jill interrupted him. "He's got a very controlling wife. If he's not home soon, she'll do much worse than give him time to calm down."

"If you're sure."

"I am. Is there a way you can just let this drop? I don't want to make this a bigger deal than it is."

He stared at her for a few seconds. "That can be a fatal mistake, ma'am."

"I know that," she admitted, "but this is a unique situation."

He rolled his eyes. "A guy wants what he can't have. That's not unique."

"In this case, the guy doesn't want me to be in love with his sister. He just found out, and he's freaked out about it."

"Oh." His eyebrows lifted. "I haven't heard that one."

"Yeah, that's probably not the most common reason you're called. I'm willing to give him some time to calm down. He's got a wife, kids, parents and three brothers nearby. I'm sure they can reason with him."

"All right," he sighed. "But I'm still going to write this up, just in case."

"Oh, shit," she grumbled. "I don't want him to have a record."

"I'm just doing an operations report. I'll need ID, names and addresses from both of you."

"My name? I didn't do anything!"

"And you're not being charged with anything. But if he comes back and kicks your door down, the officer who responds will be able to look at this and see he's already had a warning. This is for your protection, ma'am." He met her eyes. "Can I see some ID?"

She took her wallet from her back pocket and produced her license. Then he walked over to Mark and the other officer and spent a minute talking to them. Jill watched him go back to his patrol car and start typing on the laptop wedged between the front seats.

When he came back, he handed her the license. "I think it's a good idea to go see a friend. Someone he doesn't know. We'll keep him here for a few minutes, then let him go."

"Great. Thanks for being so understanding."

"No problem. But if he comes back…"

"I'll stay in the house and call you. Promise."

She walked back to Lizzie's car, not making eye contact with Mark. As she started it up, she could see him standing on the porch, hands in his pockets, staring at the ground as the police officer stood with his arms crossed over his chest. Mark didn't look so imposing now. He'd probably seem even smaller when Lisa got done with him.

As soon as Jill was a few blocks away, she called Janet. "I'm so sorry," she began, but Janet jumped right in.

"You're sorry? *I'm* sorry for having my otherwise mild-mannered son run all the way up there to harass you! What in the hell happened?"

"I'm not sure," Jill admitted. "He was on my porch when I got home, beside himself with anger. When he grabbed me by the arm, my neighbor saw him and called the cops."

There was a long moment of silence, which Jill filled with anxiety that Janet would blame her for escalating this mess, but Janet yanked her right out of her musings. "*I* called the police," she said, not a trace of regret in her voice. "I'd never heard him sound like he did, Jill. I knew I couldn't trust him to be alone with you."

"Oh, shit." She let her head fall back to rest against the seat, scrambled thoughts flying around in her head. "I'm so sorry. That must have been awfully hard for you to do."

"Not in the least," she said briskly. "I love my kids, but when they act like idiots, they have to face the consequences just like anyone else. Now tell me what happened. Did he try to hurt you?"

"I don't…" Her instinct was to lie. To say she was certain he hadn't, but Janet wasn't pulling any punches, and it wasn't fair to treat her like she was fragile. "I honestly don't know. I saw a side of him I didn't know existed, Janet. I…" The stress of the awful afternoon finally got inside and she started to cry. "I'm so damned sorry for this. I should have kept my distance from Lizzie. It would have been better for your family to have her find a complete stranger to love."

"I know that you're upset," Janet said, the crisp, staccato pace of her voice now soft and gentle. "And I've got to admit I am too. But you can't put your life choices up to a vote, Jill. You girls aren't doing a single thing you should be ashamed of. So don't ever let me—and for *God's* sake don't let Lizzie—hear you say something so silly."

"I won't," she sniffled, craving a hug so badly she could taste it. Unlike her own mother, she knew Janet would give her one—a big one—the minute they saw each other again. Damn, that was a nice feeling. One she absolutely would not let Mark and his homophobic bullshit take away from her.

✑

The last thing Jill was going to do was tell her friends the police had to come force her new girlfriend's brother to leave her alone. So she drove around for a while, then went down to the pier to watch the sun set. There weren't many people around, even though most of the boats were still in the water; floating bits of hope for their owners, who were sure they were going to get another fun-filled weekend in before it got too cold.

Jill sat at the end of the dock, wishing it was June again. She'd give a lot to have a whole summer with Lizzie. How stupid she'd been to waste time, making Lizzie jump through hoops to prove she was gay enough to take a chance on. Stupid, stupid and more stupid. No doubt about that.

Her phone rang and she could immediately feel her pulse start to race. She hadn't had time to think things through and decide what to tell Lizzie—if she didn't already know about Mark.

"Hi," she said when she saw her picture on the display. She'd used the one of Lizzie kissing her cheek when they were up on Red Rocks. The one where Jill looked like she'd been hit with a shovel. It usually made her laugh, but today she simply felt a little sick.

"Six siblings. All done," Lizzie declared, sounding as perky as she had on Friday after talking to Donna.

"How did it go? You sound good."

"It went okay. You know how my brothers are. None of them ever have much to say unless you're talking about the Sox, the Pats or the Bruins. Which is perfectly fine with me. What's up with you? You sound a little…"

"Tired. I'm tired. I went kayaking with Samantha and Carly."

"Oh, cool. Where are you now?"

"I'm sitting out at the end of King Street dock, watching the sunset."

"Nice." Jill could hear the smile in her voice. "I can picture you there, trying to make the lake a few degrees warmer just by wishing."

"How'd you know?"

"I'll be home in about an hour and a half. Do you still want to go to my apartment and pick up my stuff?"

"Sure. I should have asked you to leave your keys so I could do it myself. I'm right in the neighborhood."

A soft laugh came through the line. "Will you strangle me if I admit I have a key hidden under the mat?"

"Are you crazy?"

"Not *my* mat," Lizzie corrected. "The mat in front of the rear apartment on the first floor."

"What in the hell…?"

"I have hers and she has mine. That's how I got in to bake your birthday cake, so don't complain."

"Lizzie, you're putting out the welcome mat to—"

"No, no. Burglars are too lazy to try all of the locks. It's cool."

Jill stopped herself from launching into a lecture, even though she desperately wanted to. She already had a headache and decided it was smart to forget about this extremely ill-thought-out idea. "Just for the record, I'd prefer that you didn't hide a key to my house. I'll gladly pay for a locksmith if you ever get locked out."

"Where's the fun in that?"

Jill normally would have laughed, but she couldn't summon the energy. "I'll admit it's not as exciting as never knowing who's going to be sitting on your sofa when you get home, but I like to keep my life pretty boring."

There was a longish pause. "Are you mad at me?"

"Of course not. I'm just tired. But I'll run by your house and pick up some clothes for you. Anything else?"

"I need shoes and a purse and my makeup bag. There's probably stuff lying all over the counter in my bathroom. If it could possibly be makeup, throw it into that plastic bag that's lying there. Oh, and my hairbrush. I can use the dryer in the guest bathroom, right?"

"Of course. Call me if you think of anything else."

"I will. Or I'll text you."

"Pull over before you do that, okay? I don't want you to get into an accident."

"Hmm, I guess that means you don't want me to call my mom and talk to her all the way home like I was planning, huh?"

"I'd really prefer you didn't, Lizzie. Just play some music to entertain yourself. You can call you mom when you get back." *After I tell you your brother wanted to murder me.*

⚬

The second Jill hung up, she called Janet. "Me again," she said. "If Lizzie calls you, don't tell her about Mark, okay?"

"Jill, I have to tell her. She'll find out eventually."

"I mean while she's driving. I know it'll upset her and I don't want her to drive all that way if she's not paying attention."

She couldn't see her, but Jill could sense Janet's smile. "I'm glad you're taking care of my girl," she said softly. "I appreciate that."

"She's very, very important to me, Janet. I'll do everything I can to care for her. You can count on that."

⚘

It was kind of strange going through Lizzie's personal items. Even though Jill was doing it to help her out, it was still an invasion of her privacy.

While shoving mascara, eye liner and lipstick into a battered plastic food storage bag, Jill recalled a conference she'd gone to not long ago where she'd picked up a nice set of toiletry bags. They were emblazoned with the name of a software program she was being pitched, but Lizzie wouldn't mind that. She was the kind of woman who'd rather have a nice freebie than to have Jill spend money buying her a good travel set. That was kinda cool.

By the time she had a suitcase filled with all of the things on Lizzie's list, then stopped at the store for food for breakfast, it was nine o'clock. She hurried back to her house, arriving to find Freyja sitting in her driveway. So much nicer than that big, menacing truck that had growled at her earlier in the afternoon.

Lizzie didn't have a key, so she was sitting at the patio table, shivering. "Who decided to let fall come so early?" she demanded.

"I voted against it." Jill did her best to smile naturally.

"A whole suitcase, huh? You probably got all of my clothes in there."

"No, just a couple of dresses. I wasn't sure which shoes you wanted, so I might have gone overboard with them."

"I might have to get into your tub to warm up." She pasted herself to Jill as she tried to get her key into the lock. Jill was a little chilly too, but that didn't explain why her hands were shaking.

As soon as they entered the house, the cats put on a dramatic display, crying, purring, and winding themselves around legs, managing to convey their outrage as well as their dependency.

"Are the baby boys starving?" Lizzie asked as she bent to pick them both up and let them rub their faces against her jaw. She made eye contact with Jill. "Were you out all day?"

Jill nodded, then walked over to fetch their box of dry food. After she put a little in each bowl, the boys ran to it, then studiously acted like they were now in no hurry at all as they leisurely took a few nibbles. Jill went and cleaned the litter box, and as she was washing her hands, Lizzie came to stand next to her. The big, white light over the sink shone on her face, illuminating every twitch that Jill tried to hide.

"What's going on?" Lizzie asked, gazing at her soberly. "Did you talk to Mark?"

"Long story." Grimly, Jill dried her hands, then guided a clearly puzzled and anxious Lizzie into the den. They sat down next to each other on the sofa and she began. "He came here."

"He what?" She was on her feet in a second, looming over Jill.

"He came here," she repeated quietly.

Lizzie sat down and gripped Jill's hands firmly. "What did he do?" Her words were benign, but there was a cold anger to them that made Jill shiver. She hoped she never heard that tone directed at her.

"He was angry. Furious, really. But he didn't do much. Just screamed at me and forced someone to call the police."

"The police!"

"Yeah," she said quietly. "They didn't arrest him, but they did a report with our names and addresses. I hope to god no one at work has access to that."

"Why did you have to show ID? You didn't go to *his* house and make a fool out of yourself."

"The police said they wanted our names just in case he came back. For my protection." She cleared her throat. "They wanted me to file a restraining order."

Lizzie grasped her and pulled Jill against her body so fiercely that she had the breath knocked out of her. "He scared you, didn't he."

"Yeah. He did." She swallowed, finding it difficult to get enough saliva in her mouth to accomplish that simple task. She hadn't realized how shaken up she was, but now that she was in Lizzie's arms, she found her whole body trembling.

"I don't"—Lizzie took in a deep breath—"I don't know him any more. We never spend any time together alone, and when I see them as a family he lets Lisa or the kids do all the talking. I've…lost touch." She held Jill at arm's length and gazed into her eyes. "I can't guarantee what he'll do, so if you're afraid, we should stay with one of your friends."

"I'm not afraid he'll come back. It's just—" She started to cry, the stress of the day catching up with her now that Lizzie was home. "It's hard to admit to myself how easy it would have been for him to really hurt me. Sometimes I forget how much stronger men are." She sucked in a breath. "He made me feel really vulnerable, and that's hard for me."

"Are you cold?" She rubbed her hands briskly over Jill's arms. "You're shivering."

"Just stress, I think."

Lizzie got up and held a hand out. "Let's go upstairs and take a bath. We could both use it."

They walked upstairs together, and Lizzie briskly took over, turning on the water and deciding what to add to it. She picked bubbles, and soon the tub was crowned with fluffy white mounds of them. Before Jill could do it herself, Lizzie undressed her. It took just a few extra seconds for Lizzie to strip, then she put her arms around Jill and held her tenderly. "I missed you so much." They kissed, gently, for a minute or two. "I don't want to go away without you again," she said, brushing the hair from Jill's eyes and kissing her lids tenderly.

"That makes two of us."

Lizzie helped her step in, then slid in so she was behind her, with her legs lying on top of Jill's thighs. Gently, she eased her back so she lay upon Lizzie's chest. Cupping water in her hand, Lizzie let it drip down Jill's body, keeping up the slow, steady pace until Jill was slightly mesmerized by the drops splashing over her.

"I know you were frightened today. I would have been too. But he won't come back. Once he lets it sink in how crazy he acted, he'll be too embarrassed to leave Sugar Hill."

"I hope that's true. But"—she shivered roughly—"you didn't see him. He looked like he wanted to kill me, Lizzie. I've never had anyone look at me with that kind of…venom."

"He never got over you," she said, not a note of indecision. "Having to hear that his little sister gets to have what he wants…"

"I would have argued with you before, but he said something about turning my back on the love that had been right in front of me for years. That made things clear." Jill reached up to tuck her hair behind her ear, and when she began to lower her arm, Lizzie caught it.

Jill hadn't looked at the fingerprints again, had honestly forgotten about them, but Lizzie's body turned stiff as she tenderly brushed her fingers across them. "Did he do this?" she asked, her voice low and full of barely controlled anger.

"Yeah," Jill whispered, shame filling her, even though she knew logically that she had nothing at all to be ashamed of. Having someone stronger and more powerful show how easy it would be to snap her in half embarrassed her. The image of dropping to her knees just because of the force of his grip screwed with her view of how she faced the world... of her competence...her independence. She burrowed against Lizzie, trying to forget how powerless she'd felt.

"You should have had him arrested. If I'd been here, he'd be in the fucking hospital."

"He probably wasn't trying to hurt me," Jill said. "He just wanted to stop me from leaving."

"You're defending him?" Her voice was louder now. Painfully so.

"No, he was totally out of line, and he scared the shit out of me. I just don't think he knew he was holding me so hard. When I dropped to my knees, he let go and didn't touch me again. If he'd wanted to hurt me, he could have kicked me in the teeth right then."

Lizzie was clearly not happy, but she didn't comment further. Instead, she lifted Jill's arm to her lips and placed soft kisses all over the angry marks. "I've got to call my mom," she decided after a minute. "Want me to get out? Or can I call her from here?"

"Uhm, there's one more bit I didn't tell you yet."

Lizzie's body grew rigid and Jill could feel her suck in and hold a breath.

"Your mom called right after he arrived. I handed him the phone and he basically hung up on her. She's the one who called the police, Lizzie."

Without comment, she stuck her hand out as far as it would go, snagged her jeans and dragged them over by a leg. Then she yanked her phone so forcefully from her pocket that Jill was afraid she'd rip the fabric. A few seconds later, she spoke into the phone. "Jill just told me what happened." Her voice was level and contained. "Is he home yet?" She was silent for a minute, then said, "I'm about ready to get back into Jill's car and drive down there."

Jill slid down to submerge more of herself in the warm, bubbly water. Lizzie was giving off waves of anger, but Jill was certain Janet would calm her down and give her some perspective. Consciously trying not to listen to the conversation, Jill tried to concentrate on the cadence of Lizzie's words, rather than their meaning, and, in a short time, found herself in a kind of trance. Maybe it was just lying close to Lizzie. Or the belief that Janet had a lot of influence with her kids. For some reason, despite all evidence to the contrary, she held out a surprising amount of hope that everything would eventually settle down and be all right again.

Lizzie talked until the bathwater had started to cool. One thing Jill hadn't thought of in her bathroom design was how tough it would be to add water once you were already soaking in the tub. Having it drop down onto your head from the ceiling was really unappealing.

They got out and Lizzie tenderly wrapped a big bath sheet around Jill, covering her shoulders while she patted her dry. "Could you tell what my mom convinced me to do?"

"Nothing, I hope," Jill said, watching Lizzie grab another towel to dry her own body.

"Just about. She doesn't think I'll help the situation if I call him and ream him a new one, so she's going to try to reason with him. I'm going to stand down until she gives me the go-ahead."

Jill wriggled around in the big towel until she could get her hands free. She slid them around Lizzie's body and held on loosely, leaning against her as their bodies swayed in rhythm. "I'm glad you're backing off. He knows he screwed up. Maybe struggling with the guilt's a better idea than poking him. He'll just get defensive."

"That's what my mom said." Lizzie gave her a gentle kiss. "I'll let you pacifists have this round. But if she can't get through to him, I'm going to slug him with one of those big hammers he has lying around. Fucking jerk," she grumbled, pulling away to head back into the bedroom. This was *so* not over.

While Jill brushed her teeth, Lizzie unpacked her clothes, putting them in the guest bedroom closet. She walked back into the room just as Jill was taking the decorative pillows from her bed and snapping the quilt into place. Getting organized must have improved her mood, because Lizzie seemed lighter and perkier than she had when she left.

"You did a great job of bringing clothes over for me. I won't have to go back until Wednesday night."

"Want me to borrow a truck and buy some boxes? We could get most of your clothes over here in one trip."

"Buy boxes? Look at you, Miss Moneybags. Haven't you ever heard of going to the grocery store and taking their castoffs?"

"Yeah, I've heard of that. But I like having nice, clean boxes. I'm a spendthrift."

"I'm used to having little bits of lettuce and cabbage stuck to my stuff, but I'll give it a try your way."

They both got into bed, and as Jill turned off her bedside light, the boys ran into the room and leapt upon the bed. Lizzie stuck out her arm and Jill cuddled up against her.

"I love having you here," she murmured.

"Our family's together," Lizzie said, rubbing her face against Jill's head. "All safe and sound."

"This is all I've ever wanted," Jill said, her voice catching as she spoke. "Someone who loves me, and wants to share her life with me." She peeked down at the boys, both getting comfortable by kneading a prime spot. "And a few other dependents who love me as long as I feed them."

Lizzie kissed her cheek, then nuzzled against her neck. "You've got to feed me too, but I'll love you even if you don't." She tucked Jill up against her body and stroked her skin in long smooth caresses that ran down her torso.

"I feel better," Jill said.

"I do too. And my mom obviously feels sorry for me because she's going to tell my grandparents and my aunts and uncles."

"She is?" Jill's body jerked involuntarily and she sat up. "You're okay with that?"

"Uh-huh. I have a gay cousin, so I'm not the first. And if any of them are weird about it, my mom will straighten them out."

"If you're happy to have her run interference, I'm happy too."

"I'm done," Lizzie said dramatically. "I've come out to everyone now. It was a bumpy ride, but it's over. Now we can relax and start building our life together. Here in your beautiful house."

"Our house," Jill corrected. "This is our house now."

"I like the sound of that." She giggled softly. "I also like not living in a smokey, noisy fire trap. As soon as we buy a few shotguns to keep the crazier members of my family away, we're set."

Chapter Eighteen

MONDAY WAS AN EPICALLY annoying day, with meetings all over campus, inflexible department heads, jealous managers, and a few administrators who were nice but clueless. It seemed like the day would never end, but each meeting was mandatory.

Jill always switched off the ringer on her cell phone when she was in meetings, but when her last one of the day was over she took a look. Her eyes widened when she saw a missed a call and a voice mail—from her mother. As she hit the buttons to make the message play, the thought occurred to her that her mother had never called on a workday. And she had called so infrequently in general that Jill was surprised she had this number.

There was a pause, like her mom was waiting for a cue to start. Then she said, "I need you to come home, Jill. Tonight."

Jill pulled the phone from her ear and stared at it for a second, stunned. Her mother hadn't sounded particularly upset, but this was clearly not a friendly invitation to come for dinner. More like a command. She hurried to her office and closed the door. As expected, her mother didn't answer the phone. That wasn't unusual. She only answered when she was in the mood—which wasn't often, and she didn't have voice mail or an answering machine.

Checking her contacts list, she found an entry she'd made years earlier. "Parents' Neighbors." Her mom didn't have a real relationship with anyone in their neighborhood, but Jill and, to a lesser extent, her father, at least knew their immediate neighbors well enough to stop and chat when they saw them.

Dialing Mrs. Jennings' number, she rolled her eyes when a robotic voice said it had been disconnected. It had been quite a while since she'd updated the list. The next call was a hit. "Mr. O'Reilly? It's Jill Henry."

"Well, hello, Jill. Seems like it's been years since I've seen you. How are you?"

"I'm fine, thanks. I was wondering if I could ask you for a favor."

"Sure. As long as it doesn't require me to lift anything heavy."

"No, nothing like that. If you've got time, I'd like you to go over to the house and see if my mom's all right. She left me a message, but when I call her back she doesn't answer."

"Did she say she's ill?"

"No, she didn't. But I'm worried about her. I'm going to drive down, but it'll take me a few hours to get there."

"All right, Jill. But…" He took a breath. "I can't imagine she'll answer, even if she's sitting right in the living room."

She closed her eyes, embarrassed to think of how the whole town probably thought of her mother. "I know, Mr. O'Reilly. I'm just…"

"Don't worry about it. I'll check and call you back. Give me your number."

She did, then turned her chair so she could look out the window. She had a nice view of campus, even though she was only on the second floor. Her perch was high enough to look across the street to see students scurrying around, rushing to their next class. Seeing them now, all looking so normal and predictable, somehow calmed her.

She had to go home. Her mother had never, ever asked her to come, so she had to have a good reason. Knowing her, it could be anything. Illness, financial ruin, divorce, joining the circus or even a convent. Anything at all.

After a few minutes, her phone rang and she answered quickly. "Hi, Mr. O'Reilly."

"How'd you know it was me?"

"My phone shows the number of the person calling," she said, anxious to get to the point.

"Go figure. Well, like I thought, your mother didn't answer the door. But her car's there, and I could hear the TV on. Want me to have the police come by? They can get that door open, no problem. You should've seen them hit the door with a battering ram when poor old Helen Jennings died in her house. Oh, that was a *mess*."

344

"Uhm, thanks," she said, her mind now full of gruesome images. "But my mom wouldn't appreciate the police coming by if she's all right and if she's not…" She hated to say it, but it was the truth. "A few more hours probably won't hurt."

"I'd rather have someone come in and get me if I fell or something, but your mom would probably rather suffer alone."

"That's probably true," she agreed. "I'll be down in a few hours, Mr. O'Reilly. Thanks very much for your help."

"No problem, Jill. I hope she's all right."

"Me too."

She hung up, then called one of her employees. "Cari? Can you swing by?"

"Sure. Be right there." She had to come from the other side of the floor, but Cari was there by the time Jill had her briefcase packed.

When Jill sensed her standing in the door, she said, "I've got to go down to Sugar Hill to take care of something. Can you keep an eye on things?"

"Okay. Want me to sit in your office?"

"Yeah," she said. "Good idea, given that people stop by all day looking for something."

Jill started to walk out, but Cari stopped her by putting a hand on her arm.

"Is everything all right?"

"I'm not sure," she said honestly. "My mom left me a message, asking me to come home right away."

"I hope she's all okay."

"Me too. I'll call if I'm not going to be in tomorrow."

"Take care," Cari said, giving her a reassuring pat on the back.

As Jill started her walk home, she called Lizzie, getting her voice mail. "Hi. I just got a message from my mother, asking me to come home right away. Not sure what that means, but I'm heading out." She started to hang up, but added, "I wish I could wait for you, but I think I'd better get going. Call me when you can."

❧

After an exhaustive search, she found her old house key, which would make getting into the house easy so long as her mother hadn't changed the locks when Jill left for college. She wouldn't have put it past her.

Lizzie must have been involved in an event, because Jill arrived in Sugar Hill with no return call. After she parked in the driveway, she went up to the front door. Before she could knock, the door opened and her mother stood there, looking perfectly normal. "Took you long enough," she grumbled as she went back to sit in her comfortable chair. "Did you send that nosy man over here?"

"I did. I thought you might be sick or injured."

She waved her hand dismissively. "I'm as healthy as a horse. And if I drop, I'd rather be left alone."

Well, that was clear. Strange, but clear.

Jill moved over to sit on the sofa. "Can I ask why you called?"

"I'm going to move," she said, actually turning the TV down, a rarity.

"*You're* going to move? Not Dad?"

Even though the volume was down, her muddy brown eyes stayed locked on the television. If Jill had counted the times their eyes had met and held a gaze, she probably wouldn't get to twenty.

"Yes, Jill, *I'm* going to move. To Arizona. I'm sick and tired of this weather. And since I don't have any other reason to stay, I might as well go now."

Jill had learned to parse her mother's words like a sacred text. Each one had meaning, sometimes multiple meanings that you ignored at your peril. "What do you mean, you don't have any other reason to stay?"

"Well, Jill," she said, her eyes narrowing dangerously. "Given that this whole town knows something important about you. Something you haven't taken the time to tell *me* about..."

Oh, fuck! How could you respond to that?

"Well? Would you like to explain why I had to learn about this from Lisa Byrne?"

"God damn it," Jill cursed quietly. "She's a horrible little jerk." Then Jill let the comment really sink in. Why would her mother open the door to Lisa? "How do you know her?"

"I went to school with her mother. She was a real piece of work. Slept with every boy in Bellows Falls. Probably a few sheep too."

Jill shook her head, trying to get that information, undoubtedly a wild exaggeration, out of her brain. "But do you know Lisa?"

"I made the mistake of going to church yesterday, and she cornered me. Nosy little brat couldn't wait to tell me all about you. Everyone who passed by laughed. They all knew what she was saying."

That *couldn't* have been true. Either her mother was delusional, or her paranoia had gotten completely out of control. Jill tried to think of how to respond. Wait. This had to have happened before Lizzie told Mark. Lisa was just stirring up shit because she had the opportunity, not because she was upset about her and Lizzie getting involved. Oh, crap! What would Lisa do now? Firebomb her house?

"Well? What do you have to say for yourself? You've been having sex with girls for twenty years, and I have to find out from a stranger?"

"I…" There was no way out of this that wouldn't result in casualties. "I like my privacy."

A lightening quick gaze fell on her, then slid right back to the television. "Your privacy? That's a laugh. I've never met anyone more interested in yakking about every stupid thing on her mind. You never shut up! Until you have something you're ashamed of, that is."

Oh, that hurt. How could she get in and make a surgical strike with just a few words?

"I'm not ashamed of myself, Mom. I just didn't think you'd be interested."

"I'm not! But it was obvious I didn't know. That makes me look stupid, and I won't have it." She stood and glared at Jill as she passed by on her way to the kitchen. "I'm not going to walk around this town and have people snickering behind my back."

"You're leaving town because you didn't know I was a lesbian," Jill said, raising her voice so she could be heard in the kitchen. "Even though you admit you don't care?"

Carrying a plate with two crackers and a piece of cheese, her usual evening appetizer, her mother strode by, chilling her with a gaze filled with an anger that was barely under control. "I care about looking foolish!"

"I'm sorry you looked foolish. And I'm sorry Lisa upset you."

She sank into her chair and carefully broke the bit of cheese in half to cover both crackers. "That's a damned lie! You don't care a bit. So go on and be with the people you really care for. You can change your name if you want. Jill Davis," she said, like she was testing it out to see how it sounded.

"I don't want to change my name."

"Why not? You've always thought of that woman as your mother."

"That's not true. I care for Janet, but she's not my mother. You are."

She waved her hand again. "Yeah, yeah, I know. And a lot of good it does me. So…" She took a bite of a cracker, making the same satisfied nod she did after every predictably delicious bite of food she ate. "Do you have a girlfriend? I wasn't going to act like I didn't know."

"Yes," Jill said, her stomach in knots. "I do."

"Some professor or something, I guess. Someone with a string of degrees she can lord over everyone who didn't go to college."

"No. I'm in love with Lizzie Davis."

Her mother's eyes narrowed as she carefully chewed her cracker. "Who's that?" she asked sharply.

"Janet and Mike's daughter. They usually call her Beth."

"Beth?" She stared at Jill briefly, clearly puzzled. "Those Davis girls are married. Did you break up a happy marriage?"

"Of course not. Lizzie's never been married. She's the youngest."

"The youngest." Her eyes narrowed further still. "The little one? The one with the strange hair?" Her mouth dropped open. "She couldn't be out of high school!"

"She just turned thirty, Mom. I'm not dating a high school girl."

"She's got that weird hair," she insisted. "Like she's in some kind of freak show. Is she on drugs or something?"

"I don't know what you're talking about." She pulled out her phone and paged through her photos, finally finding one of Lizzie holding the cats up to her face. Moving across the room, she showed it to her mother.

"Her hair's perfectly normal, and she doesn't do drugs." *That I know of.* They'd never discussed drugs, but it was possible Lizzie smoked a little grass...

"That's not her." She flicked her fingers, dismissing the idea as well as Jill.

She walked back to the sofa, perching on the arm, waiting for the next volley.

"I'm selling the house. Not that anyone would want it."

That also wasn't true. Their house was very well cared for, and had a huge yard that was a real showplace.

"I hope you sell it quickly." She let an uncomfortable silence reign for a minute, then said, "What's Dad going to do?"

"It's my house, not his."

"Does he know you're doing this?" She had an image of her father, returning from a sales trip, only to find another family living in his home.

"I don't need his permission to do anything."

"Okay. Are you going to divorce?"

Her eyes shot open. "Why would I do that?"

"I don't know," she said, finding that was true. There was no true north in this house or in her parents' relationship. Anything was possible.

"It costs a fortune to do something like that. And it's not as if I'm going to marry someone else. I just have to check to make sure I'll be able to get his social security if he dies when I'm not living with him. The government's always trying to screw you out of anything they can, you know."

"Yeah, I imagine that's the most important thing," she said, then mentally kicked herself. Sarcasm was never a good idea.

"Don't smart mouth me. You might be able to get away with that over at Janet Davis' house, but not here."

Her mother turned the sound back up, her focus locked on the opening notes of her favorite game show. "You can go now. I need to pay attention to *Jeopardy*."

Jill stood and had a brief fight with herself. She desperately wanted to say something—anything—to complain about being summoned two

349

and a half hours just to be treated like something her mother had tracked in on her shoe. But she couldn't do it. Her mother was either mentally ill or emotionally damaged beyond repair. If she was missing a leg, Jill wouldn't try to make her run. This was exactly the same. She was missing empathy, understanding, care and love. Wishing she had them wouldn't magically create them any faster than a person could grow a new limb.

"Goodbye, Mom," she said as she went to the door. She didn't get a response.

⊸⊚⊷

Jill couldn't make herself start the car just yet. She was shaking, the pain in her heart making her weak. She'd always known their connection was tenuous, but this made it clear in ways that fractured what few bonds they had. *All* they shared was DNA.

She checked her phone and saw six calls from Lizzie. That helped. She dialed and felt the warmth reach through the line when her worried voice said, "What happened, sweetheart? Are you all right?"

Jill started to cry, her need for comfort so strong she wanted to curl up in a little ball and have Lizzie hold her until she could regain her strength. "No, I'm not," she whimpered. "Lisa told my mom I'm gay, and she's going to pack up and move to Arizona."

"What?" Lizzie shouted. "That's insane!"

"I know. I should have forced her to go to a psychiatrist years ago, but it's almost impossible to make someone accept treatment."

"Oh, Jill, I didn't mean it like that. I'm so sorry."

"It's okay," she sniffled. "She *is* crazy. Or wounded. I don't even know. All I'm sure of is that she hurt me. She hurt me so badly, Lizzie." She couldn't control herself. Great, heaving sobs made her stomach muscles ache, but she couldn't stop. She had an ocean of pain lodged in her gut and couldn't keep it from bursting forth.

"Are you still in Sugar Hill?"

"Yeah. I'm in her driveway."

"Go to my mom's. Right now. She's at home, Jill. I just talked to her."

"I don't want to talk to anyone," she murmured. "I just want to come home."

"And I want you home. But you need to wait for a while, baby. Please go over to my house and spend just a little while with my mom. *Please?*"

She couldn't refuse Lizzie anything. Even something she really, really didn't want to do. "All right. But I've got to get myself under control first."

"No, you don't. She'll be waiting for you, and if you can't drive, she'll come get you."

"Oh, no. My mom would have a fit. That's the last thing I want."

"Go, Jill. Go now. You need to get out of there."

"You're probably right. It gives me the creeps to even look at the house." She started up the car and backed out the long drive. There was no traffic, and she easily got onto the main road and headed for the Davis house. "Okay. I'm on the way."

"I'll hang up so you can concentrate. Call me when you leave my mom's, okay?"

"I will," Jill murmured, enormously relieved to know that someone cared, deeply, for her.

⌘

By the time the car stopped, Janet was outside, hurrying towards her. Jill put the car in park, got out and was immediately enfolded in Janet's embrace.

"I'm so sorry for all of the trouble my family's caused you in the last two days. I'm ashamed of them."

"It's all right." Jill wriggled out of the hug, embarrassed at how much she needed it. She put her arm around Janet's waist and they walked towards the house. "I should have told my mother years ago, but…" She shrugged. "We've just never had that kind of relationship."

"I know, honey." They went into the house, the big, old place strangely silent.

"Is Mike out?"

"Uh-huh. He's bowling with his buddies. Or watching them while he drinks beer. His friends came to pick him up a little while ago." She let out a soft laugh. "Just like high school kids. They pull up and honk." She headed for the kitchen. "Can I get you a beer?"

351

"Mmm, no I shouldn't. I'm distracted enough." She sat on the old sofa, the exact one she recalled from childhood. It was battered, but still comfortable, and she sank into it like a favorite pair of slippers.

Janet came back and sat next to her. "Want to talk about it?" She put a comforting hand on her leg and Jill started to tear up again.

"I don't have much to say," she said, wiping her eyes with the backs of her hands as tears started to fall. "Lisa grabbed her after church yesterday. Apparently just to tell her I was gay. I'm not sure how Lisa knew that would be a surprise, but it was."

"She's the least Christian person I know," Janet said, her mouth set in a firm line. "She's in damned near every parable—as the bad example. Mark would have been better off to stay single if she was his only choice."

"But he chose her," Jill reminded her. "No one forced Lisa on him. I think he wanted someone to lead him, and that's exactly what he got."

"I think he wanted someone who didn't like you," Janet said, gazing into Jill's eyes with empathy.

"What? Why would he want that?"

"Because he had such a crush on you." She gave her a fond pat on her leg. "You had to know that."

"I didn't. I swear I didn't. I was oblivious to signals from boys." She rolled her eyes. "From girls too. It took me until I was twenty-five to really see when someone was flirting with me. I didn't have much emotional intelligence."

"Yes, you did. You've always been a sweet, loving girl. But you were a little delayed in the dating game."

"It's tough being the only lesbian in town. I had no practice."

"You weren't the only lesbian, honey, but you were probably the only one in your class."

"So why would Mark be drawn to Lisa? Just out of hatred for me?"

Janet shook her head slowly, thoughtfully. "No, not hatred. On Mark's part at least. I think he wanted someone who'd verify his belief that you were...whatever he convinced himself you were. Cruel or uncaring or dismissive of him." She took Jill's hand and chafed it between both of her own. "Mark didn't have much dating sense either, I'm afraid. I think Lisa made him feel special."

"He accused me of being a pedophile," Jill said quietly.

"Good lord!" She dropped her head back against the sofa. "Sometimes I wish I'd stopped at two kids. Which two I'd choose changes like the wind, but there's usually two I can stand."

"I hope you keep Lizzie," Jill said. "I can't imagine anyone would want to get rid of her."

"Oh, she has her faults, but you'll just think they're cute. For a while," she added. She put her arm around Jill and pulled her close, kissing her cheek. "You're the only one of the bunch I've never wanted to bean."

"How about when you caught us lying in bed together?"

"I didn't want to bean you. Lizzie? Yes. But not you."

"Why were you mad at Lizzie?" Jill sat up straight, intensely interested in Janet's answer.

"I wasn't mad so much as hurt. It's hard learning something important about your kid, and realizing you didn't know because she didn't trust you."

"She trusts you, Janet. I'm not sure what it was, but she was really uncomfortable admitting that she's easily as gay as she is straight."

"I guess I shouldn't take her hang-ups as an indictment of my parenting, huh? That's pretty self-centered."

"No, you shouldn't. This is Lizzie's issue. It has nothing to do with not trusting you or anyone else in the family. Kristen's upset with her too, not to mention Mark."

Janet's eyes closed at the mere mention of his name.

"Did you talk to him today?"

"No. He's the kind of kid who eats himself up with guilt. I'm going to let him stew for a few days. I want him to have a few sleepless nights."

She reached over and took Jill's hand. "Let me see your arm," she said, pushing Jill's sweater up. She shook her head mournfully as her eyes briefly closed. "I wouldn't have believed Mark had it in him to grab you like this." She met Jill's eyes. "Please don't tell Mike. It would kill him to think he'd done such a poor job of teaching his boys how to behave."

353

"I won't. I'd really rather forget about it, to be honest."

"More power to you, honey, but I can't let it go. I already talked to Father Dowd about this. He's going to recommend someone for Mark to talk to. I'll pay for it, but he's going to get this sorted out."

"I don't think you can *make* someone open up to a therapist."

"Yes, you can. Even though he's a mess at this point in his life, he's not going to want to lose his family. And I swear to god, if he doesn't get some of this childish nonsense out of his system, he's not welcome here again."

Jill stared at her, stunned. Having Janet stand up for her—and Lizzie —in such a defiant way made her feel as good as anything ever had. She mattered. To people she loved.

⁂

Three hours later, she was safe in her bed, with Lizzie tightly wrapped around her. They'd gotten into bed just a few minutes after Jill had returned, exhausted and emotionally battered.

Lizzie gently stroked her back, calming her jangled nerves. "It will all work out," she murmured. "And if Mark and Lisa want to separate from the family—that's their choice."

"I wish I hadn't been so oblivious," Jill said. "If I'd known he had a crush on me, I could have talked to him about it."

"That's not your responsibility. He was twenty-two years old, Jill. That's old enough to think for himself."

"I guess." She snuggled up against her, the burdens of the past few days starting to lift under Lizzie's gentle care. "Hey, my mother said something strange. She kept insisting you had weird hair."

"Huh?" After a second, she let out a laugh. "She probably hasn't seen me since college. I did a lot of wacky things back then."

"How wacky?"

"I'll show you a photo. I think I have some stuff from college in my apartment."

"Can't wait. If it was enough for my mother to recall all these years later, it must've been good."

"Let's just say I'll bet you don't beg me to do it again."

⁂

She didn't call often, but Jill had what she assumed was a valid number for her father's cell phone. "Dad?" she asked when he answered.

"Hey, hi there, Jill. I was thinking about calling you today."

He said that every time she called. He never did, but he seemed to think she'd buy the line.

"Well, I saved you the trouble. Have you talked to Mom recently?"

"Yeah. That's why I was going to call you. Do you think she's really going to leave?"

"I think so. Why? Don't you?"

"I don't know. She thinks she's going to be welcome out in Scottsdale, but she and her sister hardly ever speak. I can't see Marilyn rolling out the welcome wagon."

Jill heard from her aunt so infrequently she'd forgotten that she'd moved to Arizona a few years ago. She wasn't quite as quirky as her mom, but she wasn't anyone's idea of a warm, welcoming presence.

"Yeah, that'll be interesting. But I think Mom's going to do it. She's not the type to make idle threats."

"No, she's not." He let out a sigh. "I guess I'll get an apartment in Brattleboro or somewhere."

"How long are you planning on working, Dad?"

"I don't have much money saved, so I guess I'll keep going until I drop dead or they fire me."

This was probably where she was supposed to pipe up and offer to help him out. Even to suggest he move to Burlington and live in her spare bedroom. But she wasn't going to do that. Of course, she'd help if he had an urgent need. But there was a lot of truth in the saying that you reap what you sow. He'd shown very little interest in her or their relationship. Rich Henry always had a decent job, but had notoriously spent his money buying drinks in local watering holes and luring women to bed. It was a little late to expect her to make up for his poor investments.

"I hope you're able to work for as long as you want, Dad. Let me know where you wind up."

"Oh, I will. Everything okay with you?"

Her mother had obviously not shared her news. Just as well.

"Yep. Everything's just fine."

Chapter Nineteen

ON WEDNESDAY EVENING, THEY sat in Lizzie's apartment, a shoebox filled with photos on Jill's lap. The one she held in her hand was from college, and was taken at an angle from behind. Lizzie had completely shaved the hair on one side, all the way around to the back of her head. In the photo, it had grown back a little, the super-short fur looking more red than brown. The other side, longer than it was now, was a flat, dull kelly green, with one purple hank, just for variety, Jill guessed. It looked like cotton candy, with all of the shine and body completely stripped from it.

Lizzie sat on the arm of the sofa, gazing down at the photo. "What do you think? Should I bring it back?"

"I don't know how your poor mother stopped herself from ripping the green part out," Jill said. "What were you thinking?"

"I just wanted to do something different. I thought it looked kinda cool."

"This is as uncool as a human can be. Thank god you got this lunacy out of your system while you were still in college. You're amazingly ordinary now compared to this."

"I've still got a wild side." She went to her bitchen, reached under her bed, and pulled out a box. When she returned to Jill, she opened it and held it right up to her face.

"No way!" Jill yelped. "You can have all of the sex toys you want, but we're buying new ones. Brand new! Never been used!"

"Oh, come on. These were expensive."

"You can use them on yourself, but they're never coming close to me. She plucked out a leather harness, still fitted with a smallish dildo. "Especially this one," she said, a look of utter distaste on her face. "I know where this one's been."

～

Jill stood on a step-stool, hoisting a few boxes of summer clothes into the storage space over the closet in the guest bedroom. "It kills me to put my shorts away," she said as she came back down. "It's like I'm giving in."

"Ohh," Lizzie put her arms around her neck and gave her a kiss. "My poor summer-obsessed baby. I can put away…" She closed her eyes briefly as she thought. "A hundred and fifty a month for a beach vacation. That'll give me six hundred by January. That's enough, isn't it? We'll go to the warmest place we can find and do nothing but play in the ocean."

Jill ran her fingers through Lizzie's hair as she looked into her eyes, reflecting on how sweet it was of her to offer. "Uhm…how…uhm…do you really have to budget for everything?"

"Yep." She moved over to open one of the boxes they'd brought over from her apartment. "After I pay all of my bills, I have seven hundred and fifty bucks left. Out of that, I have to pay for food, transportation, entertainment, clothing, and gifts. I have three or four savings plans going on all the time."

"What are you saving for now?" Jill asked, finding this all pretty adorable. She sat down on the bed and watched Lizzie go through some of her winter clothing.

"I've always got a museum trip account. I've got about fifteen hundred in that one. And a wedding gift account." She rolled her eyes. "Everybody I know is getting married. It's *killing* me to go to four or five weddings a year." Holding up a hand, she added, "I swore off being in weddings a couple of years ago. I'm all for people having a great party, but if you think I'm going to pay a thousand bucks to buy a weird dress and go to a bunch of showers and make you the queen of the world because you've chosen a regular sex partner, you're nuts!"

Jill stretched out on her belly and propped her chin up with her hands. She loved nothing more than listening to Lizzie reveal her firmly held, well-thought-out, sometimes kooky beliefs. "What else? Any more slush funds?"

"I had the Red Sox fund for taking my dad to a game. I think I'll keep that one going so we can go again next year." She leaned over and kissed Jill, then ruffled her hair. "You promised he'd be well enough to go again."

"I'm gonna stick to that one. Can I kick in a few bucks to that fund? I'd really like to go," she said, blinking her eyes coquettishly.

"All right," Lizzie said, rolling her eyes. "I put in a hundred a month, but I was going to knock it down to fifty. Let's do seventy five, total. That will let us stay in Boston two nights, go to a game and have a nice dinner or two."

"Agreed. I'll have my thirty-seven fifty to you on the first of the month." She reached over and grasped a wool shirt that Lizzie was putting on a hanger. "Hold on a sec," she said. "Is this vintage?" She let her fingers brush across the red, yellow and green plaid.

"Yeah," she said, laughing a little. "Technically, it's a hand-me-down. This was my inheritance from Gramma Davis." She opened another box and pulled out a blue and black buffalo plaid Mackinaw, a pair of heavy wool spruce green slacks and a red wool vest with pewter buttons. "I really lucked out. Donna and Kristen both wanted this, but it was all my size." She laughed. "I felt like Cinderella."

"And you wear this? I don't know many people who haven't switched to down."

"My gramma bought this stuff in the thirties." She slipped the shirt/jacket on. "Look for signs of wear. You won't find one." Jill ran her fingers along the cuffs and the elbows. The darned thing looked brand new.

"It looks really cute on you," she admitted. "I've got a couple of wool shirts, but I go with down for my coat."

"Hey, I'm not antagonistic to wearing lightweight clothes. But I'll never spend money on something new if something old works almost as well. Besides," she said, turning to look at herself in the mirror over the dresser. "I think I look kinda rugged. This fits my new lesbian personae."

"Feel free to not look like a lesbian," Jill teased. "I don't want more competition."

"Ha!" She jumped onto the bed, landing across Jill's hips. Then she collapsed on top of her, effectively holding her in place. Nuzzling her face into Jill's neck, she murmured, "You'd win my heart if every woman in Grrlington was gunning for me."

"Just in case, I think I'll steal you away from Grrlington for a few days. I've got a surprise for you. One I'm sure you'll like."

"Tell me!" she said, sitting up and thrusting against Jill's hips impatiently. "I love surprises."

"Can I roll over?"

"Oh, all right." She slid off and got to her feet, then helped Jill roll over and sit up. "Spill it," Lizzie demanded, after draping her arms around Jill's shoulders.

"I'm going to a conference in New York, and I'd love to have you come with me," she said, waggling her eyebrows.

"New York?" Lizzie asked, her eyes sparkling.

"Uh-huh."

"In a hotel?"

"A nice one."

"Going out to dinner?"

"With my meal paid for," Jill said, particularly happy about that part.

"Can we go to a play?"

"Yep. I might have some evening events with a small group I run, but I'll make sure I have one night free. Promise."

"Soon? 'Cause I'm ready!"

"Mid-October. Are you in? You'll only have to take Friday off."

Lizzie ran to the hallway and Jill heard a series of thumps. She got up and went to investigate, finding Lizzie doing backflips, then a series of cartwheels, stopping at the door, where she stood, face flushed, eyes wide with excitement.

"Does that mean you want to go?" Jill asked, laughing at her antics.

"Yes, yes, yes, yes and yes!" Her gaze grew sober. "What would you say to my inviting Kristen to come along?"

"Kristen?" Jill asked, trying not to look disappointed.

"Yeah," she said, putting her hands on Jill's hips and pulling her close. Lizzie's voice dropped down a little bit and got softer, with Jill laughing inwardly as she realized this was going to be the way she was talked into things in the future.

"She loves museums, so I'd have someone to hang out with. And she loves to shop, which I know you don't."

"I don't?"

Lizzie smiled at her. "I buy all of my clothes at resale shops. Kristen and I can spend all day trying on stuff and critiquing it. Are you into that?"

"I can't say no quickly enough," Jill admitted.

"More than that, having some time alone might let us get our relationship back on track. And that's important to me."

Jill thought about it for just a moment. Her dreams of a romantic getaway were fading, but if Lizzie wanted Kristen… "No problem. I'll be involved in a lot of stuff, so you'll have plenty of time to kill. Having Kristen along will be nice." She put her hands around Lizzie's waist and drew her close. "We'll go to bed early so we have our alone time."

"Uhm…" Her smile took on extra warmth, clearly a prelude to asking for something not on the menu. "Would it ruin the weekend if Kristen stayed in our room? She's as broke as I am."

"Stay in our room, huh?" She gazed into Lizzie's eyes, seeing the longing in them. "I can live with that. How about taking Thursday off too? I'd love a day with just you."

"It's a deal. Happy?"

"Very."

Lizzie leaned into her and gave her a long kiss. "I'm particularly happy that you're not complaining about my bringing my sister. I know that's not what you had in mind."

"I like Kristen," Jill insisted. "This will work out great."

Lizzie took a look at the clock on the dresser. "Ooo. Time for bed."

Jill started for the bedroom. Firmly believing they needed plenty of time for pillow talk, Lizzie had insisted their bedtime should be nine No one had ever demanded that kind of idle time before, but Jill found herself looking forward to it. No TV, no electronics, either. Lizzie allowed the use of phones, but only as alarms. Other than that, they just lay together and talked—usually after making love.

When they were both ready for bed, they got in and took their usual positions; with Jill lying on her back, Lizzie resting her head on Jill's outstretched arm. It had been such a short time to have these little habits already ingrained, but they gave a structure to Jill's life that she found she loved.

Her hand tangled in Lizzie's hair and she slid her fingers through the strands as she spoke. "Tell me about your day."

"Nothing big. I was on the phone all morning, trying to line up some more sponsors for our big Christmas open house. Did I tell you about that yet?"

"Nope."

"Well, you've got to put it on your calendar. It's December the fourth. That's a Friday night. It's a big deal. Formal. You're my date, of course."

"Cool. I don't know if I have anything dressy enough, but you can help me buy something."

"The suit you had on when I came by your office is dressy enough. You just need the right kind of blouse. Silk or satin would be perfect."

"Done. Will you and Kristen pick me up something? I trust your taste."

"Excited!" she said, wriggling like a puppy. "I haven't been to New York in at least two years. Maybe three. And that was just one day before I went to The Netherlands."

"You've been to The Netherlands?"

"Museums. Me." She interlaced her fingers. "They've got some great ones. I went with a friend from the Gardner. I'm kind of a Van Gogh nut, so I was in heaven."

"I want to learn more about art. When we're in New York, will you show me how to appreciate it more? I feel like I don't know what I'm looking at, so it kind of goes over my head."

"Sure. On Thursday afternoon we'll head for the Frick or the Neue Galerie. A smaller place is better for talking and taking it slow."

"That'll be cool. I'll never be able to spend eight hours in a museum, but I'd like to be more informed."

"I'm your girl," Lizzie said, rubbing her face into Jill's neck. "In many ways."

"I haven't kissed you much today," Jill said, flexing her arm to pull Lizzie even closer. "Let's make up for that oversight."

Lizzie immediately put her hand up to Jill's head as their lips met. She had the most delightful habit of running her fingers along Jill's scalp when they kissed, and she found herself enjoying the tickling nearly as much as the kissing. Both made goosebumps break out on her arms and legs.

"I love kissing you," Jill murmured. "This is the highlight of my day."

"You know one thing I love about you?"

"Tell me. I'm a terrible guesser."

Lizzie smiled and touched Jill's face, tracing along her features as she spoke. "I love that you don't give me a hard time about things. Even things you don't like."

"Mmm. Not sure what that means."

"Like when we went on the boat ride. You didn't like the guy—who shall remain nameless—and you didn't like how I interacted with him, yet you've never brought it up again. I *love* that."

"Who wants to go over stuff like that? I told you I didn't like him. I told you I never wanted to go out with him again. What else was there to say?"

"Exactly," Lizzie said, giving her a kiss. "People I've been with in the past couldn't let things go. If that had happened with Joel, I would have had to reassure him a hundred times that I was never going to see…that person again, that I agreed he was a slime-ball. All sorts of stuff."

"Well, Joel sounds like he was pretty insecure. The fact that his equipment stopped working after you hooked up with a woman showed he had some pretty significant insecurities."

"You don't seem to." Lizzie slid across Jill's hips and sat up, facing her. "You looked at that box of toys today and hardly batted an eye. Most people would want to know all of the dirty details."

"No." She blinked in confusion. "They would? Why?"

"I don't know. Just curiosity. Or they might want to make sure they're not falling behind on the job. Or maybe they're pervy like me and like to fantasize about how you've been with other people."

Jill playfully touched the tip of her nose and laughed. "You're going to have to continue to fantasize. Because I'm not telling."

"And you're not curious about me?"

"Nope. I am completely uninterested in imagining you bending some poor soul over a chair and having your way with him." She laughed a little louder. "Although I've got to give you mad props for having the guts to do it."

Lizzie leaned over and pressed her hands against Jill's shoulders, then leaned down until their faces were close. "Big secret? I've only done that once."

"Once? I thought you were frightening men all over New England!"

"Nope. Just once. In retrospect, that might have been a contributing factor in Joel's equipment breaking."

"Because he hated it?"

"No, because he liked it too much. I suspect he started to think he was gay. Which he wasn't," she insisted, rolling her eyes. "Guys have been socialized to think getting pleasure from their butts makes them gay. So dumb."

Jill rolled her over, winding up on top. Hovering over her, she looked down at Lizzie's glittering eyes. "How about you? I already know you're gay, so we don't have to worry about harming your tender psyche." She slid a hand under Lizzie's butt and squeezed a cheek. "Have I neglected an erogenous zone?"

"Yes. But it's not always erogenous. It has to be seduced."

"Isn't that true for all of your erogenous zones?" She moved her hand up and caressed a hard nipple. "They all like a little build-up."

"That one in particular likes a lot of build-up. If I'm really, really turned on, but can't quite get there, that can send me over. It's like an afterburner on a rocket."

"So…that's something to keep in reserve? For a special occasion?"

"Yeah. Unless that's something that really works for you. I can easily go along with anything that trips your trigger."

"I'm a little like you. I'm not antagonistic to it, but it's not something I crave." She started to work her way down Lizzie's body, not stopping until she was between her legs. "*This* is something I crave."

"That's your version of foreplay?" Lizzie teased, slapping at her back. "Sweet talking my girly bits?"

"Uh-huh." She looked up, catching the loving smile that met her eyes. "If I catch you before you're turned on, I'll be able to stay down here longer."

"Too late. Just lying with you turns me on. You're my irresistible boo."

"Boo?"

Shrugging, Lizzie said, "That's what I call you in my head."

"I like it," Jill decided. She parted Lizzie with her fingers and spent a moment gazing at her luscious flesh. "Changed my mind. *This* is the best part of my day."

⟰

The next evening, Jill came home when Lizzie was in the kitchen making dinner. Even though she was cooking, she was also talking, animatedly, using her hands to put exclamation points onto her words. "I know!" she said, nodding. Her focus shifted to Jill, and a kiss was quickly sent her way via one of those quickly moving hands. "He's going to try to sneak away to see a therapist—without telling the she-devil!"

Jill knew exactly who was being talked about, but she wasn't sure who was on the other end of this conversation. Moving over to tuck an arm around Lizzie and give her a hug, she listened for a moment, hearing either Donna or Kristen. They sounded an awful lot alike. Dinner was clearly well in hand, so rather than listen to the sisters talk about Mark, Jill went upstairs to change and get ready for dinner.

The boys were up in the spare bedroom, their favorite place for late afternoon sun. Jill put on a pair of jeans and a T-shirt and went into the room to snuggle with her guys.

She wasn't antagonistic to hearing about Mark, but Lizzie was a ball of energy tonight and Jill needed to ease into things. She went back into her room and found a metal comb they liked, then spent a long time grooming the boys, with each one trying to gnaw on the comb while his brother was enjoying the attention.

Lizzie appeared and lay down right in front of Jill. "Do me next."

Playfully, Jill put the comb up to her hair, but Lizzie didn't blink. "Go ahead," she said. "They don't have fleas."

"I will not touch your hair with a flea comb!"

"Such a wuss." Lizzie sat up and wrapped her arms around Jill. "Ready for dinner? I was in a vegetable mood, so I thought I'd take advantage of it. I've got red, orange and green vegetables, all thrown into a spicy Indian sauce." Her eyes widened. "Do you like spicy stuff?"

"I do. I've never met a cuisine I couldn't be happy with."

"I bought some naan too, and I made rice."

"I've missed having a girlfriend who can cook," Jill said, cuddling against Lizzie's warm body.

"Have you had one before?"

"A couple. Becca in particular. She was a real homemaker."

"I'm not that, but I can cook well enough to get by." She stood and held a hand out for Jill to take. "I went by the co-op and bought everything they had on the day-old shelf. Our whole dinner cost six bucks. Cool, huh?"

"That's very cool," Jill agreed. She draped her arm around Lizzie's shoulders as they walked downstairs. "Which sister were you talking with?"

"Kristen. She had a shitty day, and she called while she was driving home from Wyatt's lacrosse game."

"Do you guys talk a lot?"

"Yeah. Probably at least once a week. I feel all disconnected when we don't keep in touch."

"Same with Donna?"

"No, not as much. Probably once a month or six weeks. And we never talk as long. Kristen and I are the real chatterboxes in the family."

"What's the news on Mark? Still thinking of going to Sugar Hill to kick his butt?"

"Both Mom and Kristen have talked me out of that." They were in the kitchen now, and Lizzie took out a pair of plates. "But you could whip me into a frenzy again if you wanted to."

"No, I'm happy to let things play out. You said he's in therapy?"

"Yeah. Mom made him go. He's too much of a wimp to tell Lisa, so he's got to sneak out of the shop twice a week and hope she doesn't notice."

"She notices every leaf drop!"

"I know. But that's his deal. I'm just glad he's seeing someone. Maybe something will sink in and wash away some of the stupid bullshit he's been fed for the last twenty years."

"Yeah. That would be nice." Jill was also pretty sure that wasn't going to happen. Going to therapy because your mom made you wasn't the key to making permanent, positive changes.

On the last Friday of September, Jill raced around the house, trying to get the place ready for bridge. Lizzie was setting the glasses out, making sure there were no spots on them. The bell rang, and Lizzie went to open it. "Welcome!" she said, offering hugs to Karen and Becky.

"Hi, Lizzie," Karen said. "I was hoping you were going to be home tonight."

"I'm not staying. There's a movie at Main Street Landing that I'm going to see." She turned and stuck her tongue out at Jill. "One my girlfriend refuses to see with me."

"I said I'd go," Jill insisted.

"I know. But you didn't say it with enthusiasm."

Skip and Alice came in while the door was still open. Lizzie greeted them both, then collected all of the coats and took them into the den. When she returned, she flitted around for a few minutes, arranging for drinks for everyone while making small talk.

The whole scene played out again when Kathleen, Mary Beth and Gerri arrived. Then Lizzie went upstairs and came back a few minutes later. She was wearing a beat-up black leather motorcycle jacket, a tight white T-shirt and her usual snug jeans. They were rolled up really high tonight, with colorful socks sticking out of the tops of her lineman's boots. Jill stood there just looking at her until Skip gave her an elbow and whispered, "She'll be home later. Stick your tongue back in your mouth."

She shook her head and tried to stop blushing. Everyone said goodbye to Lizzie, then Jill went to the front porch with her. "I don't really like bridge," Jill whined. "I'd much rather see that stupid…I mean, really cool movie with you."

Lizzie gave her a big wet kiss, turned her and patted her on the butt. "Have fun, boo. Save some energy for me. This movie's supposed to be super sexy."

"You didn't tell me that," Jill complained. "You just said it was French."

"Bye bye now," she said as she started for her car. "See you later."

When Jill walked back in, Kathleen rolled her eyes and said, "Who remembers standing on the front porch, trying to be together for one last minute?"

A bunch of hands went up. When Skip's didn't, Alice reached across the table and gave him a punch in the arm. "Don't be a jackass."

Tossing a chip into her mouth on the way past the bowl, Jill took her seat. Because of Lizzie's bad influence, Jill hadn't even made an attempt at healthy snacking. No more hummus and raw vegetables. Tonight they'd whip through everyone's preferred fare of chips and salsa and popcorn. The snacks may have changed, but these were her chosen people, and she was going to stop being such a lovesick teenager and appreciate them, warts and all.

Chapter Twenty

A FEW WEEKS LATER, ON a Thursday afternoon in October, Jill sat on a bench at the Frick Gallery, watching Lizzie look at a painting. It was a Vermeer, and Lizzie had told her a lot about it and the artist. But she didn't get much after a long time studying it, so she sat down and watched Lizzie. She was a lot more interesting than a painting anyway.

Ever since Jill had told her, in very clear terms, how much she loved her leggings, Lizzie wore them frequently. Today a long striped shirt just covered her butt, but every inch of her gorgeous legs were on display. At least half of the women they'd passed on the street also wore leggings and boots, but the others were pretenders to Lizzie's rightful place as the queen of legs.

She stood close, very close to the piece. The nearby guard watched her like a hawk, probably worried that she was going to take a bite out of it. Jill had to agree that's how it looked, given her rapt attention.

From the angle she was at, Jill could see Lizzie's eyes. They moved slowly, then stayed in one place for quite a while, obviously taking in some small detail. Her lips, tinted with a gorgeous shade of peach-colored gloss, were slightly open, the way they often were when they made love. The tiniest of smiles curled those lovely lips, making her look completely sated.

Then she moved back, crossed her arms over her chest and stared. Now her eyes swept across the painting from top to bottom, then side to side. The slight smile remained, but now her head nodded as if she were having a discussion with herself and was agreeing with a point. Stepping back a few more feet, she continued to caress the painting with her eyes, ignoring the other people who leaned in close, took a peek, and departed. Finally, she'd backed up as much as she could, but still didn't look away. She was truly mesmerized, and Jill longed to feel what she felt. To get into the painting as Lizzie was so clearly able to do. But it just wasn't in her. Lizzie would have to delve into the art, and Jill would have to satisfy herself with delving into Lizzie. That was a deal she'd make any day of the week.

❦

They'd had a drink with one of Lizzie's museum travel friends, a glitteringly gay guy named Nathan, and were now eating sushi out of clamshell plastic containers while people watching in Washington Square Park.

"Nathan really knew what he was talking about," Jill said as she bit into a piece of spicy tuna.

"Seventeen bucks for everything!" Lizzie said, clearly as happy about the price as the flavor. "Nathan rocks. That's why he's so great to travel with. He's not above splurging, but he can also track down the best quality bargains anywhere. He's the guy I went to Amsterdam with."

"I liked him. You should invite him up to visit."

Lizzie laughed. "He's not the type who'd enjoy Burlington. He hates the outdoors, and he gets bored in two seconds flat. But I guess I could invite some of my other friends up. I haven't had the room since I was with Jon, and I always hated that I couldn't have my Boston friends up."

"Any time you want," Jill offered. "I really enjoy having house guests."

"You're just about perfect," Lizzie said. She leaned back and took a good, long look at Jill, as if she were seeing her for the first time. "Yeah, I can't think of a thing I'd change about you."

"Just one thing I'd change about you," Jill said thoughtfully. "I'd like for you to eat faster so we can go back to the hotel and make love." She leaned close and spoke into Lizzie's ear. "I've been fantasizing about you all day. I want to see if we can break your orgasm record. What is it now?"

Lizzie held up four fingers and wiggled them, while she used her other hand to shove three pieces of sashimi into her mouth at the same time. Then she stood and gathered up all of their trash, took Jill's hand and headed for the subway. She was the perfect girlfriend. Exquisitely responsive to every suggestion.

❦

The next evening, Jill got back to their hotel room late. Lizzie and Kristen were nowhere to be found. Four shopping bags stuffed with clothing and shoes had Jill wondering where they'd put it all on the train ride home. She picked up the note Lizzie had left. "We're in the bar. Come on down!"

She'd already had wine with dinner and had a brandy practically forced on her. But she felt obliged to spend some time with Kristen, so she picked up her room key and went back down.

The bar was packed, mostly with people from her conference, identified by their purple lanyards that held their name badges. She'd taken hers off, hating to walk around looking like a kid on her first day of kindergarten. In the corner of the room, the Davis sisters had procured a small table and two low chairs. Jill walked over and found herself being pulled down for a kiss. They were obviously not going to give Kristen time to adjust to their being intimate.

"Sit right here," Lizzie said, tugging her down so she sat on the arm of the chair.

"Hi, Kristen," Jill said, not sure if she should offer a hug or not. Kristen didn't get up, so she let it go.

"Good to see you, Jill," she said, her smile very relaxed and open.

"Did you have a good day?" Lizzie asked.

"Sure. Some of the presentations were boring, but a couple kept me awake. How about you two? Did you do anything fun?"

"Kristen's train didn't get in until two-fifteen, so we didn't have much time. We hightailed it down to a resale shop that had so much good stuff!" She was bubbling with excitement. "I got two dresses, a plaid jacket, three blouses and a hand-knit sweater. Guess how much?"

"Gosh, I can't begin to—"

"Two hundred bucks! I had to bargain my ass off, but I'm so stoked!"

"Did you find anything for me?"

"No, but we've got another day. MOMA in the morning, shopping in the afternoon."

"Thanks for letting me crash with you, Jill," Kristen said. "This is my first solo vacation since I've been married."

"No problem, Kristen. I'm glad you guys are getting to hang out."

"I am too," she said, her speech not very crisp. "We need time to talk." She narrowed her eyes as she gave Jill a long look. "I like you," she said thoughtfully. "But I can't imagine stopping liking men for you. Does that make any sense?"

Jill's eyes widened. How in the hell was she supposed to answer that?

Lizzie's hand was on her leg, and she beamed a grin up at Jill. "I would have jumped years ago if I'd met her earlier," she said. "I just didn't have a chance until this year."

"So you can just be going along, living your life, loving men. Then you run into Jill and you're…poof! A lesbian?"

"Yep," Lizzie agreed. "Good thing I saw her before you did, or you'd be getting divorced right about now."

"Lizzie," Jill said, a warning tone in her voice. "I think your sister's really trying to figure this out. Give her a break."

The remnants of Beth the Brat were all showing in the devilish grin Lizzie gave her. But then she faced her sister and said, "Do you remember my friend Elena? From high school?"

"Elena? The chiropractor's kid?"

"Uh-huh." Lizzie leaned forward. "We were more than friends."

"Shut up!" Kristen yipped. "Are you serious?"

"Uh-huh. Jill's the first woman I've ever loved, but she's not the first woman I've ever—you know."

"*Now* this is starting to make sense!" Kristen looked up at Jill. "Not that you're not a really nice person, but…"

"I understand," Jill said. "You two keep talking. Do you need another drink?"

Lizzie looked at her empty glass. "Maybe just one more. We've had a couple," she added, unnecessarily. Handing Jill her empty glass, she said, "Bourbon and Pepsi for both of us."

"Be right back." Wrinkling her nose in distaste at the sound of that combination, Jill went to the far end of the bar, and flagged down a bartender.

"Two Pepsis and a shot of bourbon, please."

He nodded, poured the sodas, then set a shot glass down and filled it. "That'll be twenty-five."

Jill gulped as she handed him thirty, then portioned the shot between the glasses. She hated to supervise, but she knew Lizzie. If she had to get by with less than eight hours of sleep, she couldn't add a hangover to the mix and have a good day. "Hey, are those two women running a tab?" She pointed at the Davis sisters and he turned to spot them. "If so, I'd like to pay it."

"Hold on," the bartender said. He looked through a stack, then handed it over. "They're charging it to their room."

"Can I pay separately?" She whipped out her credit card. "I'm in the same room. I just don't want the drinks on the bill because I have to submit it for reimbursement."

He shrugged. "Sure. I wouldn't normally do this, but I understand how it is to work for a place that keeps tabs on you."

The bill wasn't too horrible. Just ninety bucks. Jill laughed to herself, thinking of how hard it was to pry a hundred from Lizzie's wallet. But she was really invested in repairing her relationship with Kristen, and if she wanted to use alcohol to ease her way back into her good graces, it seemed like a small price to pay.

Jill moved back across the room to deliver the drinks. She kissed Lizzie on the top of the head and said, "I'm going to bed. I've got a session at nine that I can't miss."

"We'll be up soon," Lizzie said. "Well, soonish," she added, smiling impishly.

Jill leaned over and quietly said, "I paid your bar tab. I didn't want a bunch of drinks on the receipt I have to turn in."

"I'll pay you back," she said forcefully. "I will."

"I know, sweetheart. I just didn't want you to be confused when you tried to settle up."

"I love you," Lizzie whispered, her breath hot and moist against Jill's ear. Nice. That was probably the only intimacy they'd share, but they'd filled their tanks up very well the night before. She didn't have a thing to complain about.

❧

Jill woke in the middle of the night, slightly disoriented. Even though she had the blackout curtains drawn, a sliver of white light filtered through the space where the drapes met. She should have brought an eye mask rather than ear plugs. As she turned away from the wall, another stripe of light shone from under the closed bathroom door. She shut her eyes, and waited for Lizzie to come back to bed. The next thing she knew, her alarm was ringing. She reached to shut it off, then rolled over to cuddle for a few minutes. But the other side of the bed was cold. Jill sat up, and blinked to clear her eyes as she gazed at her lover, sharing a bed with her sister.

Slightly grouchy, Jill got up and went into the bathroom to take her shower. Her dreams of a romantic getaway were not turning out quite like she'd hoped. Luckily, Lizzie only had two sisters, and Jill was certain they'd never have to share a room with her brothers. You had to draw the line somewhere.

❧

Lizzie ran hot, as she liked to say, and they'd taken to leaving the window open a crack. Jill could tolerate it, but she had to wear a shirt to bed to keep her shoulders warm. She'd started with a T-shirt, and had recently switched to a thermal shirt, the kind she wore skiing.

On a Saturday morning in November, Jill woke to that shirt being firmly tugged. Still half-asleep, she followed the pull and wrapped herself around Lizzie's body. The bare butt that she pressed into was ice cold, not unusual since Lizzie often threw the comforter off during the night. But Jill didn't mind trading a few seconds of icy skin for that full-body hug.

Weekend mornings had become her favorite time of the week. Lizzie was very disciplined about getting up for work, sliding out of bed so stealthily that Jill rarely noticed her absence. But on the weekends, they both loved to spoon. One would wake, chase the other one down, cuddle until they were too warm, separate, then repeat. The cycle could go on for an hour or even two, but sleeping away the early morning seemed like a perfectly reasonable way to blow a chilly, overcast day.

They were sound asleep when Lizzie's phone rang and she grumbled, "Sorry, boo," before grabbing it and answering. "Hey, Mom."

Jill sat up and rubbed her eyes, getting a look at the clock. The boys came running into the room and leapt onto the bed, both of them complaining that their humans were taking too long to feed them.

"Can I put you on speaker?" Lizzie asked. "I hate to have to repeat everything you've told me."

She hit the button and Janet's voice came through the small speaker. "Hi, Jill. Did I wake you?"

"Just a little. But the cats agree we should get up, so it's all good."

"I was just telling Lizzie that I've got the final number for Thanksgiving. You can bring a side dish or bread. Your choice."

"Bread," Lizzie said before Jill could speak. "There's a bakery here that I love. I'm addicted to their dinner rolls. For seventeen, right?"

"Right. Adam and Donna won't be with us."

"Or Mark," Lizzie added quietly.

"No, but I'm confident he's making progress. I've been going by the shop when I know it's slow. That way he can't avoid me," she said. "He's talking more than he has in years. I think therapy is helping him learn how to speak for himself again."

"But he still doesn't want to be with the family," Lizzie said, a sour look on her face.

"That's not true. Well, it might be, but I didn't give him the option."

"What?"

"I didn't," Janet said. "There's no point in pushing him, Lizzie. Besides, I thought it would be too tense with them here, and I don't want that."

"But this is my favorite holiday," she said, an uncharacteristic whine coloring her voice. "I love having the whole family together."

"Oh, we never have that and you know it. My parents always go to your Aunt Eileen's house, and one of the boys always has to go to his in-law's. This year, it's Mark."

"But he's never gone before," Lizzie reminded her. "Thanksgiving was always with us."

"And it can be again. Speaking of in-laws, are you going to spend time with your parents, Jill?"

"I doubt it. I called my mom the other day to check on her, and she said I had to come by and pick up anything I want from the house by the end of Thanksgiving weekend. She didn't mention cooking."

"Then we'll have you all to ourselves," Janet said, amping up her enthusiasm.

"It's okay if we stay with you?" Lizzie asked.

"Okay?" A few seconds passed in silence. "Are you seriously asking if we want you to stay?"

"Well, Kristen's going to be there and I'm not sure what she's told her kids… I should ask, but I've been chicken."

"That's Kristen's issue, isn't it. All of my kids are welcome to stay—if they can find a spot. That will never change."

"Thanks, Mom," Lizzie said, giving Jill a watery smile. "I'm really looking forward to being with you guys. Is Dad okay?"

"He's fine, honey. He's still having very good luck with his new inhaler. Actually, he went over to Bellows Falls with Scooter this morning. They go over to the diner, drink coffee and gab for hours, like a couple of old hens."

"Don't complain. At least he's out of your hair for a few hours."

"Hey," Jill teased. "Is that how you feel about me when I go out?"

"Isn't she cute?" Lizzie asked. "Like I could ever tire of that sweet face."

"You're both cute," Janet said. "And we're looking forward to having you stay for a few days. Don't even think of leaving before Sunday."

"We won't," Lizzie said.

"Okay, honey. Talk to you later. Love you both."

"Thanks, Janet," Jill said. She was still a little skittish about declaring her love for the Davises. She knew it was illogical, but doing so felt disloyal to her own parents. Or maybe it was an even less logical instinct telling her that her mother would know. Either way, she was going to get over that hurdle. She loved Janet and Mike and needed to express that often.

On the day before Thanksgiving, Jill drove to Hollyhock Hills to pick up Lizzie. She found her on the big stone porch of the main house, chatting with a couple of guys who were dressed for outdoor work. Jill honked and Lizzie came dashing down the stairs, a big grin on her sunny face.

"Hi," she said as she threw her bag into the back seat. "I was just telling the fellas that I was leaving my car here for the weekend. I didn't want them to think I'd been kidnapped or something."

"Maintenance guys?"

"Farm ops. We were jawing about how we can make sure we've got a good skating pond this year."

"Skating pond?"

"Uh-huh. There's a low lying area right down at the base of that hill," she said, pointing. "Last year was a little dry and we didn't have enough standing water to freeze. This year they're going to pump some water up from the lake if they need to."

"Do you charge people to skate?"

"Oh, no, it's not for guests. Just us." She gave Jill a speculative look. "I guess I could bring a friend."

"Then I'll sharpen my skates."

"Winter's on its way. No doubt about it. Time to load all of my gear into my trunk. Now that I can park in the garage, I won't worry about having my car broken into."

"Gear? What kind of gear do you need?"

Lizzie snuck her chilly fingers up under Jill's sweater, tickling her ribs. "You're just gonna have to wait and see, aren't you."

Jill laughed as she pushed Lizzie's hand away. "Don't kill us before winter gets here." After turning onto the main road that would lead them to the interstate, she asked, "Will you play DJ? We need some good driving music."

Lizzie fussed with her phone, looking for a good playlist. Jill kept taking glances her way, loving how she bit her bottom lip when she was thinking.

Obviously satisfied, Lizzie leaned her seat back and stuck a foot up on the dash.

"Is that a good idea?" Jill asked. "Some trucker's going to drive off the road."

She grasped her skirt and fanned it playfully. "No one can look up my dress from behind. It'll be all right."

The tone Jill had used stuck in her head. Damn, she hated being a scold. "Sorry I'm picking at you. I think I'm a little edgy."

"I know." She put her hand on Jill's leg, then brushed her fingers across her jeans. "If you've changed your mind and don't want me to come with you, I won't be mad."

"You're mad for wanting to come," she grumbled. "It's not going to be fun."

"Jill," she said softly. "We're not partners only when we're having fun. Come on now. Get your head on straight, bucko."

Jill turned and gave her a brief smile. "How many nicknames do you have for me? I've lost count."

"Those aren't nicknames. Just names. They don't stick for long."

"True. I'm not complaining, by the way. Jennifer used to call me babydoll. Almost exclusively." She turned enough to let Lizzie see her raised eyebrow.

"Nice," Lizzie teased. "Good way to make you feel the age difference."

"Ick! I never thought of it like that. I focused more on the 'doll' part. Since I never felt like a doll, it always seemed like someone else's name applied to me."

"Now that name's going to be stuck in my head. You can slap me if I use it, but I probably will."

"Yeah, that's just what I'll do," Jill said, rolling her eyes. "You're the mistress of hyperbole."

"Awful nickname. Really awful. You've gotta keep working on that, babydoll."

"Ooo, it's gonna be a loooooong weekend."

After pulling into the family driveway, Jill tried to make her fingers release their death-grip on the wheel. "I don't want to do this," she said, her voice tight. "I'm happy to let my mother throw everything of mine away."

"That's not fair," Lizzie said gently. "Your mom's got a lot of work ahead of her to pack up a house. How long has she lived here?"

"Forty-one years, I guess. She inherited some property when her father died, and sold some of it to buy the house when she got married."

"Free and clear?"

"Yeah, I think so. I guess she might have had a mortgage, but she owns it outright now. I do her taxes."

"Interesting. I'm surprised she lets you see private stuff like that."

Jill thought about that for a second. "That is odd, isn't it? I've been doing them since I was in high school. I assume she'd rather have me know her business than someone in town, but I bet it was a close call."

She opened the car door, stood and took a long look at the property. It wasn't a spectacular house, mostly because neither of her parents cared about decorating or upgrading the interior. But the yard was awesome by any standard. Four seasons of color, with lots of texture and visual interest. It was at a low point now, but she knew she'd truly miss it in the spring, when the bulbs her mother painstakingly overwintered burst into life.

Lizzie came around and took her hand. As they went up the walk, the door opened and her mother appeared, squinting at them like she wasn't quite sure who they were. Lizzie kept holding Jill's hand, which was kind of nice. There was no reason to act like they were just friends.

"What were you doing standing out there for so long?" her mother asked, already cross.

Jill ignored the question. "Mom, this is Lizzie."

Lizzie removed her glove and extended her hand. "We've met before, Mrs. Henry, but it was a long time ago."

"Where would I have met you?"

Jill flinched. She'd been hoping her mother could suck it up just once and be cordial, but that was obviously hoping for too much. At least she'd responded to Lizzie's extended hand.

"At church. Like I said, it was a long time ago."

Jill put her hand on Lizzie's back and urged her inside. "Let me take your coat," she said, after helping her remove it. By the time she'd returned from placing their coats on a chair in the den, Lizzie was walking through the living room, commenting on the decorating.

"I love how clean and pared down everything is," she said. "It's so easy to let things build up."

"I can't stand mess. Never could. People keep a load of crap. Do you watch those shows? About hoarders?"

"Oh, I couldn't," Lizzie said. "I'm not the cleanest person in the world, but I can't stand to look at that kind of chaos."

A smile lit her mother's face, making Jill start. She was certain those muscles, seldom used, had atrophied. "Oh, you should watch. You'll never feel cleaner."

"Maybe I will."

"Do you live at Jill's?"

"Uh-huh. I just moved in last month. She has a lovely home. Very clean," she added. "I bet she learned how to keep a neat house from you."

"Certainly not from her father! He'd live in filth if I didn't clean up after him."

"Where will you be living in Arizona?"

"Scottsdale. In a townhouse. It took me a long time to find a place with a little yard that I could take care of."

Lizzie stood in front of the picture window that overlooked the backyard. She turned and gave Jill's mom such a warm smile it had to have melted her heart a little. "I don't think I've ever seen a prettier yard. You must work on it every day of the year."

"Just about," she admitted. "You've got to keep on top of things. Thank god the leaves have almost all dropped."

"I'm sure you couldn't find a place with a yard anywhere near as nice as yours, but I have a feeling you'll have it in shape before too long. How many times did you have to go out to Arizona?"

Acting like that was a strange question, she said, "I've never been there. I did it all on the internet."

"Never?" Lizzie's face betrayed her surprise.

"No. But I read the weather report. It never snows, and that's all I care about at this point."

"Then you should be good to go," Lizzie said, her smile so charming and nonjudgmental that Jill could see her mother begin to thaw. "I'm sure you'll love it."

"I've got a sister there, but I don't think we'll be bosom buddies or anything like that. She can be a royal pain in the butt."

"I've got two sisters," Lizzie said, speaking softly, as though they were conspiring. "I know just what you mean."

"Where do you work?" she asked, giving Lizzie as careful a look as she did a tree at the nursery. "You didn't get all dressed up to come see me."

"I work at Hollyhock Hills. I try to talk people into giving us money."

"I've never been there. They say it's nice, but…" She shrugged. "I guess I should have gone to see the gardens."

Lizzie frowned and bit at her lip. "I wish I could have taken you on a tour while the gardens were still in bloom. It's beautiful, isn't it, Jill?"

"It is," she said, knocked out of her passive viewing of the conversation. "It's great."

"Did you used to have funny hair?"

Good lord!

"I did," Lizzie said, laughing. "Really funny. I thought it was cool, but I'm sure I looked like a fool."

"I *knew* that was you! You're the last of the bunch, right?"

"Uh-huh. Two girls, then four boys, then me."

"Well, you look a lot better than you used to. I would have cut that mess off your head while you were sleeping."

Lizzie smiled warmly. "I'm sure my mom wanted to, but I'm a light sleeper."

"Do you want some tea? I've got cookies too."

"Sure. We've got all day, right, Jill?"

"Uhm…sure. I guess we do." Watching Lizzie thoroughly charm her mother, Jill followed along as they made their way into the kitchen. It was absolutely weird. Disconcerting. But also really nice to be able to lurk in the background and observe. Much better than being on the firing line.

⚜

After drinking tea and eating Fig Newtons, they put their coats back on and went into the garage. One wall was filled with boxes labeled "Rich," the other, with far fewer, had Jill's name on them.

"I have a dumpster coming on Friday. So if you don't want any of this, just leave it right here. They'll take everything that's left."

"What about Dad's stuff?" Jill asked. "Is he coming?"

"He'd better." She crossed her arms over her chest, as if daring her to take his side.

Jill was about to ask more questions, then realized it was none of her business. Her parents had always had a very odd relationship. One she'd never understood. It was too late to catch up now.

"I can look through this, if you want to go back inside," she said. "It's awfully chilly out here."

Lizzie met her eyes for just a second, then turned back towards the house and said, "Let's go have another cup of tea. Jill can take her time and we won't have to freeze."

"I hate the damn cold," her mother agreed, scurrying back inside. Lizzie paused on the threshold and raised an eyebrow in question. Jill waved, giving her permission to go. She wouldn't have minded Lizzie staying, but she didn't want her mother commenting on the things she'd saved. It was, undoubtedly, curated with her own unique take on things.

As expected, there was very little that Jill would have chosen. Lots of clothing, all of it outdated and child sized. Knowing her mother, she'd saved everything that had a lot of wear left in it. She hated to throw away perfectly good things. But she also hated to give things to charity. That let people in town see what they had and possibly comment on it.

In a box, she found every card she'd ever given or sent; birthday, mother's day, and later, Thanksgiving and Christmas and Easter. Every one still in its envelope. With Jill's childish hand slowly growing into her current one. Why had she saved them? And why throw them away now? One more question she'd never have answered.

The next boxes had some real treasures. Books. Loads of books. Some from her mother's youth, and a few from her grandmother. Five books, obviously old and fragile, were written in French. Those must have been her great-grandmother's. Hardbound, high quality, well-used. Inside the covers, the name Elizabeth Bergeron was written in a fine, elaborate hand. Her great grandmother shared Lizzie's name. So cool!

Jill didn't really have room to display all of these books, but she was keeping them. Books had been her oasis when she was a girl, providing a place to get away, to dream, to fantasize. If not for reading and the Davises… She shivered, thinking of what would have happened to her.

The last box, clearly in her section, bore things from her mother's youth, along with some of her grandmother's keepsakes. A number of photos, chronicling a rural Vermont girl's Depression-era life. There were several of a nicely dressed couple, assumably her great-grandparents. One might have been taken when they were newly engaged, another at their wedding, staged and very sober. Then a series of photos of her grandmother and her siblings, taken at a professional photographer's studio. Jill held one out at arm's length, reading the tiny gold script. "Smith Bros., Bellows Falls, Vermont." She'd never seen any of these things. Had no idea they existed.

Then her mom's high school yearbooks. She searched through, finding a photo of her mother as a freshman, looking a little wary of the camera. She was the kind of girl Jill wouldn't have approached. Chilly, defended, she looked like she'd be unfriendly at best. Paging through to the seniors, she found her father. Rich Henry, in his blazer, wide tie and moderately long hair. He was a very good looking boy, a winning smile making him look like he'd easily reach the title his classmates bestowed on him, "Most Likely To Succeed."

The invitation to their wedding, just over three years later. Jill's birth announcement four years after the wedding. A tiny white dress, probably from her baptism. A pair of well-worn high top white leather shoes. Her high school graduation announcement. All things signifying mileposts. Cast aside.

Without waiting for Lizzie, she opened the garage door and hustled the books and the mementos into the trunk. Then she came back inside, took her phone from her pocket and dialed. "Dad?"

"Hey, Jill. What's up?"

"I'm at Mom's and I wanted to make sure you knew she was going to throw all of your stuff away on Friday."

"Throw it away?"

"Yeah." She opened a box, labeled "clothing." "All of your suits, dress shoes…"

"God damn it!" He was quiet for a moment, clearly thinking. "Can you pick it up for me? I wasn't planning on spending the holiday driving over there."

"Uhm…no," she said, even though she could have put at least his suits and shoes into her trunk. "Give her a call. She might let you go through it later. I've got to go now. Have a nice Thanksgiving."

"Yeah. Right. You too. Hey, someone told me you're dating one of the Davis girls. Is that true?"

"Uh-huh. Lizzie. The youngest."

"The youngest?" He must have had a memory of her from years ago, given how filled with surprise his voice was.

"Yeah. She's thirty, Dad."

He laughed. "I guess she is. Time flies, doesn't it? Well, I hope you're happy together. Have you always been…?"

"Always," she said, cutting off the question.

"Wow. Didn't know that. Well, whatever makes you happy."

"Thanks. Gotta go," she said, then added, "Happy Thanksgiving," before hanging up.

Jill tried to compose herself before going back inside. Luckily, her mom didn't read physical cues very well, so she wouldn't notice Jill was shaky and shell-shocked. Lizzie would, but she'd keep her questions until they were alone. Working in development had given her a great education in how to hold your tongue until the time was right.

❧

At ten to seven, Jill's mom stood and carried the bag of cookies and mugs into the kitchen. "You two are probably hungry," she said over her shoulder as she put the mugs into the dishwasher. "Are you going to Janet's for dinner?"

"Uhm…yes?" Lizzie said, looking at Jill.

"Yeah. We'd better take off," Jill agreed. When her mother came back into the room she eyed the television, with Jill realizing her favorite show was about to begin. Every night at seven, from the time she could recall, the familiar theme song would begin, and all chatter had better stop.

A commercial was playing, giving them a spare minute or two to wrap things up.

"Do you have my new address?"

"No," Jill said. "You haven't given it to me."

Sharp eyes darted to the TV. "I'll send it." She put her hand on Jill's back and prodded her along. Then Jill dashed into the den, grabbed their coats and helped Lizzie put hers on.

The door opened, then Lizzie stuck her hand out. "It was nice to meet you again," she said.

"Me too." Jill received a brief hug, then a hand on her shoulder gave her a gentle push. "Goodbye."

As they hurried to button their coats against the bitter wind, the door closed behind them. Jill stared at the door, stunned, as the porchlight went out. "That might be the last time I see her," she said, her heart pounding in her chest as a wave of anxiety pulsed through her. "That's… how can she…?"

Then Lizzie's arms were around her, squeezing so tightly it hurt. "I wish she could give you more. I want so many things for you, but that's the biggest one. I'd give anything for you to know what it's like to be certain your mother was crazy about you."

It was nice. Really nice to have someone you cared for want you to experience that deep, primal kind of love. It wasn't close to actually having it, though. Jill was sure of that.

They walked to the car quickly, trying to get in before the wind pushed them down the driveway. Jill sat perfectly still for a minute, trying to get centered enough to drive.

"It's really warm in Scottsdale in the winter," Lizzie said quietly.

"I know. That's why she's leaving."

"I bet her townhouse complex has a pool."

"She doesn't like the water."

"You do." Lizzie reached over and took Jill's hand, then tugged firmly, until she was holding her. "If you want this to be the last time you see each other, I'd understand. If you don't... I'd happily take a trip to Scottsdale with you. *Happily*," she emphasized.

Jill nodded, unable to even consider going to visit at this point. Lizzie's offer was just about the most generous gift she'd ever received. No one in her right mind would happily visit someone so shut off, so emotionally unavailable, so unable to connect on almost any level. But Lizzie loved her enough to make the offer sound absolutely sincere, and that was a huge gift. Truly huge.

⁂

After dinner, a sad tuna casserole, followed by a fantastic lemon cake, as light and tart as you could ever want, Janet and Lizzie sat at the dining room table, watching Jill reveal the treasures she'd taken.

When everything was laid out, Janet shuffled through the papers to pull out the oldest photos and look at them carefully. "You really don't know anything about your mom's family?" she asked gently.

"Nothing. I know my grandmother was dead by the time I was born, but that's it."

"Interesting." Janet quickly pushed the photos back across the table, like she didn't want them near her.

Jill watched her carefully, noting how Janet moved onto more recent things in the pile without further comment.

"Do *you* know much about my family?"

A strained look flashed across her face. "A little," she admitted. "But nothing concrete. Just things I heard at church. Gossip, really."

"Want to tell me what you know?"

She finally met Jill's gaze. "It's not a happy tale. Your mother obviously didn't want to talk about it, so maybe it's better to let it—"

"I want to know. Really."

Sighing, Janet reached over and went to the last photo in the album, the one where the girl in the family was about ten, with four younger boys all lined up behind her. "This must be your grandmother, since she was the only girl. They lived out in the country, outside of Rockingham. I think they raised dairy cows."

"They were farmers? Really?"

"I'm pretty sure that's true. Anyway, the mother died, probably around the time this photo was taken." She sifted through the pile, finding no others. "This is the last one, so that makes sense. When a man raises five kids alone, he doesn't take them into town to have their pictures taken."

"Sad," Jill said, looking at the girl, clad in a dark sailor-style dress with a big white collar, a neckerchief, and a low belt. "I guess my grandmother had to take her mother's place?"

"I suppose so. I only heard this later. After people started to talk…"

"About?" Jill led.

"This is the bad part. Your grandmother ran off when your mom was a baby."

"Ran off?" Jill's heart started to beat faster. Critical information was coming in, fast and hard, and she stiffened, waiting for it. "What does that mean?"

"I'm not sure if she left with a man, or if she just couldn't handle being a mother. But she left. As far as I know, no one ever heard from her again." She stopped and looked away. "Although there were rumors for years. Some people thought your grandfather…"

"Killed her?" Jill's eyebrows shot up as Lizzie turned and met her startled gaze. "Holy fuck," she muttered.

Janet waved her hand dismissively. "I think that was just idle conjecture. Your grandfather wasn't thought of as the best husband, and people wanted an answer. This was the fifties, and it wasn't common for women to abandon their children."

"I hope it's not common now!" Jill said, finding herself a little breathless.

"I knew I shouldn't have talked about this." She reached out and covered Jill's chilled hand with her own. "Now you're upset."

"I'm upset because this is all news," she said. "I should have known these things. My mother said my grandmother was dead, but she could be on a beach in Rio!" She looked again at her mother's wedding invitation. No parents were mentioned. "Did my grandfather remarry?"

"I don't think so. He had a lot of women friends, though. Not that that should be a surprise. He had a good job, at a time most people were really struggling to get by. Before the Foundation started buying up property, our population was shrinking every year. Things were grim."

"What did he do?"

"He sold insurance. I think he was just about the only insurance salesman in the county at the time. Smart businessman too. Invested in land and made a nice profit when he sold a lot of it to the Foundation."

"And he died…when?"

"I'm not sure. I think your mom was at least in high school. She's almost ten years younger than I am, so we weren't friends."

"Yeah," Lizzie said, soberly. "Who'd want to hang out with someone ten years older? Yuck!"

Janet reached over, grabbed a hank of her hair and pulled it, making her yelp and slap at her hand.

"Stop!" she cried, giggling fiercely.

"You're such a smartass, Elizabeth Anne!" She rolled her eyes at Jill. "I'm not sure how you stand her."

Jill put her hand out and instead of taking it, Lizzie got up and sat on her lap.

"I've got the patience of a saint," Jill said. She was a little uncomfortable having Lizzie display their usual intimacy, but Janet seemed fine with it, so she tried to act naturally.

"When your grandfather died, he owned a lot of property. They say he invested in the stock market too, and if he did, he was unique for this area. I think your mom and your aunt each got half of a pretty substantial sum."

"Do you have any idea what he died of?"

"He ran into something one night," she said, her brow furrowed in thought. "A deer or a moose. They say he had a very hefty insurance policy too."

Jill studied the photos, noting that there wasn't a single one of her grandmother as an adult. Nor of the man she married, her mother's father. "You know an awful lot about them, given that they lived a half hour from here."

"We were from the same parish," Janet said, shrugging. "And in a small parish all people do is talk about each other. It's not much different now."

"I guess my mom paid for her house with her inheritance," Jill said. "Up until now, she's had some undeveloped land, but she might have sold that. I guess I'll see when I do her taxes." She rested her chin on Lizzie's shoulder, thinking, then looked at Janet again. "Is it true your sister dated my dad?"

"She did. I thought they might get married, but he met up with your mom and they married not too long after she graduated from high school."

"I bet he thought he'd hit the lotto," Jill grumbled.

"That's what people said," Janet agreed. "That's just gossip though," she added quickly. "Maybe it was love at first sight."

"I don't think so. My dad's always looking for the easy way out, and my mom doesn't have a warm bone in her body. He was probably cheating on their honeymoon."

"They have their quirks," Janet agreed, putting her hand on Jill's shoulder and giving it a squeeze. "But they created a very special girl. You have to give them some credit for that."

"Thanks," Jill said, ducking her head. Lizzie leaned against her and Jill rested her cheek on her back. It had been a pretty awful day, but having Lizzie's support had made it all so much better than it might have been. Of course, that was true every day of the week.

⌇

When Lizzie was born, Donna was heading off to the U. Tim graduated to Donna's big bed, Lizzie took over the crib, and it was moved to Donna's spot in the first floor bedroom, currently repurposed as the den. When Lizzie was just two, Kristen went to college. The other kids rebelled at the baby having a big room to herself, so she was reassigned to the smallest of the upstairs bedrooms, really just a large closet. It was laughably small, with a single bed and a white painted dresser filling it. Jill stood in the tiny room, assessing it. "God knows I don't want to go back to my mother's house, but we'd at least have a full-sized bed."

"This will be fun," Lizzie insisted, her smile so fetching Jill couldn't help but return it.

"I guess I can find another spare bed to crawl into if you knock me to the floor."

"That's true for tonight. Tomorrow, Kristen and Dave will be here. Five more people squeezing into two bedrooms."

"Well, I always say I love to cuddle. This will be the ultimate test of my capacity."

"You're a good sport," Lizzie said, tickling under her chin. "Want to come into the bathroom with me to brush your teeth?"

"I don't want to get caught," she said before she could censor herself.

"Caught?" Lizzie stood close and put her hands on Jill's hips. "Are you embarrassed about our relationship?"

"Not embarrassed," she said, hedging. "I just want to give everyone time to get used to it. I'm trying to be sensitive."

"You're being a dope," Lizzie said, smiling so sweetly it took all of the sting from her words. "If my mom's uncomfortable, she'll say something. You know that."

"I do," Jill said, annoyed by her own whining voice. "But I don't want to make her get to that point."

Lizzie tapped the tip of Jill's nose with her finger. "You're forbidden from worrying about that. I know you always had to be on the lookout for land mines at your house, but you don't have to do that here. Promise." She pulled her close and placed a tender kiss upon her lips. "Come on now."

"You go ahead," Jill insisted. "Since I'm not allowed to worry about them, I'm going to avoid any potential land mines, just to be safe."

Lizzie rolled her eyes, grabbed her toiletries and went to brush her teeth, leaving Jill to unpack her clothing and try to find a place to lay it all out so it wouldn't get wrinkled. Not an easy task with so few horizontal surfaces. She took the few things on the dresser and put them on the floor, then stretched her slacks across it and placed her shirts atop them. How had Lizzie managed without a closet?

After Lizzie returned, Jill went to get ready for bed. When she came back, she opened the door to find Lizzie on her side, in bed, and pressed up against the wall. The bedclothes were folded down, just like in an ad, waiting for Jill to climb in.

"The window's open wide enough for something to fly in," she said, starting to lower it.

"I know. But I'll get really hot since I can't roll away from you to cool off."

"Then let me be by the wall. You'll have more room to move, and you'll be closer to the window."

"Sure?" Lizzie was already scooting over. "I was trying to be polite."

Jill lowered the window until it was open just a crack, then climbed over her, squealing when Lizzie reached up and pinched her butt. "I knew you'd have to grab something," she grumbled.

"Then you should move faster. You can't be slow around here."

Jill stuck an arm under Lizzie and tumbled her onto her chest. "This is better. Lots more room."

"My favorite position." Lizzie started to kiss her, quickly shifting into a gear Jill knew would lead to sex.

"Slow down there, two-pack. We're not going to do it when your parents are right next door. No way. No how."

Lizzie looked down at her, obviously puzzled. "Why not? They can't hear us. My dad's oxygen makes a lot of white noise."

"Not enough to cover the noise *you* make."

Raising an eyebrow, Lizzie said, "Are you really complaining about the feedback I give you? Ask some of my old boyfriends how it felt to be met with utter silence."

"You know I love to make you squeal," Jill said. Lizzie was still lying on top of her, and she found her hands roaming all over her butt, unable to stop herself from exploring that fantastic asset when it was right under her fingers. "But I can't relax enough to be myself."

"Then be someone else," she purred. She lowered her head and captured Jill's lips, letting out the softest of moans when they started to really get into it.

"Mmm." Jill nearly let herself be pulled along, but she stopped and wrapped her arms around Lizzie, holding her in place. "I keep thinking about your parents. I'd hate to know my kid was next door having sex."

"They *assume* we are," she said. "At least my mom does. Why not make her right?"

"I don't think so," Jill said, urging Lizzie onto her side. "Don't be upset with me, but I can't let go enough to enjoy myself."

"Can I at least kiss you for a while?" She put her hand on Jill's hip and started to pull her forward. "I promise I won't touch a single erogenous zone." Her hand went to Jill's hair and she threaded her fingers into it as she started to kiss her. "I've never gotten this far with a woman in this bed," she murmured. "Elena insisted we sleep head to foot just to keep me from trying anything."

Jill started to feel like a jerk for not being more flexible. But Lizzie didn't seem upset. Not even a little. She gave every indication that she was having a very good time making out like teenagers.

After they'd kissed for a long time, Jill started to feel a definite pulse between her legs, her resolve weakening. Then Lizzie's knee lifted and she let out a soft gasp. Jill reached down to feel Lizzie's hand moving between her own legs. "I can be very quiet when I do this," she said, a satisfied smile on her face.

Jill tucked one arm around her shoulders, pulling her close so she could increase the intensity of her kisses. Then she mirrored Lizzie's pose and touched herself, smiling through their kiss. "If you can't beat 'em, join 'em," she murmured, as they quietly but enthusiastically fulfilled one of Lizzie's girlhood dreams.

On Thanksgiving day, Jill assumed the role of hors d'oeuvre tray refiller. She and Lizzie had spent the morning at the kitchen table, cutting up celery and carrots and cheese cubes and making dip for the platters now scattered around the living and dining rooms. Now she kept an eye on them, amazed at how quickly seventeen people could plow through food.

Kristen and her husband Dave seemed perfectly normal, with none of the awkwardness that Lizzie had worried about. Chris and Tim and their families also treated them the same as any other couple, teasing Lizzie about old childhood adventures, including Jill when they could. It was a lovely group, one Jill was thrilled to be a part of.

The only thing that took some of the gloss off the day was that Lizzie was a little off. Thanksgiving was her favorite holiday, and it clearly bothered her that Mark and his family weren't there. If Jill hadn't pushed her to come out when she did, Lizzie could have had the whole group together. Of course, Jill wouldn't have felt comfortable about tagging along, and that would have sucked.

No, being in the closet wasn't the answer. Sometimes people disappointed you when they knew your truth. But you couldn't let that be the deciding factor in what you revealed about yourself. Better to be authentic and let people react as they would. Just because it's a better situation doesn't mean it won't suck. It will.

~

Even though Janet had demanded they stay until Sunday, she was pushing them out the door the second they'd eaten breakfast.

"Everybody and their dog's on the road on the Sunday after Thanksgiving. The sooner you get home, the better. If you leave now, you'll be home to see the Pats."

Cornering her mother, Lizzie asked, "What's really going on? You've got something up your sleeve."

"Well, I wouldn't put it that way, but Mark and Lisa are coming over for a delayed Thanksgiving. I'm just making a couple of chickens, but I thought I should invite them to make up for not having them on Thursday."

"It's okay," Lizzie said, giving her mom a long hug. "I know you've got to juggle things to keep the peace."

"Not for long," Janet promised, placing noisy kisses on Lizzie's cheeks. "He's making progress. By next year, I know he'll be back at the table."

"We'll see," Lizzie said, grasping Jill's hand and heading for the door. "But if he isn't, I'm going to go over there and drag him back home. My patience has its limits."

⁂

They got home early, with the whole afternoon available for play. Lizzie had a dozen ideas, but her eyes lit up when she said, "I know! Let's go get a Christmas tree!"

Jill hated, truly hated to douse that bright smile, but she had to deliver the bad news. "I can't have one," she said, wincing as Lizzie's smile deflated.

"Why? Are you allergic?"

"No, of course not. But the cats don't know the difference between a Christmas tree and a toy. I had one when they were kittens and it was a mess. They climbed it, knocked it over a bunch of times, wouldn't stop playing with the ornaments, drank the water in the tree stand. All bad," she insisted.

"They're older now."

"True. But they haven't changed much, Lizzie. They're still pretty wild. I guess…" She hesitated, thinking. "I guess we could get a tree for them to play on. If we put it in the corner by the stairs and used piano wire to hold it up…"

"No lights?"

"No," Jill said, shaking her head. "I'm worried they'd break them or unplug them."

"No ornaments?"

"Nothing breakable. If we could find really sturdy ones…"

"I wasn't thinking of sturdy." She made a sad face, then took Jill by the hand. "If I can't put up a Christmas tree, you have to take me ice skating. I'm awesome, by the way, so prepare to be struck mute."

"I'm already looking forward to being awestruck," Jill said, so very, very glad that Lizzie's disappointment's never lasted long. She was the very definition of resilient.

Chapter Twenty-One

JILL SPENT A RIDICULOUS amount of time getting ready for Lizzie's open house. After going to get her hair trimmed and blown out straight, the way Lizzie liked it, she fussed in front of the mirror for a half hour, trying on different earrings, necklaces and bracelets. She owned very little jewelry, but Lizzie had a lot of inexpensive stuff she'd picked up at thrift shops that always looked good on her. On Jill? Not so much.

Lizzie was too swamped to come home before the event, so Jill took one last swipe at her dark suit with a sticky roller to get any stray cat hair off, put on her coat, and went to the car, determined to be there early to help in any way she could.

The parking lot by the main house was almost full, even though it was an hour before the event was supposed to start. Jill hated to have her car dinged, so she moved down the road and pulled over to the side. Better to walk another hundred yards in the cold than have a scrape on Freyja.

The kid at the front door was wearing a heavy parka, with Hollyhock Hills embroidered on the breast. "Good evening," he said, smiling brightly. "May I help you?"

"I'm here for the open house."

"Great! The party's not for an hour, but—"

"I came early to help out. I'm with Lizzie Davis."

His smile brightened even more. "I just saw her swing by. Lizzie's the best."

"She certainly is," Jill agreed, her possessive nature coming to the fore as it always did—much to her annoyance. "Mind if I go find her?"

"Oh, no, go right on in. There's no one to take your coat yet, but you can hang it on the coat tree right inside the door." He opened the huge, finely detailed oak door and she walked in to find the cool, dim, breezy room of the summer now sealed up tight, with a roaring fire, and a big, beautifully decorated Christmas tree filling the room with the scent of fir and some kind of spice.

Her gaze went to a group of servers, setting out glasses and mugs upon a couple of long tables covered with red fabric. *That* was the smell. A spiced wine or cider in big bowls. Nice. And much easier than having to make mixed drinks or juggle dozens of bottles of wine.

After stashing her coat, Jill turned to see Lizzie coming down the stately staircase right next to the entryway. A gorgeous stained glass window, probably twenty feet square, was lit from the outside, rendering the cool blues and greens in sharp detail. It was stunning, but it paled in comparison to Lizzie, gliding along purposefully, a notepad in her hand, followed by a couple of kids, probably interns.

Lizzie was likely only six or seven years older than her followers, but she looked like the elegant lady of the manor, trying to inculcate her young servants with enough polish to get them through a major gala.

She wore a dress Jill had never seen. Probably because it was far too fancy to wear on a regular work day, and they'd never been to a state dinner at the White House. It was scarlet red, in a clingy jersey knit that highlighted every delightful curve of Lizzie's body. The long-sleeved dress just covered her knees, but its modest length didn't reduce its sexiness one bit. In fact, having her so covered up made it even sexier. It let Jill think about what that lucky dress was hiding.

She was certain she was perfectly composed, but when Lizzie met her eyes and raced down the last few stairs, she leaned close and whispered, "Someone likes my dress."

"You think? How can you tell?"

"If it were summer, flies would be headed straight for your mouth." She reached up and playfully closed it, then placed a very chaste kiss on her lips. "Fifty bucks at that resale shop in New York."

"A million bucks," Jill said. "That's what you look like tonight."

"Oh, that's sweet of you to say. But you're the one who's going to make heads turn. You look lovely, sweetheart."

Jill stared at her, still a little awe-struck by how gorgeous she was. "I had no idea your hair was long enough to have it in that... What do you call that?"

She reached up and touched her neck, bare and delectable. "Just an updo. Nothing special." She turned, displaying her creation.

A laugh, a loud one, came out. "Leave it to you…"

Lizzie had crafted a delightfully whimsical hairdo, with a cherry red ball peeking out from a neat knot of auburn hair, a pair of googly eyes on top of that, with what looked like pipe cleaners fashioned into small antlers on the very top. Somehow, the few little doodads looked remarkably like a reindeer. It was such a contrast to her sexy, formal dress that Jill decided it was absolutely perfect for her—and the exact definition of her personality. Quirky, playful, yet deadly serious about a few specific things.

When Lizzie turned again, Jill leaned in and kissed her cheek. "If a thousand women show up, you're the prettiest one. No contest."

"Aww, you're full of it, but I appreciate the thought."

"I bet you're swamped. I came early to help."

"We're in good shape, but if you want to help, you can hand out name tags." She led the way to a small table where a young woman sat, frantically spreading the tags out, clearly trying, but failing, to organize them in alphabetical order.

"Jessie, this is Jill. She's going to help out." Lizzie kissed her one more time. "I've got to run. But I'll be back soon. Get ready to meet a zillion people."

"Okay," Jill said to thin air as Lizzie swept across the space, looking like she was about to take the stage.

Jill focused on the kid she was supposed to help. "Okay then, what can I do?"

"Have you ever done anything like this before? I usually milk the cows."

Stifling a laugh, Jill said, "Yeah, I've handed out name tags before. We'll figure it out."

After getting the tags into proper order, Jill walked over to the front door to find three young women tasked with checking coats. It looked like a bottleneck would be created as soon as more than two guests arrived at the same time. "Mind a suggestion?" she said to the woman closest to her.

"Feel free. I think this is going to get screwed up fast."

"If I were doing this, I'd welcome the first guests by leading them as far into the room as I could get them. Keep pulling groups inside, because it's chilly out there and people get annoyed when they're cold."

"Good one," the woman said. "I'll try to make that work. We don't have a lot of experience."

"What do you normally do here?"

"I move the sheep around to different grazing pastures. Kelly and Annabelle both make cheese."

"People are just like sheep," Jill said. "They like to be led."

Lizzie appeared at Jill's elbow right at seven o'clock. "I noticed you getting the kids in order. Thanks for that."

"They're not much younger than you," Jill teased. "Do you get to call them kids?"

"Anyone younger than me is a kid. And nearly everyone around here is younger than me."

"Why's that? I'm used to having a lot of seniors volunteer for things."

"These kids aren't volunteers for the most part. They're employees or interns, and most of them are in college." She leaned close and whispered, "My primary task tonight is make sure our donors are treated like royalty. These kids don't have a lot of experience kissing ass."

"I have to settle a lot of disputes between departments and schools, so I've got some experience there. I'm also good at seeing when kids look like they don't know what they're doing. There's a lot of that at a university."

"Then we'll make a good team. Feel free to step in whenever you see something out of whack."

"It's a deal. I'm good at making things whack."

Jill really did feel like she'd gotten to meet a zillion people. They spent a few minutes with Lizzie's boss, a cheerful guy who didn't seem much older than her, then the director of development came over and joined the crowd. You could just tell when people truly liked their co-workers, and Jill was certain Lizzie was a favorite.

It took a while to even say hello to all of the higher ups who ran the Foundation, all of the board members, including the creep with the boat and his dad who didn't seem creepy at all. It must have skipped a generation. Most of the best-known names in Burlington dropped by at some point during the night, with Lizzie working hard to charm each and every one of them.

Jill watched her work, proud of her for devoting so much of her energy to learning how to separate people from their money. Using her natural gifts to keep a cultural treasure running efficiently was a good way to make a living, even though she was sure Lizzie was leaving a lot of money on the table. She could have made several times her salary selling something—a product or a service. But she was more interested in doing something that resonated with her soul, and that made Jill respect her all the more.

Most of the guests were gone by eleven, with only the most die-hard partiers still slugging down the wassail. All of the staff was hanging in there, even though many of them looked as though they'd been put through the wringer. In Jill's experience, guests who stayed until the bitter end were the easy-going types, who you could act naturally around. The staff seemed to agree, since shoes started to come off, and jackets were ditched to lie across the sofas.

Someone switched the music from Christmas-themed songs to pop tunes, then cranked it up. The sofas and chairs were pushed to the walls, then the staff started to let their hair down.

The people who worked with the livestock were the first ones on the newly-created dance floor. Most of them were farm kids themselves, uninhibited and more than a little drunk by this time. Lizzie seemed to know them all, and she catcalled from the sidelines, clapping her hands and urging them on.

"You're not going to just stand there, are you?" Jill asked. She poked at her playfully. "Your whole body's moving to the beat. I have this image of you doing a few back flips, then hitting the floor doing the splits."

"You want to dance with me?" she asked, eyes glittering in the flickering candlelight.

"I was thinking of watching you. You're so much better than I am..."

"Come with me," Lizzie said, her voice dropping into a seductive growl. She took Jill by the hand and led her to the far end of the cleared space, close to the big windows that would have revealed the lake if it hadn't been so dark. There were fewer people standing there, and they had some distance between themselves and the rest of the rowdy dancers.

Lizzie kicked off her heels and set them atop an upright piano. Then she linked her hands behind Jill's waist and started to move to the sappy, romantic number currently playing.

"This is nice," Jill said. "I can keep up with you." She twitched her head towards the crowd by the fireplace. "No one seemed to bat an eye when you introduced me."

"Why would they?" she asked, tilting her head questioningly.

"Have things really changed that much?" Jill asked, a puzzled smile curling her lips. "Can a woman switch from men to women and not even get a second look?"

"I'm sure you'd get a lot of flak at a few places around Burlington, but you'd have to look for them." She laughed, her eyes almost closing when she did. "We've got nothing but idealistic, conservation-obsessed, do-gooders at Hollyhock. If they despised gay people they'd never admit it. Not cool."

"I like that. It's time for intolerant people to be afraid to speak their minds."

"I wouldn't work at a place that tried to supervise my private life. They don't pay me enough for that kind of bullshit."

"They like you," Jill said, beaming at her. "Everyone seems to perk up when they see you. That's really cool."

"Not *every*one," she scoffed. "But I really do like the people here. We've got some dopes and some people who can't organize a three-man parade, but no one's mean-spirited or impossible to get along with. I think I'll stay for a while. I fit in."

Jill pulled her a little closer and spoke into her ear. "Sometimes I wish you didn't like it. It'd be cool to have you at the U. We could always use someone like you to help raise our endowment."

"You just *think* you'd like that." She pulled her head down and gave her a very brief kiss. "Trust me to steer this relationship into safe waters. You'll have us going over the rapids if I let you be in charge."

Jill gave her a long, thoughtful look. "How did I get into the position of having a girl I met when she was about two days old be in charge of my life?"

"Just lucky, I guess." The music changed pace and Lizzie released her snug hold, then started moving more decisively. "Let's move over and dance with the guys from farm ops. They're the fun ones around here."

Jill followed along, grinning as Lizzie really got into it. She didn't show off—even though she could have. Jill had seen some of the moves she could effortlessly execute, and if she pulled any of them out, the whole place would stop and stare. But Lizzie wasn't like that. She liked being part of a team, not the star. Still, she moved those curvy, sexy hips like she didn't even realize she was in public. Jill was mesmerized by her, thoroughly charmed by her complete lack of self-consciousness. Part of that had to be the fact that she'd been dancing her whole life, and part of it was just Lizzie—fun-loving, pull-out-all-the-stops Lizzie. The coolest kid on Hollyhock Hill. And Jill got to take her home.

Two days later, Jill came home to find a truck leaving her driveway. She paused, letting him out, then pulled in and put her car into the garage. Lizzie's car was already there, sipping from the power cord nestled into its nose. It was rare for her to be home so early, and Jill hustled into the house to see what was up.

When she opened the back door, Lizzie was already in her play clothes. She was still wearing jeans, but her favorite winter pair was roomy enough to let her add some long underwear. Atop her jeans she wore a dark blue turtleneck, with her grandmother's red, boiled wool vest over it. Her big work boots covered her feet, making her look both adorable and a little tough. "You look like you're about to head outside," Jill said. "You usually jump into a pair of my flannel pajamas two seconds after you get home. What's up?"

She pulled Jill in for a kiss, unable to contain her excitement. "I got you a Christmas present," she said, grinning like a kid.

401

"You did? Isn't it a little early?"

"Nope. It needs to be early. Now we have to go decorate it."

"Decorate it?" Jill cocked her head, trying to figure out what in the heck Lizzie was talking about.

"Uh-huh. Go put on some warm clothes. And your boots. It's cold out."

Not wanting to waste time questioning her, Jill followed orders, returning a few minutes later in her snowboarding jacket and pants. "Good enough?"

"To eat," Lizzie said, pulling her close for a long kiss. "Don't make plans for around nine. I'm going to be devouring you."

"You're on my calendar," Jill agreed, already thinking about what she'd like to do and have done.

They went out the side door, where Lizzie had stacked a dozen boxes of tiny multi-colored lights. "We're decorating the house? In the dark?" Jill asked. "Did you buy a really big insurance policy on me?"

"Nope. We're decorating our tree." She led her to the far corner of the yard, where Jill found a good-sized fir tree, recently planted.

Lizzie was beaming with delight and Jill snaked an arm around her and pulled her in for a kiss. "I love it. Our first Christmas tree. And we'll be able to enjoy it all year." She put her hand on a branch and ran her fingers down it, watching the needles spring right back up. "Healthy. I like this a lot better than cutting one down."

"Good. Because I'm buying one every year. This place is going to look like a Christmas tree farm by the time we're done."

"I think our yard will make a very nice Christmas tree farm. We'll start a new trend. Urban forestry."

"Do you really like it?" Lizzie asked, putting her arm around Jill's shoulders. "It was stupid expensive, but I wanted to get you something that lasted."

"I love it," Jill insisted. "And I love you for making plans for our future. One day we'll have so many trees the whole neighborhood will go dark when we switch the lights on."

"Let's make a dent tonight. I've got a super long extension cord and a timer."

"We're really going to do this at night?"

"Yep. I'll go get the ladder. You start taking lights from the boxes."

In just a few minutes, Lizzie was standing on the first step, with Jill cautiously holding the ladder firmly.

"The tree isn't very big—yet," Lizzie said. "If I fell off the first step, I'd be just fine."

"Just making sure. You're too precious to let you risk breaking a nail."

They worked together, with Lizzie holding the top of the strand in place, and Jill running around the tree to drape it just so. They didn't use all of the strands, but the tree was so chock full of lights it couldn't take a single extra bulb.

Then Lizzie ran the extension cord into the garage, and came to stand next to Jill. "Ready?" she asked.

"Ready." Lizzie held the last plug, and Jill held the extension cord. When they met, the tree burst into color, with the tiny lights making the whole corner of the yard glow with festive warmth.

"I love this more than I can say," Lizzie murmured, her voice catching a little. "Our first Christmas tree."

"Come with me," Jill said. "We've got to rearrange some furniture."

A half hour later, they were in their pajamas. Or, rather, they were both in Jill's pajamas, since Lizzie didn't own any of her own. The sofa from the den had been moved to the window in the dining room, where they now sat, sipping cocoa and cuddling as they stared, mesmerized by the color-bedecked tree.

"I was torn between all white and colored lights," Lizzie mused.

"Color. Definitely color. Perfect choice."

"You'd say that even if you didn't agree," Lizzie decided. "That's why you're the perfect girlfriend. You always go out of your way to support me."

Jill nuzzled against Lizzie's sweet-smelling neck, rubbing her face so hard that Lizzie started to giggle. "That's because you're always right. It's easy to support perfection."

"Such good answers you give." Lizzie cuddled up closer and tucked a blanket more fully around Jill. "Warm enough, boo?"

"Uh-huh. But you could make me warmer."

Lizzie turned and looked into her eyes, a devilish grin making the corners of her mouth turn up. "Are you suggesting we get busy right here? In the dining room?"

"We haven't made love on this sofa yet. How we've missed it is a mystery, but…" She popped her eyebrows up and down, always a way to make Lizzie laugh.

"I think I could be persuaded." She cuddled closer, then placed a long, gentle kiss on Jill's lips. "Oh, yeah, I'm already persuaded. You have amazing powers."

"I have an amazing amount of love for you, Lizzie Davis. And touching you while looking at our tree is going to be the high point of the Christmas season. The twelve days of Lizzie."

"I say we leave the lights on until Epiphany. That gives us a month to sit right here every night and dream."

Jill placed her lips right next to Lizzie's ear, a sure way to give her goosebumps. "My dreams came true the day I kissed you. Every day has been Christmas since then."

Lizzie didn't respond with words. She simply slipped her arms around Jill and pushed her down, while covering her with kisses. The perfect end to a perfect evening.

Chapter Twenty-Two

LIZZIE WAS SWAMPED LEADING up to Christmas, with Hollyhock Hills putting a full-court press on their donors, trying to get them to give just a little bit more for that last minute charitable tax deduction.

That required more site visits, more tours, and more cocktail parties and luncheons. She was so tired that some nights they went to bed after just a few minutes sitting in the dining room, gazing out at their tree.

There were just two weeks left until Christmas, and Jill was starting to freak out. As they lay in bed that night, she said, "I know you haven't had time to buy any presents for your family, so I'm willing to pitch in. Who should I start with? The younger kids?"

"Start what?" Lizzie asked, her voice already starting to slow down and get a little fuzzy.

"Coming up with ideas for gifts! Two weeks," she said, holding up her fingers. "That's no time at all."

Lizzie blinked, her eyes taking on some sharpness. When she spoke, it was clear she'd shrugged off her sleepiness. "It's all the time I need. We don't give gifts to everyone. We'd go broke."

"So what do you do?"

"Donna's in charge. She creates a spreadsheet and makes assignments. This year I'm buying for Grace, Mark's oldest, and Tim's two-year-old Ava. Most of us just buy for one kid, but I take two, since I don't have to buy for any of my own."

"Just one gift for each kid?"

"Uh-huh. But we can spend up to a hundred bucks. That's enough to get something good. And, yes I've already budgeted. I've got my money ready to go."

"The kids don't mind? I'd think they'd rather have gifts from six aunts and uncles."

"If that happened, they'd get a pair of socks or something. We've got nineteen kids, Jill. Even those of us who do pretty well couldn't keep up with that."

"I guess that makes sense. How about your parents? Do you buy for them?"

"They don't like us to spend money on them, so I make something. Want to help me make peanut brittle? That's my dad's favorite."

Jill nodded absently. "Sure. But I feel like I should buy them something for being so welcoming. Is there anything they need?"

"Need? Sure. Lots of things. But they wouldn't like that. You're one of us now. So go along with the program."

"Are you sure? Matching sweaters? Fruit of the month? A year's supply of Pepsi?"

Lizzie laughed. "My mom would love not having to lug soda home, but no, we don't do that. I'd really rather you just fit in with the group, unless this really means something to you."

"I can restrain myself, but I can't guarantee I won't drag you down there some weekend and take them over to Brattleboro for a nice dinner."

"Okay, Ms. Moneybags. I'll give you that one. They'd like it too. They don't spend money on dinner out very often."

"Then we're set. I never would have guessed that Christmas in a big family would be such a breeze."

"I know!" Lizzie sat up and slapped at the bed. "We'll buy a ham and roast it here. My mother would love not to have to juggle getting a ham and a turkey done on the same day."

"Done. I'll go buy the biggest one I can find."

Lizzie lay down and placed a long kiss on Jill's lips. "Thanks for helping me think of that. Adding a little new blood to the family's going to shake us up. And I *love* being shaken up."

A week before Christmas, Jill came home after attending a Christmas concert at the U with Mary Beth and Kathleen. As usual, she stopped in the kitchen to take a peek at the mail lying on the counter. Before she could begin, Lizzie walked into the kitchen already in her pajamas. "Hi. Good concert?"

"Good enough. Would have been better with you there, but Hollyhock Hills seems intent on working you to death." Jill took off her scarf and mittens, then started to unzip her coat. "What's up? Are you feeling okay?" She dropped her coat onto a stool and moved over to put her hands on Lizzie's face, then tilted it up towards the light.

"I'm fine," she said, allowing the inspection. "Well, I'm not fine, but I'm well."

"Translation?" Jill asked, gazing into her eyes with concern.

"I texted Grace a couple of days ago, asking what she wanted for Christmas. She didn't respond, so I called her today." Her features contorted, the pain in her heart revealing itself on her face. "My number was blocked."

"What? Why would she…?"

"I called Mark and eventually harassed him into telling me." She bit at her lip, clearly to stop herself from crying. After a few seconds to get her emotions under control, she said, "Lisa told her she wasn't allowed to talk to me anymore."

"Oh, God." Jill shut her eyes hard, reeling from the implications. "Because you're with me."

"Because I'm with a woman. I assume she thinks I'll drag her into the cult. You know. The way we recruit."

"God damn it, Lizzie." She put her arms around her and held her tightly as Lizzie lost control and started to cry.

"Why are people so mean? Grace and I are close. Until that kid was in school, I spent a few hours with her every single day. God damn it, I'm no different now than I was three months ago. Than I was seventeen years ago!" She pulled away and looked up, her pain so evident it was like a punch to the gut. "But I'm happy now. Is that what Lisa really hates? That I've found love?"

"I don't know," Jill murmured, pressing Lizzie's head against her breast. The boys walked into the kitchen, wandered around aimlessly for a minute, then both jumped onto the counter. David pranced over and stuck his face against them, then Goliath started to rub against Jill's arm. "The boys don't like it when you're sad," she murmured.

"I don't like it either, boys." Lizzie lowered her face, letting David nuzzle into it. "But I feel better knowing my whole little family cares for me."

"We all do. Especially me," Jill said, holding on even tighter. If only there were a way to protect her family from small-minded jerks, her life would be perfect.

⁂

Jill's winter break started on Monday, and as soon as Lizzie left for work, she drove by the coffee shop in Lizzie's old neighborhood, got a big cup to go, and started for Sugar Hill. The normal two and a half hour trip was going to take much longer, due to the snow that was coming down just hard enough to limit visibility. But that was fine. It would give her longer to work herself into a lather.

In her fantasies, she grabbed Lisa by the shoulders and shook her so hard the obviously broken parts of her humanity snapped back into place, rendering her a decent person. It was kind of fun to picture her head whipping around like a rag doll's, but she knew nothing even close to that could happen. For one thing, she wasn't going to see Lisa. You couldn't make a complete jerk into an empathetic person. You had to have some raw material to work with, and Lisa was as emotionally arid as Jill's mother. Her only hope was to kick some sense into Mark.

Her first stop was the Davis house, looking a little magical with snow covering the roof and providing a fluffy-looking topping on all of the evergreens that fronted the house. She hadn't called first, not absolutely sure she'd stop by. But on the drive she'd decided she needed some support, and Janet was just the person to give that to her.

After knocking, Jill waited in the gusty wind for the door to open. "Hold on," Janet called out. As she opened the door, she stared at Jill for a second. "What's wrong?"

"Nothing." She leaned over and brushed the snow from her hair and the shoulders of her coat, then walked inside. "I came down to talk to Mark." As she slipped out of her coat, she told the real truth. "Actually, I came down to kick his butt, but I thought I'd better talk to you first."

Janet took her arm and led her into the kitchen. "Cocoa or tea or coffee?"

"Cocoa?" Jill's eyebrow rose.

"Mint flavored. It's addictive, but...what the hell?"

"Set me up. Should I have a shot of something in it to steel my nerves?" She looked at her watch. "It's nearly eleven."

"I can give you beer. How does that sound?" She walked over to the stove, laughing at her joke as she put some water in the tea kettle before turning on the burner.

"Lizzie called me to tell me about Lisa's edict," Janet said. "I stormed over to Mark's shop so fiercely I left divots in the turf. But the little jerk wouldn't say a word. He absolutely stonewalled me!"

"Little jerk?" Jill's brows hiked up. "I've never heard you talk about one of the kids that way."

She came back to the table and put her hand on Jill's shoulder. There was a faraway expression on her face as she said, "I've never been this angry with one of them. I try to protect Mike from all of this drama, since his emphysema gets worse when he's agitated, but I think I have to bring him in. Maybe he can reason with the kid."

"I thought Mark was making progress," Jill said, watching Janet move back to the stove to monitor the kettle.

"So did I." She shrugged. "Maybe I was just hoping we weren't throwing away money we don't have to waste." Her expression turned grim. "Lisa's always going to run his life, so it almost doesn't matter what he thinks, does it." She took a mug, added some chocolate powder and poured boiling water over it. As she stirred the drink, she added, "It's awful to lose respect for one of your kids. Just awful."

When she put the mug down, Jill tucked an arm around her waist and gave her a hug. "I bet it is. I've had to reassess what he and I had growing up. For so many years, he was my rock. I was sure he'd always be there for me. That we'd be friends until the end. But he dropped me like a bad habit when Lisa told him to. I rationalized that then, but now..."

Janet sat down across from Jill, her glum expression muting whatever Christmas spirit she'd been able to manage. "I gave him a lot of room when that happened. I knew he was really struggling when you told him you'd never be his—"

"I never told him that!" Jill shivered as she took a drink of the hot, delicious cocoa. "I told him I was with a woman and that I was probably gay. I *never* thought he considered me his girlfriend."

"You two were a pair," Janet said, smirking as she shook her head. "He thought you were already his. I know he did. And you just wanted to find a nice girl, but you didn't know how."

"I'll admit I was clueless," Jill said. "But did he notice we never kissed? Not once? I like a little more connection with my romantic partners."

"I think he assumed that would come over time. That you were…" She frowned and shook her head. "I can't guess what he thought. But it was screwed up, whatever it was."

"I'd say so. He knew…he *saw* me making out with other guys in high school. Wasn't that a clue we weren't together?"

"I think he was waiting for you to get that out of your system and realize he was the best choice. I don't think he's ever asked a girl out, Jill. Lisa was over here as soon as he got home from the U after graduation, throwing herself at him."

"And you think he took her just because she was here?"

She nodded decisively. "I do. He realized he couldn't have you, so he took what was offered. The fact that she agreed you were a terrible person probably made him feel like he had an ally."

"Be careful what you wish for," Jill said as she took another sip. She held the mug up. "How do you stop yourself from drinking that whole box at once?"

"I've already had two mugs today. If caffeine didn't give me the shakes, it'd be gone in a day."

The drink really was delicious, but even its ambrosial sweetness didn't quell Jill's sour feelings. "I feel like a jerk for pushing Lizzie to tell everyone we were together. If I'd kept my mouth shut, the family would all be here for Christmas."

"Nonsense. That's utter nonsense. Lizzie's not the type to sneak around. And God knows she wouldn't want to be here without you."

"True. But…" She folded her arms on the table and lay her head on them, like a disappointed child. "At least now I understand why she didn't want to come out as bisexual. She was trying to put this kind of thing off for as long as she could."

Janet looked at her for a minute, a puzzled expression on her face. "Do you really think that's… Is bisexuality a real category? I've always thought it was just something gay men claimed when they didn't want people to know they were gay. Sort of a placeholder while they worked up the nerve to come out."

"It's definitely a category. And Lizzie's definitely a member."

"So you don't think she's gay, and just afraid to say so? That's been worrying me. I hope we've never done anything to make her feel it wasn't safe to be herself."

Jill let out a wry laugh. "I think it's easier for people to understand homosexuality, so, no, I don't think this is an easy way out for her."

"I know almost nothing about this, Jill. Do you think I should ask Lizzie about it, or find a book or something."

"Both might be good," Jill said, thinking that over for a second. "I have a friend who teaches gender studies. I'll ask her for a good reference."

Concern filled Janet's expression. "You're not worried about this, are you?"

"I'm not. Lizzie's simply able to love both men and women. Luckily, she's chosen me."

Janet reached over and patted Jill's cheek. "She couldn't resist her first crush."

"That might have been what drew her to me at first," Jill admitted, "but that went away quickly. Now I know she loves the adult me—who I am now."

"You don't have a single doubt about her, do you?" Janet asked, reaching over to grasp Jill's hand and squeeze it.

"Not one. I've never felt more loved."

"Best idea I've ever had was inviting you to that party," she said, smirking. "I love being a matchmaker. Even inadvertently."

"You know I agree, but now I've got to go see someone who definitely doesn't. Do you have any advice? I can say things you never would, since I don't care if we ever speak again."

"I wish I knew," Janet said, clearly at a loss. "I guess I'd like it if you could remind him of who he used to be. He was the most kind-hearted of all of my boys, but he truly seems to have lost his way."

"That sounds right. He's taken a wrong turn and can't find his way back."

∽

There were customers at Mark's shop when Jill opened the side door and walked in. He started visibly when he caught sight of her, but didn't acknowledge her presence. She wandered around the shop while he handled his customers, a pair who seemed more interested in talking about smithing than buying anything. After a long while, the wife dragged her husband out, even though it was clear he would have been happy to spend the day.

Mark looked at the door longingly, like he wanted to jump into the departing car and take off.

Jill walked over to stand right in front of him. She didn't fear him any longer, but decided to be close enough to grab one of his heavy hammers in case he started acting crazy again.

"I thought maybe I'd get an apology," she said, realizing she hadn't let the incident go—at all. "You scared the hell out of me and left bruises on my arm."

"You know I'm sorry," he grumbled. Turning, he went over to the bigger of his workbenches, placed a rough-looking metal piece in a vise, and started smoothing it down with a file. Metal slivers flew from the piece, giving the small room a metallic tang. "If I wasn't sorry I wouldn't let my mother coerce me into driving over to Brattleboro twice a week to tell my darkest secrets to some stranger."

"I guess I'll take that as an apology. It's lame, but…"

"Yeah, I know," he snapped. "I'm lame too. What more do you expect from me?"

She stood still for a few seconds, watching him. He looked angry, but this time he wasn't directing that anger at her. This time it seemed like he

412

was angry with himself. The file raked across the metal, sounding uncomfortably like a slow-moving drill in a dentist's office.

"What did I do to you?" she asked, once again getting in front of him so he couldn't look away. "You were the best friend I'd ever had, Mark. I know that wasn't just my imagination. We were closer than siblings."

"I never thought of you as a sibling." He shrugged, his shoulders so much bigger and more powerful looking than they'd been in school. "I had plenty of those."

"You thought I was going to be your girlfriend," she said, deciding to just throw it out there and stop beating around the bush.

His shoulders slumped noticeably. "I thought we'd just, you know, figure out we were supposed to be together."

He finally met her eyes, and she could see all of the anger he'd shown that summer had vanished. Now he just looked weak.

"My therapist says that's what I do. Decide I want something, then wait for it to happen."

"Think he's right?"

"What do you think?" he asked, his expression filled with disgust. Definitely at himself. "I thought we'd both be accountants and have good jobs. We'd live in a big city and do things. Go out to dinner. Travel around. I used to picture us in Boston. We would have had season tickets at Fenway," he added, looking even more depressed. "How am I doing on that list?"

"Pretty bad. But you act like you're too old to change. You're not," she insisted. "I could help you out if you want to get back into accounting."

"No thanks. I don't have much self-respect, but I'm not going to work for you."

He was so literal! "That's not what I meant. The U is a huge place. You could work there and never see me. And I know a lot of people in the state government. You could live in Montpelier and get some experience. Eventually you could work your way down to Boston. Good accountants don't grow on trees. They're tough to find."

"I can't leave," he insisted. "I'm stuck here, making nothing, just so Lisa can be close to her parents. I screwed up, and it's too late to fix it."

"Fine. So you're stuck in Sugar Hill. And now you're cutting yourself off from your family. Got any more bright ideas? 'Cause the ones you've had so far suck."

"I'm not cutting myself off from my family!"

"You most certainly are. Do you really think your mom's going to banish Lizzie so you and Lisa feel more comfortable? If you do, you're delusional."

"Lizzie doesn't come down here very often. Other than that, it'll be the same."

"Bullshit," Jill spat. "Once Lisa knows she can separate you, she'll do her best to keep you away. She wants to control you, Mark, and you're letting her."

She went to stand right in front of him, getting in the way of the piece he was working on. "Look me in the eye and tell me you think I'm a bad influence on your kids. Convince me you think I'm going to hell for being gay. I *dare* you," she demanded with a pulse of venom she didn't know she had in her.

"I don't think that," he said, unable to meet her gaze. "I hear so much of that crap from Lisa that some of it came out when I was at your house. But I don't believe it."

"I bet your kids are going to believe it. Is that how you want them to grow up? With hatred in their hearts?"

"They won't," he grumbled. "They can think for themselves."

"They're looking for guidance, Mark. From you. Staying away from your family because your sister's in a lesbian relationship gives them the very clear message that Lizzie's a bad influence, or a bad person. What else are they supposed to think?"

His voice was soft, and he spoke like he was trying to convince her of something even he didn't believe. "Lisa tells them they should still love her. They just can't see her."

"Great message. Just super."

He finally lifted his chin and met her eyes. "What do you want me to do? I'm stuck in this marriage, and I'm stuck in this town. It's not like I can do what I want."

"Of course you can! You can stand up for yourself. For your family!"

"They don't need me," he grumbled. "They're fine."

"Lizzie does. You have no fucking idea how much you've hurt her. And now you're allowing Lisa to cut Lizzie's tie to Grace. How much bullshit are you willing to take?"

"If I stay out of it and let Lisa make the decisions, my life is easy," he said quietly. "She stays off my back."

"That would work just fine if you didn't have a conscience. But you do. And it's going to eat at you. I promise you that. It's going to eat away at the self-respect you claim to have."

"I have self-respect!" He gripped the vise handle, the veins on the back of his hand sticking out.

"Then use it! When you were a kid, you stood up to bullies. Remember when the other kids in the neighborhood didn't want to let Freddie Giger play whiffle ball? You stuck up for that chubby, near-sighted, slow-footed kid, even though we always lost when he was on our team. I respected you for that. I respected the hell out of you then, Mark. You stood up and did the right thing."

His shoulders slumped and he held onto the bench with both hands. "I've let this go on for twenty years," he whispered, like he was revealing a shameful secret. "If I start standing up to her now, it'll destabilize my marriage. And there's no way I could pay alimony or child support! No way!"

"Look," she said, moving close enough so she could see his pupils dilate, "you made a mistake in marrying Lisa. That's just the damned truth. But she's like a vicious dog. You can try to stay out of her way, to not make her mad, but one day she'll bite you."

"Thanks," he grumbled. "Thanks for calling my wife a dog."

"I could call her a lot worse, but I've made my point. Once you've broken things off with your family, it'll be hard to come back. *If* they'll take you back."

"They're my family! Not yours!"

She let that sting for a moment, then the truth came to her. It was so simple. "That's where you're wrong. A family is just the people you can turn to when you need support. I get that from your mom and dad. Given that I never got it from my own parents, I've realized it's not about blood. It's about love."

"My parents will always love me!" His cheeks were nearly as red as his hair. "There's not a doubt in my mind about that."

"Probably true. But they won't respect you. If you cut your kids off from Lizzie, and stop attending family get-togethers, you'll lose their respect. I'm certain of that."

He stared at her, a mixture of fatigue and anger still coloring his face. "Why couldn't you have stayed away? Things were fine before you came back."

"Doubtful," she said, moving to the door. She stopped and looked at him one more time. "I wish this didn't have to be so hard for you. I really do. But my life changed for the better the day I met you, and I'm forever grateful for the friendship we once had. Being a part of your family helped make me the person I am today." Their eyes finally met. "Don't turn your back on them. That'll be the biggest mistake you've ever made."

On Christmas Eve, Jill watched Lizzie rustle around the Davis family home, organizing the multitude of presents now tucked under the tree. They'd gotten through the dinner Janet had assembled, bland chicken and potatoes, then lit into the Christmas cookies, each one lovingly and perfectly assembled. Janet's dinner was often purgatory, with dessert nearly always a bite of heaven.

The whole family was expected for their traditional gathering early on Christmas day, with breakfast and present opening starting around eight.

Now, in the lull before the storm, Lizzie sat crosslegged on the floor, with the huge tree providing Jill a nice backdrop to study her by. The Davis family had always gone for big trees, as big as would fit into the room, and this year was no exception.

The decorations were from several different eras, large, old-style colored lights, a string of bubblers, probably from the sixties, many strings of mini-lights, and a few new ones, their blue cast revealing them to be LEDs. It was, frankly, a mess when it came to style. But it showed how long they'd been at it, with Jill giving them high marks for longevity. Janet and Mike were going to celebrate their fiftieth anniversary in the spring, and Jill was filled with confidence that Mike was healthy enough to not only make it, but enjoy it.

After watching her work for a while, Jill realized Lizzie was grouping presents according to family, lining them up under the tree just so. Her hands landed on the one Jill had watched her wrap at home. The one for Grace. Not the type to linger on upsetting topics, Lizzie hadn't mentioned her niece since she'd found out her number had been blocked. But Jill knew how much it hurt her. She'd spent a long time wrapping the gift, making it prettier than all of the others by leaps and bounds. It was like she was trying to show Grace how much she cared, given she couldn't actually tell her.

Even though Lizzie had been upbeat about the holidays, Jill could see she was a little off. Not quite her perky self. Even now, sitting by the tree, there was a certain melancholia in her attitude. Nothing glaring. Just a little slump to her shoulders, some fatigue in her expression.

With a burst of cold air, the front door opened. A sheepish Mark stood in the opening, with his kids' heads peeking around his shoulders. His gaze traveled around the room, finally landing on Lizzie. "Got room for a few more?"

Leaping to her feet, Lizzie ran across the room and threw her arms around her older brother. For a moment, Jill saw the old Mark, the one she'd loved, in his tender expression. His eyes were closed, his chin buried in Lizzie's shoulder as he clearly tried to control his emotions. Jill wanted to jump to her feet and get in on the hug, but she stayed right where she was, letting the siblings have a moment. Movement from the kitchen caught her eye, and she saw Janet in the doorway, dabbing at her eyes with a dishcloth.

Mike broke the tension when he called out, "Will you come in and shut the door! You'll give us all pneumonia." His bluster was just for show, and his voice softened immediately. "Come over here, Grace and give your old Grandpa a Christmas kiss."

The girl strolled over to him, acting like she was oblivious to the emotion pulsing in the room. But Jill was certain she was taking it all in, maybe deciding how to process it. Her brothers, both tall and gangly, stood next to their father, looking around like they were visiting a place they were unfamiliar with.

Jill decided it was time to make an overture. She stood, walked over and said, "Let me take your coats, guys."

Mark gave her a thin smile, then he and the boys handed over their coats and stocking caps. She put them in the den, then came back and heard Mark explain, "Since we're going to be with Lisa's family tomorrow, we thought we'd better come over tonight." He shrugged, looking a little uncomfortable. "Lisa's not feeling well, so she's staying home to get some rest."

"Good," Mike said, a little too enthusiastically. "I mean, it's good that she's taking care of herself."

"Yeah." Mark came farther into the house and sat on the sofa. "Got anything to drink?"

"I'll get it," Jill said. "Beer?"

"Yeah. And soda for the kids?"

"Got it," she said, continuing on her way.

When Jill came back, Lizzie was perched on the arm of the sofa, leaning against her brother. Jill didn't have many memories of Lizzie as a kid, but she recalled this exact scene from at least twenty-five years ago. With Lizzie soaking up every bit of affection she could pull out of Mark. He'd always been her favorite brother, and that made it Jill's business to pull Mark back in. They'd figure this out. It wouldn't be quick, but they would do it. If it would make Lizzie happy, Jill would do damned near anything—just as Lizzie would do for her. They were partners. In every way.

❦

Sixteen kids. Fourteen adults. All bundled up against the cold, waiting to enter Sugar Hill Ponds, the Nordic, tubing, and snowshoeing center right on the edge of town.

418

Mike and Janet had bought season passes for everyone for Christmas, and they were queued up according to age, just as they'd done as kids. Jill recalled sitting with her parents at church when the Davises came in, Mike and Janet leading, sometimes carrying Tim and Lizzie, with Donna, Kristen, Chris, Mark, and Adam following behind like little red-headed ducks.

The guy at the entry point checked their tickets, noted the number in the party, then waved them on. By the time he got to Lizzie, his hand was probably cramping. "Another Davis? How many of you are there?"

"We're the last of the bunch. And there's only two in the Davis-Henry family." She let out a chuckle. "Well, there are two more, but they'd be terrible on a tube. Real scaredy cats." She leaned over and said in a stage-whisper, "See what I did there? Scaredy cats."

"You are a clever, clever woman," Jill agreed. She took the pass from Lizzie and looked at it for a minute. Seeing their names together, as a family, warmed her heart more than any gift could have. They didn't even need to use the darned thing, though they definitely would. It wasn't the gift itself that was so cool. It was being considered a family of their own as well as members of the larger group that gave her chills. She zipped the pass into her jacket pocket, already thinking of what she'd do with it at the end of the season. Maybe she'd get a cork board for the rear entryway. Then they could save each pass and look back on them years from now, spending a moment recalling this visit to the Ponds. Their first as a family.

They'd brought their skis, both anxious to get out on the trails and test the fresh powder. Nearly everyone else was going to go tubing, but Jill and Lizzie took off after Donna's oldest boys.

They both preferred skate-skiing to the classic style, so they were able to stay side-by-side as they started off from the warming house. Donna's kids were racing one another, and they disappeared around the first curve and were never seen again. Jill didn't mind. Skiing with Lizzie, out in the clear, cold sun, the wooded terrain shrouded in near silence was way, way up on her list of favorite things to do. Lying on a beach would always be at the top, but the gap was narrowing. Maybe that was because Lizzie seemed to enjoy winter sports a little more, and if Lizzie liked it, it was instantly more fun.

They kept up a brisk pace, their skis cutting across the groomed trail with a rhythmic scratching sound that soon became hypnotizing. They didn't speak much, their pace keeping them on the edge of breathlessness. But Lizzie would occasionally turn and give Jill a big, sunny smile, clearly enjoying the hell out of the day. After a half hour, Jill was about to beg for mercy. Luckily, that was close to Lizzie's limit too, and they slowed down substantially. After a few minutes they reached a modest summit, allowing them to look down at the criss-crossing trails, with a few colorfully dressed skiers gliding along below them.

"Is this fun, or is this fun?" Lizzie demanded.

"This is fun. I'm going to need to lie down in about two minutes, but I'm having a ball."

"Winter sports kinda kick ass," Lizzie said. "I love summer, but this?" She held her hand out in front of herself, her pole dangling from her wrist, as she gestured at the vista. "C'mon!"

"No arguments. It's quiet and peaceful and I feel like we're all alone. And you know how I love to be alone with you."

"You know," Lizzie said, lowering her voice to speak conspiratorially. "If you were going to ask a woman to marry you, you could do a lot worse than dropping to a knee right here."

Jill's eyes nearly popped from her head. She must have looked as stunned as she felt, because Lizzie let out a long, hearty laugh. "No, I'm not proposing. I'm just saying…" Her smile was adorably cryptic, with Jill puzzling over her comments.

"What *are* you saying?"

"Just something to think about. You wouldn't necessarily need an engagement ring, right? I mean, are you the engagement ring type?"

"I've never thought about it."

She nodded. "Then you're not. But you'd have to have something prepared. You know. Some romantic words to knock a girl off her feet." She took her pole and gave Jill a playful whack across the seat. "I'm just giving you some food for thought."

"Are you an engagement ring kinda girl?" She narrowed her eyes. "If I had to guess, I'd say yes."

"You are correct!" Lizzie beamed at her. "So that's something you'd have to consider. You don't want to buy the wrong kind of ring. You'd look like a dope, right?"

"Oh, right. No one wants to look like a dope."

"Right. So if that's the kind of thing you're thinking of doing, you might want to start doing some research. I know you're a planner, so... Maybe you should get to planning."

"I appreciate your insights. Just...you know...if I was thinking of doing something like that."

"Yeah. Just in case." She took a few small sidesteps, getting right next to Jill. Then she leaned in and gave her a long, sweet kiss. Her nose was cold, as were her lips. But that only lasted a moment. Then her lips molded to Jill's and grew warmer as the seconds passed. Lizzie's hand went to rest on the back of Jill's stocking cap and she pressed gently, lengthening the kiss. Finally, she pulled away, but stayed very close. "You still love me, right?" she asked, the question having become an almost daily joke.

"I think so." Jill closed her eyes halfway, then nodded. "Yeah. I'm pretty sure I do."

"Okay then. Let's get a move on and get back so we can drink some of that cocoa my mom made."

"It's a deal. Ready?"

"For anything," Lizzie agreed, her laugh carrying across the broad expanse that lay in front of them. She took off, with Jill right behind, rushing to get in sync.

Proposing while they skied *would* be pretty cool. And while they both loved Sugar Hill, it would be awfully nice to be up at the top of a hill. Killington would be good. But Mt. Mansfield was a little taller. She'd have to do some research. This wasn't the kind of thing you could just do on the fly. It was critical that they have peace and quiet, and were completely alone. Jill smiled as she thought of standing on a windy peak, surrounded by snow, looking down at miles and miles of natural beauty. It had to be special. As special as Lizzie was to her. *That* was going to be a tall order. But she was up to it. And if she couldn't get it organized, Lizzie would drop a few not-so-subtle hints, since she clearly had it all worked out in her head. It would be a fantastic day. One to remember for the rest of their lives. Of course, today wasn't half bad either. No surprise there. When Lizzie was next to her, every day was one to remember.

The End

What comes next?

Read the epilogue at: www.briskpress.com/homecoming-epilogue.html

By Susan X Meagher

Novels

Arbor Vitae
All That Matters
Cherry Grove
Girl Meets Girl
The Lies That Bind
The Legacy
Doublecrossed
Smooth Sailing
How To Wrangle a Woman
Almost Heaven
The Crush
The Reunion
Inside Out
Out of Whack
Homecoming

Serial Novel

I Found My Heart In San Francisco

Awakenings: Book One
Beginnings: Book Two
Coalescence: Book Three
Disclosures: Book Four
Entwined: Book Five
Fidelity: Book Six
Getaway: Book Seven
Honesty: Book Eight
Intentions: Book Nine
Journeys: Book Ten
Karma: Book Eleven
Lifeline: Book Twelve
Monogamy: Book Thirteen
Nurture: Book Fourteen
Osmosis: Book Fifteen
Paradigm: Book Sixteen
Quandary: Book Seventeen
Renewal: Book Eighteen

Anthologies

Undercover Tales
Outsiders

Visit Susan's website at
www.susanxmeagher.com

Go to www.briskpress.com to purchase any of her books.

facebook.com/susanxmeagher
twitter.com/susanx